PUFFIN BOOKS

THE DARK ARMY

After several incident-filled years of travelling the world, Marcus Alexander decided to pack in all serious attempts at reaching maturity, and instead embraced the much more suitable world of parchment scribbling for a living.

Marcus has a fondness for causing mischief, knows how to run really, really fast when he's in trouble and knows how to duck out of sight when someone points the long, bony finger of blame.

Find out more about him and Charlie's adventures at

www.keeperoftherealms.com

Books by Marcus Alexander

The **Keeper of the Realms** series:
CROW'S REVENGE
THE DARK ARMY

THE DARK ARMY

MARCUS ALEXANDER

PUFFIN

PUFFIN BOOKS

Published by the Penguin Group
Penguin Books Ltd, 80 Strand, London WC2R ORL, England
Penguin Group (USA) Inc., 375 Hudson Street, New York, New York 10014, USA
Penguin Group (Canada), 90 Eglinton Avenue East, Suite 700, Toronto, Ontario, Canada M4P 2Y3
(a division of Pearson Penguin Canada Inc.)
Penguin Ireland, 25 St Stephen's Green, Dublin 2, Ireland (a division of Penguin Books Ltd)
Penguin Group (Australia), 707 Collins Street, Melbourne, Victoria 3008, Australia
(a division of Pearson Australia Group Pty Ltd)
Penguin Books India Pvt Ltd, 11 Community Centre, Panchsheel Park, New Delhi – 110 017, India
Penguin Group (NZ), 67 Apollo Drive, Rosedale, Auckland 0632, New Zealand
(a division of Pearson New Zealand Ltd)
Penguin Books (South Africa) (Pty) Ltd, Block D, Rosebank Office Park, 181 Jan Smuts Avenue,
Parktown North, Gauteng 2193, South Africa

Penguin Books Ltd, Registered Offices: 80 Strand, London WC2R ORL, England

puffinbooks.com

First published 2013
001

Text and character illustrations copyright © Marcus Alexander, 2013
Inked by Muhammad Zulkipli
Internal illustrations by Zul Kamarrudin
Map by David Atkinson
All rights reserved

The moral right of the author and illustrator has been asserted

Set in 10.5/15.5 pt Sabon LT Std
Typeset by Palimpsest Book Production Ltd, Falkirk, Stirlingshire
Printed in Great Britain by Clays Ltd, St Ives plc

British Library Cataloguing in Publication Data
A CIP catalogue record for this book is available from the British Library

ISBN: 978–0–141–33978–8

www.greenpenguin.co.uk

ALWAYS LEARNING   PEARSON

For the awesome Moll who decided to fly,
for A & J and their heart-warming faith
in their bad-boy son,
for all my peeps and their constant support
(OMG, look-look! Tommy, Mac, Leafy & Dan-I,
your names are in a book!
With pages, a front cover and all. Whoop-whoop!)
. . . and of course for my gorgeous wife
(and her Puerto Rican va-va-vooOOooom x),
my love,
Your Boy
M

WESTERN
MOUNTAINS

GREAT
PLAINS

SLUMBERING

Western
Mountains
(City of)

HILLS

Alavis

Idle Wind

Stubborn
Citadel

Opal Hold

Shidden Vale

BELLANIA

Charlie's Waterfall

DEEPFOREST

Sylvaris

Alacorn

THE
WINGED
MOUNT

Southern Cities

Contents

1

Rusty Manacles

Charlie Keeper was not happy. Not by any means.

It had been two days since the Stoman army had killed the Treman guards assigned to protect her. Two days since they'd separated her from her friends and two days since they'd left her in a rotten, rat-infested cell.

'If you chumps don't let me out of here this instant,' she screamed, 'I'm going to get really upset and, trust me, you don't want to deal with me when I'm angry!'

To underline her determination Charlie kicked her heels against the wall. (She would have preferred to stamp her feet, but the spiteful guards had left her hanging two metres above the floor.) For the hundredth time she screwed her eyes shut and tried to focus her Will, but nothing happened. Since she'd crossed the divide from Earth to the realm of Bellania, life had been nothing more than one hard lesson after another. Now with her magical ability refusing to materialize, it appeared she was undergoing yet another painful and inconvenient lesson.

'Why don't things ever work like they're supposed to?' she muttered irritably to herself.

It felt like a lifetime ago that she had been living in

London, but in reality it had only been several weeks. And in those short turbulent weeks she had discovered that her house was a Gateway between realms, that her parents had passed on a secret to her that people were more than willing to kill for, and that her family name was more than just a name; it was a title. With that title came a genetic talent known as the Will and the Way that granted her the power to open portals to travel through and to increase her own strength to the point where she could hold her own against foes who were bigger, badder and more vicious than her.

But the Will and the Way had not been an easy thing to study. It had taken long days of gruelling practice before Charlie had been able to wield the writhing golden energy that burst from her hands . . . But now, when she needed it most, it refused to appear.

Dull weariness and a constant, throbbing headache pounded at the inside of her head, making it impossible to summon the concentration that her Will required. The fatigue from opening a Portal to the University of Dust in Alavis, the beating she'd suffered at the hands of the Stoman soldiers and having to endure hanging by her wrists for so long had all taken their toll upon her body. All she could muster were little bursts of yellow light that frittered and fizzed from her fingertips. And without the power of her Will to tear the manacles from her wrists or open a Portal back to Sylvaris she knew she wasn't going anywhere.

She felt drained and useless.

Why had she been left for so long and what had happened to her friends Jenson, Kelko and Nibbler? Why hadn't anyone come to see her or even interrogate her? And why did prison cells always have to have creepy-crawlies and mouldy straw strewn across the floor?

'I hate stereotypes,' she grumbled.

Muttering to herself she began to grind her heels against the rotten brickwork so that mortar and small shards of plaster crumbled to the floor. The rats scurrying beneath her feet squeaked as they dodged the downfall.

Charlie peered blearily down at the rodents. 'I hate rats.'

As she continued to kick and grind her feet, the movement caused the iron manacles to rub deeper into her skin. She scowled up at the restraints. 'Handcuffs, manacles, Isiris Bracelets and chains . . . I hate them too! I hate all of them! I hate them!'

Realizing that she was growing close to losing her temper Charlie took a big, deep breath. And another . . . and then another. Gradually she felt her anger receding.

'That's better . . .' she murmured.

One of the rats, unhappy with the amount of dust and debris raining down on it, chose that moment to scamper up the wall, on to Charlie's foot and up her trouser leg.

'Aaaaaaaaaaaaaaaaahhh!' she screamed in disgust. She kicked and thrashed her legs, dislodging the rat so that it fell to the floor. The motion caused the manacles to cut deeper into her wrists.

'Gaaaaaaaaaaah!' That was it. Charlie really lost her temper. 'Get me out of here! Get me out! Out! Out! OUT!'

Kicking and screaming, she jangled on the end of her chains as sputters of Will fizzed from her fingertips, and her face went red then purple.

'Let me out of here you low-down, good-for-nothing, chumpaholic idiots –'

A rumble and creak of stone from the opposite wall stopped Charlie mid-flow as small fractures appeared across its surface.

'Huh?'

The cracks grew, the stonework moaned and Charlie could hear the faint sound of what seemed to be whale song mixed with the distant rumble of thunder. As the song grew in volume, the wall began to bulge and shake. A large circular hole peeled open in the brickwork to expose a dark and forbidding tunnel. The singing stopped and a bulky figure wrapped in a black hooded robe strode confidently out of the passageway.

'B-Bane!' stuttered Charlie, feeling the blood drain from her face. The Stoman Lord was the reason she was in Bellania. It was, after all, his twisted ambition and his shadowy servants, the Shades, who had chased her from London, intent on trying to kill and even eat her. Bane seemed to think that the pendant Charlie had worn round her neck ever since her parents went missing seven long years ago was key to controlling the realm. With the pendant in his power he could ensure his mastery over Bellania and, knowing this, he would stop at nothing to get it. It had become clear that keeping it in her possession and discovering its secrets was the only way Charlie could save the realm from his evil rule, as well as her only hope of seeing her parents again.

Right now she could feel its reassuring presence round her neck. Whoever was holding her captive clearly didn't know what the necklace was. It seemed like the only piece of good luck she'd had since she'd opened the portal to Alavis.

Striding forward, the figure loomed over Charlie. Large hands reached up and pulled down the hood to reveal the characteristically gnarled skin of a Stoman. The stranger's face was hard and rigid and he had the coldest grey eyes Charlie had ever seen.

'No, not Bane,' said the large visitor. 'My name is Darkmount. Edge Darkmount.'

Charlie blinked in astonishment. Edge Darkmount was the Stoman bishop she'd been trying to find: the one person who could reveal the secret of her pendant. The bishop was rumoured to be one of the most powerful Stomen in all of Bellania, with stonesinging abilities that could manipulate even the hardest rock as if it were nothing more than clay. Now that Charlie was face to face with him she was relieved that it wasn't Bane, yet she didn't necessarily feel any safer for she could see that he carried his own darkness. However, as she stared back at the hulking figure, instead of fear she felt the familiar stirring of fury within her. It was like the welcome return of an old friend.

'You chump! You sold us out! You were supposed to help us, but you stabbed us in the back!' she shouted. Lashing out, she tried to kick the looming Stoman, but he was out of reach. 'If I ever get down from here I'm going to rip that cloak off you and stuff it up your nostrils, you lousy back-stabber!'

'Silly Humans, you are all the same,' snarled Darkmount. 'Only an idiot chained to a wall would insult a stranger.' Raising a clenched fist he sang a powerful note that caused his hand to glow a deep, baleful red. 'Indeed if you aren't careful you might be forced to learn a painful lesson.'

Jensen groaned and did his best to gain some control of his torn and bruised body. Spitting mud from his mouth, he clenched his fingers into the dirt, pushed his knees under his chest and struggled to his feet.

'I won't ask again. Tell me wot yer've done with Charlie!' he demanded through swollen lips. He staggered defiantly upright to face the Stoman guards in their shining armour. 'Where is she?'

The Stomen were tired of the repeated questions. Grown used to the Treman's plucky determination, they did what they always did. With a nod from a nearby sergeant one of the Stoman soldiers stamped his way from beneath the shelter of the overhanging roof into the pouring rain. Casually he lifted his heavy war axe and, using the thick shaft of the handle rather than the sharp business end, clubbed Jensen back to the ground.

The soldier stared down at the captive. 'You better stay down and be quiet!' he growled, nudging his boot into Jensen's ribs.

'I'm getting tired of repeating meself,' mumbled Jensen. Raising a shaking arm he waved it in the general direction of the astonished guard. 'Tell me where me little Hippotomi –'

The guard slammed his foot into Jensen's head, cartwheeling the Treman over on to his back. As Jensen lost consciousness, the courtyard finally fell silent.

The Stoman grinned and raised a thumbs-up sign to the rest of his squad.

'Ya didn't answer the man,' said a voice interrupting the moment. 'Where's the girl? Where's Charlie?'

Snarling, the soldier snapped round. Furious, he broke into a run that quickly covered the distance between him and the second prisoner. Slamming shoulder-first into the girth of Kelko's stomach, the guard once again brought the shaft of his axe into play and knocked the fat Treman into another unconscious heap. When the chubby Treman was down the soldier ruthlessly kicked him several times.

This was getting way beyond a joke. The two Tremen were insulting the might of the Stoman army with their lewd jokes and constant demands to know where the young Keeper was. A sound beating was the least they deserved. The other Stoman soldiers looked on in approval as he continued to kick and grind his heel into the unconscious prisoners.

A flurry of activity at the far end of the courtyard announced the arrival of a lightly armoured messenger. Ignoring the beating, the messenger jogged past the ranks to the colonel.

'At last,' snorted the colonel once he had absorbed the message. 'I thought we would have to babysit these fools all season long.'

Indicating that two of his men and the messenger should follow him, he strode over to the prisoners, who were slowly regaining consciousness. 'I would like to thank you for gracing us with your constant wit and banter, but we no longer require your presence. Lord Bane has commanded that you be taken with all haste –' the colonel punctuated his speech with a well-placed kick in Kelko's stomach – 'and ceremony –' and another kick for Jensen – 'to the Soul Mines of Zhartoum, where you will work till your fingers are worn to stubs, your teeth drop from your mouth and your hair withers like rotten wheat. Welcome to the end of your days.'

With a nod of his head he watched his men drag the two Tremen off.

'The dog too?'

'Yes, Colonel.'

'Good, that beast was a real pain in the neck. It mauled three of my men before we could muzzle it. So what about the Keeper and the Hatchling? Can we get rid of them too?'

'They are to remain here, Colonel. Lord Bane has further plans for them. He has dispatched a pack of Shades to usher them to the Western Mountains where he will oversee their fate in person.'

'Excellent,' muttered the colonel, who felt that guarding prisoners was a waste of his time. 'And then what of me and my men?'

'What else but back to the fray? The Human cities are almost ours for the taking and once they have fallen we can turn our sights to Deepforest and that cursed city, Sylvaris.'

2

An Introduction and a Deal

Hands glowing, Darkmount grasped first one manacle, then the other. At his touch the metal peeled back, releasing Charlie so that she fell to the floor in a puff of dust with a startled 'Oof!'

'Huh?' gaped Charlie, too shocked and too tired to register the pain in her backside. 'Why'd you do that?'

'Would you rather I had not?' said Darkmount. 'If you prefer that I leave you to your fate it will take but a moment to reattach the manacles.'

Charlie managed to compose herself, but only just. 'But why would you want to set me free after betraying me?'

'You weren't betrayed. Alavis simply had the misfortune to fall faster than anyone expected.'

'Come again?'

'The Stoman army invaded the city and when you opened your Portal you were unlucky enough to open it into one of the courtyards that the Stomen were using.'

'Yeah, a courtyard you picked!'

'When I picked it,' reasoned Darkmount, 'Alavis was still a free city. Let me repeat myself, you weren't betrayed; it was just . . . poor fortune.'

'What?' sneered Charlie, still angry and suspicious. 'Like you couldn't send me a message or at least give us some kind of warning!'

'And how would you have suggested that I do that?' Darkmount held up his hand and ticked off points on his fingers. 'One, Bane's forces were far larger than predicted. Two, the city was surrounded so no message could get out. Three, even if I had sent a message it wouldn't have reached Sylvaris in time to stop your arrival.'

'OK, so if you didn't betray me how come you weren't there to warn us?'

'So I could be captured too? Pah! You are either innocent or idiotic, and neither personality trait is acceptable, particularly in a Keeper. Fortunately for you I am no fool, which is why I used my time wisely.'

'Yeah, doing what?'

Again Darkmount ticked off points. 'One, moving my research and books to a safe place. Two, keeping an eye on the guard movements and, three, planning a safe method of extraction.'

'Extraction?'

'Escape! I'm helping you escape, you foolish child! Enough of this idle chit-chat. Now that you are in a position to make a bid for freedom it is time for us to discuss the requirements for our deal.'

'Deal?' said Charlie. 'What deal?'

'I believe you wanted your pendant examined, did you not?' rumbled Darkmount. 'You and your Lady Dridif from the Jade Circle believe that it holds answers, answers that only I can provide, and in return for this information you and I must discuss the matter of price. A deal must be made.'

'Right,' muttered Charlie, who had come to expect such things from strangers in Bellania. 'What kind of deal would that be?'

'Do not be sarcastic, little girl. Remember, we all have different paths to walk.'

'Oh, sure, paths that require you to force me to make a deal while me and my friends are still imprisoned. That really seems fair, doesn't it?'

'Who ever told you that life was meant to be fair?' asked Darkmount. 'I am offering you something, I require something in return and I believe that is the basis of a "fair" deal.'

Charlie stared hard at Edge Darkmount. It was true that he should get something in exchange for his knowledge and since she was half rescued thanks to him she should, she supposed, be grateful. But there was something very unlikeable about him; he was too cold, too distant. But as with so many things that had happened to her in Bellania, she knew when she had little or no choice.

'So what do you want from me?'

'I need you to fetch me a vessel. A holy vessel. It is a sign, an embodiment of my religion and with it in my hands I can begin to repair the damage that Bane has done to the true faith of Bellania.'

'True faith? Bane? What has Bane done to you?'

'What has he done?' growled Darkmount, and for the first time he revealed some genuine emotion. 'What has that dog *not* done?' A flickering anger swept across his face, causing veins to pulse across his forehead. 'He has made a mockery! A mockery of the Stoman religion. His new so-called god has usurped the true faith and led the righteous astray. Bane must be forced to see the error of his ways.'

'So I take it you're not pals, right?'

Darkmount let out a sigh of frustration. 'Your constant, infantile witticisms are wearying to my ears, but in this you are indeed correct. Bane and I share a hatred so sincere, so pure, that the darkness of night pales in comparison.'

'So is this an "enemy of my enemy" kind of deal?'

'If you wish to see it like that,' replied Darkmount, once again in control of his emotions.

'So what's in this vessel then?'

'My god.'

'Say what?' Charlie rubbed at her ear, thinking that she had misheard.

'I said it contains my god,' growled Darkmount. Lightning seemed to flicker across his eyes. 'The vessel is merely the physical casing that contains my god.'

Charlie frowned as she tried to get her head around that idea. 'What, like a genie in a bottle?'

'That is a crude and irreverent way of putting it, but . . . yes.'

'Oh, right,' muttered Charlie, 'cos that really makes sense . . . a god in a bottle.'

'What was that?' snapped Darkmount.

'Uh, nothing,' said Charlie, carefully eyeing the bishop. 'So, um, tell me more about this deal. Why can't you go and get this "vessel" yourself?'

'Because Bane has hidden it beyond my reach. However,

your abilities as a Keeper allow you to open doors that others cannot. So . . . for this deal to go ahead you must accompany me to the Stubborn Citadel. Buried deep inside the citadel is a door, a Gateway if you will. This Gateway leads to one of Bellania's lower dominions and in it lies my vessel. I need you to use your Will to break into the dominion, find my god and return it to me. Do this for me and I will tell you everything that you want to know about your pendant.'

'Waaaaaait a minute.' Charlie crossed her arms and threw Edge Darkmount a suspicious look. 'You make it seem all too simple. Why do I get the impression this is going to be harder than it sounds?'

'Oh, it will be difficult. More than difficult. The Stubborn Citadel is one of Bane's strongest fortresses. Its walls are thick and impenetrable. The soldiers that garrison it thrive on brutality and the lust for blood. Once past these soldiers there will be Shades and perhaps worse within. Yet getting past these obstacles will be easy in comparison to what lies within the lower dominion. The denizens that inhabit it are full of guile and poison. Pah! Little girl, retrieving the vessel will be difficult in the extreme! But once my god is returned to me all things are possible.' A look of hunger flickered across his face. 'With the vessel in my hands the guards, the soldiers, the things that scurry in the darkness of the lower dominion will tremble before us. So all you have to worry about is getting in; everything else you leave to me.'

Charlie's eyes had been growing wider as Darkmount described the danger. 'Hang on a second. You want me to break into an impenetrable fortress that is guarded by insane-sounding soldiers and Shades . . .'

'I do.'

'And then head past more creepy-crawlies to find a door that leads to a dominion full of wackos . . .'

'That is correct.'

'Where I have to hunt around, no doubt while I'm being chased, grab your "vessel", which incidentally holds a god, and then make it back past these nut-jobs who probably won't be happy to see me leave.'

'Yes.'

'And you want someone of my height and shoe size to go there?'

'What needs to be done, needs to be done.'

'You're joking, right?'

'I do not joke.'

Charlie eyed the grim-faced Stoman up and down. 'No, I guess you don't. One thing I don't understand: what is a "lower dominion"?'

'It is what you would call a hell.'

Charlie's mouth wobbled, she laughed nervously then went pale. 'Look, I know you don't joke . . . but you're joking, right? Hell's not real. Not really.'

'What?' sneered Darkmount. 'There are many hells in Bellania – seven of them to be exact – and if you don't believe in hells on Earth then be assured that ours are very real.'

'With daemons and everything?'

'Of course. Do you think Bane would entrust the guarding of a god to furry rabbits, jovial cherubs or pretty unicorns with ribbons wrapped round their horns? Bah! It is the Daemon Kindred who Bane made a deal with and it is the Daemon Kindred who guard my god.'

'And you think I'm going to go anywhere near a place with daemons? You're crazy!'

'Do you want to find the answer to that which lies round your neck?'

'Yes, of course I do, but . . .' Charlie stumbled to a halt. She stared around at the depressing walls and remembered all that she had seen and done, all that she had experienced within Bellania. The magic, the sights, the smells, the sheer adventure of it all. She had accepted it, acknowledged this wonderful world so different from London and Earth, yet what was now being asked of her seemed unreal, almost ridiculous. She was sure the task ahead of her was beyond her abilities. 'You really want me to go to this hell? Like, for real?'

'Enough of your weak-minded blather. Young you may be, but nonetheless you are a Keeper. Your blood ensures that you carry the burdens that Bellania delivers your way. Only your family has the ability to open the gates that stand between me and my god, and this is the price I demand for deciphering your pendant. If you want me to help you escape this city and move forward on your journey then this is what must be done, no more no less.'

With those words hanging between them Charlie knew he was right. Not a nice person, not a fair person, but still right in what he said. She wanted – no, she *needed* – to unlock the secret of the pendant. If she was ever going to stand a chance of defeating Bane, of seeing her parents again, then this was what she had to do.

As soon as she had acknowledged this, the calmness of responsibility settled once more upon her shoulders. She would do this, she would succeed and she would do the right thing. 'So I get you your god, you give me my answers.'

'Yes.'

'And what about my friends?

'What of them?' asked Darkmount.

'They are here, prisoners like me. There's two Tremen, Jensen and Kelko, their dog, Sic Boy, and Nibbler, a young Winged One who you've met already.' Even as Charlie talked her mind continued to churn. She still couldn't believe that she was friends with a talking dragon. A real dragon! Nibbler had woken early from his hibernation and answered her call for help, but all the other Winged Ones – the elders who could restore peace to Bellania – were prevented from returning by the powerful hand of Bane, the Stoman Lord. It was Nibbler who had flown to Alavis and set up the arrangement with Darkmount on behalf of the Jade Circle. Wherever Nibbler was now Charlie could only imagine how furious he must be, knowing that everything had gone so spectacularly wrong. 'You've got to help me free them too.'

'That isn't part of the deal,' rumbled Darkmount.

'Deal? There is no deal until we agree on the details and you don't know me if you think I'm leaving my friends behind.'

Darkmount – so tall that his head almost scraped the ceiling – stared down at the young Keeper with a baleful expression. Charlie, determination overcoming her trepidation, stared right back.

'Good,' grunted the bishop. 'I admire your strength of spirit, little girl; you will be needing it where you are going.

Very well, I accept. If your friends are imprisoned in this city I will aid you in freeing them.'

'And you will tell me half of my pendant's secret before I get your god,' demanded Charlie, mindful of Lady Narcissa's painful lesson in betrayal. 'And the other half when I return with this vessel of yours. Agreed?'

'Agreed,' said Edge Darkmount in his mournfully deep voice.

Charlie held out her hand, Darkmount mirrored the gesture and the two of them shook hands, sealing the deal.

Kelko and Jensen had been thrown, battered and bruised, into the back of the prison wagon. Their wrists and ankles had been secured in wooden stocks and as a parting gift from their Stoman guards their mouths had been gagged with an old pair of the colonel's sandals. A bustling knot of muscular soldiers, heaving on chains and knotted rope, half hauled, half heaved Sic Boy into the courtyard. With great effort they got the huge dog on to the wagon too.

Once the grumbling, kicking – and in one case barking – prisoners were secure, two of the guards swung into the driver's seat. With a crack of the reins they set the large horses moving. Trailing a cloud of dust, the cart passed beneath the city gate of Alvaris and out into the countryside.

As the dust from their passing began to settle, a Shade slunk into the courtyard. It slipped past the soldiers and its shadowy form eased beneath the door that led to the colonel's temporary office. Familiar with Lord Bane's personal guard, the colonel looked up from his paperwork as soon as he noticed the drop in temperature.

'Yes?'

'I have come to oversee the transfer of our lord's prisoners.'

The colonel carefully lowered his raised quill to stare at the black shadow that coiled and bristled in the darkest corner of his office. 'The two idiotic Tremen and the beast have been transferred to the Soul Mines as instructed. The Hatchling and the Keeper remain within our custody. Again, as instructed they have been jailed separately.'

'Good. Take me to them now. Our lord has requested that they be sent with haste to the Western Mountains. The Keeper and the Hatchling have fates to face.'

'It shall be as you say. I shall send for a runner to show you the way.'

'No, I think not,' said the Shade with a dry, acidic tone. 'You shall take me yourself.'

'As you wish. Please follow me.'

The colonel, muscles bunching beneath his ornate armour, strode through the courtyard towards the prison cells with the Shade writhing, half-hidden, by his side. It was time for the Keeper girl and the Winged One to take a trip.

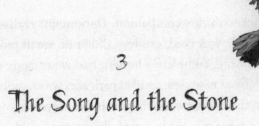

3

The Song and the Stone

Darkmount used the power of his stonesinging to carve a tunnel beneath the city.

When she had been in Sylvaris seeking help from the Jade Circle Charlie had witnessed the beauty of treesinging and had admired how it could craft and create the ornate towers and sweeping bridges of the ancient Treman city. But she had to acknowledge that the Stoman art of stone-singing was equally awe-inspiring.

The bishop's deep, melodic voice and fiercely glowing fists sculpted the rock, pushing it aside and easing it into a smooth passageway. The light from his fists doubled as a means of illumination, allowing Charlie to admire the different grades of rock and ore that were swirled into fresh patterns by his song. An occasional flash and flicker of amethysts, tiger-crystal and unrefined gold brought the walls to life with their sparkle. Once, to Charlie's delight, the fossilized bones of some prehistoric monster momentarily reared up, before being rearranged and incorporated into the tunnel.

But for all the subterranean wonders and the fact that this was the first chance she'd had to witness stonesinging, travelling beneath the city was not a pleasant experience, at

least not with this companion. Darkmount really creeped
her out. He was cold, grumpy, didn't do small talk and, if
she was being completely honest, had weird body odour.

The joy of new sights and experiences was rapidly fading.
In fact, this most recent chapter in her travels across Bellania had been miserable, painfully miserable, which, when
Charlie thought about it, was putting it mildly. Charlie's
mind started to wander. Old and new concerns flickered
through her mind. Were Nibbler, Jensen, Kelko and Sic Boy
OK? What of her gran left behind in London? Was this guy
Edge Darkmount really going to solve the pendant's riddle
so she could free her parents? Why was her luck always so
bad? And why did she always seem to get hurt no matter
how hard she tried to do the right thing?

She was so caught up in these turbulent thoughts that
Charlie failed to realize that Darkmount had stopped, and
walked into his back. It was like walking into a lamppost.
Bouncing off him, she peered up in surprise at the Stoman's
hard face. Glancing past his broad shoulders, she saw that
the tunnel ended in a brick wall.

'We are here,' he rumbled. 'Prepare yourself.'

And before Charlie could ask where exactly 'here' was
and what she had to prepare herself for, Darkmount smashed
the wall apart. Moving quickly, he leaped forward,
surrounded by a cloud of dust and flying fragments of brick.
Charlie peered through the wreckage into a dungeon so wide
that its far side was hidden in shadow. Halfway down the
room a group of startled Stoman soldiers slowly drew their
weapons, intent on investigating the cause of the explosion.

The thick cloud of debris and dust obscured Darkmount.

All that could be seen was a faint outline and the soft glow from the bishop's fists that pulsated and throbbed with the unspoken promise of violence.

The tone of the bishop's song abruptly deepened and grew in volume. Its aggressive melody rolled along the length of the room and echoed off the walls.

Menacing.

Haunting.

As it swelled to a crescendo, Darkmount's fists and forearms burst into thick shafts of green flame. With a terrifying roar he burst from the dust and charged forward.

One of the soldiers staggered and tripped at the sudden sight of Darkmount hurtling towards them. The others slowed and licked their lips as they re-evaluated the balance of power, but their sense of duty and natural aggression quickly quashed any doubts. Screaming defiantly, they raced up the dungeon with their weapons raised.

With the lack of sleep and dust stinging her already bleary eyes, Charlie couldn't quite count the soldiers, but she thought there might have been eleven or twelve. Surely too many for Darkmount to take on alone? Hurriedly she tried to dig deep and find the rage that had fuelled her through so many occasions before, but fatigue meant her Will still failed her. All she could do was stand there and stare.

Sprinting forward Darkmount dipped his blazing hands into the floor and ripped free jagged clumps of rock. As he pounded across the room, he flung these crude missiles, knocking soldier after soldier off his feet. Then he was amidst the warriors, moving with raw efficiency. Kicking and stamping, hurling punches, bone-crunching elbows and vicious headbutts against his opponents.

Charlie's mouth gaped open. Edge Darkmount didn't move with the elegance of a martial artist but with the fury and brutality of a bar-room brawler. He used any and every part of his body as a weapon to strike and pummel the soldiers. When they tried to strike back his glowing fists and forearms deflected their blows in an explosion of sparks.

Darkmount was a tidal wave of destruction.

As he made short work of the Stomen, unconscious, twitching and moaning bodies fell to the floor until only three remained. The warriors hesitated at the obvious strength of their foe. Adjusting their grip on their weapons they lowered their stances and began to circle their adversary.

'Idiots!' snapped Darkmount with a sneer of disdain. 'You face a Bishop of the Faith! A true Master of Stone!'

Again reaching his hands into the floor he tore free a length of rock. Quickly passing his hands up and down its surface, he shaped it into a long mace. Then, raising it above his head, he began to whirl it round and round, all the while feeding his power with his stonesinging.

The first warrior made his move. The others, gaining courage from his action, also darted forward, but Darkmount was quicker. Much quicker. Punching the mace forward like a spear, he thrust its blunt head deep into the first soldier's gut. Lashing the club backwards, he struck the second warrior on his shoulder, hip, knee and wrist in quick succession, before spinning it round to crack against the remaining soldier's skull.

He grunted in approval as he surveyed his work. Seeing that the majority of the guards weren't moving and that those who did were writhing in agony, he allowed his song to slow and the light to dim from his hands.

Moans of pain filled the silence and, apart from the occasional twitch from one or two of the fallen guards, the dungeon was still.

Charlie stared at Darkmount with a combination of awe and alarm. Creepy he might be, but she got the impression he might be better than having a battering ram or armoured tank on her side. Much better.

'Mmmmmmmmmmggggg!!' protested a familiar but muffled voice. 'Mmmmmmmmhhh!'

Charlie moved across the mouldy dungeon where, to her surprise, she found Nibbler. He was struggling between taut lengths of chain. A leather harness had been forced over his muzzle, preventing him from opening his mouth, and all that escaped his lips were the peculiar murmurs that groaned their way across the room.

'Mmmmmmmmmmmg, mmh-nng-mmmmmmmmhhh!'

'Oh, Nibbler,' breathed Charlie, partly in relief at seeing her friend still alive and partly in dismay at finding him in such a bedraggled condition. She wanted to crack a wise joke, something to make everything better, but the sheer scale of failure that had accumulated over the past couple of days weighed heavily on her heart. All she could say was, 'Oh.'

Stumbling over on leaden feet, she stroked the side of his face. The sight of the cruel harness was enough to push her Will into a tight knot of concentration that twisted and burned within her soul. It swept out from her mind, down her arm and flickered with a wobbling intensity from the tips of her fingers. It was a puny display of power, nothing compared to her normal abilities, but it was enough to tear the harness from Nibbler's face and the cruel chains from his wings and legs.

'Ppfffft!' spat Nibbler. He staggered backwards on unsteady feet with a wild look in his eyes. 'Ugh! Yuck, yuck, yuck!! Do you know how long I've been dying to spit? That harness tasted of sewer fish! It stank of rotten underwear and mouldy broccoli and . . . and . . . two days I had it stuck in my mouth!' Nibbler hopped up on his back legs and used his forepaws to wipe at his tongue. 'Two days, you know! I can't believe it. Ppft!'

'Oh, Nibbler, are you –'

'Ack! Eurgh! Ick!' coughed Nibbler as he tried to spit out the taste. 'Two days of foot cheese and toe jam in my mouth!'

'Nibbler, did they hurt –'

'Two!' snorted Nibbler. His eyes spread wide with horror and he waved one paw above his head in protest.

'Nib–'

'Aaahh . . . urgh . . . ppft!'

The young dragon continued to prance around, shaking his head in disgust and gesturing wildly. He was so caught in the moment that he failed to catch the look that crossed Charlie's face. When Charlie finally opened her mouth it was like an explosion going off.

'NIBBLER!'

'Huh? Oh . . . uh, hi, Charlie. How're you doing?' The silence, combined with Charlie's tip-tapping foot, caused Nibbler's eyebrows to wriggle in concern. His shoulders hunched forward and a flustered look passed across his face. 'Uh, the, uh, taste . . .' he tried to explain, realizing a little too late that he was in trouble.

Charlie's frown deepened. 'Do you have any idea how concerned I've been? I've been stuck in a manky, rat-infested cell worrying about what might have happened to you and all you want to do is have a sissy fit about a bad taste. Do you have any idea what it feels like to be that stressed about the safety of your friends?'

'Er . . .'

'Do you?'

'Well . . .' began Nibbler, then paused to look around with a cheeky expression. 'Before I answer your question I have one of my own which is . . . are you my momma?'

'What?' said Charlie, the unexpected change in conversational track causing her to mentally stumble. 'No, of course I'm not! What kind of stupid question was that?'

'Well, it's just that you're nagging me like an old woman and doing that squinty thing with your eyes . . . so I kinda thought it'd be wise to check.' With an air of innocence he went on to shrug his shoulders. 'Y'know just on the off chance.'

'But . . .' Nibbler's rude grin caused her own lips to twitch and she could not stop a large smile creasing her face. 'Ahhh, Nibbler, you're a joker through and through.' Reaching over she rubbed his muzzle. 'I'm glad you're OK, I was getting really worried and . . . well I'm just glad you're safe.'

Nibbler laughed at the sudden release of tension. 'I missed you too.' Leaning forward he batted his head beneath Charlie's arm and pulled her into a hug. 'So you're not my momma then?'

'Oh my gosh!' huffed Charlie and pushed him away. 'Two days of being tied up and you're still a fool!'

Nibbler chuckled in delight, secretly pleased to see her still smiling.

'Enough of this idiotic prattle!' snapped Darkmount. 'Your companion is safe. It is time we hastened and freed the other three. Hopefully they won't all be as foolish as this young Winged One.'

'Who's this?' asked Nibbler, giving the brooding Stoman a look.

'He's Edge Darkmount –'

'What! The one wh–'

'And, no, he didn't betray us,' interrupted Charlie before Nibbler could go off on another verbal rampage. 'To cut a long . . . well, medium, story short he's trustworthy . . .' She paused to look over at the Stoman bishop who, having picked up one of the unfortunate guards by the scruff of his neck, was now cruelly demanding the location of her friends. 'Well, maybe trustworthy isn't quite the right word for him. But I think he'll help us in the short term. I've made a deal with him and till it's sorted out he's going to help us.'

'Deal? What, are you crazy? I wouldn't invite a dude like that to my birthday party, let alone consider making a deal with him!' exclaimed Nibbler. He flinched as the huge bishop casually threw the guard across the room. 'What kind of deal was it?'

'I'll tell you on the way. I think he's found out where the others are.'

Edge Darkmount strode back across the room. 'Your friends are being held in the Autumn Winds Courtyard. It's on the northern side of the university, next to the city gates.'

'Did the guard say if they were OK?'

'I didn't ask, but knowing the Stoman army I would assume that they have been treated harshly – probably beaten or whipped.' He shrugged. 'We won't know for certain until we get there.'

Charlie scrunched her eyes shut at the thought of her friends taking such punishment.

The bishop continued. 'I would suggest we continue to be discreet and tunnel our way beneath the university. We don't want to deal with every guard and soldier between here and there.'

'Agreed.' Charlie nodded, seeing the wisdom of his words. 'Lead the way.'

Darkmount grunted, turned round and strode back the way they had come, his voice blossoming into song and his fists erupting into light. Charlie and Nibbler shared a quiet look of determination before following the Stoman bishop into the tunnel.

The colonel and the Shade passed from the well-kept corridors of the university into the dusty, darker vaults that lay beneath the city. Two bored guards straightened as they caught sight of the colonel. Throwing a hasty salute at him they opened the heavy door that led to the cells.

'Which one is she in?' queried the Shade.

'This one,' said the colonel, pointing at one of the doors. It took both of his hands to open the bolt, but once it was free he swung the door back and allowed the Shade to enter first.

'You bungling idiot!'

The colonel frowned. Dipping his head beneath the door-frame he glanced inside. It only took him a second to realize what had occurred. 'Guards! You –' he pointed to one. 'You are to attend me, and you –' he pointed at the other – 'go and raise the alarm. Someone has freed the Keeper.'

Drawing his sword and indicating that the remaining soldier do likewise, he began to jog briskly down the tunnel.

The Shade stared venomously at them, but swiftly followed. Punishment for this idiocy was something that could be dealt with later; first, the Keeper had to be secured.

Flitting from shadow to shadow the Shade overtook the two Stomen. Moving faster and faster, it charged on until it came to a split in the tunnel. It hissed in frustration; the scent of the Keeper was fresh in both directions. Slashing at an offending piece of rock, it spat in fury. The Shade didn't like having to make hasty decisions. When it hunted it preferred certainty, not doubt. Now it would have to split its meagre forces. Tail coiling, it waited for the two Stomen to catch up.

'The tunnel has split. You two will take the northern direction; I will continue along this path.'

'Wait, what of your brethren?' asked the colonel. 'I was informed that a full pack of Shades would be arriving at Alavis. If there are more available, now would be a good time to call upon them.'

'Sssssss . . . my brothers and sisters are on their way,' spat the Shade. 'They will arrive shortly, but for now I suggest you shut up and continue with your search!!'

The colonel nodded his head in compliance before racing north with his guard. The Shade leaped to the wall and, using it as easily as the floor, sped down the other tunnel.

4

The Courtyard

Edge Darkmount folded back the brickwork with a flicker of his hands. When he was satisfied that the way was clear he stepped from the tunnel into one of the narrow corridors that bordered the Autumn Winds Courtyard. Nibbler slipped past and tiptoed to the corner so he could peer out.

'I can't see Kelko or Jensen,' he whispered. 'The square is empty!'

The courtyard, with its rearing stone columns and impressive statues of great scholars and heroes, was indeed empty. Two guards patrolled the square, and another pair could be seen guarding the far gate, but that was it. No prisoners, no captives and certainly no friends waiting to be rescued.

A small fragment of hope plunged from Charlie's heart to wrestle its way into her stomach where it coiled uneasily like bad indigestion. What had happened to her friends?

Darkmount frowned as he too peered out. 'Perhaps they have been moved elsewhere. I will have to question those two soldiers to clarify this matter.'

'What makes you think they'll tell you anything?' asked Nibbler.

'The last guard I questioned gave up this location pretty quickly. I doubt that these soldiers will prove any different.'

'Wait,' hissed Charlie. 'I thought we were going to be subtle about this? Marching out there and demanding directions is going to bring the whole army down on our heads!'

Darkmount fixed his cold eyes on Charlie. 'What makes you think I won't be discreet? Little girl, we have all seen how weak your Will is. You will need sleep and food before you're of any use and as we don't have the time to pamper you back to health. I suggest you stand aside!'

'But –' began Charlie.

'Bah, there are only two!' snapped Darkmount.

'What about the two by the gate?'

'They will not see me.'

'I can help,' offered Nibbler.

Darkmount turned on Nibbler. 'I doubt, Hatchling, that you would be able to stalk those two half as well as I. You will stay here.'

Without waiting for a reply he softly sang two notes of power, causing his hands and feet to glow. Walking to the nearest wall, he plunged his fingers and toes into the rock and swiftly scaled the side of the courtyard.

Charlie gaped in astonishment as the Stoman bishop swept up the side of the wall, hands and feet actually sinking into the stone, giving him an unbreakable grip. Clinging first to the side of the courtyard, then the underside of the hanging eaves, he swung on to the roof then sneaked forward from gargoyle to gargoyle.

Charlie couldn't help but think that he moved like a creeping spider. She shivered in disgust and also a little in delight; it was like watching an evil superhero in action. The excitement of the moment briefly washed away her weariness and for a while she felt like her old self.

'Charlie,' hissed Nibbler.

'What?' she whispered, eyes firmly fixed on the events unfolding in the courtyard.

'I know we need to work with this guy, but he's powerful, I mean really powerful,' continued Nibbler. 'Do you really think we can trust him? What happens if he decides to turn on us?'

Charlie was quiet for a minute as she considered Nibbler's concern. As promised, she had explained the deal she'd struck with Darkmount as they'd approached the courtyard. The Winged One had not been pleased with the arrangement, and after witnessing the bishop's display of stonesinging power Charlie wasn't too sure how she felt about the matter herself.

After a moment's consideration Charlie had to admit that Nibbler was right; Edge Darkmount was brutally powerful, stronger than anyone she'd encountered since arriving in Bellania. As Charlie continued to weigh up her options, she reached for the pendant hidden round her neck. All she knew was that her parents had been kidnapped by Bane for the secrets it held and now they were trapped in his macabre Tapestry, which kept them in a terrible state of suspended animation. The Tapestry itself was beyond reach, heavily guarded by Shades and Stomen deep within the darkness of Bane's Throne Room. Life had played a cruel trick in leaving

Charlie's parents' fate in her hands. Surely parents were supposed to rescue their children, not the other way round? Charlie's knuckles whitened as she tightened her grip on the pendant.

'I don't think we've got a choice,' she said with resolve. 'We need to know what the pendant does – without it we can't move forward. As for trusting him, I don't.' Charlie could still remember the beating that Lady Narcissa and her twisted sons, the Delightful Brothers, had given her in pursuit of the bounty Bane had placed on her head . It would be a long, long time before she was stupid enough to trust a stranger again.

'And what if he turns on us?' insisted Nibbler.

'I don't think he will.'

'Why not?'

'Because he needs me to get his "god" for him. If he turns on us before then he'll lose out. Until I actually hand this vessel thingy over to him we should be safe.'

'Are you sure?'

'No!' chuckled Charlie with a wry laugh. 'I'm not. Nothing ever seems to go the way I hope, at least not in Bellania. But it makes sense. Edge Darkmount knows he's on to a good thing with me; it'd be crazy for him to do anything stupid before he gets his half of the deal. Besides, I think we're stressing too much. As soon as Sic Boy, Kelko and Jensen are back, he'll be outnumbered and outmatched. Right?'

'Right . . . I guess, but don't let your guard down. I don't like the feel of him. He's hard and he's cold, and even I know that's a bad combination.'

'Yeah, tell me about it. But you watch my back and I'll watch yours.'

'Always.'

Nibbler raised his paw, Charlie raised her hand and the two of them exchanged a high five. Sharing a grin they turned to watch their formidable, but uncertain, ally in action.

Darkmount had nearly reached the pair patrolling the courtyard. Slinking head first down the wall he paused just within arm's reach and waited.

Silent. Still.

Then he blurred into action. Grabbing one guard by the head, he slammed his unsuspecting victim against the wall. Snapping his hand back, he gripped the second guard before he had a chance to react and knocked him unconscious in a similar manner. Checking to see that the soldiers guarding the gate hadn't noticed his ambush, he stuffed his catch beneath an arm, retreated back up the wall, on to the roof and out of sight.

Charlie's mouth dropped open. She shut it, then opened it again. First the fight in the dungeon and now this.

'Have you ever . . .' she began, blinked, then shook her head in disbelief. 'Wow. That was amazing. Just amazing.'

'That's one bad man,' agreed Nibbler.

'No kidding, it's like he's part ninja or something.'

'What's a ninja?'

'You know those guys that dress in black, do *Hong Kong Phooey* and get all sneaky at night?'

'Huh?'

'Ninja!' Charlie slipped into a bad impression of a martial artist, 'You know, kung fu! Hi-yaaa!'

'What are you going on about?'

'Aw, I don't know why I bother,' grumped Charlie. 'Ninjas, they're deadly assassins that creep around, a bit like Darkmount was doing just now, they –'

The unconscious body of one of the soldiers slammed down between them, making them both jump in shock.

'What is it with you two?' hissed Darkmount as he crept down the wall with the other guard still firmly in his grip. He glared ruthlessly at them. 'Every time something needs to be done you two brats open your squabbling, petty mouths.'

'Squabble? We weren't squabbling we were talking about –'

'Enough! I am not interested. Now be quiet while I interrogate this faithless fool.'

Darkmount removed the guard from beneath his arm and shook him like a tambourine.

'Er . . . are you sure that's the best way to wake someone up?' asked Nibbler, looking on with wide eyes.

'Knocked out many Stomen lately?'

'Er . . . no, I tend to flame them.'

'So you haven't knocked any out and had to revive them?'

'Um . . . no.'

'And would you consider yourself intimate with the physiology of the Stoman body?'

'I'll, er . . . just shut up and leave you to it, shall I?'

'Answer the question!'

'Ah . . . no.'

'Well, why don't you close your prattling mouth and leave

this to me?' snapped the bishop. Bending over, he glowered at Nibbler. 'Or would you like to spend the rest of the day standing around cracking foolish, immature jokes?'

'Stop picking on him,' said Charlie, stepping forward. 'He's sorry, I'm sorry and I'm pretty sure that guard is going to feel sorry when he comes to. Let's just please get on with it. I need to know what's happened to Jensen and Kelko.'

'Hey, he's waking up!' Nibbler pointed enthusiastically at their prisoner.

'Gaaahh,' groaned the guard, his head lolling around and his eyes unfocused. 'What happened to me?'

'I happened, you unrepentant worm,' rumbled Dark-mount, the baritone of his voice rolling off the wall like an avalanche.

The soldier, realizing his predicament, reared back his head and opened his mouth. Darkmount slapped him before he could cry for help.

'Enough of that nonsense! Tell me what happened to the two Tremen being guarded here or I'll stuff your head into that wall and leave you hanging there like a festive orna-ment.'

The guard's eyes flashed to the wall then back to the bishop's serious face. It didn't take him long to crack.

'They've been taken to the Soul Mines of Zhartoum,' he babbled, then flinched as Darkmount raised a threatening fist.

'When did this happen?'

'This morning,' gabbled the soldier. 'They got processed pretty quickly and –'

'And what of the dog that accompanied them?'

'It went with the Tremen!'

'You mean they've gone?' asked Charlie, putting her hand on the soldier's wrist.

'Y-yes!'

'So they're not in the city?'

'No.'

'Well, where is this mine?'

'It's to the north-west of –'

'Be silent,' snapped Darkmount. He gave the guard an idle shake to emphasize his demand, then turned to Charlie. 'If your friends have gone then that is that. It no longer affects us.'

'What do you mean it no longer affects us?' protested Charlie.

'It means that they are beyond our immediate reach.'

'Well, we'll just have to go after them then!'

'There is no "we" in this matter, little girl!' spat Darkmount. 'I agreed to help you in this matter provided that they were still in the city.'

'What are you saying?'

'Pah! Your ignorance is despicable! We have a deal. I have done my half now it is up to you to honour your side of the bargain.'

'What! But my friends need help, we need to go after them, we need –'

In a fit of anger Darkmount smashed the guard against the wall. 'Listen, child, a deal is a deal! You. Will. Uphold. Your. Side. Of. The. Bargain!'

Charlie and Nibbler backed off at the sight of the enraged

bishop. Black waves of anger shimmered above his head, shoulders and clenched fists.

'A deal is a deal!' he repeated. 'If you want to find out what your pendant is capable of you will hold true to your side of the bargain or I will walk, right here, right now and you will never – so I swear by Rock and Crystal – *never* learn its secrets!'

Charlie staggered backwards as she stared at the incensed Stoman. Thoughts and emotions cascaded through her heart and mind. Jensen, Kelko, Sic Boy, her parents, Bane, Bellania, her grandma, Lady Dridif and all the other tangled threads in her life. What could she do? She stared at Darkmount and knew, just knew, that this was a make-or-break moment. If she wanted the pendant's secret, she'd have to go with him, but at what cost?

'Nibbler.'

'I'm here, Charlie.' He was hunched into a taut, stream-lined pose, as if he were ready to spring on Darkmount at any moment.

'If I go with him will you sort out the others?'

'No.'

'What?'

'I said no.'

'Nibbler, this isn't the time to be joking! I need you to do this.'

'I'm sorry, Charlie,' he said with genuine concern in his eyes, 'but I'm not going to leave you to do this by yourself. No way, no how. Kelko and Jensen can look out for themselves, they're adults, they've got Sic Boy with them and they're experienced. They know what they're about and they

know how to survive. You're a Keeper, you're new to Bellania, you're my responsibility and above all you're my friend.
I'm not leaving you.'

'But –'

'No buts on this one, Charlie. We'll do this together, we'll
do this right and then we can get the others later.'

Charlie stared at him: all proud, loyal and every inch a
dragon. She wanted to slap him. She wanted to kiss him.
She settled for a little sigh instead.

'All right, Darkmount, we're with you. Let's go get this
god of yours.'

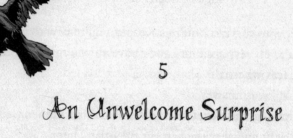

5

An Unwelcome Surprise

The Shade was almost shaking with fury. First the Keeper had managed to escape and now the Winged One.

'What happened?' it hissed as it surveyed the wrecked dungeon.

The guard swallowed as he warily eyed the angry shadow. He looked for some support from his friends, but after Edge Darkmount's brutal attack he was the only one still capable of standing. 'She had a Stonesinger with her – a bishop, I think, but strong, stronger than any other I've seen.'

'Sssss . . . a renegade?'

'Yes, he . . . well, you can see for yourself. He cut through us like a flame through a haystack.'

The Shade eyed the carnage, listened to the moans and groans, watched as a soldier tried to lever himself off the floor using his axe as a crutch.

'Uselesssss!' it snarled. Coiling and spiking its black flesh in frustration it quickly took stock of its options. They were limited.

It reared up on its back limbs and stretched open its mouth. A scream of hunger, need, desire, hatred and, above all, fury, spat from its jaws. The sound snapped around the dark recesses of the room, shivered through the bricks, sank into the rock, slithered into the earth and reached into the dark places where the Shade's brethren waited.

His call was answered.

The crying and echoing call of his siblings grew nearer, filling the dungeon with dread and horror. The bruised and battered soldiers huddled closer to their companions, clenching their weapons with white-knuckled fists, and stared uncertainly towards the dark corners of the room, which began to move, tremble and shake. Heaving and writhing, Shade after Shade leaked out from the cracks and gullies and other secret entrances hidden in the ancient stonework to join their brother. They slunk into the light, covering the floor as they gripped and groped at each other like a mound of blackened and rotten fruit.

As the noise grew to almost unbearable levels, the soldiers flinched from the snarling pack of Shades. Then, with a final hiss, the mound of constricted black flesh broke apart and, like a rushing river of black silk, the Shades sped off in pursuit of Charlie and her powerful new guardian.

'Good. You have chosen wisely,' said Darkmount, and for the first time something like a smile cracked his lips. Not a great smile, not a nice smile, but a smile that seemed to indicate . . . something. Success maybe. 'We will travel from here to the Southern Citadel and there I will tell you half of the pendant's secret.'

'And the other half when I get you your god, right?'

'Correct, little girl.'

'How are we going to get to this place?' asked Nibbler. 'And . . . wait a minute, where's this "Stubborn Citadel" anyway? Is it near here or what?'

Darkmount turned to the Winged One. 'It's on the southern tip of the Western Mountains, where the mountains dwindle into the low rise of the Slumbering Hills.'

'Er,' said Charlie as she tried to put her limited grasp of Bellanian geography to use. 'So how far away is that?'

'Far enough,' he said. 'Fifteen days' walk. But I am not prepared to undertake a long, risk-filled journey. We will escape this fallen city and walk to my place of refuge where you will rest and recover your Will. Once your strength has returned you will open a Portal to the Slumbering Hills.'

'And then what?' said Charlie. 'How are we going to get into the Southern Citadel? Are we going –'

The tolling and clanging of alarm bells interrupted her question. They could hear raised voices and a distant trample of booted feet that grew nearer.

'Pah!' grimaced Darkmount. 'Those buffoons have finally realized what's happened. It is time for us to be gone.'

Darkmount raised a fist and opened his mouth in preparation to stonesing, but as he did so the colonel, accompanied by the Stoman soldier, leaped from the tunnel's mouth. Both warriors had raised swords that they aimed at Darkmount's chest and it was only by hastily jumping backwards that the bishop avoided being skewered. Again he opened his mouth to sing, but the colonel backhanded him in the mouth with the pommel of his sword. Darkmount tried to sidestep the next blow, but the cramped width of the corridor restricted his mobility. As he attempted to draw breath, the colonel once again slipped past his defences and struck him in the gut, winding him.

'Back! Fall back!' gasped the bishop, gesturing at Charlie and Nibbler to give him space to manoeuvre.

The three of them staggered backwards into the Autumn Winds Courtyard. The colonel and Stoman warrior sprang forward, pursuing and harassing Darkmount and doing their utmost to prevent the bishop from opening his mouth or drawing a full breath. As large and as ferocious as the Stoman bishop was, without his stonesinging to give him the edge he was losing this fight against the two experienced and formidable swordsmen.

Nibbler, realizing that this was potentially more a game of wits than skill, slipped past Edge Darkmount and snapped at the colonel. Gusting out a small jet of flame, he forced the two warriors to scrabble backwards. The Winged One grinned in victory as he heard the bishop's voice breaking into song behind him, the wave of light reassuring him that his mighty ally was now ready to fight.

'Well, well,' chuckled Nibbler, shooting a cocky look at the colonel. 'Looks like we've got a big, bad Stonesinger on our side! Whatcha going to do now?'

The large doors lining the courtyard burst open, spilling bloodthirsty soldiers and snarling Shades into the square.

'Well, well,' said the colonel with deadpan humour and an eyebrow raised to perfection. 'Looks like I've got a big bad army on my side. The question is, I think, what are *you* going to do, my winged friend?'

6

A Clash of Arms

Shocked and caught off guard, Charlie stared at the charging soldiers.

Puffs of dirt kicked up around their shins. Sunlight glinted off their swords and spears. Shades snarled and screeched as they coiled and bristled between the soldiers' legs. The sound of boots trampling on the flagstones thundered in her ears. But rising above it all were the steady, chanted notes of Darkmount's singing.

Statues and chunks of rock spun across the courtyard, slamming into the Stoman troops as Darkmount ripped free whatever was close to hand to use as makeshift missiles. As the ranks drew closer, Nibbler opened his mouth to spit crackling jets of flame that turned spear shafts and bows to ash, ignited clothing and scorched the eyebrows off more than a few unfortunate warriors.

Shielded between Nibbler and Darkmount, Charlie hesitated, well aware that her Will had deserted her. She felt useless. Without the power of the Keepers she was just a normal girl. Uncertain, and pretty sure that her K'Changa wouldn't cut it against armoured Stomen, she reached down and picked up a clump of rock, a fragment from one of Darkmount's crude missiles. Maybe she could knock out a Stoman or Shade if she got close enough, or lucky enough. Maybe.

She licked her lips and realized just how dry her throat had become. Looking up she saw that the spears and swords were drawing nearer, and she wondered what it would feel like to have one of those strike her. Would it hurt? Would it be quick? She felt nauseous. Butterflies swept around her stomach and she had to fight the urge to vomit.

'YOU FAITHLESS CURS!' roared Darkmount in a voice that eclipsed the courtyard. 'HAVE YOU ALREADY FORGOTTEN THE POWER OF THE TRUE FAITH?!'

Scowling, the bishop sucked in a deep lungful of air and increased the power of his song. The flames billowing from his arms erupted into vivid shades of green as his feet and legs shone with power. Marching forward, he lifted one foot high and stamped down heavily.

The square shook as the flagstones round his feet shattered, statues fell from their plinths and the courtyard erupted. Pressure waves swept outward, knocking over the few remaining sculptures and bowling the troops and Shades off their feet.

Lifting his other foot Darkmount stamped again.

And again.

The courtyard rippled and rocked like a pond disrupted by a thrown brick. Nothing stood still. The statues, screaming Shades and fallen warriors were flung repeatedly off their feet as wave after wave of rock rippled across the square. Charlie and Nibbler, sheltered from the epicentre by Darkmount's bulk, stood and stared, their mouths gaping in disbelief.

Finally, the courtyard fell silent. Several Shades shook themselves upright and one or two Stomen staggered to their feet, eyes dazed and unfocused. Others crawled around disorientated and dizzy, trying to find weapons and lost helmets.

'It is as I thought,' growled Darkmount. 'They have lost their way; they –'

He was interrupted as the sound of singing wafted from the doors that lined the square. Glowing figures shone in the buildings' darkened interiors. As the lights drew closer, they took shape and Charlie realized that they were Stomen. Nine of them, wrapped in armour and ornate flowing robes.

'Stonesingers!' exclaimed Darkmount. 'Too many of them for me to take on alone. We need to go – now!'

Stepping into the courtyard, the Stonesingers formed loose ranks. Their voices intermingled, creating a tapestry of sound that stretched from wall to wall. As the singers began to gesture with their hands, Charlie could feel the strength of their power. Her ears popped, her skin tingled and the hair on her neck began to curl. One by one the Stonesingers pointed downward. The cracked and ruined flagstones by their feet began to shift and heave as though some great, buried beast was beginning to stir.

'Winged One,' snapped Darkmount, realizing that it was too late to flee. 'Give them fire while I block their approach.'

'On it,' said Nibbler.

Charlie noticed that Nibbler didn't appear fazed by the turn of events. He did after all have his wings and fiery breath to rely on.

Unfurling his wings, he leaped into the sky. Circling over the Stonesingers, he spat out a bright jet of flame. Three of the singers turned to meet him. Tearing large slabs of paving from the floor to use as temporary shields, they defended themselves and their company from Nibbler's flames. The remaining six continued with their efforts, their song growing more complex, more ornate. Their voices built to a crescendo and with a fierce cracking noise the courtyard's floor burst apart. A gigantic head lurched upward, followed by a huge shoulder that squirmed its way free of the constricting flagstones to reveal a massive groping arm. Controlled by the song, the stone monstrosity began to tear its way from the ground, revealing more and more of its hulking body.

'A behemoth,' growled Darkmount, grimacing at the new threat.

The thing looked vaguely man-shaped, like a mannequin that had been carved from rough clay. Charlie's legs buckled as she gawped at the looming giant brought to life and puppeteered by stonesinging. Such a thing couldn't be real. It just couldn't.

Darkmount's voice crashed into the square, breaking the power of the moment. His deep voice sliced through the singers' chant, causing the behemoth to stumble. Taking advantage of their momentary confusion, he stamped over to the nearest building and plunged his arms into the brickwork. Grasping hold of the building's supports, he strained, his voice catching with the effort. The building quivered and shook as the bishop took a step backwards and pulled it with him. Its walls hung at a crazy angle, cracks appeared across the brickwork and a small waterfall of tiles cascaded from the roof to shatter on the flagstones below. As the stone behemoth finally tore itself free and began to lurch upright,

Darkmount gave another massive heave, ripping the building from its foundations. With a groaning roar, all five of its floors crashed down on the behemoth's head, burying it and the Stonesingers beneath its fallen masonry. A cloud of dust billowed outward, covering everything.

The sudden silence was shocking.

Nibbler flapped over, folding his wings as he skidded to the floor. 'Oh my gosh, that was awesome! Pulling a whole building down? A whole building! Wow, when you get a job done you don't do it in halves, do you?'

Darkmount paused to catch his breath. 'Faith gifts the righteous with strength,' he rasped as he surveyed the ruined courtyard. In the distance they could hear a clamouring alarm bell. 'I have no desire to face more Stonesingers. Come, it is time for us to bid this place farewell.'

Gesturing for them to follow, he retreated to the tunnel. Taking one last look at the devastated courtyard Charlie and Nibbler returned to the subterranean passageway. Darkmount, hands still aglow, pulled the mouth of the tunnel shut behind them, preventing any further pursuit.

The Shade stared at the ruined courtyard and the devastated remains of the demolished building, and hissed. 'How could you allow this to happen?'

The colonel shrugged, then immediately regretted it. His broken collarbone didn't allow for such gestures. 'Every soldier must face a defeat now and again. In our business it is unavoidable.'

'In war perhaps, but this is unforgivable! You were to watch a child. A child!'

'Who had the aid of a renegade bishop. And by the looks of the damage and casualties involved I would have to say no ordinary bishop either. Rarely does one encounter such power.'

'Is that all you have to say in your defence?'

The colonel turned to the Shade. 'Look at what he did! One man against a pack of Shades! One man that took out nine Singers! Nine! The fact that some of us are still alive . . . well, I consider that lucky.'

'Lucky?' hissed the Shade. 'Lucky?! Ssssss . . . count yourself lucky that we need all our officers for the invasion of Deepforest, otherwise I would be gutting you for such a miserable failure! Our lord will not be happy with this news and if I have to pay the burden for your failure, be sure that my brethren will ensure you share a part of the pain.'

Spitting and shrieking in anger, it slunk from the courtyard, leaving the colonel to reflect on his threat in the wake of Darkmount's destruction.

A Journey Underground

Charlie groaned as she staggered along the tunnel. Her body felt like it was beginning to shut down. The pain and hardship she had endured over the last couple of days was catching up with her, and the adrenalin that had kept her going was long gone. Her wrists and shoulders screamed with every step, her ribs cramped and spasmed from where she had been beaten and the lack of sleep meant she stumbled with nearly every step.

'How much longer are we going to walk for?' she moaned. Darkmount had been carving their way underground for what had seemed like hours. 'C'mon, Darkmount. I'm knackered! You said you were taking us to a place where I could rest and recover my Will. Well, if we carry on like this it's going take two weeks of sleep and lie-ins for me to be able to remember my own name, let alone summon my Will.'

'We are almost there,' rumbled Darkmount. He didn't bother to turn round.

'You said that two hours ago!' complained Charlie.

Darkmount suddenly stopped and turned to fix his cold grey eyes on her. 'Well, if you didn't drag your feet we would be there already. We are a mere five miles from Alavis and Alacorn. The ground above will still be a hotpot of activity and if we were to walk up there we would soon be caught like piglets in the butcher house! Do not forget that Bane's forces control this land, which is why we must continue to travel underground.'

He skewered Charlie with a piercing look, before turning his attention back to the path. Muttering under his breath about 'infantile youths' and 'spoilt children', Darkmount stamped ahead.

Charlie licked her lips. The fatigue weighed down on her like an anvil, more pressing than before. The pain in her body grew, her legs felt weak and her vision began to blur. As she took several staggering steps forward, nausea churned in her stomach and up her throat.

'Nibbler,' she mumbled through numb lips. 'Nibbler, I think I've got to stop for a bit –'

As the world grew dark, she slowly toppled over. The last thing she remembered seeing was Nibbler's sudden look of concern as he sprang forward to break her fall.

The driver hitched up his trousers, threw the dregs of his coffee into the bushes and kicked some dirt over the fire, then both he and the guard clambered back on to the wagon.

'Well, you green-skinned sacks o' lard, we're almost there. Another day and you'll be able to admire your new home.'

The guard chuckled. 'Think they'll like it there?'

'Oh, sure, what's not to like? Fourteen-hour shifts of hard

labour? No daylight, no warmth, a hard floor to sleep on and food so bad that not even a dog would eat it. Course they'll like it, it's a real holiday camp.'

The guard laughed yet again. He loved his job. It was easy, they got to take their time travelling from place to place and he could torment the prisoners to his heart's content. Reaching over, he hooked a finger under Jensen's gag. 'So tell me, are you looking forward to your stay in the Soul Mines?'

Jensen worked his jaw from side to side, trying to release some of the cramp. Once he felt he could speak coherently he beamed up at the Stoman. 'Oh, of course. The faster we can get there the better.'

'What?' sneered the guard. 'And why would you tree-fairies be so keen to get there? Think you might bump into your momma?'

'Possibly, possibly.' Jensen grinned. 'But ta be honest the sooner we get there the sooner we can hope ta stumble across some real humour. Listening ta ya guys trying ta rustle up some witty banter is killing me. I've never heard anyone butcher a joke as bad as ya guys. Maybe if I slipped ya a little cash ya could give us some ear plugs?'

With a roar the guard jumped from the seat into the back of the wagon.

Cursing, the driver sprang after him. 'Stop that!' he urged, grabbing the guard's raised fist. 'You know we'll lose our bonus if they turn up more damaged than they already are!'

'Shatter that! They're already black and blue with bruises, the sergeant-at-arms won't notice a couple more. Besides, you know they've got it coming!'

'No doubt they do, but either way I'm not risking it. I'm not going to lose my bonus over this green idiot's mouth!'

The guard's eyes narrowed into slits. 'All right, but no food or water for them; they can suffer a little for their impudence!'

'Sounds fine ta me. Ya can't cook anyway!' Jensen smirked. 'An' don't forget the ear plugs!'

'Why you –' snarled the guard. Spinning round, he drew back his fist only to have it grabbed once again by the driver.

'Stone Gods and Crystal Daemons, but I've had enough of this!' Reaching down he gagged Jensen then pushed the protesting guard back to the front of the wagon. 'No more noises, burps or farts out of you two!' He glared at Jensen and Kelko, then turned to the guard. 'And, you, you better keep a hold on your temper.'

Settling back into his seat the driver shook his head. This trip was turning out to be a lot more bothersome than he had first thought. Just one more day to go. Trouble was, he had a sinking feeling that it would be an insufferably long final day.

'Tremen,' he said. Leaning over he spat into the mud-churned road.

Bane roared and slammed his fist through the wall.

'Again? AGAIN? You insolent dogs! How could you allow that childish bag of flesh and bones to escape? Have none of you learned from your previous, inexcusable failures?' Bane snatched up the Shade and flung it at the nearest group of men-at-arms. All went down in a tangle of limbs. 'I should tear your stomachs from your backbones and feast on your innards!'

Black waves of anger writhed above him like a dark halo. He began to pace the Throne Room. 'The time has come to stick a nail in that young Keeper's luck. Pages and scribes, attend me! Ensure that the following proclamation is carried across the land: I, Bane, Lord of the Western Mountains, declare Charlie Keeper to be an outcast and outlaw. I will pay whomever brings me her head and her pendant fifty baskets of emeralds, a hundred baskets of sapphires and a thousand fistfuls of gold coins. If her head is delivered still fresh and bleeding I will double the sum offered. If she is delivered whimpering and broken to lie at my feet I will triple the sum and bestow the title of Lordship of Alavis on whomever succeeds in this undertaking.'

The scribes worked furiously as they took note of their master's words. When their quills had finished scratching they bowed their heads.

'Good,' growled Bane, his anger and black halo abating. 'If my own servants cannot see the task done then I will see that all of Bellania is turned against that annoying maggot. Make sure the proclamation is carried far and wide. Ensure it reaches the ear of every assassin and mercenary in Bellania. Is this understood?'

The scribes and pages bowed again in silence.

As they trailed from the Throne Room, Bane clapped his hands together. 'Send for my generals. I want to know how Alacorn and the remaining Human cities fare against my banner.'

'Wake up,' growled a voice.

Charlie roused herself and slowly sat up. Her head felt muzzy.

Darkmount sat beside her. Blinking, she realized she was on a bed. The Stoman held a steaming bowl and a spoon, which he pressed into her hands, urging her to eat. As she swallowed the warm pleasantly spiced food, she began to feel stronger. Looking around, she saw Nibbler asleep at the foot of the bed. Her wrists had been wrapped in bandages and her clothes, folded neatly on a nearby chair, had apparently been washed while she slept. Her sluggish brain held ghost memories of being fed before.

'How long have I been asleep?'

'It has been nearly two days since you passed out in the tunnel,' said Darkmount, taking the empty bowl from her hands. He passed her a glass of water. 'I've been feeding you every six hours to rebuild your strength and I've attended to your various cuts, bruises and sprains.'

Charlie slowly flexed her arms and shoulders. They were still stiff, but obviously better than before. She felt stronger too; tired but no longer exhausted.

'Where are we?'

'My place of refuge.'

'Where is –'

'Bah! No more questions from you. At least not now. It is the middle of the night and although I woke you to feed you I did not intend for a full-blown conversation.'

'Pfft.' Charlie rolled her eyes. 'It's not like you've ever been one for long heart-to-heart talks.'

Darkmount let that one slide.

'What about Sleeping Beauty over there? Is he OK?'

'Ha! Other than his empty head that Hatchling has no worries. With the ridiculous amount of food he's been wolfing down do not be surprised if he starts to show rapid signs of growth.'

'Really? Will he grow big?'

'Big? You've obviously never seen an adult Winged One. Your companion has a lot of filling out ahead of him. But for now, enough words.' He held up his hand, silencing her next question. 'I would suggest that you continue to get what sleep you can. Tomorrow we will discuss strategy and in the evening we will make our move.'

'That quickly?'

'Your strength appears to have recovered and I do not wish to dawdle. My god awaits and Bane deserves to face judgement followed by swift and serious penance.'

'Yeah, well if we're going to get your god tomorrow I'm going to want half the secret to my pendant before we go.'

'So the deal was made, so it shall be,' said Darkmount with a nod of his head. 'Tomorrow, then, we shall talk of strategies, of gods and of secrets.'

'Tomorrow,' echoed Charlie.

8

The Pendant's Secret

'Charlie, wake up!' insisted Nibbler. He pulled back one of her eyelids to peer into her bloodshot eyes.

'Ppff, huh? Whuddya want?' Charlie stared around with a dazed look then hastily sat up. 'Where are we? How'd we get here?'

'Darkmount carried you here, remember?'

It all came rushing back to her. 'Yeah, yeah I remember,' she yawned and knuckled her eyes. 'You know, I don't think I've had one night of decent sleep since I got to Bellania. I've got to do something about all these dark dreams I've been having.'

'Too right you do,' snorted Nibbler. 'Have you ever tried sleeping in the same room as someone who fidgets as much as you?'

'Is it that bad?'

'Charlie.' Nibbler's eyes grew wide. 'You have no idea. If it's any consolation at least you don't fart in your sleep.'

'Nibbler!'

'Well it's true – you don't. You kinda make up for it though by snoring like a bad-tempered volcano.'

'I do not! Well, maybe I snore a little, but I don't think

it's as crazy as you're trying to make out.' She did her best to ignore Nibbler's wicked grin. 'So where's Edge Darkmount?'

'He's outside. This place is amazing; you'll love it! Here, let me show you.'

As Nibbler led the way through several rooms and corridors, Charlie soon realized they were in the home of a scholar. Books and scrolls lined shelf after shelf. There were blackboards, thick with scribbled notes and mathematical symbols and maps of far-off places. Detailed diagrams of Winged Ones hung from the walls. Some were sketched details of their wings, others showed close-ups of their heads and yet more showed them in varying postures of flight and rest.

Nibbler caught sight of Charlie's questioning look. 'Darkmount said he started moving all his stuff here as soon as Alavis came under siege. You won't believe it, there's hundreds and hundreds of books on Winged Ones, histories of old empires and encyclopaedia of strange creatures that live thousands and thousands of miles away. It's awesome! If I stayed here long enough I reckon I could catch up on the education I'm missing. And check this out . . . Apparently, half the books Darkmount wrote himself! But if you think the house is cool wait till you see what's outside.'

Nibbler pushed a door open and light came spilling in.

They were still underground, but in a cave the like of which Charlie had never seen before. The cavern was so large that it dwarfed Darkmount's house. Charlie gazed around with a sense of wonder and delight.

Fat stalagmites reared upward like great tree trunks to

touch a roof of amethyst that glowed and flickered with a light of its own. Several chuckling and trickling streams meandered between the large stalagmites to gently fill an oval pond. Looking into the crystal clear waters Charlie could see lazy carp swimming in circles. Moths the size of eagles flapped close to the ceiling, the strange light from the amethyst giving their wings a soft, lantern-like glow.

'So our sleeping Keeper finally awakens,' said Darkmount, appearing from behind a stalagmite.

'Erm . . . yeah.' Charlie fidgeted as she realized she owed this unlikeable man a debt for the care he had given her over the past days. 'I wanted to thank you for carrying me here and for all the cooking . . . That was . . . nice of you.'

'We are partners in the undertaking of a deal,' grunted Darkmount. 'It makes sense that I look after you. So today is the day for action. Are you ready?'

'Yes, I think I am. But if we're making a move today then today is also the day you tell me about my pendant.'

The Stoman bishop nodded. 'And so I shall. But first you must show me that you have regained control of your Will. Show me that, then we will talk about your pendant and then, well, then we shall talk about retrieving my god.'

'OK.' Charlie could already sense that using her Will wouldn't be a problem. The rest had finally restored the familiar energy that nestled like a deep pool within her body. 'So what exactly do you want me to do?'

'First show me your talent. Show me you can hold your Will.'

Charlie reached deep then grinned as she felt her Will coiled inside. It was like the welcome return of an old friend.

Golden flames flowed from her hands and forearms. 'Is this what you were looking for?'

'Good,' grunted Darkmount. 'Now open a Portal.'

'Where to?'

'Anywhere, it matters not.'

Charlie hesitated. By the rules that governed her Will it needed to be a place she could visualize. Reaching a decision, she gestured with her hands. A slice appeared in the air. She teased it apart so that it formed a circular portal; through it they could see Deepforest and the slender towers of Sylvaris, the Treman capital. The sound of tree song and the scent of orchids breezed into the cave, filling her with a welcome sense of déjà vu. Memories and flashbacks flickered in her mind's eye: the Jade Circle informing her of her parents' fate, Lady Dridif's no-nonsense approach to leading the Circle and ruling the city, eating exotic new foods with Kelko, and the day that her mentor and friend Azariah Keeper had first saved her from Bane's Shades . . . and how he had ultimately died while trying to protect her from Mr Crow.

'Good. Now open another,' demanded Darkmount, snapping Charlie out of her daydream.

Charlie closed the first Portal, then, gaining confidence, swiftly opened one more. Through it they could all see the waterfall and cave through which, after being chased from her home by Bane and Mr Crow, she had first arrived in Bellania. Mist from the waterfall sprayed through the Portal.

'Good. Now open two.'

'Two?' Charlie's face grew pale. 'I've never opened two! I didn't even know it could be done.'

Darkmount shrugged. 'Well now would be as good a time as any to try it.'

Charlie tensed her shoulders and hustled forward like a wrestler limbering up before confronting an opponent. Keeping the Portal with the waterfall open, she gestured with her left hand and to her delight a second Portal opened to reveal the grassy clearing where she had first met Kelko and the other Tremen.

'Excellent. I believe that you are up to the task that lies ahead.'

Charlie smiled. Having her Will back felt wonderful. After the low moments in the Alavisian prison and during the escape she had felt weak . . . useless. But now, now she felt whole. Her grin nearly split her face in two. 'So now it's time for the pendant!'

'Very well.' Darkmount put out his hand.

Charlie felt the twin emotions of nervousness and excitement. Excitement that now, at long last, she would learn the pendant's secret. Nervousness about entrusting it to someone she barely knew. Realizing that she would have to trust someone at some point in order to have it examined, she took a deep breath and with the insistent throb of excitement urging her on she pulled it from round her neck and placed it in Darkmount's outstretched hand.

He held it up to the light, gave it a close look, then began to stroke it with his eyes closed. After a few brief moments of the slightly odd stroking he grunted thoughtfully and passed it back to Charlie.

'Is that all?' she blinked. 'No magic, no flash of light?'

'"Magic"? Bah, why do children always believe in magic?'

'Well, I thought it was, you know, a magical item,' insisted Charlie.

'Of course it's not a magical item! It is a Winged One's artefact and it is my long years of study that allow me to plumb its secrets, not because I spent my youth daydreaming about "magic"!'

'So what is it?'

'It is a key.'

'Yeah, I know that already.' Charlie raised an eyebrow. 'But a key to what?'

'A key to free the Winged Ones.'

'Huh?' Charlie turned to stare at Nibbler. 'But I thought Bane needed to completely take over Bellania before he could block their return? That's what Lady Dridif told me.'

'Bane's power has increased far beyond anyone's reckoning. My sources tell me that Bane has already managed to block the Winged Ones' Gateway back. They cannot return, at least not through their traditional route. Hatchling, you must have returned to Bellania before this happened.'

'What? Bane has blocked their return *already*?' choked Charlie. Her dreams that the pendant would unlock some secret weapon – perhaps a magical wand or a super cannon – or give her the ability to control a legion of undead ninjas, were dashed. And now this news! 'How are we supposed to do anything if we can't get the Winged Ones back? I thought they were supposed to save the day and kick Bane's backside! And what's up with the pendant? I thought it was supposed to be a key to a weapon of some sort. A really powerful weapon that was going to defeat Bane and end this war!'

'Wait,' insisted Darkmount, holding out a hand to calm

Charlie. 'Wait before you jump to conclusions. Yes, Bane has managed to block their Gateway, but that doesn't mean that there aren't other ways for them to return. Have you listened to anything I said? The Winged Ones knew that Bane was rising too quickly. They knew the threat he posed. And although you might not appreciate it, a key to return the Winged Ones to Bellania is a tool more powerful than your feeble reckoning. Imagine if the Winged Ones could return, especially if Bane wasn't expecting it. What would happen to him then? All his dreams of conquest would come to nought. The Winged Ones could snuff out his empire like the wind does a candle.'

'But how did he manage to block their Gateway?'

'Pah! Easily! Do not forget how powerful he has grown and how large the forces that march beneath his banner. I should imagine that sending a small part of his army to the Winged Mountain was a simple task met with very little resistance. I doubt it would have taken his soldiers long to slit the throats of the sentinels that guarded the Winged Ones' sanctuary. Since then I hear he's kept a cadre of Stone-singers garrisoned there, where they funnel their energies day and night towards the Gateway, ensuring that it remains closed.'

Charlie rubbed her forehead in an attempt to dispel her growing headache. The pendant's secret wasn't all she had hoped it would be. She had wanted a quick fix. Not this. 'So if the Winged Ones can't return that way, what's this other route you're talking about?'

'Well, the Winged Ones weren't stupid. They prepared another Gate to be used in dire circumstances.'

'What, like a secret door?'

'Yes.'

'And you know where it is?'

'Yes I do. The pendant reveals the location, but if you recall our deal was half the secret now, half the secret later. My god first, location second.'

'OK, that sounds fair. But how'd you know about this Gateway?' asked Charlie with a suspicious frown. 'It's not like that pendant came with a map and an instruction manual.'

Darkmount chuckled. 'Yes it did.'

'Ppft. No it didn't.'

'Yes it did. The instructions are written upon it.'

'What? No they aren't!'

'Yes they are. They have been written in Hydraic script.' Darkmount sighed when he saw her puzzled frown. 'Feel it, feel the pendant.'

Charlie rubbed it. 'I can't feel anything.'

'Idiot child. The pendant is not smooth is it?'

'Well no, it's got lots of little bumps on it.'

'Those "bumps" are Hydraic script.'

'Huh?'

'It is meant to be read with your fingers. By touch.'

'Oh . . . like Braille? For the blind?'

'I am not familiar with this "Braille", but, yes, it is a script meant for the blind.'

'Slick!' Charlie turned to Nibbler and grinned. 'How cool is that? Darkmount, one more question. How do I use the pendant once you give me the location?'

The Stoman shrugged. 'Much like a normal key. Take it

to the Gateway, where you will find a keyhole in the Gate itself. Place the pendant in it and use your Will to power it open.'

'Right . . . I'm still not a hundred per cent with this Keeper stuff. I know how to open a Portal and how to use my Will to boost my K'Changa. But I'm not sure how to do other stuff with it. Last time I managed to use the pendant to call Nibbler and Azariah it was by accident.'

'I am not a Keeper; my strengths and studies outside stonesinging are limited to Winged Ones. Opening the Gate is something that you will have to work out for yourself.'

Charlie bit her lower lip then forced a confident grin. 'Nothing is ever easy, huh? OK, that's something that I can sort out on my own.'

'I'll be there too,' said Nibbler. 'If it's a Winged One's Gateway then maybe I can help too?'

Charlie flashed him a smile. 'Thanks, Nibbler. So that's it, then. Once we've got your god you'll give me the location, right?'

'Correct.'

'Then all I have to do is travel to the Gate, plonk in the pendant, use my Will on it, bring the Winged Ones up to date on what's been going on, then go give Bane the beating he deserves and rescue my parents?'

'Pah! I do not care what you do – just help me get my god.'

'Still not one for small talk, are you?'

Darkmount gave her a long level stare.

Charlie sighed. 'OK, then, let's talk about what we're going to do tonight.'

'We will talk over a meal. You will need all your energy for what comes next. It will not be easy and shall most assuredly be dangerous.'

'Oh, great.' Charlie grimaced, rolling her eyes at Nibbler. 'I can hardly wait.'

9

Planning Ahead

The three of them sat in the middle of the cavern. Darkmount's cooking, although no five-star affair, was filling and hearty.

Charlie stretched the kinks from her back then leaned back to enjoy the feeling of being suitably stuffed. Her eyes narrowed as Nibbler, having polished off his bowl, pulled out a great slab of ham.

'Where'd you snatch that from?'

'I didn't "snatch" it,' he protested. 'Darkmount gave it to me in exchange for allowing him to sketch my wings.'

Charlie looked at her friend. 'Darkmount's right you know. You've got bigger.'

It was true. Nibbler had bulked up. No longer was he the size of a mastiff; he was more the size of a tiger.

Nibbler paused in his efforts to bury his face in the ham. 'What? Is that a bad thing?'

'No, no, Nibbler.' Charlie couldn't help but laugh. 'It's not a bad thing. It's just a surprise that's all. I guess Winged Ones do "growth spurts" slightly differently from Humans.'

'Well, Nibbler by name, Nibbler by nature,' he smirked.

'Enough,' interrupted Darkmount, 'Enough of this pointless chatting. We have work to do.'

'Sorry.' Charlie sat up. She knew she'd need to pay attention if she hoped to keep her skin in one piece while retrieving the bishop's god. 'So what's the plan for tonight?'

'Tonight will come in two parts. Firstly, we have to gain entrance to the Stubborn Citadel and, secondly, you will have to enter the Gate that leads to the lower dominion while we keep the soldiers occupied. But before we delve into details you will need to know some geography. The Stubborn Citadel lies on the southernmost part of the mountains, where the Western Mountains join the Slumbering Hills.' With a few notes of stonesinging and a wave of his hands, Darkmount caused the floor to ripple and move. At his insistence the ground pulled itself into a three-dimensional map.

Charlie blinked at the phenomenon. It was very detailed, more a work of art than a topographical map.

Darkmount stood and, like a teacher giving a lecture, began to point out locations. 'Deepforest and Sylvaris lie here in the east.' His fingers then tracked to the left, indicating a range of jagged-looking mountains that ran from north to south. 'The Western Mountains, obviously in the west. This great expanse that lies between them and Deepforest is the Great Plains.' He pointed to two city-like bumps to the south of the Great Plains. The bumps were separated by a river. 'Alavis and Alacorn, the twin cities. And even further south, right here, is the Winged Mount.'

'That's where the Winged Ones live, right?'

'Yes, and that is where Bane has posted his Stonesingers to seal their Gate.'

Charlie stared at the mountain. It held the one thing that would destroy Bane and free her parents. If only she –

'Pay attention!' snapped Darkmount, jerking Charlie from her thoughts. 'Now, if we travel up from Alavis, across the Great Plains, we reach the Slumbering Hills. And here, right where the Slumbering Hills meet the Western Mountains, is the Stubborn Citadel.'

He sang another note and a miniature citadel appeared on the mountains. Charlie leaned forward for a better look.

'Take a good look at this map. Remember it, because tonight when I ask you to, you will open a Portal to this location.'

Charlie looked long and hard. 'Deepforest to the east, then the Great Plains, then the Western Mountains and where they join the Slumbering Hills . . . the Stubborn Citadel. Got it.'

'Are you certain?'

'Yes.'

'Excellent. Now for a closer look.' Singing softly, Darkmount zoomed in on the citadel. As it grew, the other features of the map dwindled until only a perfectly formed model of the fortress remained.

'That's one mean-looking place,' said Charlie.

The citadel sat on top of a craggy, sheer-sided hill. The main building was a squat-looking tower that was encircled by three high stone walls. The place was thick with battlements, guard towers, arrow slits and murder holes. If Jensen's tower was the epitome of fairy-tale architecture, then this was the complete opposite. No one in their right mind would ever want to visit this place.

'How are we going to get in?'

'The citadel is guarded to prevent any unwarranted

Portals so you will have to open your Portal down here, at the base of the hill. We will then climb these cliffs and scale the walls here.'

'That's a long climb,' said Nibbler, looking doubtful.

Charlie was quiet as she attempted to estimate how high the cliffs were, then tried to add the height of the walls on top of that. 'There's no way –'

'That will not be a problem,' said Darkmount. 'I will carry you.'

An image of the bishop climbing the courtyard in Alavis flashed through Charlie's mind. 'Er, OK. Will you be able to carry me over the other walls as well?'

'Yes.'

'What about me?' asked Nibbler.

'Fool, just fly in! It'll be dark and the last thing anyone would expect is a Winged One.'

'Er, yeah. OK. So fly in where?'

'Here.' Darkmount pointed to a secluded side of the main tower. 'The portcullis and main entrance is over on the other side so there will be fewer guards here. Once you meet us I will carve a door inside –'

'Wait,' interrupted Charlie. 'You're making it sound too easy. Won't they spot us once we're inside, and won't they hear your stonesinging first or at least be able to detect it?'

'If we stumble across any guards I will silence them, and as for the stonesinging do not forget I am a Stone Bishop. Stone is my element and my faith gives me power. Real power. Keeping my voice quiet enough to remain undetected, at least long enough for us to get over the wall, will be child's play. Of course once we're inside the citadel . . . Well, that's where the real danger begins.'

'Oh, great.' Charlie laced her words with a healthy helping of sarcasm. 'After all, we wouldn't want it *all* to be child's play and sweet eats. So what makes the inside scarier than the outside?'

Ignoring her scorn, Darkmount replied. 'Firstly, there's a whole garrison of soldiers, Shades and Stonesingers inside. And, secondly, I don't know where the Gate to the lower dominion is, so we will have to find that when we get in.'

'By beating the directions out of the first soldier you can get your hands on, I'm guessing?' suggested Nibbler, who had grown used to Darkmount's ways.

'Of course,' snorted the Stoman. 'I only use methods that produce results. Why do otherwise? Of course, on this occasion we won't have the luxury of taking our time. Once we break in all the citadel's forces will come raining down on us.'

'Isn't that going to be a problem?'

'Possibly. But provided this Hatchling –' he gestured at Nibbler – 'and I can find a narrow passageway to bottleneck the opposition, it shouldn't be. Between his flames and my stonesinging we should be able to keep any threat at bay long enough for you to return with my god. Once my god is in my hands there will be no power in that fortress that can prevent us from leaving.'

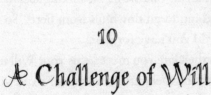

10

A Challenge of Will

Charlie knuckled her head in an effort to stay focused.

'Right,' she said. 'If you and Nibbler are keeping the citadel's forces at bay I'll be going on alone, in which case I want some real instructions on where I've got to go and what I've got to do. And when I say instructions I mean the kind that are step by step, childproof and impossible to fail.'

'Do not worry, Charlie Keeper. The task ahead will be dangerous but not impossible. You are the one who is going to bring me back my god. Of this I am certain.'

'Well . . . good. So tell me what I've got to do once we're inside.'

'There are seven lower dominions in Bellania, or as you'd call them, seven hells. The realm you require is inhabited by the Patchwork Kindred, and it will be as different to your eyes as Bellania is from Earth. Be aware that it will be unlike anything you have ever seen.'

'Anything?'

'It will be like a dream made real.' He paused as he gave the matter some thought. 'Or a nightmare.'

'Oookay, then.' Charlie had a sinking feeling that things were only going to go downhill from here. 'So what other good news do you have for me?'

'To open the Gate you must focus your Will upon it. You told me that the Delightful Brothers forced you to use a mirror to open a Portal to your own world. Well this is the same. Force it to open and it will reveal the path. Once you have passed through the Gates you will find yourself in a mist, so visibility will be limited. Beneath your feet you will feel a stone path; do not wander from this – turn neither left nor right, but follow it straight ahead. It will lead you to a bridge and on the other side you will find a temple. Remember: stay on the path and do not look down when you cross the bridge.'

'Why not?'

'Because it is said to span a bottomless pit. Those who look into it become mesmerized and fall. Once you have entered the temple –'

'Wait, wait, wait. This all sounds too easy. I'm supposed to just walk on in? No guards with three heads? No devils with horns and tridents? No portcullis that turns into a mouth and tries to swallow me whole? Nothing like that?'

'The scriptures say nothing of –'

'Scriptures? You mean you don't know? Have you never been there?'

'Silly child, of course I have never been there! If I had do you think I would have any need for you and your idiotic sidekick?'

'Hey!' said Nibbler, who was quickly silenced by Dark-mount's thunderous glare.

'May I continue?'

Charlie nodded, still unsure what she was letting herself in for. She pouted and crossed her arms.

Darkmount stared right back. 'I can tell you nothing with certainty,' he continued. 'All I can tell you is what has been written. The temple will be open and unguarded. Once inside you must take yourself to the highest floor. There you will find a corridor lined with many doors. Those on the left will be marked with a burnt cross; the doors on the right will be marked with a burnt circle. The vessel you seek will be in one of the last three doors on the right. Precisely which of the three neither I nor the scriptures can say for certain. Under no circumstances must you attempt to open any door marked with a cross.'

'Why not?'

'The scriptures did not say why, only that it was forbidden.'

'Fine. No doors with a cross. What does this vessel actually look like?'

Darkmount sketched an outline in the dirt on the cave floor. It looked like a classical Greek vase, the kind with a pointy base. 'It is an honest and humble stone urn. Dull brown in colour with no lid, and if you were to gaze inside you would see the night skies.'

'What, with stars and all?'

'With stars and all, Charlie Keeper.'

'So shouldn't be too hard to find, then, huh?'

The Stoman bishop gave her a measured look, trying to discern whether or not she was mocking him. Charlie stared back and did her best to look serious.

Pulling a sour face Darkmount nudged over a beautifully crafted leather satchel. Charlie opened it and peered inside.

'Er . . . is it supposed to be empty?'

'It is for the urn. Its padding will keep the vessel safe and will allow you to keep both hands free.'

Charlie slipped the satchel over her shoulders so she could wear it like a backpack.

'Most importantly,' he continued, 'Touch nothing, eat nothing, drink nothing. Remember these words and remember them well.'

'Touch nothing, eat nothing, drink nothing. Sure. But this still all sounds a little too easy. C'mon, Edge, there's got to be some monsters or guards or . . . well, something! What about all these "Daemon Kindred" you talk about?'

'I was coming to that.' Darkmount picked up a long bundle. He carefully unwrapped it to produce an ancient, rusted and seemingly useless sword.

Charlie looked at it carefully, waiting for a flicker or a sparkle to suggest a hidden sharpness, but she was disappointed. It really was just a rusty sword.

'Oh, great, I feel safer already!' she snorted. 'Not only are you sending me to hell, you're giving me the worst sword I've ever seen in my life and what's twice as ridiculous is that I've absolutely no idea how to use it. Ha! If there's any hungry daemons in there they might as well sit back and enjoy the show cos the only person I'm going to be a danger to is myself.'

Charlie crossed her arms and sat back in an obvious grump, not caring who saw her pouting.

'Young Keeper, nothing in any realm is what it seems. Nothing. The same can be said of this sword.'

'What, you mean it's going to turn into a lean, mean, slicing machine, then?' she said with thick sarcasm.

'It is a Hell Sword. It bears a nasty surprise and if it looks like nothing now that is because it is deceptive.'

'But what am I going to do with a sword? I don't know how to use one!'

'Well you'd better learn fast as it is the only thing that kills daemons.'

Charlie leaned over and took the heavy sword in her hands. It felt as useless as it looked. 'What about the scabbard?'

'There is no scabbard.'

'So what am I supposed to do with it?' said Charlie, unimpressed. 'Hold it all day long until my hand goes numb?'

'Just slide it between the straps of the satchel so it rests between your shoulders.'

She sighed despondently, but did as he suggested.

'OK, so are you going to give me some more info on these daemons? Like what do they look like and how do I stop them doing . . . well, whatever it is they do to little girls who trespass in the lower dominions.'

'The Daemon Kindred are a jigsaw race. No two are the same and each has been modelled upon a nightmare. Legends speak of creatures and critters half-man and half-beast or half-man and half-insect. Some of the wilder stories suggest that they are even more versatile than this, maybe even half-elemental.'

'Elemental?'

'Half-man and half-smoke, or wind, or fire, or soil or –'

'OK, I get it. Half-not-very-nice, then. I can hardly wait. But why are they all half-man, why not half-hedgehog and half . . . I don't know . . . half-*Tyrannosaurus rex*?'

'Some fables whisper that the Daemon Kindred strive to become that which they hate the most. Man.'

'Yeah, is that Human, Treman or Stoman kinda man? I always get a little confused now that I'm in Bellania.'

'Take your pick, each race is as capable of sin as the next.'

'So you don't know.'

'I tell you what, young Keeper. Why don't you take notes while you're down there and then when you come back you can enlighten us all with your insights.' He gave her another one of his measured looks – he seemed to have a lot of those to spare.

'Right, well, then,' said Charlie. 'Any last words of advice for me, like what I should do after I have your "vessel"?'

'I would run like you've got all the denizens of hell hot on your heels.'

'Ha. Ha. Ha,' grumbled Charlie with as much sarcasm as she could muster.

'I do not joke about this, Charlie Keeper. Run and run for your life for all the Kindred will come for you. They always welcome those into Hell with deceit and wiles, but they will not so easily let you go. So run, Keeper, run back with my god as fast as you can.'

'Run.' Charlie nodded like it was the wisest thing in the

world to do. Truth was, she was beginning to get scared. She had known that going to hell was part of the deal, but a large part of her mind hadn't been able to accept the reality of it. She gripped the hilt of the useless Hell Sword to stop the sudden shaking in her hands. It didn't help, but at least it hid her fear from the others. 'Right, running I can do. Any other last words of wisdom?'

'Yes. Your Will will not help you in the lower dominions.'

'What!' choked Charlie and Nibbler in unison.

'Your Will will only get you through the Gate and back. Nothing more.'

'Please tell me you're joking. Please tell me that was just bad Stoman humour.'

'As I have told you several times: I do not joke.'

'No, no, of course you don't,' said Charlie, white-faced. The shakes were now starting in her arms and legs. 'You don't joke.'

'Hold up,' growled Nibbler. 'Charlie, forget this. There's no way you're going in there. Not without me and not without your Will. Listen, Darkmount, the deal is off! Definitely off! What kind of idiot are you and what kind of idiots do you think we are? We don't need this; we can find the location of the Gate another way. We don't –'

'A deal was made!' said Darkmount, his angry voice crackling around the cavern. The shadows seemed to darken, the light grew dimmer and the bishop appeared to grow in size.

'Yeah, well who makes deals like that with little girls?'

yelled Nibbler. 'Got to be some kind of twisted person to pull a fast trick like that!' He stared fiercely at the bishop. Small puffs of flame burst from his mouth.

Darkmount jumped to his feet, his stonesong already building. Rage made the veins in his face and neck bulge. 'So you would revoke a deal?'

'That wasn't a deal, that was a trick!'

Nibbler, just as furious, reared up on his back legs, spread his wings wide and gushed out a torrent of bright flame that burned and flared across the room. Dark green and bright yellow flames crashed together with the explosive sound of a thunderclap.

The two adversaries snarled and spat wordlessly at one another. Darkmount drew his arms over his head and increased the passion of his song. Nibbler sucked in a huge breath of air, widened his mouth and tensed his legs ready to jump forward.

'Enough!' screamed Charlie. Jumping upright she sent a sheet of golden Will between the two. 'Enough! I will do it!' she shouted. 'I will do it. I will see this through. A deal is a deal and if this is what it takes to beat Bane then this is what I shall do.'

'Charlie, are you sure?' asked Nibbler as he settled back on to all four paws. 'Are you sure this is what you want to do? There's always another way.'

'No, it's not what I want to do. I'd rather be chilling at home with my parents or hanging with you, Jensen and Kelko back in Sylvaris, but this is what's gotta be done. If we want to keep moving forward then this is the way.' Charlie forced out a dry laugh. 'This is the Will and the Way. Ha.

You know Azariah would be laughing if he could only see me now.'

Hands clenched by her sides, she swallowed her fear and prepared herself for what was to come.

11

A Lawyer's Touch

The crows cascaded through the air like a ragged scarf caught in the wind. Wheeling this way and that, their movement was fierce but discordant. Overhead, ominous clouds churned with the promise of thunder and lightning; below, the apparently never-ending grasslands of the Great Plains stretched as far as the eye could see.

As the flock sped onward, their flight became more chaotic, more disorganized, as though they were having trouble acting as one. At the point when it seemed as though the birds would break off in different directions, an abrupt change came over them. Cawing nastily they spiralled downward and, nearing the ground, burst into one large flailing mass of inky feathers. With an odd sound of breaking glass Mr Crow stepped on to the grass.

Still dressed in his suit and tie, and still slightly transparent after his battle royal with Nibbler – the distant horizon could be seen through his body – Charlie Keeper's lanky lawyer and legal guardian looked very out of place.

Truly, Mr Crow was a stranger in a strange land.

Almost immediately he began to pace up and down. A perplexed expression crept across his face and as he strode

back and forth with jerky motions his angular nose began to quiver.

'What to do? What to do? What to do?' he asked.

Ignoring the fact that he could see the grass through his shoes and refusing to acknowledge that his fluttering fingers appeared more ghostly than Human, he began to gnaw at his knuckles.

'What to do?' he asked the grass.

'What to do?' he asked the clouds.

'What to do? What to do?'

Thoughts, fears and anxieties raced through Mr Crow's brain. It was obvious that he had failed in his task. As far as he was aware, Charlie Keeper still ran free and still had that pesky pendant hanging round her smug little neck – a fact that would no doubt infuriate his master, Bane.

And that was the crux of the matter.

Mr Crow did not, under any circumstances, want to return to face an enraged Stoman Lord. He knew from his previous encounters how powerful, ferocious and unforgiving Bane was.

The lawyer's beady little eyes bulged with alarm. He really did not want to be ripped limb from limb or pummelled into a bloody pile of fleshy scraps – a fate that he suspected was waiting for him in the Western Mountains. He had no idea how he might return to Earth from Bellania, but he knew that even there he would not be safe from Bane's wicked revenge. Something stronger than greed swelled inside Mr Crow's soul.

Cowardice.

'WHAT TO DO?' he screamed.

The answer came to him, not in a flash of brilliance, but in a sluggish wave of gutlessness.

He would do nothing.

He would hide and wait.

Surely, thought Mr Crow, an opportunity would arise if he waited long enough or was patient enough?

Having made his decision, he raced forward and leaped into the sky. Bursting into his alternative form, the cawing, shrieking crows sped across the grasslands beneath the tempestuous skies. Banking left and right they searched for miles and miles until they at last found what they wanted.

A dank and dark cave.

Circling round the entrance once, twice, three times, they flew back the way they had come until they hovered above a herd of wild cattle that they had seen while scouting for their hideout. Descending venomously, the flock pulled one of the cows kicking and bellowing into the air. Whipping round, they sped back to the cave and disappeared inside with their writhing catch.

To wait.

And to feed.

Three Stoman generals entered the Throne Room, stamping past the guards and the long line of footmen. The rattle of their swords and the clink of their chainmail resounded across the great space, yet oddly didn't echo back. Each man was grizzled and war-torn, but they wore their scars and marks from a hundred different battles proudly. Heads held high, hands on pommel or belt, they marched to the foot of the great dais. Slamming their feet together and holding clenched fists above their heads, they saluted.

'My lord!' they said, standing ramrod straight. Each of them knew the punishment for failure. Each had seen lesser men, beasts and creatures snapped across Bane's knee or torn to shreds between his powerful hands for failing to deliver his wishes. But each cared not. They stared up at their master with shining eyes. Bane, the Stoman Lord, was the man who had led the forces of the Western Mountains to rule Bellania, and for this they would worship him forever.

'Report,' commanded Bane.

'The Second has taken Alavis,' said the general with a milky eye and a scar that curled his lip in a perpetual sneer.

'The Third has taken Alacorn,' said the one with the cleft in his jaw. 'Both Human cities now lie beneath the shadow of your banner, my lord.'

'Good,' said Bane. 'And do the Tremen still believe that our forces intend to use Alavis and Alacorn as launching posts from which to invade Deepforest and Sylvaris?'

'Our spies report this to be so,' said the milky-eyed general.

Bane settled back into the Devouring Throne. He appeared pleased with the news. 'Excellent. You will command both the Second and the Third to make preparations to move, but they are to take their time. Allow the Tremen to believe they will have weeks – if not months – in which to prepare for the arrival or war.'

'As you wish, my lord.' The milky-eyed and cleft-jawed generals both bowed their heads in acknowledgement of their orders.

'And what of the First?' growled Bane. 'How does my prime army fare?'

The last general, larger and more ferocious-looking than the others, peeled back his lips to reveal blackened teeth. 'The First has already departed the Western Mountains, my lord. As you commanded, they will loop northward through the Great Plains to strike at Deepforest from an approach that the Tremen will not suspect.'

'You have scouts and outriders scourging the way?' asked Bane.

'Yes, my lord. Once the army leaves our land and enters the Great Plains they have been instructed to butcher any who stands in the way. There will be no witnesses to warn the Tremen of our coming. Sylvaris will be caught unaware.'

Bane rumbled in delight. The sound carried across the Throne Room and unlike the clink of the general's armour it echoed back, growing louder and louder until it sounded like a war drum pounding out its malicious and blood-fuelled intent.

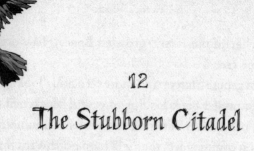

12

The Stubborn Citadel

Keeping the image of Darkmount's map of the Stubborn Citadel in her mind, Charlie summoned her Will, raised her hands high and tore open a Portal. It revealed a night-time landscape and a series of gently rolling hills that disappeared into the darkness. Darkmount eased his bulk through the Portal and after a quick look gave a nod of approval.

'Good. This is the place.' With a beckoning gesture he indicated that Charlie and Nibbler should join him.

Jumping through, Charlie took a quick look at the hills then turned to see if the fortress lay behind them.

'Oh,' she murmured as she came face to face with a sheer cliff. She craned her neck back and there, at the very top, where her vision began to blur, she could make out the Stubborn Citadel.

Charlie gulped. The place was huge. No army in its right mind would ever attempt to scale these walls. She was very glad that Darkmount would be doing the climbing.

'Quick,' hissed Darkmount. 'Close the Portal. The light will give us away.'

Charlie allowed the Portal to wink out of existence.

'Right,' continued Darkmount. 'You –' he pointed at

Nibbler – 'get going and remember to stop flapping your wings once you are over the citadel.'

'Stop flapping my wings? Are you crazy? How am I supposed to stay airborne? Hold my breath and hope I float like a balloon?'

'Idiot!' snapped Darkmount. 'Glide in! Gain enough altitude outside the fortress then glide down. Those big wings of yours make a lot of noise.'

'Oh,' said Nibbler, seeing the wisdom in his words. 'OK, good idea.'

'Well don't stand there dawdling all day. Get on with it.'

Charlie could see that Nibbler was hesitant. Not because of any concern for his own welfare, but fear for hers.

'Don't worry, Nibbler. I'll be OK. We'll meet up on the inside.'

'Are you sure?'

Charlie flashed him a nervous smile. 'Yes.'

The two of them exchanged a hug.

'By Stone and Spit!' cursed Darkmount. 'This isn't nursery school. Stop wasting time and get on with it.'

Nibbler threw him a dirty look. Then with a hop and skip he launched himself into the night sky.

Once Nibbler had disappeared Charlie turned to confront Darkmount, but before she could utter a word Darkmount held up his hand. 'We're not friends, we're business partners. Nothing more. Best you remember that.'

Anger seethed within Charlie. She wanted to say something, but knew that now wasn't the time.

Darkmount walked over to the cliff and knelt down. 'Climb on,' he said.

Charlie twisted her sword belt so the Hell Sword rested against the back of her leg. Not caring if she pinched Darkmount in the process, Charlie clambered up the bishop's broad back, hooked her arms round his thick neck and jammed her feet into the small of his back.

Once Darkmount was certain she was secure and not likely to fall he stood and began to chant softly. His hands and feet glowed a soft dark green, which seemed to melt into the darkness. Charlie didn't doubt that it would be hard to see from a distance.

Darkmount plunged his hands and feet into the rock and with a surge of his powerful muscles began to climb effortlessly upward.

Charlie swallowed as the ground dwindled into the distance. The fear of an imminent fall rushed through her and as their ascent continued her sense of vertigo only intensified. Even the bunch and tense of Darkmount's prodigious muscles beneath his cloak didn't reassure her, and as they climbed higher and higher she was sure that at any moment she would topple off and fall to the ground in a mass of flailing limbs.

Darkmount's gravelly voice shook her from her thoughts. 'The cliff ends here and the wall begins. Hold on tight, the ride won't be smooth.'

Charlie's stomach lurched as Darkmount began to push his hands into the stonework. Little flashes of dim light met his every contact and as he pushed his fist into the stone it seemed to resist. Charlie began to bounce and shake as the Stoman bishop did his best to climb smoothly.

'They have treated the walls,' hissed Darkmount through

gritted teeth, 'to make it resistant to stonesinging. We will have to hope that no one sees the sparks.'

'Are . . . are we going to fall?' squeaked Charlie.

But Darkmount refused to answer, instead saving his breath for the climb ahead.

Higher and higher they went. As the ascent became increasingly difficult, Darkmount's muscles started to ripple in an unsteady rhythm, making it harder for Charlie to maintain her grip round his neck. She soon felt her own muscles begin to cramp and tire.

'Hold on,' panted Darkmount, sensing her fatigue. 'We are nearly there. Nearly there.'

Charlie took one last look at the moon-drenched landscape that swayed hundreds of feet below and decided that now would be a good time to shut her eyes.

A sudden lurch made her eyes spring open and she was terrified that they were about to fall. But instead of plummeting to their deaths she realized that Darkmount had heaved himself up and was now lowering his legs over the other side of the wall. He changed his song subtly and released his hold on the stone so that only the tips of his fingers and toes touched its surface, allowing them to slide rapidly downward.

As they descended, Charlie had a brief view of the main citadel with its jutting battlements and jagged turrets, but before she could examine it further it fell out of sight behind a second wall.

Darkmount's feet touched the ground and, ducking low to hide their silhouette, he hastened to the next wall. Charlie, white-faced and high on adrenalin, clung to his back like a racehorse jockey. On reaching the far side Darkmount once again began to climb.

Halfway up Charlie pounded on his back. 'Guards!' she whispered. 'There're guards.'

'Where?' growled Darkmount.

'Below,' she hissed, then realizing that was obvious added, 'Down, to our left.'

The two of them watched as a small troop of Stomen marched by. The tread of their feet and the clatter of armour echoed eerily into the night.

They soon passed, allowing Darkmount to continue upward undetected.

Soon they were up and over the second wall with another nervous wait at the bottom as another patrol passed. Then they were climbing the final barrier.

The citadel swept into view. Charlie's heart, already panicked from the treacherous climb, almost skipped a beat. The fortress seemed to defy the rules of perspective. It was gigantic – a mountain of stone. Thick, impenetrable and very, very intimidating. The battlements and spiked walls cast fierce shadows that seemed to lash out at the moonlight.

'Calm,' she whispered to herself, and did her best to slow her panicked pulse. 'Stay calm.'

Darkmount shifted his grip on the wall so that he could see her. 'Get a hold of yourself! This is not even the beginning. You cannot afford to feel fear, not at this stage.'

'I-I'm trying my best.'

'Well your best doesn't seem good enough!' he harrumphed. 'You're supposed to be a Keeper, so behave like one!'

Charlie felt her fury rise at the remark. She'd heard it too often since arriving in Bellania and hated the fact that everyone had unrealistic expectations of her simply because of her name. Although Azariah Keeper, her mentor, had taught her so much about the powers she could command, she still felt woefully underprepared for what lay ahead. The reminder of Azariah's death fuelled the fury inside her, and although the sudden warmth of her anger buoyed up her courage, it wasn't quite enough to blanket her fear. It remained within her breast, heavy and sullen, like bad heartburn.

'I've got it under control,' lied Charlie. 'Let's get going, OK?'

Darkmount gave her a wary look, grunted in annoyance, but continued their descent. At the bottom Charlie slid off Darkmount's back, massaged some feeling back into her fingers, then squatted down beside her unpleasant companion. Together the two of them hid in a pool of shadow.

She almost screamed as she felt a talon squeeze her shoulder.

'Nibbler, you idiot! What are trying to do, give me a heart attack?'

'Sorry.' His eyes flashed in the darkness. 'I've been waiting ages.' He grinned in relief, obviously glad to see her.

'Are you two ready?' asked Darkmount.

'As ready as I'm ever going to be,' said Charlie. Nibbler nodded in agreement.

'Good. Then it's time for us to make our entrance.'

Throwing his previous caution aside, Darkmount strode across the gap between the wall and citadel. Raising his arms over his head he began to sing. His hands started to glow and as his song increased in strength the light intensified so that it went from a deep green to a pearly white that was almost painful to look at.

With a roar he clapped both hands against the citadel and, amidst an explosion of sparks, started to push. The wall juddered and moaned in response to his onslaught and slowly, ever so slowly, his hands began to push a section of the citadel's stone blocks inwards.

The stonesinging and twisted shriek of the tortured wall didn't go unnoticed. Cries of alarm and shouted orders could be heard in the distance.

'Darkmount . . .' Charlie began, but stopped when she realized the huge strain he was under.

Veins were popping across his forehead, tendons stuck out along his neck, sweat dripped from his nose and his eyes had narrowed into slits of concentration.

Begrudgingly the section of wall sank deeper beneath his fingers.

A spear slammed into the floor by Charlie's feet as a troop of Stoman guards rounded the corner. With shouts of anger they rushed towards them.

'Better hurry that up!' shouted Charlie to Darkmount as she watched the soldiers narrow the distance.

Nibbler reared back on his feet and pawed at the air. Unleashing a torrent of flame that crackled into the night he prepared to jump into the skies.

Charlie grabbed him by the tail. 'No! We can't afford to get separated. I'll deal with it.'

Stepping forward and summoning her Will, she crouched into a loose K'Changa pose and waited for the first Stoman to come within striking distance. Charlie licked her lips in anticipation. She was determined that after her last confrontation with Stoman soldiers – back in Alavis where her Will had failed her – this time would be different. This time she wouldn't act like a scared little girl.

But before she could put herself to the test a shuddering screech came from the citadel as Darkmount, with a final grunt, forced his way inside. There was a boom as the section of wall he had been pushing fell forward.

'In!' he roared. Grabbing a loose rock, he flung it so that it deflected a thrown spear that had been intended for Charlie. 'Get in!'

Charlie and Nibbler took one last look at the running soldiers before ducking through the hole in the wall.

Veins still pulsating and with sweat coursing off him, Darkmount knelt down, heaved up the fallen slab and, with a final bellow of stonesinging, slammed it back into place.

13

Dark Forces

The young Stoman boy lay awake, wrapped in his blankets. Something unusual was happening and it took a while for his sleep-befuddled brain to work out what exactly had woken him. There – a rhythmic pounding, so low pitched he could hardly hear it, but he could certainly feel it as it rippled through his bones.

Wide awake and curious, he threw off his blankets, made certain his pannier was secure and added an extra log to the fire to ensure it would still be alight when he returned. The night sky was clear and the stars twinkled overhead, but over towards the Red Moon Canyon – where the rhythm seemed to be coming from – was an odd glow. With his curiosity growing, the young boy crept forward past thick stalks of wild amethyst bamboo and beneath the softly glowing leaves of crycarry trees. As he neared the canyon, the pounding noise grew in volume and the light intensified. Scrambling down on his hands and knees, he edged forward right to the canyon's edge. Peering over he looked down and gasped in astonishment.

Below, a Stoman army flowed through the canyon like a scarlet river. The pounding he had heard was the measured step of hulking soldiers as they marched in order, battalion after battalion sweeping past amidst flickering torchlight.

Each Stoman soldier wore polished scarlet leather armour and was armed with an axe, sword or mace. Black circular shields embossed with a clenched fist were strapped to their arms, and at the head of each battalion marched a hooded figure who carried a blood-red pennant that flapped in the rushing canyon wind.

As the army marched on and on, seemingly endless, the Stoman boy gazed in wonder at its sheer numbers. After what seemed like hours, the infantry passed and the young boy was just about to rise from his vantage point and return

to his bed when a rustling, scuttling sound froze him in his tracks. Once again, torchlight lit the canyon and rounding the bend came the Stoman cavalry, different from anything that had preceded it.

The boy's eyes went wide with fear. It was the Widow Brigade, infamous throughout Bellania for their savage attacks. Not on foot, these were mounted soldiers, in horned helmets and spiked stone armour. They handled their charges with pride and studied nonchalance, but as seasoned warriors the Widow Brigade knew just how much terror their steeds evoked. Instead of horses they rode giant, bloated arachnids, whose venom dripped to the ground to form a poisonous wake. The spiders marched across the canyon floor and even along the walls, the crunch and thud of their claws echoing back and forth.

The boy turned even paler as fear and revulsion gripped him. He hated spiders, even the smallest kind. 'Sweet Sapphire Gods, please don't let them see me,' he whispered.

Luck was with him, for the Widow Brigade passed without incident. Breathing a sigh of relief and with a promised blessing to the gods, the young boy headed back to his campsite. But as he retreated he could hear the rumbling of stone wheels along the canyon as even more troops and wagons passed through, and the Stoman army tirelessly and relentlessly marched to war.

14

The Descent

Charlie took stock of their surroundings within the citadel.

They were in a long corridor that was decorated with a series of snarling gargoyles and intersected at regular intervals with other pathways. Curious, Charlie leaned forward to examine the nearest figurine, which had been skilfully carved as part snake, part fox, and set into the wall. She jumped in horror as it opened its glowing red eyes and began to howl. The two gargoyles on either side opened their eyes too and, seeing the intruders, joined the cry. The cacophony of yowls and screams swept down the corridor as all the other gargoyles awoke and fixed the small group with their glaring eyes.

Panicked by the bizarre alarm system, Charlie turned to Darkmount.

'We won't have long,' he said. 'You –' his finger thudded into Charlie's chest – 'go that way and you –' he pointed at Nibbler – 'go in that direction. I will wait here. Bring me the first soldier you come across and be quick!'

A hundred questions flitted across Charlie's mind, but the urgency of their mission and the awful racket spurred her into motion. Sprinting down the corridor, she slipped round a corner and, to her shock, ran straight into an approaching Stoman soldier.

Charlie bounced off his armour and fell backwards to sprawl on the floor.

'Whoopsy,' she said. It was a stupid thing to say, but she couldn't help it after the shock of the collision and the constant screech of the alarm. As the soldier drew his sword, her brain finally kicked into gear.

Summoning her Will, she kicked the Stoman in the knee and, while he flailed around trying to regain his balance, jumped to her feet. Falling into a loose K'Changa pose, she skipped aside to avoid the first swing of his sword and blocked his second. Before he could reverse the blow, she punched him in the solar plexus, robbing him of air. As he doubled over, Charlie instinctively followed through with another blow to his chin.

The guard spun around, bounced off the wall and fell unconscious in a heap.

Charlie grabbed him by the ankle and dragged him back round the corner. 'Hey! Darkmount! Over here.'

The bishop hastened over. 'Good. Now get your Winged friend while I find the Gate's location.'

Charlie nodded and ran off in the direction that Nibbler had taken. She stumbled to a halt as Nibbler rounded the corner in front of her. He was dragging a soldier along too.

'Wud-hop?' Realizing that he couldn't talk with the soldier's sleeve in his mouth Nibbler spat it out. 'What's up?'

'Got one already,' Charlie panted. 'Let's go.'

In his haste to follow her, Nibbler got his hind leg tangled in the soldier's clothing. As he stumbled forward, an arrow snapped past his face and splintered against the wall. He turned to see a horde of enraged Stomen stampeding towards him.

'Run!' shouted Charlie.

Racing back up the corridor, they saw Darkmount give his captive a final shake before smashing him into one of the gargoyles.

'Darkmount, we've got company!'

Seeing the charging Stomen, Darkmount hurled the unconscious soldier like a javelin towards them. Charlie and Nibbler hurriedly ducked out of the way, but the Stomen behind them went down like bowling pins.

'This way!' Darkmount hastened off down the corridor, and for all his bulk moved with surprising speed.

Charlie was shocked to realize that without her Will she probably wouldn't have been able to keep up with the nimble bishop. Nibbler, however, had no such problem. Wings half spread and with all four talons striking sparks from the floor, he easily kept up.

The three of them ducked into a passageway, tore open a door and burst into a wide stairway that spiralled down into the gloomy guts of the citadel. They ran on, taking the steps two and three at a time.

A roar came from above. Charlie glanced over her shoulder and saw a jostling wave of soldiers burst into the stairwell. At their feet was a telltale dark swirl of Shades as they too joined the chase. The cry and curse from the Stomen and the shriek of the Shades were so loud that they overwhelmed the howl of the gargoyles that also lined the stairwell. Charlie faltered at the piercing sound.

'Keep going!' insisted Nibbler.

Somehow Charlie managed to keep her momentum as arrows whistled past them. Leaning forward, she pumped her arms and ran for all she was worth.

The Shades, hungry for a taste of flesh, leaped ahead of the Stoman soldiers and closed in on the trio.

'Faster!' cried Darkmount. 'We need to go faster!'

Mustering the Stonesong so that his feet glowed as brightly as his hands, he jumped on to the thick banister that lined the stairs and began to slide downward. He quickly picked up momentum and was soon flashing past floor after floor. With Darkmount out of his way Nibbler had more room to spread his wings. He too picked up speed, the whistle from his wings mingling with the klaxon sound coming from the gargoyles.

Which left Charlie in the rear.

The bowmen switched their focus to her.

'Right,' scowled Charlie as a hail of arrows fell around her. 'Skank this!'

She fanned her Will so that it started to burn brighter. The golden sheets of flame that billowed from her fists surged and, taking hold of her courage, Charlie leaped.

She soared over the banister, over the terrible gap that led to the depths below, and landed with a thud on the far side of the floor below where she had started.

'Ha!' She grinned in jubilation.

Bunching her legs beneath her she jumped again. And again. Skipping from side to side and from floor to floor she descended.

All three of them, Darkmount with the green glow of his

stonesinging, Nibbler with his wings spread wide and Charlie with a haze of golden light surrounding her, sped downward and deeper. The soldiers and Shades, although still in pursuit, soon dwindled from sight.

As they headed deeper, the staircase began to change. The steps were carved with less precision, the banister grew rougher and the walls that lined the shaft became craggy. The gargoyles grew further and further apart until eventually they disappeared altogether.

Finally the stairway ended and, looking back up, Charlie realized that they must have descended not just the height of the citadel's walls, but also the cliff that it rested upon. In fact, she guessed that they must now be hundreds of metres beneath the ground.

A tunnel led away from the stairs. Ugly statues, cruder and very different from the gargoyles of the citadael above, lined the way. Made from a rough unglazed terracotta clay, each one held its head and appeared to be in the process of screaming. Darkmount, ignoring the grim artwork, walked a small distance into the passageway before stopping.

'This is it. The Gate lies that way. Your Winged friend and I will hold Bane's forces here.'

'But what –'

The screech of Shades and the sound of booted feet grew closer as their pursuers approached. The shrieking of the Shades and the clink of weapons were joined by the ominous rumble of stonesinging. It sounded as though the whole weight of the Stoman army was descending on them.

'There is no more time!' snapped Darkmount, preparing

himself to face the onslaught. 'Remember everything that I have told you. Now go.'

'Wait,' said Charlie as a final thought came to mind. 'What does the Gate look like?'

'Pah! You will know it when you see it. Now go!'

A spear whistled into the tunnel, only to be stopped by a swipe of Darkmount's glowing hands.

Nibbler gave Charlie a despairing look, a choked, 'G'luck!' then turned to stand next to Darkmount.

With a burst of crackling yellow flames and a flash of Stonesong, they rushed forward to meet their foes.

With a great clash the two sides met. Charlie stood dumb-struck as Nibbler began to rend and tear at armour. She watched as Darkmount smashed a shield in half and battered two soldiers to the ground. Nibbler's flames pushed back Shades, and Darkmount's hands shaped weapon after weapon from the stone floor with which to attack his opponents. Looking over their heads she stared at the torrent of enemies that filled the tunnel and swept down the staircase like a never-ending tide.

Shaking herself free from her stupor, Charlie turned and ran.

Down the tunnel towards hell.

15

Bounty Hunters

Jensen, Kelko and Sic Boy, cramped and tired, were slowly lulled into a shallow, fitful sleep by the rocking and bumping of the wagon. Occasionally they were slapped awake by the cruel guard, but soon returned to their restless slumber. They had tried and tested their bonds, wiggled fingers at each other in the hope of communicating some formula for escape, but other than that there was very little with which to occupy their minds.

A slow rumble intruded on their hazy dreams, growing in volume until it reverberated into a resounding *tha-thud, tha-thud*.

The wagon driver called out, 'Whoa-whoa!' and with a crack of his whip forced the horses off the side of the road. Jensen and Kelko craned their necks over the side of the wagon to stare in disbelief as the Widow Brigade, very much unexpected this far into the Great Plains, marched past.

'What's your business?' snarled a captain as he rode up to the wagon on a rearing rhinospider. 'State it quickly or see your heads parted from your necks!'

'W-we're c-carrying prisoners to the Soul Mines of Zhartoum,' stammered the driver as he watched the sharp tip of the captain's halberd swaying mere inches from the end of his nose. 'On express orders from our lord himself.'

'Show me your papers,' snapped the captain.

The guard hastily rummaged through the small box secured beneath the driving bench. Finding the papers, he presented them with a smug look on his piggish face.

The captain scanned them and, finding them legitimate, relaxed somewhat. 'Apologies for the rough approach, lads. But we've strict orders to silence all eyes that witness our passing.'

The driver and the guard shared a panicked look.

'Don't worry!' snorted the captain as he caught the exchange. 'That doesn't apply to our militia going about legitimate business.' The driver and guard let out a thankful sigh.

The driver stared at the passing banners and military standards. 'I thought the Widow Brigade was stationed at the Western Mountains?'

'We were.' The captain grinned. 'But now we're on a path to greater things. In alliance with the First Army we're on our way to stamp the towers of Sylvaris into the ground. Our lord has offered to pay all his soldiers a blood price for every Treman nose delivered to his Throne Room.' The captain pulled two sacks from his saddlebags. 'If I can fill these with green noses I'll be rich beyond my wildest dreams!'

With a throaty laugh of delight he turned his arachnid mount and galloped off, adding the dust of his passing to the great cloud already kicked up by the passing of thousands of booted feet.

The guard turned to look at the two prisoners with a speculative eye only to get a slap round the back of his head.

'Stop that!' insisted the driver. 'Take their noses and we'll not only lose our bonus, but we'll lose this cushy job. And if you think that's worth it, imagine where you'll be drafted to next.' The driver waved a thumb in the direction of the First Army. 'Right in with that lot of grunts. Is that what you want? Marching for miles each day on an empty stomach, being ordered around by snotty-nosed colonels and gut-punching sergeants?'

'No. Now that you mention it . . . no.' The guard pushed his dagger back into its sheath and settled into his seat.

In the wagon, Jenson and Kelko, gagged as they were, needed no words to express their horror at what they had heard. Powerless to act, they had to wait three long hours before Bane's mighty army had snaked its deadly way past them towards their beloved home of Sylvaris.

Bane's bounty for Charlie Keeper was carried across the land. Heralds in elegant livery and town criers in rich robes shouted the announcement in hamlets, villages, towns and cities. Word began to travel far and wide and those motivated by the colour of gold and the twinkle of jewels pricked up their ears. Mercenaries, bounty hunters, cutpurses, bandits, soldiers of fortune, bootstraps and backstabbers gathered in throngs.

The Scarlet Poison Gang, the Scaramanga Triplets, the Forty Swords, the Band of Thirteen, the Liver Eaters and many, many more listened eagerly as Bane's bounty was described.

'. . . sapphires!'

'. . . enough rubies to swim in!'

'. . . a thousand fistfuls of gold!'

Grinning and slapping each other on the back as though they had already earned the reward, they began to disperse in trickles and then droves as they started their quest for Bane's elusive fugitive.

In a dusty square in some nameless village the herald's words caused a riot as three competing gangs clashed over foolish boasts of what they would do with the reward.

On the outskirts of the piazza, a tall stranger with an unusual wide-brimmed hat and a shabby cloak ignored the violence and walked straight across the square. Those who saw him coming leaped out of the way. The fighting stopped and silence spread as the hoodlums cleared a path for the stranger and shouted warnings to those still brawling.

'Fe-fi . . .' whispered a heavily muscled Stoman.

'Fo Fum,' gasped another.

'Watch out, watch out,' chanted all the gang members in unison, 'the bad man comes.'

Planting his heavy staff against the side of a building that edged the square, the stranger pulled a compact wooden box from beneath his robe. Inside was an ornate compass, the beauty and craftsmanship of which was most unusual. Its great age was also apparent, suggesting it had been constructed not just in a different time, but perhaps in a different realm. The man pulled the compass to his lips.

'Charlie Keeper,' he whispered in a dry, croaky voice. 'I want Charlie Keeper.'

The compass wheel spun one way, the needle the other. Round and round they went, then suddenly snapped to a standstill, the needle pointing unerringly towards the Slumbering Hills.

The stranger folded the lid over the compass before carefully stowing it away.

Taking hold of his staff and ignoring the shouts and curses of the amateurs who resumed fighting behind him, the man strode off.

He had a fugitive Keeper to find and a bounty to earn.

16

Final Preparations

At the end of the tunnel was a chamber, crudely hewn from the bedrock. Thick candles crouched on lumps of rock and hung from stone outcroppings. Grey smoke and the putrid smell of burning fat oozing off the candles created a gloomy atmosphere and offered little in the way of illumination. The scent of rotting carcasses and stagnant water clogged Charlie's nostrils and the only thing that stopped her from crying out in disgust was the sense of . . . something. She couldn't quite put her finger on it, but beneath the terrible stench lay a feeling of suspense. As though something was lurking nearby, like a shark hidden in the murky depths waiting for someone foolish enough to dangle their toes in the water.

She wished that someone was there with her. Someone to talk to and help break the eerie atmosphere, but she was alone. At least she thought she was; she had the unpleasant sensation that something was watching her.

As her eyes grew accustomed to the gloom, Charlie examined the chamber. On the far wall a skin of some sort had been stretched taut over the craggy surface. Drawing closer Charlie realized the terrible smell was coming from the stretched piece of hide. She could see bits of fat, scales and hair clinging to it and, to her disgust, what looked like big pimples.

'Eeurgh!' she complained, unable to keep her mouth closed any longer. 'That thing is gross! Gross! And look it's even got zits on it, how naaaaaaaasty is that?'

She realized that she was talking to herself, but she didn't care. Standing here, in this place, in total silence was more than she could bear.

'This has got to be the Gate,' she muttered. 'There's nothing else.'

She called forth her Will and smiled slightly as the gorgeous golden light pushed back the darkness. She reached towards the skin, her fingers not quite touching its horrendous surface. As she focused her mind and gritted her teeth, her Will shot out, covering the skin in golden light. It rippled and changed, becoming translucent. Through it she caught a brief glimpse of a cobbled stone pathway and a hanging rope bridge before a thick mist descended and obscured everything from view. All that remained were a few short metres of visibility that allowed her to see the path lying tauntingly in front of her.

She squeezed her eyes shut and thought of her parents, Azariah, Jensen and Kelko, and everything that had led her here. Grabbing the useless hilt of the Hell Sword and finding little comfort in its decrepit appearance, she gathered all the courage she could muster and leaped through the Gate.

The tunnel was narrow enough to prevent the Shades and Stoman soldiers using their weight of numbers to their advantage. That and the sheer brutish strength of Dark-mount and his stonesinging caused Nibbler to grow cocky.

'Well, come on then if you think you're hard enough!' he called out in a sing-song. A flight of arrows whistled towards him. He casually burned them to a crisp. 'Ha! Even my grandma could have done better than that! Is that all you've got? Do you want to stop for tea and biscuits?'

'Winged One,' interrupted Darkmount.

'Er, yeah?'

'You're a Hatchling. You don't know your grandmother.'

'Well no, no I don't. But it's just a saying. You know, just to get into the feel of things.'

Darkmount shook his head. Tearing a lump of rock from the wall, he flung it down the tunnel, knocking a Shade and two Stomen off their feet.

A flash of golden light from behind caused the two of them to pause.

'Was that . . .' began Nibbler.

'Yes, that was the Gate. She's gone through.'

'Does that mean –'

A chorus of Stonesong washed down the tunnel. The Shades and Stomen parted to make way for a line of angry-looking Stonesingers.

'Enough questions,' said Darkmount, hurling another lump of rock at his adversaries. 'More flame.'

17
Hell

The mist felt wrong.

It was cold and clammy yet smelt like a hot greenhouse. The scent of lilies, freshly ploughed soil and the tang of exotic plants tickled at Charlie's nose, which she knew couldn't be right as the few things she could see were barren and lifeless. Sounds seemed to behave oddly too; one minute her footsteps would sound muffled, the next too loud. But what bugged her the most was the wind. It howled around her constantly. But she couldn't feel it on her skin and the mist didn't move at all.

Nothing behaved as it should.

Looking back Charlie could see the Gate and through it the faint outline of the cave beyond. It was like trying to peer into a bathroom mirror made foggy from condensation. Squaring her shoulders, she ventured deeper into the mist.

At first she was troubled by the idea that she might become lost, but the pathway was easy to follow. The same screaming statues that had lined the corridors were here too, their outstretched arms pointing the way, and it wasn't long until Charlie found herself at the bridge.

It was a rope bridge, the kind that she had seen in travel

magazines and documentaries. Rough wooden slats formed the walkway and the handrails were made from thick ropes. Unlit lanterns had been tied not only to the side of the bridge, but also to a guide line that hung overhead. As she planted her foot on the first slat, the closest lantern flickered alight, its oddly cheerful flame warming the mist with its glow.

Charlie gaped up at it foolishly. She peered along the bridge, then looked over her shoulder to check that someone wasn't watching. But she was alone.

'Huh,' she muttered.

Shrugging, she took a couple of hesitant steps. More of the lanterns came alive, illuminating the bridge as though eager to show her the way.

Charlie raised an eyebrow, but, growing more confident, continued to make her way across. Something skittered past; she felt the weight of its passing on the handrail. The thick rope thrummed and vibrated beneath her palm. She spun round, trying to locate the source of movement. But there was nothing to see: only the fog, the lanterns and the eerie feeling that something was out there.

Then she felt it again. The vibrations in the handrail, the flash of shadow in the mist and the very definite sense that she was not alone. She took a firmer grip on the Hell Sword and crouched low. Waiting. Listening.

The bridge heaved upward. It felt as though some giant hand had grabbed the end and was whipping it up and down. Charlie squawked as she was flung through the air. She landed face-first on the wooden slats, one of them actually giving way so that her arm plunged through. Staring down into the mist, she resisted the urge to scream. Instead she wrapped her free arm round the handrail, heaved herself up and rode the shaking bridge. Charlie was certain she could see movement, but each time she whipped her head round to catch whatever was out there she was too late. All she saw was a ripple in the mist and a hint of passing shadow.

Something touched the back of her neck. The horrible and totally unexpected contact spurred her into motion. She jumped forward and ran, moving faster than she had thought possible.

Sprinting along the bucking bridge, she kept one hand firmly on her sword and the other round the rope. Leaping over missing slats and ducking beneath the bobbing lanterns she darted forward.

She stumbled to a sudden halt as the mist abruptly ended, launching her into sullen sunlight. The bridge was calm and as she looked back into the solid wall of fog she could no longer detect any movement.

She breathed deeply, shut her eyes and counted to five. Regaining her composure, she stared around.

The bridge continued for another forty or fifty metres then ended against a gigantic cliff that reared up into the dull skies. Charlie rubbed at her eyes and looked again. It wasn't a cliff; it was a temple. The sheer size and scale made it seem unreal, as though someone had torn a mountain free and dumped it here in the middle of nowhere, then carved it into the shape and suggestion of a building.

She rubbed at her eyes again.

There were many, many floors, each one separated from the one above by its own graceful rooftop. The bricks were orange in colour, the slates on the roofs green, and dotted here and there on narrow balconies were gardens. But everything appeared dull and dead. The bricks were faded, the paint on the slates peeling and the gardens full of grey brittle leaves.

Unable to help herself, Charlie traced the building downward and before she could stop herself, and against Darkmount's explicit words of warning, she found herself staring underneath the bridge.

There was nothing beneath her. Nothing. She could trace the line of castle all the way down until it blurred into the distance. She could see the cliff wall on the other side too. The view was good, and her sight wasn't obscured by haze so she could see for miles.

It was bottomless. Absolutely bottomless.

Her stomach lurched, her knees gave way and the only thing holding her upright was her hand. She grasped the rail so hard that she could feel the rope cutting into her palm.

Desperate for an anchor, she draggd her gaze back to the castle like a drowning man striving for land. Following the line of the building to the very top, she noted that the pinnacle had a spire that soared into the gloomy clouds.

Then everything slammed into focus. Those weren't clouds. They were cobwebs.

The sky was made from spun silk.

As her numbed brain began to function after the terrible sights both beneath her and above her, she reached an abrupt decision and ran for all she was worth. Towards the castle and away from whatever lurked in the mist. She really, really didn't want to meet whatever had made those webs and she had a suspicion that she had had a close encounter with the spinner already.

Then she stumbled to a halt.

What if the spinner wasn't in the mist? What if she was running from phantoms and the real source of the cobwebs was waiting for her in the castle?

Sweat prickled her forehead and goosebumps crested up and down her arms. But there was no choice. In order to retrieve Darkmount's god she had to follow the path and deal with whatever she encountered. The bridge lurched again, almost knocking Charlie from her feet. Instinct told her that forward was safer than back, so she pushed her fears aside and sprinted into the temple.

18

The Hard Sell

The wagon drove through the mine's main entrance, past the bored eyes of the watchmen and rumbled down a dim and stinking tunnel. It crunched to a stop in front of a barbed gate.

There was a clanking of bolts and the sound of heavy locks being turned before the gate swung open to reveal a chamber with further tunnels leading deeper into the mine.

A pair of brooding Stomen came lurching up to the wagon and silently manhandled Jensen and Kelko off the cart.

'Have they been searched?' one of the guards enquired gruffly.

'Yeah,' drawled the driver. 'Back in Alavis. All their wood was burned. You won't be having any trouble from these two even if they are Tree Singers.'

'Good.'

'A friendly word of advice,' warned the driver. 'Send up a team of eight to take the dog. The two of you won't be enough.'

The two Stomen took a look at Sic Boy, weighing up his streamlined muscles and huge incisors. They nodded.

'We'll take these two down first. Then we'll come back with some help.'

'Just be sure to bring our bonus back up with you,' leered the wagon guard. He leaned over so he could stare at Kelko and Jensen. 'Goodbye, little monkeys. I hope you have fun in the mines.'

The two Tremen were dragged away to the sound of the barking laughter of the wagon guard and driver. They were carried, prodded and pushed down tunnel after tunnel. They heard screams, moans and the lash of whips. They passed chain gangs of huddled slaves, cruel-looking guards and endless passageways that snaked off into the stinking darkness.

After what seemed like an endless period of time, the two were forced into a smoky, fire-lit cavern and thrown to their knees in front of the largest Stoman that either of them had ever seen – even bigger than Lady Narcissa's adopted son Stones. He was clad in trousers and boots, but wore nothing over his top, leaving the taut muscles on his torso exposed. A puckered scar ran from forehead to chin, passing over the ruined pit of an eye that was covered by a patch before continuing down to end near his navel. An axe hung from his belt and in his hand dangled a long whip.

'New fish,' he drawled with a lazy predatory smile. 'My name is Jook the Attentive. And seeing that I'm the boss of this mining venture it is only fitting that I be first to welcome you to the Soul Mines of Zhartoum. It is here, in my mines, that you will begin your new life. The ceiling above will become your sky, the rocky walls your horizon and the scream of your companions shall be the only music to grace your ears. Be sure to please me or –'

Jensen, in what seemed like a moment of madness, decided that now would be a good time to make himself heard. He interrupted the overseer's speech by doing his best to speak through his gag.

'Huw-whuddya-ike-tabe-ich!'

The guard nearest to him spun round and raised a hand, but Jook stopped him. 'Wait, let's hear what the little fish has to say.'

The guard removed the gag and for the second time in several days Jensen worked his jaw until he felt able to speak.

'Hold on a minute,' said Jook with a warning wave of his sausage-like finger. 'Before you open that pipe hole of yours let me warn you that if I'm not pleased with the words that drop from your mouth I'll cut the tongue from your head and feed it to your fat friend.'

Jensen returned the overseer's smile with a cocky one of his own. 'How would ya, me big brooding friend, like ta become very, very rich?'

Jook's eye bulged then he roared out laughing. 'Rich? I'm rich already! I'm the boss of the Soul Mines of Zhartoum. Ha! Well I hope your chubby friend has an appetite to match his fat stomach cos he's about to be fed your wriggling tongue.'

One guard grabbed Jensen's shoulders while the other reached for his mouth. Jensen bobbed his head aside to avoid the guard's fingers and with that sure little smile still plastered firmly on his face he looked Jook dead in the eye. 'But how much do ya get paid?'

Again Jook's eye bulged at Jensen's forwardness, but once again he chuckled, clearly delighted by the idiocy of his latest slave. 'A yearly stipend of two baskets of gold, one of sapphires and two slaves delivered to my house every half year to break as I please.'

Jook grinned in self appreciation and watched with interest as the second guard finally managed to grab Jensen's jaw. The first guard pulled a knife from his belt and waited for the other to grasp Jensen's tongue.

'Grmp-grng,' gurgled Jensen. He maintained eye contact with Jook, and even though his tongue was in the process of being wrestled from his mouth managed to appear calm.

Jook was impressed. 'Wait,' he said.

The two guards paused. The knife hovered over Jensen's tongue.

'What was that, little fish?'

'Grmp-grng.'

'Let him speak.'

Jensen shook his head free. With an insolent look at Jook he said, 'Chump change.'

'What?'

'I said "chump change". Two baskets of gold and one of sapphires a year is nothing.'

'He gets four slaves a year too,' muttered one of the guards who, fascinated by the bizarre turn of events, felt the need to add his two cents.

'Well, if slaves are your thing, four a year ain't much to go by, is it? I've heard that even the Northern Shamen get paid double that and all they do is guard Bane's borders from a few ice tigers and the occasional snowstorm.'

'What is this?' sneered Jook. 'A tit-for-tat comparison of incomes? You're a slave. A fish. And a fish who's about to lose his tongue. Why on Bellania should I listen to your crazy opinion on money?'

'Because I'm Jensen the Willow.'

Jook and the two guards shared an empty look.

Jensen sighed. 'Ya guys don't get out much, do ya? I control the Moreish Powder trade, which makes me the richest man anywhere east of where Bane happens ta be standing.'

'You?'

'Well, I know I don't look like much, particularly as yer've got me all trussed up like dis.' He smiled disarmingly. 'But yeah, I'm the only one who knows how ta distil Lindis flowers. And ya, my friend, might be the Daddy of the Soul Mines of Zhartoum, but I'm the First Merchant Prince of Sylvaris and money don't flow faster than when it dances around me.'

Jook frowned. 'What are you offering?'

'Freedom for me and me mates. Food and enough supplies ta get us back to Sylvaris, and in return I'll set you up with some Lindis seeds and the secret ta distillation. Just think, ya could control the trade across all of Bane's empire!'

'He's lying, boss,' said one of the guards. 'All of his wood was stripped from him in Alavis.'

Jensen chuckled. 'Yeah, well let's just say that the soldiers know how ta give a good beating, but don't exactly have an eye for detail.'

'Huh,' mused Jook. Stepping closer, he loomed over Jensen. 'What's to stop me torturing the secret out of you or cutting your fat friend here into little pieces until you tell me what I want to hear?'

'Well, I'm offering wealth beyond counting and ya are offering us a chance to dine with death. Sounds like ya and I are at the negotiating table, in which case I think there's room for a little haggling.'

Jensen smiled confidently up at Jook. Kelko, kneeling behind him in the dust, smiled subtly too. No one could beat Jensen when it came to a deal.

19

A Sword of Swords

The inside of the temple was as dead and as decrepit as its exterior. The long corridors were lined with cracked and shattered statues. Piles of dead leaves filled dusty corners and the occasional painted mural was faded and blistered, making it impossible to see their original images.

The place stank of lost secrets, but Charlie didn't want to hang around and find out what they might be.

'In and out,' she whispered to herself. 'In and out and be quick about it.'

She trotted down the empty corridor and into a massive but desolate room with a wide staircase leading up into the pagoda. Keeping Darkmount's directions in mind, she hurried towards the stairs, but as she took her first step she felt the Hell Sword lurch in her hand.

She stared at it in amazement. It was growing.

Its steel began to gleam as it stretched thicker and longer. The hilt became more comfortable to hold, almost like it belonged there, and as Charlie examined it she noted that the pommel had morphed into the face of a snarling eagle.

'Ooooooooohh,' she breathed, unsure whether to be delighted or shocked.

Her free hand wandered towards the edge of the blade, but stopped at the last second as common sense took over. Instead she tested the blade on the banister.

'Guuuuurgh!' she gulped, staring at the severed lump of wood that now lay by her foot. She had only touched the sword edge to the banister, and gently at that, but it had passed through the wood like a knife through butter. Charlie grinned wildly, a new self-belief washing through her. Checking she was still alone and did not have an audience, she began to chop and lunge with the sword.

'Whoooooosh! Whoosha-whoosha-whoooooooosh!'

She couldn't help it. Really she couldn't. There was just something about holding the sword that brought out the wannabe ninja in her.

She began to mix the sword play with her K'Changa stances. Growing more confident, she started to flip and tumble, weaving the blade in intricate patterns. She even practised raising an eyebrow after she finished each combo. And it was all going so well until she tripped over a hole in the floor and fell flat on her back. The sword flashed out of her hand, lurched into the air and began a perilous arc straight towards her . . .

Before Charlie could react, the sword drove straight into her chest, from which it rebounded and dropped to the floor.

'Huh?'

She patted her chest to make sure there weren't any gaping holes in it.

She looked at her hand.

'No blood?'

Picking up the sword, she tested it against the nearest

wall. A section of wood and bricks tumbled to the floor in a shower of dust.

'Wha . . .' she mumbled, her mouth opening and closing in shock.

Gathering her courage she touched a finger to the sword point. The blade flowed backwards, bending like rubber. She tested her finger against the long edge. It was like playing with soft candle wax, but when she hacked at a banister it went straight through.

'Awesome!' she breathed. 'Awesome. Now that's what I call a sword!'

Grinning wildly and perhaps with more confidence than was wise she made her way up the stairs.

The noise in the tunnel was appalling. The clang of weapon striking weapon mixed with the enraged shouts of Stoman soldiers created a giant cacophony. The flash of light from Nibbler's flames and Darkmount's glowing fists did little to aid illumination and if anything only added to the chaos. Soldiers tried to force their way deeper into the tunnel with swords and axes as Shades scampered over the walls or clung to the ceiling. Stonesingers puppeteered behemoths that, too large to enter, had to crouch down on hands and knees and force tree-trunk size arms with outspread fingers into the tunnel in an attempt to grasp the trespassers.

Darkmount tore a Shade off the wall and hurled it spitting and screaming into the face of a soldier. Whipping his mace overhead he brought it cracking down to shatter the stony fingers of a behemoth's fist. The behemoth withdrew its mangled arm only to be replaced as another of the huge mannequin-like figures was ordered to take its position. Darkmount hurled his ruined mace aside in disgust. Reaching into the wall to fashion yet another he paused to look towards the distant Gate.

'What is it?' panted Nibbler as he noticed the bishop had halted his barrage of missiles.

'She's taking too long,' said Darkmount.

Nibbler puffed out a huge jet of flame that cleared the Shades off the ceiling and walls and momentarily forced the soldiers back.

'What do you mean too long?' asked Nibbler with a startled look of concern. 'She's going to be OK, right?'

'That's hard to tell.'

'Well what are we waiting for? Let's go!'

'Bah! And do what?' snarled Darkmount. 'If we leave this position, who will hold back the garrison? Who will prevent them from rampaging into the cavern to stab your precious Keeper as soon as she returns?'

'I-I . . . well,' stammered Nibbler as he struggled to think it through. 'Well you should stay here. You're powerful enough to hold this lot at bay. I'll go and check on Charlie.'

'Pah! I knew you were as stupid as you looked! What will you do if Charlie has been taken by daemons? What will you do if they come screaming out of the deeps like a horde of locusts? Do you have the necessary expertise? I think not. No, you will stay here and hold back these faithless Stomen and I will ensure that your friend is safe.'

Without waiting for a by your leave Darkmount stamped his way into the darkness, leaving Nibbler alone.

Screaming and shrieking, hooting and bellowing, the throng of Stomen charged down the tunnel. Shades streaked between the feet of the lumbering Stomen; Stonesingers joined ranks to raise glowing hands high and behemoths once more plunged their monstrous hands deep into the tunnel like grown men trying to sink their hands into a mouse hole.

Nibbler took a deep breath to settle his nerves.

'She's got to be OK. She's got to be,' he whispered to himself.

Breathing out, he reared up on to his back legs and unleashed a jet of crackling flame.

20
The Daemon Kindred

Charlie breathed a sigh of relief once she reached the top floor of the temple. Staggering over, she leaned the Hell Sword against the wall and knuckled both hands into her stiff back. Once her back felt as though it had relaxed slightly she shook each of her legs in an attempt to loosen up the cramp in her thighs.

Lady Narcissa's tower in Sylvaris had been high, but it was nothing compared to this. Nothing.

Wiping the sweat from her brow, Charlie stared down the long corridor. It was as empty as the rest of the temple: no furniture, no nothing. The only things to be seen were little clumps of dried leaves and small clouds of dust that swirled in the weak light.

Just as Darkmount had predicted, there were doors on either side: scores of them. Those on the left had been marked with a cross, those on the right with a circle. The corridor was long, making it hard for Charlie to distinguish the last three doors on either side, which blurred together with distance. But she remembered from Darkmount's instructions that it was one of the final three circled doors that she was headed for to find the vessel.

'No doors with a cross,' she recalled to herself. 'Simple, right?' Sighing, she picked up the sword, slung it across her shoulder and trudged forward.

Hell was turning out to be a lot more boring than she had expected. Not a soul in sight and after her fright on the bridge she had not seen a flicker of movement other than the stirring of debris. No noise, no movement, no people and definitely no Daemon Kindred.

Charlie wasn't certain whether it was a good thing that she was bored or not. At least boredom indicated a certain level of safety, but still everything was just so, 'Booooooooring,' she huffed, completing the sentence aloud.

As if in response to the sound of her voice, the door closest on her left suddenly rattled and shook on its hinges, making Charlie yelp and jump. She scampered a couple of steps down the corridor before her bravado caught up. Spinning around, she unsheathed her sword and hesitantly made her way back to the door. It clattered in its frame, then fell silent.

Charlie stared at it accusingly. Slowly she reached for it, thought better of it and slowly backed away.

It rattled again, but the further she moved away the quieter it became until finally it stopped.

Charlie stood there, sword still raised, and waited.

And waited. But nothing happened.

She gave the door a dirty, speculative look then continued on her way. When barking, howling and scratching noises came from behind a door marked with a circle she jumped again. With the sword at the ready she edged past.

A few doors further down she heard a whistling voice:

'. . . sit, stir the blue one. Yes, sit, stir the blue one. Yes, sit, stir the . . .'

Again she backed away from the repeated nonsense until it faded to nothing.

For a while after that she heard nothing, although she did see odd neon colours glistening beneath a door and felt an intense cold emanating from another. She hastened past both until finally she saw the end of the corridor and the last three doors on the right.

'Oh, Leaf and Sap, is someone there?'

Charlie froze in her tracks, she slowly turned to face the door with the voice. It was marked with a cross.

'P-please . . . is someone out there? Someone?'

Charlie hesitated, unsure what to do. She stared first at the door with the cross then turned to look at the three marked with a circle. She took a step towards the circled doors.

'Wait, please don't go. Don't leave me, yer've got ta help me.'

The voice was definitely Treman and it sounded young. Really young. Like that of a little girl.

'Please, please help.' The voice was desperate. 'Blessed Sapling, don't leave me here for them!'

'Yeah right!' said Charlie. 'Do you think I'm stupid or what?'

'Wot?' said the voice. 'No wait, ya can't leave! Look they dragged me here, they took me! And . . . and, wait, who are ya? Are ya one of them? Ya are aren't ya? Yer taunting me, aren't ya?'

'One of who?'

'One of . . . Green Sap, if yer not one of them, yer've gotta get me outta here! Yer've gotta get me home! Please . . .'

As the voice choked off into tears and sobs, Charlie felt something catch in her throat. She tightened the grip on the sword, swallowed and perhaps against her better judgement reached for the door handle.

'Listen up, whoever's in there,' said Charlie. 'If this is a trick, you're going to upset me and, trust me, when you see what I've got in my hands you're going to be real, reaaaaal sorry if I lose my temper.'

'Wait! What do you mean by a trick?' went the voice; it sounded panicked. 'What are ya going ta do ta me?'

'Well, if I open this door and find out you're nothing more than a daemon trying to trick me, I'm probably going to cut your head off.'

'Oh . . . uh, well, I'm not a daemon so hurry up and get dis door open and let me outta here!'

Charlie quickly transferred the sword to one hand, turned the latch, grabbed the sword again between both sweaty palms and kicked the door open.

Jumping forward with the sword raised, she stumbled to a halt when saw the young Treman girl tied to the wall. Charlie's mouth fell open then, remembering where she was, she spun round looking for any hidden daemons, even going so far as to check behind the door. When she was certain they were alone, she gave the girl a good looking over to make sure she wasn't a daemon in disguise.

The girl was indeed a young Treman, perhaps about seven or eight. Her dishevelled hair was still in some semblance of a topknot and she was dressed in typical Treman fashion:

three-quarter length trousers, waistcoat, jewellery and all. The girl must have spent some time crying, as her eyes were red and puffy, tear tracks showed in the dirt on her face and dried lines of snot had crusted her upper lip.

'Um . . . I'm Charlie. Charlie Keeper.'

'Yer a Keeper? Ya can get me outta here?'

'Well . . . yeah. I guess.' Charlie moved forward then stopped. 'Wait a minute. How'd you get here?'

'Oh, Sweet Sap, I don't know! One minute I was asleep at home then the next thing I know I'm on some misty bridge with these creepy-crawly looking people. They stuffed me in ta a sack then the next thing I remember is being dragged up some stairs and being chained in dis room! I ain't heard nothing or seen nothing since! All I wanna do is go home.' The young girl began to cry.

The sight tugged at Charlie's heart. She knew the feeling of being in a strange land only too well. 'OK, OK, I'm gonna get you down from there. Just remember that if you do turn out to be some kind of daemon I'm going to make sure you're sorry.'

'I'm not a daemon,' sniffled the girl.

Charlie used the sword to cut the girl's bindings and did her best to catch her as she fell. 'So what's your name then?'

'Lallinda,' said the girl rubbing at her wrists. She stared up at Charlie with wide brown eyes.

'How old are you, Lallinda?'

'Seven.'

'Seven, huh. Well it wasn't too long ago that I was in the same position as you.'

'Wot, ya were grabbed by the creepy-crawly people too?'

'Oh no. I was chained to a wall too, so I know how your wrists hurt.'

'Why were ya chained to a wall?'

'Disagreement with a bunch of Stoman soldiers.'

The girl stared at her like she didn't know what to think. 'But yer a Keeper right?'

'Uh, yeah.'

'So ya came ta get me out?'

'Er, no.'

'But . . . wot am I gonna do?'

'Look, uh, Lallinda,' said Charlie, slightly flustered and none too sure how to handle the role of rescuer. 'I'll get you out of here, but there's something I need to do first. So, um . . . you can either wait here for me or –'

'I'm not staying here!'

'You can come with me, then.'

'Where are we going?'

'To the end of the corridor.'

'We're in a corridor?'

Charlie rubbed at the bridge of her nose. She didn't remember being quite so dense when she was seven, but then again she appreciated that the girl was scared and remembered only too well how terrified she had been when she found out monsters were real. She would never forget the first time Mr Crow had come to give her a beating.

'Look, honey, I've got to be honest. We're not in a good situation, but there's something important that I've got to do. Really important. So what I need you to do is stay by my side, be really quiet and I'll make sure the two of us get out of here in one piece. Think you can do that for me? Stay quiet?'

Lallinda nodded silently, keen to show that she knew how to keep her mouth shut.

Charlie couldn't help but notice that her eyes were very wide. Very innocent.

'And, Lallinda, I know how horrible it is when someone asks you to be quiet, particularly someone older than you, but I really, really need to keep my wits about me. I need to listen and I need to stay on my toes so, uh, just keep quiet and be ready to move fast. OK?'

'OK,' said Lallinda, doing her best to flash a brave smile even though her eyes were still wet with tears.

'Great.'

Charlie took the girl by the hand, poked her head out of the door to double check the corridor was still clear, then headed towards the last three doors on the right. As she approached the first, she released Lallinda's hand, grabbed the handle and pulled it open.

A huge mouth lunged at her, all sharp teeth, rotten breath and rolling tongue. The mouth was the size of the doorway and the tongue unfurled towards her.

Charlie hurriedly slammed the door shut.

'Not that one, then.'

Ignoring the slobbering and scritchy-scratchy noises coming from the first door she headed to the next. Taking a deep breath she eased it open.

At first she thought the room was empty, but then she noticed a painting on the wall. It was a portrait of a woman with her eyes closed; something about it reminded Charlie of a pre-Raphaelite exhibition she'd seen on a school trip. So beautiful, but also so very, very sad.

The woman's eyes opened and looked directly at Charlie. Tears began to track down her face and dripped silently off the frame.

Something about the painting – the woman's eyes and her tears – dug at Charlie's heart, but she honestly didn't know if she should do something about it. Confused, she slowly backed away and closed the door.

The experience cut her deeper than that of the lunging mouth. Hesitantly she made her way to the last door.

When she opened it she was surprised to see that there were no beasties inside and no paintings – just a plinth, and on it a simple stone vessel, just as Darkmount had described.

Charlie approached the pedestal and stood on tiptoes so she could peer into the urn.

Stars. It was full of stars.

Her hands trembled a little as she reached for it.

As she plucked it from the plinth, a dry, rasping chuckle filled the room. The voice was promptly joined by others until the whole temple seemed to echo with wicked laughter.

'Not good, not good,' muttered Charlie, realizing that time had suddenly run out.

Moving as quickly as she could, she stuffed the vessel into her backpack, grabbed Lallinda by the hand and ran into the corridor before staggering to a halt.

The walls were sliding upward to reveal a forest of thick purple plants. Their fat leaves glistened with sticky-looking dew drops and stretching from plant stem to plant stem were thick strands of silk. The plants were so tightly packed and the light so poor that Charlie couldn't tell how far the plants stretched, but she got the impression that the forest was big. Really big. Which considering they were inside a building made no sense, but then again, she thought, nothing about this place behaved as it should.

The sounds of leaves being brushed aside reached Charlie's ears as slowly and stealthily the temple's inhabitants began to push their way through the foliage to step out into the corridor.

The Daemon Kindred.

They slunk, skittered and crawled into view. Hybrids. They were all insane and ghastly-looking hybrids.

Tremen who scuttled on hairy arachnid legs, Stomen who lurched on spindly grasshopper joints and Humans who scurried around with millipede propulsion. None of them were the same, all slightly different and each more twisted than the last.

They lined up along the length of the corridor and in unison their mouths twitched upward, their blackened lips peeled back and suddenly they were all grinning.

'The creepy-crawly people!' gasped Lallinda.

'Good description,' agreed Charlie, unable to tear her gaze away from their mottled skin, pointed teeth and ravenous eyes.

One by one the daemons put out a hand to gesture down the corridor towards the distant staircase, as though daring Charlie to run their gauntlet.

'SweetSapBudandLeafSweetSapBudandLeafSweetSapBud andLeaf,' chanted Lallinda in terror, scrunching her eyes shut.

'Come this way,' smirked one of the Kindred in a taunting voice. It pointed past the length of its brethren to the possible sanctuary of the stairs. 'Oh, won't you come this way, little girls, and play our games?'

Charlie's mouth opened and shut. Her mind struggled to accept the reality of the situation, but her heart, far faster than her brain, was already bursting with fear.

'Come, come this way,' chuckled another in a voice that sounded like metal twisting and buckling. 'Won't you come and be our playthings?'

'Come, come, come,' chanted all the daemons on one side of the corridor.

'Play with us, play with us,' sang the others.

Their smiles grew wider, their eyes glittered with sickly hunger and their long fingers began to twitch as though eager for unspeakable delights.

Charlie could feel her fear sink deeper, feel her stomach flutter and the muscles in her lower back quiver and tense. She couldn't take her eyes from their teeth, couldn't bear to think what their idea of playing might be. But more importantly she didn't know what to do, didn't know where she could run to, didn't know –

And then the anger suddenly took over.

'I'm not playing your games!' she snapped. 'And if I've got to play any sort of game it's going to be by my rules!'

She spun round, grabbed Lallinda and sprinted back to the room that had held the urn. Wielding the Hell Sword she carved a large square into the wall, knocked it outward with a firm kick and peered through the makeshift exit to the ground below. The influx of wind ruffled her clothes, tore through her hair and brought that odd greenhouse scent to her nose. Looking out she could see the bridge to her right, the spider-web clouds in the sky above and the tiered roofs with their garden balconies below.

Sudden cries of rage burst down the corridor and punched into the room. The cruel shrieks gave strength to her determination and speed to her actions.

'Lallinda!' barked Charlie, her unexpected voice of command startling the terrified child from her vacant gaze. 'Put your arms round my neck and jump on to my back.'

'But –'

'No questions, do it now!'

The scrabble of insect legs at the doorway caused her to look up, but she didn't hang around. Making sure that Lallinda had a firm grip, Charlie edged backwards until her heels hung over the precipice. She flashed the first daemon that came into view a rude grin and an insolent wave then jumped backwards.

Out into the void.

21

Sting in the Tale

In the end Jook the Attentive agreed to allow Jensen, Kelko and Sic Boy to leave the Soul Mines of Zhartoum with suitable supplies (and with all their limbs intact). But before any of this was to happen Jensen had to provide his half of the bargain. To this end Jensen and Kelko had been hauled through the despairing tunnels of the mine to Jook's office.

It was a luxurious room that had been split into two parts. One held a line of empty prisoner cells while the other had thick carpets, plush seats and an impressive-looking desk backing on to a long window that looked down across the hellish cavern of the main mines. The distant sound of lashing whips and slaves crying seeped into the room. The two guards had tagged along, and seeing that Jensen and Kelko were, for the time being, still prisoners, had wrapped them in chains.

'Show me these Lindis seeds,' insisted Jook.

'I'll need Sic Boy for that.'

Jook raised the eyebrow over his patched eye.

'I've hidden the seeds on the dog.' Jensen shrugged apologetically. 'Really, wot better place ta hide them and keep them safe?'

'You've got to be kidding if you think I'm letting that beast of a dog in here,' sneered Jook.

'Put him in one of those cells if yer worried about security,' suggested Jensen.

Jook grudgingly nodded his assent. One of the guards left and after a short period returned with another eight Stomen who, swearing, grunting and groaning, hauled Sic Boy into the office. The dog immediately perked up when he saw the two Tremen.

'Calm down, Sic Boy,' said Jensen soothingly. 'Don't worry, Boy, everything will be all right.'

Sic Boy allowed himself to be guided into the cell before a guard slammed the door shut, sealing him in.

Jensen turned back to Jook with a disarming grin. 'Happy now?'

'Just get on with it.'

Jensen coughed into his fist.

'What now?'

Jensen rolled his eyes towards the mass of guards. Jook, quick to realize the value of sharing secrets with as few as possible, grunted in agreement.

'You lot. Out.'

'Boss, are you sure?' queried one of the guards.

'What? You think two little Tremen in chains are a danger to me? Curse your ears, you fool!'

The guard's shoulders drooped. He trudged after the others and pulled the office door shut behind him. However, once the guards had departed, Jook grabbed Kelko and shoved him into another of the cells. 'The man had a point,' he said. 'Risks should always be kept to a minimum.'

'Quite right,' agreed Jensen. 'Now back to business . . .' He held out his hands.

Jook stamped over to the Treman. Leaning over him in an obvious act of intimidation, he placed one large hand round both of Jensen's. 'Don't forget, we might be acting at being pals, but if I suspect for one second that you're trying to play me for a fool I'll gut you like a rabbit and strangle you with your own intestines.'

'I wouldn't have it any other way,' said Jensen, staring the huge Stoman straight in the eye.

Jook paused, grunted, then finally released Jensen from his shackles.

'Ta business, then,' said Jensen.

Striding purposefully forward, he made straight for Sic Boy's cell.

'Come here, Sic Boy,' he urged. As the large dog came closer, he pushed his hands through the dog's fur to detach a small box hidden beneath his collar. He opened it, checked the contents and as he turned back to Jook he gave Sic Boy one final pat. 'These, me large friend, are the seeds of yer future success. Allow me to demonstrate their worth.'

He placed a seed on the desk. Closing his eyes he began to softly chant. The sound of his voice and the warmth of his Treesong carried across the room. It weaved its way through the bars of the cells, tickled at Kelko and wafted past Sic Boy's great ears. A scent of sap and freshly cut grass seeped into the office and with it came an odd feeling of contentment. The seed responded. Bursting open, it released small tendrils of greenery that weaved up into the air. As Jook leaned closer to watch the magic unfold, his face betrayed a mixed array of emotions: wonder, delight and good old-fashioned greed.

As Jensen continued his chant, the tendril grew fatter, roots pushed their way into the desk and into cracks in the floor. Leaves blossomed and finally the shoot swelled into a small sapling large enough for its branches to scrape against the ceiling.

Jensen, with a very large smile on his face, allowed his song to fade.

Side by side, the small Treman and large Stoman admired the new growth in silence.

'So this is it? This is a Lindis plant?' asked Jook. Leaning over he took one of the leaves in his hands to gently rub between his thumb and forefinger.

'Ah . . . no. Actually it's an elm tree. Me old friend Stotch was fond of them. In fact, his family name was Elm.'

'What?' growled Jook.

'Well wot did ya expect ta find in the collar of my late friend's prized dog? If ya really wanted ta find a Lindis seed ya should have come ta see me in Sylvaris.'

'You . . .' snarled the Stoman. Rage building, he reached for his axe.

'Hold up,' suggested Jensen with a grin that was so cheeky it would have made angels weep. 'Ya might want ta know that dis ain't the only elm tree in yer office.' The jaunty Treman jerked a thumb over his shoulder towards the cells. 'In fact, you might find a second one over there.'

Jook turned.

There was indeed a second elm in the room. It sprouted at an odd angle from the ruins of Sic Boy's cell lock.

Jook, slightly overwhelmed at the state of his office, stared disbelievingly from one elm tree to the other, then finally settled his furious eye upon the small figure of Jensen the Willow.

'I palmed the other seed inta the lock when ya weren't looking. And, uh . . . before ya reach any further for yer beloved axe ya might want ta take one last look over there.'

TTTWANG!

The lock shattered as Sic Boy gently prodded the door with one of his paws. It swung open with a long creak. The huge dog padded into the office with a truly terrifying expression of malice on his face.

'And dis,' said Jensen, 'is wot is known as the payback. Sic Boy . . . do yer thing.'

The dog leaped forward with a ferocious growl.

Once it was over Jensen released Kelko.

'The ol' Lindis seed trick, huh?' grinned Kelko.

'Never fails,' smirked Jensen. 'Hate to end these things so violently, but I figured it was either him or us.'

Kelko stepped over Jook's remains to stare out at the Soul Mines. 'So how do ya plan ta free that lot? There's a lot of people down there who need saving.'

'We're not going ta save them,' said Jensen.

'Wot?' asked Kelko with a startled look. 'Why not?'

'It's too big a project. Sweet Sap knows how many guards and soldiers are down here. Surely too many for us ta take on.'

'But we've got Sic Boy with us. That'll –'

Jensen held up his hand to silence his large friend. 'Kelko, I know wot yer gonna say and I know how that big heart of yers works . . . But it ain't gonna happen. The risk is too great and the cost of failure a price that we cannot afford ta pay.'

'Yer gonna say "think of the big picture" aren't ya?' grumbled Kelko.

'Yes I am,' admitted Jensen. 'And it's by looking at the big picture that we can achieve the most. Ya know wot's at stake here. Ya know we can't afford ta get caught and ya know with all the guards and soldiers out there there's a high chance that things could go wrong. If we get caught who would save Charlie? Who would see that the pendant is kept safe? Who would warn Sylvaris about Bane's attack?'

Kelko sighed so heavily that his stomach almost burst the buttons off his shirt. 'OK, I get it. I do. I just wish . . .'

'I know, Kelko, I know. But freeing the Winged Ones is the quickest way of getting rid of Bane. And once Bane is out of the picture places like dis will disappear too.'

'So wot now? How're we going ta get outta here?'

'Well we know there's ten guards waiting outside dis door and a whole lot more between us and the exit so I think we should carry on with wot we've started here.'

The two turned to admire the small tree emerging from the ruins of Jook's desk.

'Wot about the guards?' asked Kelko. 'Won't they knock down the door as soon as they hear wot's going on?'

'Probably,' admitted Jensen with a mischievous look. 'But there's still some seeds left in Sic Boy's collar. I think we can put them ta good use.'

Kelko watched with a befuddled look that swiftly turned into amusement as Jensen placed another seed in front of the door into the office.

Standing back with a grin to mirror Kelko's own, Jensen asked, 'Are ya ready?'

'Ya can't even begin ta imagine how ready I am. Let's do this!'

Jensen was first to start singing, Kelko – waiting a moment to follow the melody – joined in shortly after. Guiding their Treesong, they teased the seeds and sapling into growth. Pushing their roots deeper into the ground, they found added sustenance and beneath the urging of the Tremen's song the saplings swelled into mature trees. Their branches pressed against the ceiling and with a groan, a creak and a crack they forced their way upwards.

Eyes twinkling in delight and buoyed up by the idea of escape, Jensen and Kelko increased the power of their song. The trees, already impressive, grew even larger.

There was a sudden pounding of fists on the door, but the guards could not get in. The seed that Jensen had placed in front of it was now a tree and barred their entrance more efficiently than any lock.

Snapping, splintering and screeching, the rock above was forced apart. With a final roar the roof was split open to reveal a chasm that led to a ribbon of blue sky.

'That's it!' yelled Jensen, sheltering from the falling rock at the base of the giant elm. 'Let's get outta here! C'mon, Sic Boy, let's go!'

Clambering up the trunk, the Tremen scampered from branch to branch until they at last reached the welcome sunlight. Sic Boy scrambled up behind them, his huge claws gripping the bark.

'What the –' growled a startled voice. 'Why, you green-skinned monkeys! Trying to escape are you? We'll see about that!'

It was the wagon driver who had shipped them here. After eating a meal and collecting his bonus, he had just turned the wagon round and was in the process of returning to Alavis when the road in front of him burst open with a flourish of branches. The guard too was still by his side, an incredulous look plastered across his face.

Jensen and Kelko merely grinned and crossed their arms. The tree branches that emerged from the crevice shook and rustled. The movement got fiercer and in an explosion of green leaves Sic Boy jumped free.

The guard and the driver, already halfway off the wagon seat, froze in astonishment.

'Er . . .' began the guard.

'Eep,' wheezed the driver.

Kelko and Jensen's grins grew even bigger.

'Leave yer clothes and weapons behind and we might let ya leave here with yer skin intact,' smirked Jensen. 'But be quick; we ain't got all day.'

The two Stomen looked at each other, but a menacing growl from Sic Boy soon had them pulling the belts from their trousers with trembling fingers.

'And yer weapons,' insisted Jensen when the two stood in nothing but their underwear.

There was a clang as a short sword and two daggers hit the floor.

'And let's not forget yer bonus, eh, boys?' sniggered Kelko.

The guard tried to bluster a response, but Sic Boy snapped his teeth mere inches from the man's backside.

A handful of coins joined the weapons.

'Good . . . now beat it!' said Jensen with a snap of his fingers.

They watched with interest as the two scampered back towards the entrance to the Soul Mines of Zhartoum.

Chuckling, Jensen and Kelko helped themselves to the fallen booty before swinging themselves on to the wagon. As they retreated back towards the Great Plains, the leaves of the elm tree gently rustled in the wind.

22

A Devilish Betrayal

As they fell from the temple, Charlie caught a brief flash of the bridge, a dizzying glimpse of the bottomless drop beneath and felt more than heard Lallinda's terrified scream as the young girl pressed her face into Charlie's back. The wind tugged at her hair, vertigo lurched in her stomach and her eyes watered as the temple wall flashed by.

Gripping the sword hilt as tightly as she could, she reared back then lunged forward, driving the blade into the brickwork. The sword sank deep, but with Charlie and Lallinda's combined weight hanging from the hilt it didn't stop their fall, only slowed their rapid rate of descent so that they fell like two pirates with a knife in a sail. From floor to floor they slid, the sharp blade cleaving a huge chasm into the wall. They crashed through roof after roof and in a cloud of mortar, loose bricks and wayward slates they continued downward.

Charlie, unable to restrain herself, grinned jubilantly at the dwindling faces of the Daemon Kindred.

'Haaaaa!' she screamed. 'Catch us now, you suuuuuuuuuuuckers!' She cackled in delight.

Then her eyes bulged as the Daemon Kindred scampered

down the wall on their insect and spider-like limbs. Hundreds of them burst from the top floor, their claws and talons giving them unbreakable grips. Spreading out, they almost obscured the temple walls with their sheer weight of numbers. They streamed downward, mouths agape and screaming like hyenas.

Growing desperate, Charlie searched for a new avenue of escape. Spying a rapidly approaching balcony coming up on their left she reached a sudden decision. Pulling the blade from the wall she kicked outward with her feet. The two girls flew through the air to land on the parapet in an explosion of dust and sprawling limbs. Checking that the urn was still in one piece, Charlie hauled Lallinda to her feet, sprinted to the end of the parapet and jumped on to the roof below.

Loose tiles scattered on impact and Charlie instinctively rolled forward, but Lallinda – slower and lower on luck – broke through the timbers and fell part way through the roof. Staggering backwards, Charlie grabbed the young girl by the shoulders and helped drag her free.

'Quick! Quick!' snapped Charlie, hurrying the crying girl forward.

'I can't, I can't go –'

'Yes you can! You can!'

'I can't!' wailed Lallinda, collapsing into a sobbing heap. 'Dis is just a dream. It's a dream. A dream . . .'

Charlie glanced back at the approaching horde. They had almost reached the balcony. Half cursing, half bemoaning her luck, she ran back. Heaving the sword overhead she swept it through the large supports that formed part of the parapet's foundations. With a groan of tortured timber and the *snap-snap* of cracking bricks, the balcony plunged into the abyss, taking scores of daemons with it. Unfortunately the demise of their brethren didn't slow the others or dull their enthusiasm for pursuit. Hooting and screaming, the daemons scuttled closer.

'Get up, Lallinda! Get up! I'm not leaving you here. Now up on your feet!'

Grasping the girl by the arm, Charlie lurched forward and, reaching the end of the roof, half flung, half lowered Lallinda to the bridge then swiftly followed after.

'Come back and plaaaaaaaaaaaaaay with us!'

'We have games, such games. Delightful games!'

'Yeah, I'll show you chumps what to do with your games,' gasped Charlie as she staggered across the bridge, doing her best to prod the terrified Treman girl forward.

The mist closed round them, hiding the temple and their pursuers from view. The taunts and cries of the approaching Kindred now sounded muffled and distant.

'C'mon, Lallinda, we're almost there. Almost safe.'

Reaching the end of the bridge, Charlie slashed at the ropes then gleefully watched as the bridge and its annoyingly cheerful lanterns disappeared into the mist.

'Catch us now, you –'

The sight of the grinning daemons spanning the void with lines of spun silk caused Charlie to fall silent. Even from a distance their teeth looked awfully sharp.

'Come back!' they cackled in unison. 'Join us! Join us and plaaaaaaaaay!'

As she stared at their gaping mouths and multi-jointed legs, the fear suddenly returned.

'R-run!' The word escaped her lips as a gurgled whisper.

With the aroma of hot greenhouses catching in their noses and the feel of the clammy mist on their cheeks, Charlie and Lallinda sprinted up the cobblestone path. Puffing and panting, they headed towards the soft golden glow of the Gate.

The sound of insane laughter, the scuttle of insect feet and the anticipation of something grabbing at her shirt gave Charlie an extra burst of speed. Grabbing Lallinda by the hand, she jumped for the welcoming glow of the entrance.

Landing back in the cave, adrenalin pumped through Charlie's veins. The thick stalactites, smoky air and screaming statues still littered the area, giving it an unwelcoming atmosphere. But Charlie didn't care. She'd made it back and with the vessel too! She felt delighted; at last something was going right!

Something suddenly tugged at her hand. The motion pulled her up on tiptoes and almost lifted her off her feet.

Befuddled, she turned to look at Lallinda.

But the Treman girl was gone. In her place was one of the Daemon Kindred and it was grinning madly like a fisherman having just landed the catch of a lifetime. It was half-human, half-millipede and much larger than those she had left behind. It loomed overhead and Charlie was shocked to realize that she was holding the creature's hand. She blinked in astonishment.

'Lallinda?'

The daemon, with its hag's face and long matted hair that floated in the air like seaweed caught in the tide, giggled in delight. 'Ah, little Charlie, so innocent and sweet. Did you really think you could get away without being my play-thing?'

'B-b-but where's Lallinda?' stuttered Charlie. Dismay, exhaustion and confusion prevented her brain from putting two and two together.

The daemon found this uproarious. Rearing backwards on its millipede's tail, it stretched its free arm to the ceiling and laughed like a thing possessed.

'Oh, sweet Charlie! Your innocence is a prize. A real prize! I shall enjoy sucking it from your soul. Souls such as yours are a rare gift indeed.' Seeing that Charlie still hadn't grasped the truth of its trickery it allowed its face to morph back into that of the young Treman girl. 'Oh, Sweet Sap please save me, Charlie Keeper!' it lisped mockingly. 'Please be my hero!' Once again it chuckled wickedly before morphing its face back into that of an old hag. 'I am Lallinda, Queen of the Patchwork Kindred and you, Charlie Keeper, are the only mortal foolish enough to have fallen for my trick in millennia. Millennia, I tell you! Everyone who steps into our realm knows better than to believe their eyes and ears. At least everyone but you.'

'So you tricked me.'

'Easily, little Keeper – you are as naive as a puppy and now –'

Charlie didn't wait for the daemon to finish. Fuelled by anger and horror at what she had allowed to escape from hell, she swung the sword overhead and sliced clean through the creature's neck. There was a brief moment when the daemon managed a look of disbelief before its head toppled one way and its body the other.

Charlie watched with mixed feelings as the sword in her hand shrank back to its original rusted form and the daemon's body withered into a pile of purple leaves. Charlie noted that the leaves were the same as those from the forest hidden within the daemons' temple.

'I'm an idiot,' she muttered. She was disappointed in herself; her stupidity had almost ruined everything she had fought for. Darkmount had warned her about the crossed doors. 'How could you have been such a sucker?' She resolved in that moment not to tell the bishop about Lallinda. The last thing she needed was for him to think even less of her than he already did.

She shuddered in revulsion and had to fight the urge to empty the contents of her stomach across the floor. Suddenly unable to bear the weight of the sword, she threw it so that it landed amongst the scattered leaves. Wiping her hands on her shirt, she slowly backed away.

The sound of battle echoing down the tunnel from the Stubborn Citadel reminded her that Nibbler and Darkmount were still fighting for her. She took a hesitant couple of steps in that direction then stopped. Thoughts rampaged through her head, thoughts of hard lessons learned and bitter betrayals suffered. Reaching a sudden decision, she swept the backpack off her shoulders, opened it and drew forth the urn.

Taking a deep breath she stared into its depths. The stars within lit her skin with a soft glow, yet the stone surface of the vessel itself felt cold. Very cold.

'Hello?' she said. She was aware of how ludicrous it was to hope to hear a voice coming from an urn, but with all the events unfolding around her she didn't care. 'Is there anyone there?'

'What is it you desire?' asked a voice, which sounded not from within the vessel or from within the cavern but resounded loudly inside her head. 'Speak and let your request be known.'

It's more like a genie than a god, Charlie thought to herself. There was something seductive about the voice, something honey-rich, but at the same time alien and insect-like. As the god spoke to her, she felt a wet trickle of something running down her nostrils, over her lips and off her chin. With a start she realized it was blood. Once again Charlie felt slightly sick, but drawing more upon necessity than courage she voiced what she thought needed to be asked.

'Do you know why my pendant was made?'

'Yes.'

Charlie felt the stirrings of excitement. 'I want to know the location of the Winged Ones' secret Gateway. I want to know where I have to go to release the Winged Ones back to Bellania.'

'The Serpent's Tail,' the god answered without hesitation.

Ha! This was much easier than dealing with Darkmount. No wonder he hadn't mentioned this little perk to her before.

'Where is –'

But the god, pre-empting her question, was already answering. 'The Serpent's Tail lies within the Winged Mount's shadow.'

'Yessss!' Charlie punched at the air. She knew where to go now! She knew how to free the Winged Ones and now,

now she really was on the path to rescuing her parents. At last she had uncovered the final piece of the pendant's puzzle. However, one last question remained unanswered. She took a deep breath and clenched her fingers knuckle-white round the vessel before continuing. 'One more thing: does Edge Darkmount intend to betray me?'

'Yes.' Even as the voice echoed within the confines of Charlie's head she felt as though she had already known the answer. It was, after all, her doubts that had caused her to ask the god the question. All she had really wanted was confirmation.

'Well done, Charlie Keeper. Perhaps you are not quite as infantile as I had first thought,' growled a voice right by her ear. 'Now give me my god!'

23

Greed

Charlie tried to pull away from Darkmount's grasping hands, but he was too quick and she too surprised by his sudden appearance. His large fingers wrapped round the vessel, overlapping her own.

'Give me my god!' repeated Darkmount, a fevered look shining in his eyes.

'So you can betray me just like everyone else? Not a chance!' snapped Charlie. Her hands burst into flames as she summoned her Will.

Darkmount, matching her move for move, sang several notes of power so that his palms too billowed with flame. With the urn clutched between their glowing hands, the pair stared at each other with hate-filled eyes.

'I'll ask you once more and once more only: *give me my god before I snuff out your life!*'

In response Charlie grinned mirthlessly. 'Have you forgotten that my Will makes me just as strong as you?'

'Maybe it does,' acknowledged Darkmount, 'but perhaps you have forgotten that I am more experienced than you, YOU LITTLE WHELP!'

With a roar he released the urn with one hand. Scooping

up a handful of dirt, he flung it at Charlie's face. She countered his move, but it had been a bluff. Lunging forward he slammed his foot down. His heelstrike sent explosions of rock rippling out in circles and Charlie, caught off guard, was sent cartwheeling through the air.

'Ha!' said Darkmount as he secured his prize. 'My god! Once again my god is mine!'

Grinning ecstatically he tucked the vessel inside his robe. Composing himself, he turned to face Charlie as she jumped to her feet.

'So now, my little adversary,' said Darkmount as he eyed his foe. 'I believe the time has come to end your life.'

Digging his fists into a nearby stalagmite, he pulled free a chunk of rock that he fashioned into one of his characteristic clubs. Swinging it in large circles, he began to pace after Charlie with a determined look upon his face. The club thrummed and whistled as it whipped through the air.

WHUUUSH!

WHUUUSH!

Dancing out of reach, Charlie's eyes widened as Darkmount stepped between a stalagmite and one of the screaming statues.

KA-KRAAACK!

KRAAACK!

Both stalagmite and statue burst apart in a shower of dust and splinters, but Darkmount and the brutal club didn't slow at all. Merciless and unstoppable, he stomped forward leaving a trail of destruction in his wake.

Charlie tried to jump forward so she could strike the bishop with her glowing fists, but she found it impossible to get past his weapon. Calling on all her K'Changa moves and gambits she leaped, tumbled and somersaulted this way and that, but each and every move was checked. Darkmount was simply too strong, his Stonesong too powerful and, armed with his club, his long reach was insurmountable.

Charlie was outmatched and outpowered.

Realizing this, Darkmount grinned.

Switching his grip so that he held the club one-handed, Darkmount started to sing louder. With his free hand he pointed to the stalactites that clung to the ceiling. One by one they burst free to fall like spears.

KA-PHOOM!

KRAK-PHOOM!

Close to panic, Charlie jumped from side to side, doing her best to avoid not just Darkmount's club but the battery of missiles that cracked around her.

Aware that he held the advantage, Darkmount's singing grew in power to become a deafening roar. Flinging the club aside he raised both hands upward. At his gesture the largest of the remaining stalactites burst from the ceiling. Charlie dodged one, slid beneath the explosive impact of another, but was too slow to avoid the debris of the third. She squawked, then screamed in agony as a large rock slammed down on her leg with a sickening *crack*.

Charlie went down in a tangle of limbs, the pain of her broken leg extinguishing her Will. Hearing the thump of Darkmount's approaching footsteps she rolled on to her back so she could face him.

'Just tell me why?' she hissed through gritted teeth.

Darkmount leaned down to tear the pendant from round her neck. 'For this, of course.'

'You're going to sell it to Bane?' choked Charlie. 'But why?'

Darkmount snorted in derision. 'Foolish to the very last, eh, Charlie Keeper? No, Bane is no longer my main concern. With my god returned to me I can now bring the true faith to the whole of Bellania. The only fear I had was the return of the Winged Ones. They would have objected to my holy plans, but now with your pendant in my grasp I no longer have to worry. If it's any consolation, know that Bane and all who honour him will fall beneath my fist. And now, Charlie Keeper, the time has come for us to say our final goodbyes.'

Lifting his fists he called upon his stonesinging and once again gestured towards the ceiling. Charlie, seeing what was coming, screamed. Raising her hands she summoned her Will, but the pain from her mangled leg broke her concentration so that it only manifested as a jittering light that stuttered weakly across her fingertips.

Darkmount grunted with mild appreciation at her efforts. 'Still defiant? I can almost respect that . . . but it won't save you.'

With a final bellow of Stonesong, Darkmount pulled the ceiling down upon Charlie. The light of her Will grew brighter, but as the weight of rock piled up around her it flickered and finally died beneath the onslaught of stone.

When the rockfall finally ceased, Darkmount gave Charlie's burial mound a nod. Whether it was a nod of satisfaction or a nod of respect from one opponent to another it was impossible to tell. Checking that the urn was still secure in his robe he strode across the cavern, raised his glowing fists and carved an exit tunnel into the deeps.

24

Lightning

Without Darkmount by his side, Nibbler was slowly being overwhelmed. He could no longer successfully hold back all that rose up against him. The Stomen and the Shades knew it too. They slowly began to pace forward as step by step they pushed Nibbler backwards.

The Hatchling's chest heaved, his throat was ragged from spitting so much flame and his talons felt blunt from endlessly scraping them against armour and weapons. Eyes rolling and muscles shaking, he took one more step backwards then stopped.

He could not give up. He couldn't. Charlie was depending on him.

Grabbing hold of his courage, he dug deeper than ever before. He felt the gases inside him churn, then boil with the need to be ejected. Gritting his teeth, he reached even deeper. He was determined to show these Stomen and Shades what it meant to face a Winged One. He would show them what it meant to face a fire-breathing creature.

The pressure built internally as his lung and chest muscles heaved with effort, but he wasn't ready to release his wrath. Clenching and tensing, he summoned up more and more fire

within his belly and just when he thought he might explode with the effort of it he opened his mouth and ejected a crackling fork of lightning.

The spike of electricity shot down the tunnel, burning a blue line in everyone's retinas and exploding against all it touched. Stomen and Shades were flung against the tunnel walls, behemoths had their hands blown off and Stonesingers were sent tumbling through the air. One of the more fortunate Stomen who had only been grazed by the attack stumbled to his feet with wide eyes.

Nibbler stared back with a look of surprise that mirrored the dazed soldier's.

Slowly he raised a paw to touch the end of his mouth to check that everything was still intact.

It was.

What was more, he felt remarkably good, as though spitting

lightning and not flame was perfectly natural for a Winged One.

'How did I . . .' he began before falling silent.

He could shoot electricity out of his mouth! Nibbler couldn't believe it. Unable to help it and regardless of how serious the circumstances were, he burst into a big toothy smile. A grin so big that his dimples almost grew dimples of their own.

'Ha!' he roared. 'Haaaa!'

Digging deep he tensed once more, and opening his mouth he spat out another jet of lightning.

There was a whimper from one of the Stomen and a shriek from one of the Shades. The smell of scorched flesh filled the air and the gloom of the subterranean chamber was filled with the faint glow of static aftershock.

There was a hubbub of mixed voices and commands from the end of the tunnel as the Stoman garrison, having fallen back in disarray, hastily tried to recompose itself. Nibbler, not one to miss an opportunity, opened his mouth wide and hurled yet another lightning bolt in their direction, intending to scatter them even further. However, in his eagerness he had miscalculated and his aim was off. His shot burst against the arch of the wall, causing a small landslide of rock.

Nibbler blinked in astonishment at the power of his new-found ability. He blinked again as his mind kicked into gear. If he could tear down part of the tunnel he could block the way, giving Charlie all the time she needed to complete her task. Time in which he could go to the Gate and be there for her should she need his help.

Without wasting another second, Nibbler began to lay about him in earnest. He sent lightning strike after lightning strike into the tunnel ceiling. Great slabs of rock began to break free and with a terrific crash a portion of the tunnel collapsed, blocking the way.

Chuckling to himself as he heard the muffled complaints of the distant soldiers, he turned and sprinted for the cavern.

Jensen and Kelko stood on the grasslands while Sic Boy lounged on top of the wagon.

'How are we going ta do dis?' asked Kelko. 'Two goals, two different directions.'

Jensen abruptly laughed. 'We both want ta go and save the little Hippotomi, don't we?'

The two Tremen shared a rueful smile.

'All right, let's just cut ta the chase,' said Kelko. 'We both know it's gonna take brains ta find our girl and brains is something that ya have in spades. So ya go and find the little lass and I'll go and warn the Jade Circle that Bane's First Army is headed to Sylvaris. Deal?'

Jensen shook Kelko's hand. 'Deal.'

'Good,' said Kelko. 'Seeing that all I've got ta do is head in a straight line while ya'll probably have ta show a little muscle, Sic Boy should go with ya.'

Jensen struggled to hide his astonishment. 'Are ya sure?'

'Of course. It's a bad world out there now and as cunning as ya might be yer don't have anything like my manly muscle.' Kelko paused to slap his stomach. 'So it only makes sense that I lend ya a little canine ferocity.'

Jensen eyed the poor horse that was harnessed to the wagon then eyed Kelko's rounded figure. 'Are ya sure ya'll be all right on that? Horse riding was never yer thing.'

Kelko grimaced at the idea of riding day and night and more on a horse. He could already feel his bum wincing in protest. 'A Treman's gotta do wot a Treman's gotta do.'

Jensen helped Kelko unhitch the horse. Throwing a blanket and what padding they could find across the animal's back, they constructed a crude saddle. Then there was nothing left to do but say goodbye.

'Boss,' began Kelko, suddenly touched by what this parting could mean. Bellania's future appeared very uncertain while war was a cloud that hovered over the not-so-distant horizon. 'I . . .'

'Enough with that!' protested Jensen. 'Things will work out for the best, ya'll see. Just make sure Sylvaris is still standing when I bring Charlie back!'

Slapping Kelko on the back, Jensen helped his friend heave himself on to the horse. Once Kelko was secure, Jensen leaped aboard Sic Boy's broad back.

With a final wave and a hearty grin that hid doubts about the future, the two friends parted ways. Kelko headed east to warn his beloved city, as Jensen headed south-west to see if he could pick up the trail of Charlie Keeper.

25

The Darkness

She couldn't see anything, she couldn't hear anything and for a moment Charlie thought she was dead.

It was only when she hesitantly stretched out her hands and encountered the rough surface of rock that she realized where she was.

Buried alive.

A cruel crunching pain stabbed through her leg, raced up her spine and slammed into her brain. Biting back a shuddering gasp, she hesitantly pushed her hand down her thigh, past her knee and, scared of what she might find, slowly investigated further. She stopped when she felt something hard and jagged poking out from beneath her trouser leg.

'My leg . . .' she whispered, realizing just how badly broken it was. She grimaced as another wave of pain swept through her. Laying her head back down, she tried to relax in the hope that the pain would ease.

But the pain didn't ebb and neither could she relax.

'Darkmount.' She snapped, unable to constrain the sudden explosion of rage. 'My pendant!' she added a moment later as her memory caught up with her. Her rage grew as it dawned upon her just how horribly lost she was: buried alive and the pendant torn from her grasp. How on earth was she ever going to save her parents now?

The rage melted away to be replaced by bitter despair. A sob escaped her lips. Then another and another.

Charlie hated the sound of her own crying, she hated the evidence of her weakness and, most of all, she hated the idea of lying here in the dark with nothing but the warmth of her tears to keep her company. But she couldn't stop. The thought of her parents being forever lost to her was simply too overpowering and before she knew it she was sobbing uncontrollably.

Never had Charlie been so miserable. Never had she felt so lost, or so helpless, or isolated.

Images of all her past betrayers and spiteful opponents came to mind: Mr Crow, Lady Narcissa, Bane, the Delightful Brothers, the Shades and Wyrms, the Alavisian Watchmen, the Daemon Kindred, Lallinda and Edge Darkmount. All the punishment, cruelty, petty words, deceits, betrayals and terror that she had suffered at their hands flashed through her mind.

Slowly, as Charlie continued to sob for what had been and what was lost, she began to change. A darkness born back in Lady Narcissa's tower and partially unleashed in the Arena of Sylvaris began to unfold and unravel. It crept up, out of her heart and slowly, slowly began to sink its fingers deeper into Charlie's being. And there, in the pit beneath the Stubborn Citadel, buried beneath the weight of stone and misery, a new spirit of darkness was born into the realm of Bellania.

Nibbler raced into the cavern and skidded to a halt as he saw the overwhelming panorama of destruction. Stalagmites and stalactites were cracked or hanging at unnatural angles or simply missing with nothing more than a ruined stub to show that they had ever existed. Rubble lay strewn across the floor, rock dust hung in the air and what he assumed to be the Gate hung limply against the far wall, one corner completely folded over like the bent cover of a book.

Frantically he looked around for a sign of Charlie and, finding no clues to her whereabouts, he shut his eyes and let his nose guide him. It led him to a large pile of shattered stone.

'Charlie! Charlie, are you in there?'

Getting no response and fearing the worst, he began to claw the fallen rock aside. When he came across larger pieces too big to shift with a paw or shoulder he would grasp the offending obstacle with his front legs then use his rear legs in tandem with the beating of his wings to generate enough torque.

Slowly but surely he began to dismantle the rockfall.

'Charlie!' he called again. 'Charlie, can you hear me?'

There was a moment of silence before the halting reply came: 'Yes . . . Nibbler . . . here . . .'

The faint whisper was greatly reassuring; just knowing that Charlie was alive brought a rush of elation to the young Hatchling, but it was tempered by fear of what he might find. She sounded hurt. Terribly hurt.

Grasping a final boulder he tore it aside, pausing when he saw what lay beneath his excavation.

A pit of black flames waved and licked at the air, emitting

a dark energy that chilled him to the bone. Nibbler licked his lips, unsure what to make of the phenomenon.

'Charlie?' he asked.

The dark flames subsided then were extinguished to reveal Charlie's figure hunched into a tight ball. Nibbler blinked in astonishment. The unusual flames had been black – purest black – and it was only at the moment when they had disappeared that he saw any trace of the Keeper's normal golden Will.

Aware that his friend was in a dire way, he pushed his doubts aside and rushed forward.

'Charlie! Charlie! Are you OK?'

'. . . Nibbler?' Her voice was weak and scratchy.

'I'm here, Charlie. I've got you.' Reaching out, he stroked her face. 'Can you move?'

Charlie opened her eyes, 'He broke my leg . . .'

Nibbler almost bit his tongue as he looked down to see the mangled state of her shin. 'Who did?' he asked. 'A daemon?'

'No. Darkmount,' gasped Charlie, '. . . and he took the pendant.'

Nibbler growled before he could stop himself as a thousand furious thoughts blazed inside his head. Swallowing, he resisted the sudden urge to slash at the rocks. His friend needed him, perhaps more than ever before. He had to get her to safety.

The faint sound of Stonesong from the tunnel that led back to the citadel prompted an even stronger sense of urgency. The Stoman soldiers had renewed their attack and surely it wouldn't take them long to get past Nibbler's barrier.

'Can you stand? Wait, no of course you can't.' Bending his knees, Nibbler shuffled as close to Charlie as possible. 'Put your arms round my neck.'

When he felt Charlie's hands grip him he stood and tried to move forward. Charlie screamed in agony as her ruined leg scraped along the ground. Nibbler immediately stopped.

The sound of Stonesong grew louder. The scrape of boulders being pushed aside and the clink of armour echoed into the cavern. The soldiers were coming.

'Which way did Darkmount go?'

He followed Charlie's wobbly finger to the discreet tunnel half-hidden in the shadows at the far side of the cave.

'Charlie, I'm sorry, we've got no choice. You have to hold on. You have to.'

Once again Charlie screamed as her leg was knocked from side to side, but Nibbler gritted his teeth and, ignoring the terrible sound, continued to drag her forward. As they inched towards the tunnel, Charlie's cries turned into bubbled moans of agony.

'I'm so sorry, Charlie. I'm sorry, so sorry.' Nibbler repeated the litany over and over as guilt plucked his conscience. But he simply couldn't afford to leave her behind. If he allowed her to be captured by the Stoman soldiers worse things would happen to her, of that he was certain.

Reaching the tunnel, he gently deposited Charlie several metres in then hastened back to do his best to disguise their escape route.

Hearing the soldiers and glimpsing the dark flicker of approaching Shades, he set to work slashing and burning at the tunnel mouth until it collapsed in a pile of rubble, leaving the two of them in darkness. Nibbler wasn't sure how his makeshift handiwork looked from within the cavern, but he hoped it was enough to disguise the tunnel at least long enough for them to make good their escape.

Blowing a small jet of flame to illuminate the way, he trotted over to Charlie. She had passed out and no matter how much he tried he couldn't wake her. Quickly he tore part of her shirt into strips so he could bind her arms together. Wriggling his neck between her wrists, he did his best to ensure the bulk of her weight rested across his back. Struggling upright, he lurched forward and heaved Charlie along.

For what seemed like an endless, horrifying stretch of time Nibbler followed Darkmount's path until it eased its way out from the depths of the ground, to reveal an exit silhouetted against the blue of a dawning sky. Nibbler poked his head round the corner and, seeing no sign of Darkmount or any other potential threat, dragged his friend into the light.

Spreading his wings to capture the oncoming wind, he took flight with his precious cargo strapped perilously to his back.

With both the Western Mountains and the Slumbering Hills behind him the Stoman boy headed down into the low country. Walking through crooked canyons and past rocky outcroppings he made his way through the harsh landscape.

Yet as hard and as unforgiving as the stony countryside was it still felt like home. It was scenery that he was familiar with and his village, even further south, was only two days' walk away. Tired but happy, the boy felt as though his trip had been a success. He had sold his rock fruit and crystal flowers for a surprisingly high amount. With the war going on and Bane demanding that more and more soldiers join his armies, the merchants, normally serpent-tongued and oily-fingered, had been only too happy to pay twice the normal rate for his wares. His rock sisters and brothers would be happy and perhaps for once he might be able to put a smile on his father's brooding face.

A shadow flashed overhead. It narrowly avoided slamming into a rock spire, but in its efforts to right itself careered into the canyon's wall in a shower of dust and pebbles before bouncing off and losing altitude. Lower and lower the thing flew, its trajectory wobbly and ungraceful.

The boy flinched, fearing it was another Wyrm or even another pack of those wild, evil-sounding crows. But once his heart had stopped hammering and he actually managed to open his eyes, he realized that the odd shape was in fact a Winged One – with someone hanging hazardously off its back.

The boy watched open-mouthed as the odd pair barely made it over the far wall before disappearing. Without thinking he shrugged the pannier off his back and rushed down the canyon, towards where he assumed the Winged One and its passenger had landed.

26

A New Arrival

Nibbler waited for the cramp to subside before attempting to close his wings. His shoulders ached and he was sure that his skin was bleeding where the fabric binding Charlie's wrists together had cut into his flesh.

Wearily he snaked his head from between Charlie's hands, then used his teeth to gently cut her free. Shaking loose the dust that clung to his head after his brush with the local landscape, he tried to stand on unstable legs and investigate Charlie's injury. But his muscles gave way and he collapsed in a further explosion of dust. Too tired and too weak to move, he dragged himself closer to his friend.

Shutting his eyes, he breathed deeply in an attempt to recover his strength.

When he opened them he found, to his surprise, a young Stoman standing in front of him.

'Back off!' he growled, and tried once again to struggle to his feet. Failing to regain his footing, he bared his teeth and hissed out a warning jet of flame.

The Stoman hastily retreated, but didn't disappear. Instead he stood out of harm's reach and stared with curiosity at both Nibbler and Charlie. The Stoman, although somewhere in his teen years, was to Nibbler's mind still a potential threat. His long lean frame was wrapped in tight muscle and even though he didn't carry any obvious weapon Nibbler wasn't about to let down his guard.

'Back off, I said!' Summoning all his strength the Hatchling pulled himself upright and staggered forward.

Surprisingly the young Stoman didn't retreat, but bowed deeply. 'Winged One,' he began in a soft but well-spoken voice. 'I mean no harm. I-I only came to see if I could offer some help.'

Nibbler didn't know what to say. It was obvious that he was in dire straits yet he was wary of allowing anyone he didn't know close to Charlie.

'Don't . . . trust . . . him . . .' groaned a voice.

Turning round he found Charlie revived, but her eyes barely open. Disturbingly and somewhat frightening to behold, a flicker of both black and gold flames flittered and fizzed round her fingertips.

'Can't . . . trust . . . strangers . . . can't . . . trust . . .' Charlie's eyes rolled up in her head and with a long shuddering sigh she passed out. Thankfully the shadowy flames disappeared too.

Nibbler didn't know what to make of the change coming over Charlie's Will. Neither too, by the look of things, did the Stoman. Eyes wide, the boy took a step back.

'Is-is she OK?' he asked.

'What does it look like?' snapped Nibbler, fear for his friend causing him to grow angry. 'She has suffered more –'

'Winged One,' interrupted the boy. 'I can help.'

'You what?'

'I can help.' The Stoman pointed at Charlie. 'I can heal her leg.'

Nibbler hesitated. He stared at his suffering friend and her cruelly twisted shin, then back to the Stoman boy with his large brown eyes and honest expression. Realizing he was risking everything, but also aware that he and Charlie were in terrible jeopardy, he struggled to reach a decision.

'OK,' said Nibbler at last. 'But don't hurt her. She . . . she just can't take any more. OK?'

The boy nodded. Walking forward, he knelt by Charlie's side so he could better study her wound.

'It's a bad break,' he muttered, talking more to himself than Nibbler. 'It's fractured and . . . No matter. This I can fix . . .'

Shutting his eyes he began to sing, his hands taking on a soft blue glow.

'Whoa! Whoa! What do you think you're doing?' asked Nibbler, alarmed by the presence of stonesinging so soon after his fight beneath the Stubborn Citadel.

The soft blue glow disappeared when the boy stopped singing. 'It is my Stonesong. I need it if I am to heal her leg. With it I can manipulate the calcium in her bone and the iron in her marrow.'

Nibbler hesitated before consenting.

Once again the boy started to sing and when his hands glowed blue he gently placed them on Charlie's shattered leg.

'First for the difficult bit. This will hurt your friend, but it will be quick.'

Without waiting for Nibbler's permission, he yanked Charlie's shin straight. It was a violent motion and it obviously pained Charlie as, even unconscious, she arched her back. Strangely enough the boy's glowing hands seemed to have a calming effect and Charlie stirred no more after that.

Bowing his head, the boy began to chant a simple melody with a lilting voice. His hands glowed brighter, the blue colour grew more intense . . . and then he stopped.

'It is done,' he said simply. Rocking back on to his heels he waited in a crouch.

Nibbler, still eyeing him with slight misgivings, padded over to inspect Charlie's leg. Leaning in he sniffed at her leg. 'It's still bleeding,' he said accusingly.

'Of course, but I have welded her bone back together. It is as good as new. Winged One, if your friend was awake now I am certain that she would be able to walk again.'

Nibbler looked at the boy with new-found wonder. 'Amazing. But what about, you know . . . all the fleshy bits?'

'Stonesinging has its limits. I can mend bone, but healing flesh is a talent that only lies with Treman healers. Surely you should know that?'

'It's a long story,' grimaced Nibbler, not keen to explain yet again why his education was lacking. 'What are you doing?' he asked as the boy pulled a length of thread and a needle from the small bag he wore at his waist.

'This? Well with the weight of the rock fruit that I carry to the market, my pannier often breaks so I have to repair it all the time. I thought I could use this to stitch her wound and . . . oh, wait a minute! I must recover my pannier. It has my pot in it and we will need it if I am to sterilize the needle and thread.'

'Sterilize the thread?'

'Sure, to stop any chance of infection. And if I look around I'm sure I can find some Birolac Stone.'

Nibbler looked confused again. 'Birolac Stone?'

'It has healing properties in it. Please, Winged One, I will be back in a moment.'

'Wait!' urged Nibbler. 'How do you know all this stuff?'

The boy smiled brightly as fond memories filled his head. 'My uncle. He taught me everything I know about the healing ways of Stonesong.'

Nibbler nodded. 'One more thing. What's your name?'

'Crumble Shard,' said the boy. With a final smile he jogged off.

Nibbler hesitated, uncertain of what to do. Part of him wanted to snatch Charlie up and see if he could fly her all the way to Sylvaris where he knew he could get her the best medical attention. But as much as he had recently grown, he was still too small to fly long distances with a passenger. Indeed it had been pure luck that when fleeing from the Stubborn Citadel they had been gifted with strong winds and high altitude. Without similar conditions he doubted that he and Charlie would get far. He too needed to rest, find some food and grow stronger. For the moment it seemed that Charlie was, relatively speaking, safe.

What of this Stoman? he thought to himself. *Is he as genuine as he appears?*

The boy *seemed* genuine and although Nibbler was deadly serious about preserving Charlie's safety he also felt as though he had a natural intuition for reading a person's character. Narcissa, Darkmount, even Flint the Councillor had immediately struck him as people with hidden agendas. However, he felt no niggling doubts about this boy.

Besides, thought Nibbler and shrugged, *right here, right now, what choice do Charlie and I have?*

Settling down with one wing wrapped protectively round his friend, he waited for the return of Crumble Shard.

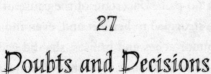

27

Doubts and Decisions

Charlie awoke with a gasp, her fingers scrabbling round her neck to find that her nightmares were indeed true.

Her pendant was gone.

'Darkmount,' she whispered and clenched her hand into a fist. 'My parents . . .'

Charlie's voice faded as she realized how completely she had failed in her task. Looking past her own family's concerns, she also had to acknowledge that she had let Bellania down too. Without any hope of freeing the Winged Ones there would be nothing to stop Bane. Nothing to stop his dreams of conquest. Or if there was, Charlie had a suspicion that it would be Darkmount with his new god and his terrifying dreams of forcing his beliefs on Bellania. Neither prospect held any hope or joy.

Thoughts, ideas and doubts danced through her brain, and the more she dwelled on recent unhappy developments the more she became aware that something had changed within her. A darkness, physical and very much alive, lay coiled within her chest. She could feel its strength, its power and somehow she couldn't help but welcome it.

Looking down, Charlie was pleasantly surprised to find

her leg cleaned and bandaged and when she wriggled her toes she felt no pain. Uncertain of the cause of this minor miracle, she struggled to her feet and, even though she felt sore from minor aches and bruises, she did genuinely feel fit. She smiled as she looked at Nibbler sleeping next to her. Her faithful companion, one she could trust beyond all others. Her smile faltered as she noticed a young-looking Stoman asleep on the far side of the camp fire.

Who's he? Charlie thought to herself. *And can I trust him?*

'Charlie?'

She turned to find Nibbler with a look of concern on his face and beyond him the Stoman boy was also waking.

'Charlie,' continued Nibbler, 'are you OK? How do you feel?'

'How do I feel?' Charlie rose on the balls of her feet, testing the strength of her recently broken leg. 'Other than being betrayed by that rat Darkmount? I feel . . . good. Really good. Who do I have to thank for mending my leg?'

'Um . . . that would be me,' said the Stoman somewhat shyly. 'The bone wasn't that difficult to fix and the gash on your leg cleaned up nicely so it should heal well too.'

'Are you a doctor?'

The boy blushed. 'No. Nothing of the sort. I just know some healing that my uncle showed me. I'm not the best Stonesinger, but fixing a bone was –'

'Stonesinging?' interrupted Charlie. 'You used stonesinging on me?'

Nibbler, sensing how upset Charlie was, quickly did his best to calm her. 'He's OK, Charlie. Really. If it hadn't been for Crumble Shard's healing talents and help making camp and catching us some dinner we would really be down on our luck.'

Charlie struggled to throw aside her suspicions and even though she knew next to nothing about this new Stoman she did know that she could trust Nibbler.

'Sorry,' she mumbled. 'Strangers and stonesinging aren't a good combination, at least not in my experience. But if Nibbler says you're OK, then for now you're OK. I owe you for fixing my leg and I hope that one day I can repay you, but right now we've got to go.'

'Go?' asked Nibbler in alarm as he watched Charlie raise her arms in preparation to open a Portal. 'Go where? Charlie, we've got to come up with a plan before we do anything! You've already lost your pendant and you nearly lost your life! Now is most definitely not the time to be doing anything rash.'

Charlie's face momentarily fell at his mention of the pendant, but swiftly hardened into a mask of determination. 'You're right, I've lost a lot and, yes, you're right we've got to make decisions, but I'm not doing it here. We're going back to Sylvaris where at least we know we'll be safe. Dridif can help us and so can Jensen –'

'They're gone, Charlie!' interrupted Nibbler. 'Jensen and Kelko got taken to the Soul Mines, remember? And I don't ever really remember being that safe in Sylvaris either. The Delightful Brothers and Mr Crow are still out there some-where and let's not forget that Bane managed to send his Shades not once but twice into Deepforest. If anything, we're safer here where no one knows us!'

Charlie squirmed uncomfortably as she realized that in

the heat of the moment she had forgotten that Jensen and Kelko were potentially in a great deal of trouble too. The burden of responsibility slammed down upon her shoulders. Friends, family, the future of Bellania . . .

'So what am I supposed to do?' she asked, finishing her train of thought aloud.

'Winged One. Keeper,' said Crumble Shard. 'I know we have only just met and I know that in your eyes I am very much a stranger, but I would like to offer my help. My uncle always said that a problem shared is a problem halved. Perhaps if you were to voice your troubles we may be able to summon suitable counsel.'

Charlie sucked on her lower lip as she gave his idea some thought. Both he and Nibbler had raised some valid points and after so many mistakes she knew she could no longer act without forethought. However one thing bothered her slightly. 'Is it Crumble Shard or just Crumble?'

'Uh, just Crumble is fine.'

'Crumble, I have to ask . . . do you always speak so formally or are you talking like that just to impress us?'

'Um . . .' Crumble blushed again, his cheeks turning crimson with embarrassment. 'No I do not, I mean, no I don't. It's just that I was always taught to show respect to Winged Ones and Keepers and now I'm talking to both of you at the same –'

'Crumble?' said Charlie, interrupting the flustered boy.

'Uh, yes?'

'Do me a favour. Talk normally, will you? I'm only fourteen, but when you talk to me like that you make me feel old.'

'You're fourteen?' squawked Nibbler. 'You told me you were thirteen!'

'I was, but I worked out the date – I had my birthday five days ago.'

'Five days ago?' Nibbler scrunched his eyes shut as he struggled with the calculations. 'What, you mean you had your birthday when we were in Alavis?'

'Yup. My fourteenth birthday was spent hanging from my wrists.' Charlie shook her head. 'Great party decor too, lots of straw, cobwebs and a fine collection of stinking, scurrying rats for party guests. Bellania really knows how to show a girl a good time. Crumble, how old are you?'

'Fifteen.'

'Great. A fifteen-year-old, a fourteen-year-old and a seven-year-old. I bet Bane and Darkmount are tembling in their boots right now.' Charlie did her best to rein in her sarcasm. 'OK, I guess talking can't hurt.' She sat close to the fire and indicated that the others should do the same.

'Seven in Winged One years isn't the same as in your years,' said Nibbler, who obviously felt honour bound to defend his age. 'Really. I'm sure if there was a mathematical equation we'd probably work out that I'm closer to fourteen or fifteen too.' Seeing the carefully polite look on Crumble Shard's face and the more-to-the-point raised eyebrow of Charlie, Nibbler squirmed on the spot. 'Fine, don't believe me, then. See if I care.'

Charlie sighed, rubbed at the empty spot round her neck then stared directly into Crumble's eyes. 'Let me tell you where we currently stand . . .'

The sun had set hours ago, but Sic Boy continued to carry Jensen across the darkened landscape of the Great Plains. Although Jensen, as a Treman, was more used to the rich splendour of the forest surrounding Sylvaris, he was none-theless a seasoned traveller and took delight in all the places that he visited. The grasslands of the plains did not have an ounce of the wildlife found in Deepforest, but if you knew where to look there were wonders to be seen: the huge herds of purple and green striped antelope, the soaring bila eagles, the crafty prairie foxes, the two-streak moths with their seven-foot wingspans and so much more than would have been believed in such a seemingly desolate place. Now that it was night Jensen found himself bewitched by the beauti-fully eerie mating song of fengris bats. In his attempt to spot the creatures his eyes had inched skyward and now he could hardly drag them away from the wonder of the stars. Bright and unmarred by any terrestrial lamps, lights or fires, they glowed supreme. Here, out in the wide, wide grasslands without trees or hills to encumber the view, the stars were awe-inspiring.

Lost in his thoughts and his eyes diverted, he trusted Sic Boy's good sense to maintain the right direction. When the large dog slowed and halted it took a moment for Jensen to snap out of his reverie.

'Wot's up, boy?' he asked.

But the cause of Sic Boy's discomfort was obvious once Jensen looked down and saw a ghoulish green glow in the valley below.

Sliding off Sic Boy's back, Jensen crouched low and slowly inched his way forward for a better look. Always making sure there was a ridge or a crest of grass or a bush between him and the glow, Jensen circled closer and closer. When he thought he was near enough he slunk down on his stomach and slowly parted the knee-high grass so he could see clearly.

At first he thought he was looking at a vista of statues. There were about twenty of them, all standing in geometric lines, but then the eerie green light flashed again. There was a moment of silence then the sound of something heavy thumping its way across the grass.

Jensen held his breath in shock.

It was one of the statues. It was moving. In fact, it was alive.

The thing thumped its way over to the others then froze, becoming as still and as silent as its companions. There was further movement, but this time it was more natural. Raising his head, Jensen spied a Stoman standing over what he first assumed to be a cooking pot, but when he looked closer he realized that it was a stone urn. It was one of the sources of green light; the other was the Stoman himself whose fists glowed the same supernatural colour.

'Stone Bishop,' whispered Jensen to himself.

The Stoman muttered an inaudible request. The urn flashed and something next to it began to move.

Jensen's eyes widened.

An egg of some sort appeared to be growing out of the ground. As he watched, it swelled and increased in size. Miraculously it twisted and transformed into one of those stony-looking creatures that he had mistaken for a statue. The thing stood upright then stamped over to join the others. Whatever these things were there were now twenty-two.

Jensen frowned. Whatever or whoever this Stoman bishop was, it was obvious that he was building himself an army.

'But why?' whispered Jensen. 'And wot on Bellania is in that urn?'

He wanted to stay longer in the hope that some of his questions would be answered, but he forced his curiosity down. He had something more important to attend to: a young friend who needed saving.

Slinking back the way he had come, he left the strange Stoman bishop with his ghost-like urn and silent but growing stone army.

28

Dark Tidings

Crumble Shard rubbed uncomfortably at his head. He had a dazed look in his eyes as though he couldn't believe what he had just heard. The three of them had talked for hours and he had to admit that he had been shocked by the problems that Charlie and Nibbler had encountered so far, but what Charlie had just proposed seemed ludicrous. Insane even.

'So let me get this right. After everything that you've been through you want me to guide you to the Western Mountains so you can defeat Bane? In his own city?'

'More or less.' Charlie nodded. 'I mean, what other choice do I really have? I have no idea where Darkmount is and as much as it hurts me to admit this . . . I don't think I'm ever going to get my pendant back.' Her voice faltered. Struggling to maintain a brave face, she continued: 'That means the Winged Ones are out of the picture and, as Nibbler pointed out, there's little reason for me to return to Sylvaris. Our ultimate goal still remains: if I'm to save my parents and keep Bellania free that means I've got to defeat Bane. We don't know where the Soul Mines of Zhartoum are so we can't come up with a plan of rescue for Jensen and Kelko, and even if we did know where they are, we don't have any guarantees that the boys are there or if they were taken somewhere else. Again, the best thing we can do to help them is end this war. End all of it and once again that means confronting Bane. Any which way you look at it the path always leads there.'

'But that's crazy!' insisted Crumble. 'Look, I've already told you that I don't believe in what Bane is doing. Most of my village don't like the idea of one Bellania beneath Stoman rule, but we all know how powerful Bane is! There's never been a Stoman lord like him before. Jugged the Great, Hook the Thunderer and Stale the Swallower are like mice next to Bane and they're mythical heroes and kings! The fact that Bane is real and stands head and shoulders above all the legendary lords makes what you're suggesting absurd.'

'Maybe it is and maybe it's not,' said Charlie. 'But it doesn't matter. I'm not asking you to join our fight. You offered to help and that's all I'm asking. All you need to do is be our guide. Azariah said that the Western Mountains would be protected against unwelcome Portals so we'll need to walk in. All you have to do is show us the way. Once Nibbler and I are there we'll handle the rest.'

'And do what?' Crumble continued stubbornly, unwilling to allow a Keeper and a Winged One to walk towards what he saw as certain death. 'What do you think that you can possibly do to Bane? Don't you understand when I tell you that he's the most powerful being that has ever sat upon the Devouring Throne?'

Charlie sat up straighter and clenched her teeth together. Without realizing it her hands knotted into fists as she imagined finally coming face to face with Bane. A dark shadow flickered across her eyes and her hair began to writhe as her Will – unsummoned this time – manifested itself as black flames that flickered round her knuckles.

'Don't worry about Bane. He and I have some unfinished business,' she said with a voice that growled with the promise of violence.

'Charlie,' protested Nibbler. 'Look, I know we've just gone over all our options, but surely there's got to be something else that we can do? There's got to be another option. There's got to be.'

'Like what?' snapped Charlie. Little sparks of darkness trickled from the corners of her eyes. 'Where in Bellania are we going to be safe? Nowhere! Can we afford to hide away and hope things get better? No! Things are only going to get worse. Either Bane conquers the land or Darkmount does. Yes we could play the waiting game in the hope that Darkmount and Bane eventually fight and we try to take the pendant from whoever wins, but the likelihood of that happening or us lasting that long are tiny.'

As Charlie continued to talk, she grew angrier and her voice grew harsher. 'So if we make a move now or later our chances are still the same. Maybe better now because no one would expect us, maybe worse later with Bellania crushed and conquered. But all of that aside I've had enough! They've taken too much from me. Too much! And I for one think that Bane needs to learn that things don't always go his way. I want to go to the Western Mountains, go to his Throne Room and show him that I mean business. I owe Bane a debt of agony!'

Seeing how alarmed both Nibbler and Crumble appeared

she abruptly grew aware of how she must look. 'Sorry,' she mumbled and rubbed at her hands in an attempt to push her Will away. Using the action of tidying her hair into a topknot as a chance to recover her composure she did her best to smile reassuringly. 'Just thinking about Bane gets me angry. Look, Crumble, honestly you don't have to worry about us. Just get us to the Western Mountains and we'll do the rest.'

The young Stoman looked concerned, but sitting in the presence of both a Winged One and a Keeper, young as they were, he found he couldn't deny Charlie's request. 'OK. We'll make a start in the morning.'

'And you'll take us to the Western Mountains.'

'I'll take you,' he agreed with an unhappy expression.

Jensen the Willow and Sic Boy were not the only ones to witness the birth of Edge Darkmount's stone army. Mr Crow, having cleared the surrounding landscape of prey, had been forced further afield in order to fulfil his constant gnawing hunger.

Spotting the odd green glow amongst the night-time drudgery of the Great Plains, he had swept out of the sky to stand on a grassy ridge that overlooked Darkmount's temporary residence.

Crow twitched his head from side to side as he watched the events proceeding below. Something about the Stoman bishop fascinated him. Perhaps it was the tantalizing display of power, or perhaps it was the possibility that something in the valley below could offer him a reprieve from Bane's wrath if only he could decipher what that was. The lawyer knew he needed something to appease his lord and he suspected that perhaps there really was something here that could aid him towards that goal.

Standing still and scarecrow-like on the ridge, he watched for several long hours. In that time Darkmount's dark army continued to grow until it could be counted in the hundreds, and the source of his power, the vessel at his feet, continued to flash with flames of green light.

The appearance of dawn's rosy fingers awoke Mr Crow from his trance. Blinking, he stared around him in alarm. He didn't want to be discovered out here in the open. Jumping into the sky in a burst of feathers, he headed back to his cave to ponder his cowardly concerns.

29

Shatterstone

Charlie awoke just as the first light of dawn began to break across their campsite. Knowing that Nibbler, always a fan of sleeping, would be the last to awake, she tiptoed away from the remnants of the fire with the intention of practising her K'Changa, only to find that Crumble had beaten her to it.

Only he wasn't practising K'Changa. He was systematically going through a series of very brutal-looking strikes. Punch followed kick and knee followed headbutt. With blow after blow, Crumble Shard moved forward, his lean muscles burning with a fierce economy of movement. His face was marred by a look of concentration and at the end of each fearsome combination he would exhale forcefully.

'What are you doing?' asked Charlie.

Crumble whipped his head round in surprise.

'Are you trying to scare me to death?' he half joked.

'I said "What are you doing?"' Charlie's face hardened, underlining her determination to get a straight answer. Whatever form of martial art the Stoman boy had been practising, it looked very effective. She wasn't sure how she felt about having someone so obviously capable travelling with her and

Nibbler. A fighter in their midst was obviously a help, but also a possible future threat.

'Shatterstone.'

'What's that?'

'The fighting style of my village. My uncle won the Western Fist Championship when he was young. I've been training under his tutelage since I was five.'

'Let me be honest, Crumble. I don't trust you.' She stared him square in the face. Feeling the darkness rise inside her she clenched her hand into a tight fist. 'I think that you being able to move and fight like that,' she gestured roughly in the direction that he had been practising, 'goes against your oh-so-nice image of last night. So let me say it again: I don't trust you.'

'I don't blame you,' he replied.

'You don't?'

'No. Of course not.' Crumble, ignoring the sweat on his brow and the hard look coming from Charlie, briefly closed his eyes and gave her a formal yet humble little bow. 'After hearing your story last night I have an inkling of what you must have gone through – all that pain and fear and heartache and anger. You know what, Charlie?'

'What?'

'I think that if that had happened to me I'm not sure I would have the strength to continue. I don't think that I could have done what you have done. And after all those betrayals? I wouldn't trust anyone either. So if it would make you happier, allow me to aid you as best I can. Let me draw you a map of the region so if you do decide to press on to the Western Mountains you can. Or should you come to your senses it'll give you other places of refuge that you can reach. I can do all of that and have my pannier packed and be gone in less than an hour.'

Charlie continued to stare Crumble in the eye, but was the first to look away as she felt something other than the pool of darkness squirm in her chest. Shamed by her own words and Crumble's honest expression she held up a hand.

'Look . . .' she began, but unsure how to continue she paused to search for the right words. 'You're right. I don't want to trust you. I don't want to trust anyone . . . but I can't allow –' She stopped as Crumble held up his hand.

'I get it,' he said. 'Really I do. You're like my younger rock sister. Sometimes she struggles with words, but she never realizes that I can read her heart by seeing what's on her face. How's this? I will stay and help as long as you like, but the minute that you feel that you cannot trust me tell me and I'll go. I will ask no question nor require an explanation. To aid a Keeper and a Winged One is honour enough and I would be more than a fool not to realize that such a task comes with many difficulties.'

Charlie opened her mouth, but found that mingled thoughts of darkness and shame clouded her judgement. Instead she gave Crumble a nod then turned to trudge back to their campsite.

'Wait,' she said and turned back to the young Stoman. 'That "Shatterstone" of yours. Is that what Stonesingers use to fight with?'

'Some do or if they don't they use a similar style.'

'Show me.'

Aware that this was a somewhat odd request, but still

keen to aid Charlie in whatever way he could, Crumble began to demonstrate. But after only a few sequences he stopped.

'Am I showing you this because you want to learn or is there another reason?'

Charlie shrugged. 'A bit of both. I've fought Shades, Alavisian Watchmen and Mr Crow and held my own, but Darkmount brushed my Will aside like it was nothing. He used a fighting style similar to yours, but when he combined it with his stonesinging it was . . . it was like he was unstoppable. Like a boulder rolling down a hill. Maybe if I can learn a little of this Shatterstone of yours, the next time I come up against a Stonesinger as strong as Darkmount things might turn out differently.'

Crumble nodded and picked up a rough-looking stone. Summoning his stonesinging, he began to chant. The stone began to bulge and flex. With a *crick-crack* the stone split and as he continued to sing a small crystal flower emerged.

Charlie's eyes widened as she gazed at the small miracle.

Crumble held up the flower for closer inspection. 'I can heal, I can shape stone and I can call forth the crystal harvest, but, Charlie, you need to know that I am no great Stonesinger. Darkmount is not just a Stonesinger but a Stoman bishop. One of the greats, one of the powerful. People like Bane and Darkmount are forever above and beyond my reach. Yes, I might be good at Shatterstone, but facing someone like me will be vastly, vastly different from facing someone of real power.'

'I know that. But show me what you can and leave the rest to me.'

Crumble smiled softly. 'OK, let me show you what I can do.'

Charlie settled down to sit cross-legged with studious intent as Crumble, blue fists aglow, began to strike and glide beneath the still starlit but gently lightening dawn sky.

Leaving the Great Plains behind, Jensen headed into the Slumbering Hills and made for the merchant town of Idle Wind. It was a suitable location that was not only halfway between Alavis and the Western Mountains but also a major cornerstone of the trading world. It was here that Jensen hoped to learn more about Charlie's fate.

Jensen was well aware of how badly Bane wanted to get his hands on Charlie and her pendant. It was only logical that if his forces had captured her in Alavis she would then be transported to the Western Mountains. What Jensen didn't know was whether she had been transferred quickly and swiftly via a lightly armoured escort or if Bane's forces, concerned about the possibility of escape, had instead chosen to transport her at a slower pace, but with more guards. If she had been transferred with a light escort, he reasoned, then she would already be in the Western Mountains. However, if she was under the watchful eye of a full military escort it was more than likely that she was still in transit.

And it was this information that would dictate how Jensen would proceed.

Riding into Idle Wind on Sic Boy's back, Jensen received some strange looks. Such a sight wasn't an everyday occurrence, but it was not that unusual either. Idle Wind was a major trading post that attracted visitors from the length and breadth of Bellania and had seen more than its fair share of exotic visitors riding in on mounts that were equally strange: Humans on painted horses; Sandraiders on mottled grasshoppers; Northern Barbarians on snowbears; Tribesmen of the Eastern Sea on mournful crabs – the list went on. Most would have assumed that the number of visitors would have decreased with the onset of the war, however the wise knew that money was to be made during times of dispute. Barter and trade was the Idle Wind's lifeblood and with the rise of Bane's empire it was more prosperous than ever.

Forcing his way through the press of the crowd, Jensen headed towards the central marketplace where he hoped to glean an insight into current affairs. If he dug deep enough perhaps he might even hear a whisper of Charlie's whereabouts.

So it came as a shock when a herald climbed on to a stage normally reserved for auctions and announced Bane's proclamation in a ringing voice that reverberated across the streets.

'. . . her head is delivered still fresh and bleeding I will double the sum offered. If she is delivered whimpering and broken to lie at my feet I will triple the sum and bestow the title of Lordship of Alavis on whomever succeeds in this undertaking.'

Jensen staggered as he heard those words. Conflicting

thoughts and emotions rushed through his head; the first and perhaps the happiest was that Charlie must have eluded Bane's soldiers. She must be free! The second was one of doubt and confusion: if Charlie was indeed free then where was she now? And how on Bellania was he to find her? The final thought that staggered through his mind was that Charlie was still in peril. With such a bounty on her head every lowlife would be after her, a fact that Jensen could verify for himself as he saw freebooters and mercenaries grin in delight after hearing the herald. Many immediately hastened off to begin their hunt.

Nudging Sic Boy through the crowd, Jensen headed to a quieter side street to mull things over.

'Wot ta do?' murmured Jensen. 'Wot ta do, wot ta do?'

Hundreds of different ideas and possible solutions clashed and clamoured through his thoughts, none of which seemed realistic or even viable. In the search for inspiration he studied the merchant's stall on the other side of the street, and it was there that he saw the flash of gold and the twinkle of coins as money changed hands.

A small smile tugged at Jensen's lips.

Jensen was the largest dealer of Moreish powder in both Bellania and Earth. He had made his fortune from trade and it had made him the foremost merchant prince in Sylvaris. It was time he remembered that.

Heeling Sic Boy round, he made his way towards the city bank. He had a transaction to make.

30

The Proclamation

Nibbler disturbed Charlie's concentration and Crumble's demonstration.

'I'm not sure what you guys are doing, but I think we need to get our bearings, have something to eat and discuss how we're going to continue. Charlie, if you're still dead-set on facing Bane in the Western Mountains –'

'I am.'

'Then we need to come up with a plan.'

'Can we not stay here until you settle upon a direct course of action?' asked Crumble. 'And if you are hungry there's still one more rabbit to be cooked.'

Nibbler squirmed before answering. 'I, uh, had some growing pangs in the middle of the night so I, er –'

'Nibbler's trying to tell you that he's already yammed the rabbit,' said Charlie.

'Well . . . yes. I did.'

'That matters not, Winged One,' said Crumble. 'You are most welcome to eat your fill. Perhaps I can catch some more later.'

'To be honest, I think we need more than food,' urged Nibbler. 'We need supplies, particularly if we're going to have to walk to the Western Mountains. Roughing it beneath the stars is OK for one night, but not all the time. We're going to need blankets and, er . . . you know what? I've never gone camping before. I'm sure we're going to need stuff, I just don't know what.'

'I've a good idea of what we'll need,' said Crumble.

Nibbler looked relieved. 'Great, so where can we get it from?'

'We could go to my village –'

'No,' interrupted Charlie with a determined look on her face. 'I don't want to get your family involved. I've lost too much of my own life to risk anyone else's.'

'But –'

'No,' repeated Charlie. 'That's final and there's no room for negotiation on this.'

Such was the look of determination on her face that neither Crumble nor Nibbler voiced any further protest.

'So what do you want to do then?' asked Crumble.

'We need a village or a small town. Somewhere where we can get our hands on the stuff we need and a place where we can find out how close we can get to the Western Mountains with a Portal before Bane's barrier kicks in and we have to start walking. That is unless you already know the answer to that, Crumble?'

'I wouldn't know anything about Keeper stuff or how Bane manages to block Portals.' Crumble shrugged. 'I can't help you with that I'm afraid.'

'No problem. Nibbler and I will find that out. Can you suggest or take us to a town? It needs to be big enough to have shops or a market, but not so big that we need to worry about stumbling across a garrison of soldiers or any more angry Stonesingers.'

'Hmmm . . . there's Opal Hold. It's more of a big village than a town, but we can get supplies there.'

'How far away is it?'

Crumble pointed to the top of the canyon wall. 'With all the canyons to cross it would take us most of the day to reach, but if we were to stand there we would be able to see it in the distance.'

'OK, let's do that.'

'What, climb the canyon? Why would you want to do that?'

'Well, if I can see it it'll make it easier to open a Portal.'

'I thought you said you couldn't open one near the Western Mountains.'

'Well, yeah, that's true, but I opened a Portal with Darkmount right next to the Stubborn Citadel and according to what you said last night that's closer to the Western Mountains than where we are right now. If I could open one there it's not going to be difficult opening one here, so let's save the walking until we really have to. But we'll have to climb up there – I don't want to waste any of my Will.'

Charlie and Crumble scaled the side of the canyon while Nibbler flapped to the top with several lazy beats of his wings. Following Crumble's outstretched arm to where the crags and gullies began to blur together into a dark line Charlie could just discern a group of buildings, but distance blurred any detail.

'That's it,' acknowledged Crumble.

'Can you describe it to me?' asked Charlie. 'It's not easy to make out from here.'

'There are two roads that run from north to south and east to west and where they meet is a small square that they use for festivals and market days.'

Charlie had shut her eyes. 'Can you describe any buildings on the outskirts? It might be best if we don't open the Portal in front of everyone.'

Crumble scrunched his eyes shut so he could better recall his last journey to Opal Hold. 'If memory serves me true there's an old statue of Hook the Thunderer in a sheltered rock garden on the far side of town from us.'

'Got it,' said Charlie and tore the air open.

Crumble eyed the Portal with slight misgivings. Through it they could make out a small garden.

'I've never been through one of these. Does it . . . hurt?'

'To step through? No. Let's go.'

Pushing through the Portal they found themselves next to a looming statue of a Stoman bishop poised in mid leap, his cloak flung out behind him. Around him was the rock garden itself. Charlie gaped in wonder as she took in the sight.

'How?' she began. 'How can this be?'

The flowers and bushes were all crystalline, with petals and leaves that glittered and glistened in the early morning sunshine. Reaching over Charlie touched a petal – it was hard and cold to the touch.

'You've never seen a rock garden before?' enquired Crumble.

'I've never seen anything like this before. How can you have plants like this?'

'Ah, they're not plants, well not in the Treman sense,

which I think is what you're used to. These are rock flowers and can only be teased from a stone or rock by stonesinging.'

'So they're real, though? I mean they'll reproduce and seed like normal plants, right?'

'No. Well, technically yes, but it would take more time than you and I ever have to see a rock flower produce seeds.'

'How much time?' asked Charlie, her curiosity unfulfilled.

'The village elders say it would take eleven lifetimes to see a rock flower reproduce.'

Charlie gazed at the small garden with a smile of delight. 'Amazing,' she whispered.

'The village is this way,' said Crumble, leading Charlie and Nibbler from the small hollow that held the rock garden.

Rounding a bend, Opal Hold was revealed. It had a quiet country village feel to it, one that Charlie, as a city girl, was not familiar with but could instantly recognize. What was unfamiliar was the type of house. Like the Treman city of Sylvaris, everything looked organic, but here the buildings had been made from stone and rock. Dark sandy-coloured structures reared upward – tall buildings that looked like they had been shaped by aeons of wind – and smaller low-slung buildings with domed roofs crouched below them. All the buildings had oval windows and strangely rounded doors, and appeared to have been formed from the ground. Which, Charlie deduced, was what had happened. These buildings had been created by stonesinging, which explained the lack of mortar or any sign of bricks or carved stone. Charlie was impressed. Her first experience of Stoman habitation – while not as overpowering as her first sight of

Deepforest – would become a memory that she would treasure.

Nibbler elbowed her in the side. 'Hey, stop daydreaming. If you stand there all day with that funny look in your eyes people are going to mistake you for the local fool.'

Charlie grinned ruefully, but followed Crumble's lead as he headed towards the village square. Nibbler, head held high, walked beside her.

They were in luck. It was market day and the small square hustled and bustled. Stalls with brightly coloured canopies lined each side of the square and in the middle was a raised dais overshadowed by yet another statue of a mythical Stonesinger. Stoman farmers, merchants, blacksmiths, potters, weavers, brewers and carpenters were busy selling their wares. Here and there the slight figure of a Human could be seen and occasionally the much smaller figure of a Treman, but they were a rarity.

As the trio headed towards the line of market stalls, Nibbler instantly began to draw a lot of attention. Some of the villagers and merchants, respectful of Winged Ones, touched their foreheads as he passed with a few words of greeting. Others, however, threw nasty looks and muttered under their breath.

'I think the sooner we get what we need and the sooner we get out of here the better,' commented Charlie.

'Agreed,' said Crumble. Walking past a fruit and veg stall he headed towards a likely looking place that appeared to stock the items they needed. He swiftly began to haggle with the merchant. 'Two silver florins and an eighth,' he called over his shoulder as he collected blankets, bed rolls and other items. 'Or the merchant will take seven Deepforest shillings if that's what you're carrying.'

Nibbler and Charlie looked at each other with guilty, startled faces. Neither one had thought about money, and neither for that matter had any.

Crumble caught their look and with a big sigh dug his fingers into his waist pouch. Eyeing his profits with a forlorn expression he handed the sum to the waiting merchant.

'That's another reason for you two to come back from the Western Mountains alive because if you don't pay back that money my father is going to beat me from house to market and back again –'

'HEAR ME, PEOPLE OF OPAL HOLD!' boomed a voice. 'HEAR ME NOW AS I BRING A MESSAGE FROM OUR GREAT LORD!'

Silence swiftly fell across the marketplace as villagers and merchants turned to look at the raised dais in the centre of the square. A Stoman herald in gorgeous black, red and gold robes stood in a pose of studied self-importance on the circular stage, an unfurled scroll between his hands. Behind him stood a small squad of soldiers and off to one side, nearly hidden by the shadows of a building, lurked a Stonesinger in full ornamental armour.

'I come with a proclamation,' continued the Stoman on the dais. Raising the scroll, he began to read aloud. '"I, Bane, Lord of the Western Mountains, declare Charlie Keeper to be an outcast and outlaw. I will pay whomever brings me her head and her pendant fifty baskets of emeralds, a hundred baskets of sapphires and a thousand fistfuls of gold coins. If her head is delivered still fresh and bleeding, I will double the sum offered. If she is delivered whimpering and broken to lie at my feet, I will triple the sum –"'

A ripe melon slammed into the herald's chest, spattering him and some of the nearby soldiers with bits of fruit. In the deathly silence that followed the herald wiped the gooey matter from his face. Picking a large piece of the offending missile from his shoulder he held it up for closer inspection. His face rapidly went from white to red and finally to a dark murderous purple.

'WHO DID THIS?' he roared. 'WHO DARED TO –'

A second melon, followed in quick succession by a Very-vaverry fruit and an oversized Mooseberry, burst against the herald's once gorgeous robes.

'I think,' rang a voice, 'that the culprit you're looking for is me.'

The herald, once he had wiped his face, the soldiers and most of the stunned villagers and merchants turned to stare at the Human girl who stood in the midst of them with her poorly kept topknot and a piece of fruit in either hand.

'I'm Charlie Keeper and I'm a bit short on money so if you've got any of that reward with you we'll be happy to take it.'

The herald could have replied with a thousand different responses, but he was so angry that he simply screamed, 'GET HER!' at the top of his lungs.

The soldiers pulled the swords from their scabbards and lifted the axes from their harnesses as they spread out in a loose semicircle.

The crowd looked at the angered herald and soldiers, then back at the small Human girl. A collective gasp rang across the village square. Charlie Keeper stood wreathed in black and gold flames. With her fists raised high and a glint in her eyes, she slowly walked forward.

'If Bane has offered all that money,' she shouted at the herald while bowling over the first soldier in a flash of dark light, 'then surely you're intelligent enough to realize that I've got to be considered a threat.' With an unusual expression that was half smile, half focused anger, Charlie kicked and punched the next two soldiers so hard that they were propelled backwards through a line of stalls. 'Surely no one would be stupid enough to try to take on Bane's most wanted with just a handful of soldiers?'

Ducking beneath the swishing arc of an axe, she tripped one opponent, flipped another and rapped her elbow against the helmet of a third while drawing closer and closer to the alarmed herald. 'Or is it perhaps –' she punctuated her sentence by bringing down the last two soldiers who stood in her way – 'that your fat mouth and ability to swagger around in a pretty costume hides the fact that you're a little bit dim-witted?'

With most of the soldiers lying scattered behind her, Charlie stood at the foot of the dais and stared disrespectfully up at the herald. Sweating profusely and looking less than regal in his fruit-splattered robes, he staggered backwards while gesturing for the Stonesinger to step forward.

Charlie grinned as, out the corner of her eye, she detected a wave of crackling flame followed by a high-pitched scream and a thud. Nibbler had taken care of the Stonesinger.

'Looks like you're all out of help,' she said, and with a sardonic smile still wrapped across her face Charlie lunged forward, driving a black-and-gold-flamed fist against the side of the dais. The stone cracked and the force of the blow caused the herald to lose his footing and fall to the ground. Charlie jumped lightly upward and, walking across the dais, stared down at the herald now suffering the indignity of lying in mud.

Groaning, he tried to sit up, but Charlie leaped to land feet-first on his chest, driving him back down. Crouching on top of the moaning herald she rifled through his robes, removing all his coins and valuables. 'What's this? No fistfuls of diamonds or rubies? No precious bounty? I'm kind of disappointed.'

'Are-are you going to kill me?' gasped the herald.

Charlie fixed him with a stare. 'I'm no killer . . . but I'm no pushover either. Go back to Bane and tell him he'll have to work harder if he wants my head.' Reaching down she patted one of his cheeks. 'Have fun getting all that mud and fruit out of your pretty clothes.'

Hastening back to her companions she found Crumble fingering a big dent in his cooking pot and the unconscious body of a soldier at his feet. Nibbler trotted over with the Stonesinger's burnt cloak in his mouth.

'Everyone OK?' she asked. Getting a nod from both she showed them her haul: a small pile of gold coins and two sapphires. She pocketed some of the gold and then gave several of the remaining coins to Crumble. 'Here's what we owe you and a little extra for the camping supplies, and here's some more in case we need to buy any other stuff on the way.'

Striding over to the group of wide-eyed merchants and

villagers, she tossed the leftover coins and sapphires at their feet. 'I'm sorry for what happened to your market day. I hope this goes some way towards paying for the damage.' Then, without waiting for a reply, she tore open a Portal so she and her companions could make a quick exit.

31

The Golden Touch

'Yes? Can I help you?' asked a haughty cashier.

'Yes, ya can. I'd like ta speak ta the master banker if ya please. It's Jensen the Willow of Sylvaris.'

The cashier looked down his nose at the travel-worn Treman standing on the other side of his counter.

'And does sir have an appointment?' enquired the cashier in a slightly mocking tone.

'Does it look like I've been in town long enough ta make an appointment?' countered Jensen. 'Of course I don't have one, but I have several large accounts with dis bank and many more with its sister banks in Sylvaris, Alavis and Alacorn. I think ya'll find that the size and merit of my accounts allow me more than ample opportunity ta drop inta any branch of the Gilded Bank as and when I want ta.'

'Is that right, sir?' said the cashier in a patronising voice. 'Are you sure you have an account with us? Perhaps you've got your banks confused?'

'Listen, sonny –'

'No, you listen, sir. This a bank for gentlemen not scoundrels! You must think me a buffoon, sir. Not one of our clients would ever dress as poorly as you or, might I add, stink of the road as much as you. I insist you leave our premises or I'll have our bailiffs escort you out!'

Jensen sighed. Reaching over he grabbed the cashier's ear.

The cashier yelped and tried to close his own fist round Jensen's, but the Treman twisted his ear even further. All the other clerks watched in alarm and one of the burly bailiffs started to lumber over.

'Ladies, gentlemen,' began Jensen in a loud but polite manner, 'I find that I am rapidly losing me respect for the Gilded Bank. Allow me ta repeat meself, I am Jensen the Willow and over the years I have deposited enough money in this bank ta warrant a little respect. Now if someone doesn't go and fetch me the master banker *right this instant* I can guarantee that I will be withdrawing me more than considerable business from this sorry excuse for a bank!'

'What, might I ask, is going on here?' A plump Stoman with thick reading glasses held open one of the doors that led deeper into the bank. She wore a concerned look on her educated face. 'And who, might I add, is the gentleman who is manhandling my staff?'

'Jensen the Willow.'

The woman blinked upon hearing the name. 'Of Sylvaris?'

'Aye, that would be me.'

The Stoman blinked yet again. She snapped her fingers at the bailiff. 'Please remove that man.' The bailiff loomed over Jensen. 'No, not that man, *that man*.'

The bailiff hesitated for a moment, but, reading the seriousness of his employer's expression, swiftly let go of Jensen and instead clamped his oversized hands round the surprised cashier's shoulders.

'Wh-what?' stuttered the cashier, unable to comprehend what was happening.

'Silence,' growled the bailiff.

All the other clerks watched in fascination as their ex-colleague was unceremoniously hurled out of the door.

'I do apologize for that,' said the Stoman once the door was slammed shut, silencing the cashier's high-pitched squawks of protest. 'Since the war broke out it has become perilously hard to find good staff. Please allow me to introduce myself. My name is Sindris the Third and I am the master banker of Idle Wind's branch of the Gilded Bank.'

Jensen's eyes twinkled.

'Sir,' continued Sindris the Third, 'you are an honoured customer and it is a pleasure to welcome you. If you would please follow me, we can retire to a room more suitable for someone of your stature.'

The clerks all watched with open mouths as the scruffy Treman walked past their desks and breezed through the door that the master banker held open.

Arriving in Sylvaris, Kelko headed towards the Jade Tower. However, when he tried to dismount from his exhausted horse he found that his legs wouldn't obey him. Groaning and doing his best to ignore the sniggers of those passing by and the whinny of protest arising from his steed, he half fell and half slumped from the saddle to land with an 'oof' by the feet of a surprised guard.

'Are ya OK there, buddy?' asked the guard.

'I can't straighten my legs,' croaked Kelko.

'Here let me help ya . . . Oh, my Sweet Sap, wot have ya been eating?' the guard grunted as he strained to pull Kelko back to his feet. 'Blight my Leaf, but ya've got girth enough on ya for two grown men.'

'Ahh,' sighed Kelko. The relief of being able to stand without a horse bumping and bruising his thighs with every step was wonderful. Straightening up, he cricked and cracked the ache from his back before fixing his sights on the entrance to the Jade Tower. 'Listen, we could spend all day discussing the merits of me manly girth over yer weedy chest, but right now we've got more pressing matters. I need ya ta help me get inside the Jade Circle right away.'

'Wot for?' asked the guard, slightly taken aback by the sudden seriousness of Kelko's demands.

'War.'

'Say wot?'

'War is coming ta Sylvaris and a lot sooner that we expect. Now stop gawking and lend me yer shoulder!'

Leaning on the guard, Kelko staggered into the tower.

All the councillors looked up in surprise as Kelko and his attendant banged against a table, knocking over a particularly graceful vase of flowers before rebounding into the table's twin and knocking over a second vase. The crash of shattered porcelain was especially loud.

'Er . . .' began the guard as he realized he had earned himself the unwanted and displeased attention of the Jade Circle. 'I'm just the help. He's the one ya want ta talk to.'

All eyes turned to Kelko.

'Oh, Bless my Oak, but I can't do this standing up. Would someone please bring me a chair? I've been riding non-stop for three days and nights, I haven't had a bite ta eat nor a sip of water and I've been bitten by just about every mosquito that lives in the Great Plains.'

'Fetch the man a chair,' said Lady Dridif in a particularly dry voice. 'We'll let Kelko the Oak sit before listening ta his no doubt golden words of wisdom . . . and if we don't value the words that pass his lips we'll have him clear up every splinter from those Tulip Dynasty vases with a pair of tweezers.'

Kelko winced as his bruised bum settled into the seat offered, then sighed in content as his thighs finally stopped cramping.

'Oh, thank me beloved Oak for that.'

'Kelko,' said Lady Dridif with a warning tone of disapproval.

'Sorry, ma'am. It hasn't been an easy week. Let me get straight ta the point. We're at war.'

There was a brief period of silence during which many of the councillors paused to stare at one another with a what's-he-going-on-about look.

'We know we're at war,' said a rather uptight-looking councillor. 'I don't think anyone would call the past couple of years' relations with the Stoman lord a "period of peace".'

'Wot? Ah, no. Look, wot I mean ta say is we're *about ta be* at war. Bane has sent his First Army across the Great Plains in the hope that we would be too distracted looking at Alavis and Alacorn to notice the danger coming from a different direction. I've come ta warn ya that we're under threat of an immediate attack.'

There was a moment of shocked silence that was swiftly broken as every councillor tried to speak at once.

'Silence!' snapped Dridif. 'Kelko, I would very much like ta think that ya would have the good sense not ta come in here with a concoction of idiocy, however having known ya since ya were a child I feel the urge ta ask ya ta repeat yerself. Do ya really mean dis? Do ya really mean that Bane's forces are bearing down on us as we speak?'

'I do, Yer Honour. And I fear that we have little more than a day's reprieve before they arrive.'

There was yet another period of silence during which Dridif held her hand aloft to prevent anyone speaking out of turn. Weighing Kelko's words against the wear and tear of his clothes and the obvious signs of a forced journey evident in the dark circles beneath his eyes, she finally spoke.

'Then we'd better prepare our defences,' she said. 'Captain?'

'Yes, ma'am?'

'Get me me generals.'

32

Brimstone and Fire

'Charlie, what's up with your Will?' asked Nibbler as they sat around waiting for the contents of Crumble's battered pot to come to the boil. 'Why isn't it golden any more?'

Charlie winced, not really willing or ready to offer an explanation. But from the look on Nibbler's face she realized he expected an honest answer. Casting her eyes skyward she sighed. As one of her most steadfast friends, she owed him the truth.

'There's something in me, Nibbler. Something dark. I can feel it in my chest and when I tense I can feel it in my muscles too.'

Nibbler's eyebrows furrowed as he looked at his friend with concern. 'What kind of "something dark"?'

'I don't know what it is. It's been there for a while.'

'How . . . long?'

'A while now. I first felt it in Narcissa's tower, but when I think about it perhaps it's been there all the time. Maybe since my parents went missing, maybe since Mr Crow came to live with Gran and me. All I know is that it's there, it's with me now. Since Darkmount broke my leg and left me for dead. And . . . and I like it.'

'You *like* it?'

'Yes. It . . . it's like a fire. A fire that rages in my chest, a fire that fuels me when I need it. It keeps me going, keeps me strong and hard.'

Nibbler, a stony expression on his face, walked over to Charlie and rested a paw on her chest. 'There's nothing there, Charlie, it's all in your –' He yanked his paw away as he felt something hammer and pound beneath his talons. His eyes grew wide, and slowly he reached for Charlie's ribcage again. 'Oh my gosh . . .' he whispered as he felt whatever it was pulse inside his friend. 'What is that? It's real, isn't it? It's really real.'

She nodded.

Crumble, who had been watching with some alarm, spoke up: 'Does it hurt?'

'No.'

'What do you think it is?' he asked.

'I'm not sure. All I know is it helps.'

Crumble cocked his head to one side. 'I've never heard of anything like this before. But what if it's harmful? What if it's going to cause side-effects or damage your body? Maybe one of the great healers could take a look at it.' He scratched his head thoughtfully. 'Might be best if a Treman healer looked at it. Are you sure you don't want to go back to Sylvaris? With your Keeper abilities you could be there and back in less than a day.'

'No,' said Charlie with a determined frown. 'I'm not moving backwards. I won't. Forward or nothing.'

Nibbler and Crumble shared a look, but neither chose to pursue the subject. Both of them knew how stubborn Charlie could be.

'So, where are we now?' Charlie asked Crumble.

'I think your Portal took us south of Opal Hold so we're a bit further away from the Western Mountains than before.'

'How long would it take us to walk to the Western Mountains?'

'To the mountains? About four, maybe five days from here and then another two to get to the city.'

'The city is called the Western Mountains too, though?'

'Yes.'

'Why is it people can't come up with original names for places?' said Charlie, pulling a face. 'It's the same back on Earth, they're always using the same names over there too. Or if they want to pretend to be creative they add the word "New" in front of the old word: New York, New Zealand, New South Wales.' Charlie paused as she pushed thoughts of Earth away. 'Look, I'd rather cut out as much of the walking as possible. Is there another village around here where we could try to get some answers to where we can and can't open a Portal?'

'Well there's –'

'Hang on a minute,' said Nibbler, cutting off Crumble. 'Why can't you just try to open a Portal to the Western Mountains? Everyone is saying it can't be done, but we don't know that for sure. And maybe if a Portal won't open in one place you can play around. If you try to open a series of Portals leading away from the Western Mountains you'll eventually find one that works.'

Charlie grinned. 'Now that's a good idea.' Standing up she clapped her hands together. Amidst rocky spires and at the bottom of one of the many canyons that dotted the land, Charlie had no line of sight from which to take her bearings.

'Crumble, which way are the Western Mountains from here?'

'There, to the north.'

Charlie turned to face where Crumble was pointing, and although she was facing a canyon wall she felt as though she could sense the mountains in the distance. Feeling confident and drawing on everything she had heard about the city, she summoned her Will. Pulling her hands apart, she teased open a Portal.

Immediately something felt wrong. The Portal felt far too heavy, as though it was fighting her. It bucked and weaved from side to side and a horrendous grating shriek burst from it. Realizing that she'd made a terrible and potentially dangerous mistake, Charlie threw herself to the side. Crumble and Nibbler, already a safe distance off, backed even further away. The roar grew to near unbearable levels and just when the three thought it couldn't get any worse they felt a vibration rumble through the air.

WHHHHUUUUUUSH!

A jet of molten lava spat from the rift, searing everything in its path, igniting the hardy cacti that grew in the canyon and turning sand and stone to glassy slag. With a final shriek the unstable Portal collapsed in on itself and blinked out of existence.

Charlie, ears ringing so hard that she thought she might now be deaf, stared at the devastation in shock. Wincing and blowing through her pinched nose to relieve the pressure in her ears, she staggered over to her friends.

'That, er . . . that didn't go too well.'

Crumble stared at her like she was mad. 'That's perhaps the worst understatement I've ever heard! "Didn't go too well! Didn't go too well!"' he parroted and shook his head in wonder.

Charlie, still unable to hear, nonetheless got the gist of what he was saying. 'I don't think I should try that again.'

'You think?' choked Crumble. 'Look, definitely no more Portals to the Western Mountains! We're going to go to another village and we're going to get a qualified answer before we attempt anything like that again. I do not want to burn off my eyebrows or get burned alive for that matter before I turn sixteen!'

'What?' said Nibbler and stared around with dazed eyes. 'Did someone say it was time to see the Queen?'

Crumble rubbed at his head in frustration as Nibbler staggered on unsteady feet and Charlie continued to alternate sticking her fingers in her ears and puffing on her nose.

'But what Queen?' asked Nibbler with a concerned look on his face. 'Will we be there in time for tea?'

Crumble clapped his hands to his face and groaned. Grabbing Nibbler by a wing in an attempt to stop the dragon walking into a pile of smouldering lava, he took hold of Charlie with his other hand and dragged them to a safe part of the canyon.

He pointed his finger at Charlie. 'No more Portals! We're going to walk to Shidden Vale. It's a bigger town than Opal Hold and it'll take us the rest of the day to get there, but NO MORE PORTALS!' Finished with Charlie, he stuck his finger directly beneath Nibbler's nose. 'And there is no Queen!'

'Really?' asked Nibbler whose hearing was returning, or at least returning at a faster rate than Charlie's. 'But what about the tea and biscuits?'

'Argh! There is no tea and biscuits! Look, just help me pack up our stuff. The sooner we get out of here and on the road to Shidden Vale the better.'

Taking charge, Crumble prodded the two into action and fortunately it was only an hour later that Charlie's hearing fully returned to her.

'What do you think that was?' she asked. 'What do you think caused that noise and all that brimstone and fire?'

'I don't know what it was or what caused your Portal to fail,' said Crumble, 'but it's safe to say that you stumbled across Bane's barrier to travelling.'

'But it was so weird,' continued Charlie. 'The Portal felt like it was going to shake free from my control and –'

'Charlie?'

'Yes, Crumble?'

'I think there are always going to be mysteries in life and for now, until we get any answers from someone in the know, this will have to be one of those mysteries that you're going to have to learn to live with.'

'Hhmpf.'

They walked in silence for a while. Leaving the red sand-stone canyons behind them, they entered a flat land covered in wind-rounded boulders and dotted with strange incan-descent trees that glimmered softly in the sunlight. Giant bumblebees the size of beach balls drifted from thorny bush to cacti flower, and insects unseen, but very much heard warbled a constant tune that followed the companions as they walked through the landscape. They came to a slow-flowing river that brought with it a sweet scent. Nibbler – still thinking about tea and biscuits – was fascinated by the brightly coloured birds that would dive into the water in search of silvered fish.

Eventually they joined a road and could soon see Shidden Vale appearing round a bend in the late afternoon sun. And just like Opal Hold, here too Charlie was mesmerized by the strange architecture: bold statues and crystal gardens that lined the streets.

'Let's try not to get into any more fights this time,' advised Crumble with a worried look. 'Let's get in and out of the town fast.'

'What about that proclo-proclee-proc–'

'Proclamation,' finished Charlie, unable to bear hearing Nibbler mangle the word any further.

'Yes, that thing. Do you think Bane will have sent any heralds here to offer that reward?'

'I guess so,' mused Charlie. 'Either way I think it would be best if we stick with Crumble's suggestion. Get the information that we need then move out.'

The closer they drew to the centre of town the more populated the streets became and once more Nibbler began to draw a lot of attention, as did Charlie. Only this time all of it was negative. Dark scowls and muttered curses followed them.

'It looks like Shidden Vale has taken up Bane's banner,' said Crumble. 'Maybe this wasn't such a good idea.'

Charlie hesitated. She wasn't enjoying the welcome either. 'Perhaps you're right. Look, how about Nibbler and I go back. You can still go on – as a Stoman you're not going to stand out so much. You can get us the information.'

'OK, that sounds like a . . . wait. Where's everyone gone?'

The street, quite busy before, was now almost bereft of people. Those still about were rapidly departing.

Charlie, immediately realizing what was coming, shut her eyes and breathed deeply. The darkness within her throbbed.

'What's going on?' asked Nibbler.

Charlie opened her eyes. 'It's a set-up, isn't it? Someone in Shidden Vale knows about the bounty and thinks they can take me to Bane.' Part of her wanted to stay and fight, to unleash the darkness and teach those who thought they could claim the reward a lesson. But the larger part of her was concerned about her friends. 'Let's get off this street before any bad guys arrive.'

She turned to lead them down a narrow side street, but they were greeted by a motley group of Stomen armed with a mixture of weapons and mismatched armour. Tridents, chunky axes, crooked swords, hooked chains, weighted nets and shields were clenched in calloused hands.

'Not that way, then,' said Charlie. 'Let's try this . . .'

But turning back to the main street she found another group of similarly armed men and women.

Charlie shrugged. 'Sorry, boys, but it looks like it's going to be fight time.'

Even as she apologized Charlie knew the sentiment wasn't genuine. She wanted to fight. The darkness inside her drove her towards it and she was only too willing to sate its appetite. She only hoped that neither of her friends got hurt in the process.

A shorter-than-average Stoman stepped forward. His belly protruded over his belt and the battered helmet thrust upon his head had seen better days, but from the girth of his shoulders and the way he held his weapon Charlie suspected that this man knew what he was doing.

'All right, squishy girl,' he rasped, 'we'd prefer it if you came with us quietly and simple-like. Course, if you don't want to play it that way we'll settle for cutting your head from your shoulders to deliver it bloodied and dripping to our lord. Either way we make enough money to go around.'

'Are you sure there's enough of you?' asked Charlie with a flippant manner.

'What? You cheeky scarab-beetle! We're the Forty Swords! That's forty of my men –'

'And women,' interrupted a dangerous-looking lady with scars along her arms and a huge warhammer clenched in her fist.

'And women,' acknowledged the man, 'who are more than willing to tear off your legs so they can carve a new set of dice from your thigh bones. You'd better pack it in and come with us now or we'll leave this fair city knee-deep in your blood and guts.'

'Oh, I'll come all right,' said Charlie, striding forward. 'It just won't be quietly.' Reaching within, she pulled the darkness from her heart, raising her hands so the mercenaries could see the interlacing golden flames and black shadows that writhed round her fists. As she plunged into the group, her voice soared above them: 'And let me tell you . . . FORTY OF YOU AREN'T GOING TO BE ENOUGH!'

33

Thornwood

'How can I help?' enquired Sindris the Third, smiling politely.

'I think,' said Jensen, 'that dis is a matter where we can help each other. Allow me ta cut ta the chase: Bane is bad for business, particularly banking. He has swamped the market with an over-abundance of gold and jewels, which has sent stocks plummeting and devalued currencies throughout Bellania. Worst of all he's single-minded. Very single-minded. If he wins dis war do ya think there would be any place in his new empire for independent banking? Do ya think that he would allow a source of wealth ta flourish that he did not in some way control?'

Sindris rose from the couch and walked across her plush study to a drinks cabinet. She poured two healthy portions of Scented Isle brandy and, returning to the couch, passed one to Jensen.

'You have a direct approach with your views, Jensen of the Willow,' she said after taking an elegant sip from her glass. 'And although I would never admit this outside this room, it is a view that I and many members of the board share. Bane, indeed, is bad for business.'

Jensen raised his glass in a salute. Sindris mirrored the gesture.

'You were intending to go somewhere with this?' she asked, urging Jensen to continue.

'I was. Obviously, we are both businessfolk so I was not going ta come out with some drastic notion or request a heroic action or appeal to yer conscience.' Both resisted the urge to snigger at that. 'However, wot I am requesting is a reasonable use of yer network.'

'Go on,' prompted Sindris.

'Bane has placed a bounty on Charlie Keeper.'

'Ah, the infamous proclamation. I'm familiar with it. My contacts have reliably informed me that Fo Fum has expressed an interest in the reward.'

Jensen paused with his brandy glass halfway to his mouth. 'Fo Fum? That raises the stakes somewot.'

'Indeed. Fo Fum is yet another character who makes business . . . difficult. Please do continue; we were discussing the proclamation, were we not?'

'We were. I would like ta raise a proclamation of me own.'

Sindris raised a perfectly groomed eyebrow.

Jensen grinned, but continued. 'But a discreet proclamation issued only within your network. I would like ta raise a considerable bounty ta be given as a reward for any news that successfully leads ta me and Charlie Keeper being reunited.'

Sindris considered the request, her face expressionless. 'Excuse me for being so brash, but I must ask . . . Why is it so important that this Charlie Keeper remains out of Bane's grasp?'

Jensen smiled grimly as he recalled their history. 'I can

think of many reasons why it would be prudent ta keep Charlie out of his grasp. I think the most pressing concern – in relation ta the Gilded Bank – is that her continued freedom ensures that Bellania remains out of Bane's control, allowing businessfolk like ourselves a continued free rein. That and, of course, the healthy commission that I will give ta the Gilded Bank for aiding me in this service.'

Sindris raised her glass. 'A toast to free markets.'

'And commissions,' said Jensen with a knowing grin.

Sindris chuckled.

'Two more things,' added Jensen. He paused as he looked down at his bedraggled clothing. 'No, better make that three more things.'

'How else can we be of service?'

'A tailor and perhaps a bath?'

'Not a problem,' said Sindris, who all this time had politely avoided acknowledging Jensen's road-weary look. 'And your third request?'

'A length of Thornwood, of Sylvarisian quality.'

'Ah, that won't be the easiest item to procure. I'm assuming that you had something special in mind?'

'With Fo Fum's arrival on the playing board? Yes, I will need something special with which ta even the odds. A length of Thornwood fits the bill perfectly. Do ya have access ta some?'

Sindris raised her glass again in respect of her esteemed customer. 'All things are possible for patrons of the Gilded Bank.'

Crumble's jaw dropped as he watched Charlie slam into the packed mercenaries, knocking them aside like bowling pins. He stared in disbelief as she broke tridents and swords, snatched thrown spears and daggers from the air and lashed at the largest of her foes with great whips of dark flame. The spectacle of it seemed unreal, like a painted battle of the furies brought to life right in front of his very eyes.

'Crumble!' shouted Nibbler, waking him from his dazed reverie. Spinning round he found the Winged One attacking three heavily armoured mercenaries with tooth and claw, while a fourth approached with a spread net.

Although he'd fought in Shatterstone tournaments before, Crumble had never been in a battle. Intimidated by the ferocity of it, not to mention all the fearsomely sharp weapons being pitched about, he hesitated.

'Crack this!' he cursed. Summoning not just his courage but his rudimentary Stonesong, he sprinted towards the fourth attacker with blue glowing fists, taking him by surprise. Making quick work of the net-bearer he ran to aid Nibbler, but the dragon already had the upper hand.

Wings rearing, Nibbler pointed at a reinforcement of five who were attempting to approach Charlie from behind. 'Take care of them!' he said. 'I'll deal with the rest.'

Nibbler took flight so he could better rain down fire and electricity from above. Which left Crumble trying to figure out how he was going to take on not one but five armed professionals. He briefly thought about using his cooking pot as he had in Opal Hold, but he knew there was no way that idea would work. Grimacing, he sprinted forward and snatched a discarded shield from the ground. Dodging a wayward bolt of Nibbler's lightning he knocked aside a hook-wielding thug, leaped over a pile of fallen bodies that had succumbed to Charlie's Will and slammed, shield first, into the five mercenaries. They all went down in a clatter of amour.

Crumble, first to regain his feet and doing his best to mask his terror, pounded both blue-glowing fist and battered shield against the attackers. Moving as fast as he could, he skipped from one to another, beating one halfway down then staggering to the next before they could recover their wits or stand upright. His whole body shaking with adrenalin, Crumble battled to stay alive.

Jensen admired his reflection. Bathed, with a freshly tied topknot and crisp clean clothes, he felt like a new man. Retreating from the polished mirror, he crossed the lavish guest room to a small side table containing a gift-wrapped item.

Humming gently to himself he carried the delivery to the centre of the room. Neglecting the plump chairs he instead chose to sit cross-legged on the floor where he slowly unwrapped the silk packaging to reveal a length of ebony-coloured Thornwood. Jensen stroked his hands across its surface and drew on its familiar aura. As his fingers traced its length, a soft scent of ginger filled the room.

Collecting his thoughts he began to sing. His melodic voice drifted through the room, filling it with a sense of intent and purpose. This wasn't a Treesong of growth, rather it was one of craft, of shaping.

As he continued to chant, he ran his hands over the wood. Excess pieces dropped away like fine shavings. Here and there the wood buckled, warped and in some places drew inward, becoming more compact. The minutes turned into hours and Jensen continued to work the wood, manipulating it into the shape he desired until eventually he held his finished piece aloft.

A sword constructed entirely of Thornwood.

Its blade was long and elegant, the point exceptionally sharp, and in truth so fine that it was hard to see. The hilt was crafted with fine ridges to provide a comfortable but sure grip and the cross guard was shaped to resemble curving leaves.

There was a knock at the door.

'Come!' said Jensen.

Sindris the Third entered. She raised her eyebrows as she saw Jensen's finished product. 'Is that a . . .'

'A Thornsword?' said Jensen, completing Sindris's question. 'Aye, it is.'

'By the Scales, such a thing is a rare sight. Perhaps one day you might have the time to allow me several questions about its making? However, I fear now is not the place to be asking as time is pressing. My clerks received word from our branch in Opal Hold that Charlie Keeper was spotted there earlier today. She did not dawdle, but left through a Keeper's Portal. Our clerks at the Opal Hold branch were unable to ascertain where she went but they have noticed an increase of bounty hunters in the vicinity.'

'Opal Hold? That's two days' ride from here, ain't it?'

'That is correct, however we can receive communication via carrier pigeon in as little as five hours.'

'Hhmm,' mused Jensen. 'Wot other towns are there between here and Opal Hold?'

'Little Storm, Shidden Vale and Yearning Tooth.'

'And the Gilded Bank has branches at each of those?'

'We have a large branch in Little Storm, a smaller branch in Shidden Vale, but nothing in Yearning Tooth. We do have ties to Yearning Tooth's post office so if your young Keeper were to arrive there I can see to it that you are informed.'

'Me thanks, Sindris. I think it would be prudent ta take myself ta Little Storm. It makes a more convenient hub ta receive local intelligence.'

'I will notify my counterpart at the Little Storm branch that you are coming.'

'Again, me thanks,' said Jensen. Unfolding himself from the floor he grabbed his backpack and with sword in hand headed for the door.

34

The Bookseller

Charlie breathed deeply, savouring the moment.

She could feel the anger under her skin. The rage, the humiliation and the fear; all of it accumulated while in Bellania. Bane, Narcissa, Crow, Stix, Stones, Darkmount, Lallinda, the Shades, the Wyrms, the daemons – all of them had contributed to the anger that bubbled within. But now, with each and every blow from her fists and kick from her legs, she got to give some of it back.

It felt wonderful.

Her fists flared darkly, leaving a trail of golden sparks as she pummelled opponent after opponent into submission. Wrenching swords from their owners' fists, snapping axe shafts and shattering maces into splinters, she danced about. Blurring from one K'Changa stance into another she left a trail of destruction in her wake.

Suddenly it was over.

The few mercenaries still capable of standing ran for cover. Ducking into side streets and alleyways they melted away, leaving a collection of discarded weapons and piles of unconscious or moaning bodies behind.

'Forty Swords?' Charlie shouted at their backs. 'More like forty chumps!'

'Charlie!'

She turned to find Nibbler and Crumble hurrying towards her.

'Are you guys OK?' she asked.

'Yes,' panted Nibbler. 'But we've got to get out of here before anyone else decides they want a go at claiming Bane's reward.'

'Why?' queried Charlie. 'We coped with those guys easy enough.'

'Are you mad?' snapped Crumble, his newly acquired shield still in hand. 'We almost got killed! There's no way I want to go through that again.'

Charlie felt the anger rise. She wanted more people to fight; she wanted to burn all the hate that resided inside her by beating anyone who stood in her way. She *hoped* that more mercenaries would come.

'Charlie, I'm serious,' insisted Crumble. 'We can't go through that again.'

Charlie noticed that his hands were shaking and saw how exhausted Nibbler looked. Suddenly she felt ashamed. Her actions had endangered her friends and it was they who had placed their lives on the line for her. Guilt churned in her stomach at the thought of Nibbler or even Crumble, a relatively new arrival to her circle of companions, suffering an injury on her behalf.

Shouts and the tramp of booted feet stirred her from her contemplation.

www.keeperoftherealms.com

'Ah that doesn't sound good,' said Nibbler. 'It sounds like half the town must be after us.'

'Or another crew of gold-diggers,' suggested Crumble with an unhappy look on his face. 'Charlie, what do you want to do?'

'Keeper! This way!' hissed a voice, making all three of them jump.

Turning, they found a Stoman lady gesturing frantically at them from the mouth of an alley. Sharing a look between them, but, realizing how quickly things could take a turn for the worse if they stayed out in the open, they filed into the passage-way.

Charlie, fearing treachery, allowed a little trickle of Will to ease on to her fingers. *Just in case*, she thought to herself.

The Stoman led them down the alley, across another street, down yet another winding backstreet and, ensuring that they weren't observed, ducked into a small garden. Charlie eyed the enclosed space with suspicion before following her.

Now they had stopped moving Charlie could see that the Stoman lady wore a brown leather kilt and a simple shirt. She had little jewellery on her person, but wore a glass monocle on a leather cord that hung round her neck. 'You shouldn't be here!' she urged. 'Word of Bane's bounty has reached Shidden Vale and it won't be long until every –'

'Relax,' said Charlie, 'we just took care of the Forty Swords.'

'They were nothing! The Band of Thirteen are here in Shidden Vale, so is the Scarlet Poison Gang and word is that Fo Fum has been seen searching for you in the Slumbering Hills.'

'Fo Fum!' choked Crumble, a look of astonishment and horror in his eyes.

'Who's that?' asked Charlie.

'You don't know who Fo Fum is?' snorted the lady. 'Ah, Keeper, the rumours about you being naive and innocent must be true.'

'What? Naive? What do you mean by that? And just who is Fo Fum? And . . . wait, who are *you* anyway?'

The Stoman had the face of an older woman, but with youthful grey-green eyes that she now used to frown at the three. 'Lots of questions there, young Keeper. Do you want to pick one for me to answer or should I just try to answer all of them?'

'Lady,' spluttered Charlie, 'did you bring us down here for a reason or did you just want to make me look like a fool?'

'I brought you down here to try to keep you and your friends alive for another day. Acting like a fool is something that you seem to be doing well all by yourself.'

'Oooh! You're as bad as Azariah!' scowled Charlie, immediately feeling the loss of her friend and mentor. 'OK, I can see you want to help and I can see you're also going to be annoyingly difficult to deal with, so let's start again. I'm Charlie Keeper, this is Nibbler and the big guy is Crumble Shard. What's your name?'

'Ottoline Lark.'

'Right. Well, Ottoline, if the rest of Shidden Vale want to kill me to claim Bane's bounty then why do you want to help us?'

'Because I'm a free thinker, child. I don't like Bane's ideas for "one Bellania beneath Stoman rule" and I still hold true to the old ways of respecting Keepers and Winged Ones.' Ottoline gave Charlie and Nibbler a measured stare. 'Although to be truthful the two of you don't look much like a real Keeper or a Winged One. You look more like a bunch of kids than anything, but you should know that I hold true to the ideals of respecting your elders so I guess that means looking after you whipper-snappers.'

'We're not children –' began Nibbler, but was cut off with a scowl from Ottoline.

'Yes, you are. Crumble Shard can't be older than sixteen. Humans I'm not so good at but I reckon Charlie can't be a year above thirteen and, Winged One, you're still just a Hatchling! Come to think of it, shouldn't you be hibernating with the rest of your brethren? Or perhaps you could kindly inform them that we could do with their help right now.' Nibbler started to explain, but she cut him off. 'Anyway – kids, you're all kids.'

'I'm fourteen actually,' said Charlie. 'But I won't argue with you about us being kids. So how can you help us?'

'How? By getting you three out of Shidden Vale as quickly as possible.'

'That's something that we could do by ourselves. We need help with other matters.'

'What sort of matters?' said Ottoline, crossing her arms.

'We need help from someone who knows about Portals.'

'Pfft,' snorted Ottoline. 'You're not going to find anyone with that knowledge in Shidden Vale. The last Keeper to visit Shidden Vale was harassed so badly that the Winged Ones had to intervene on his behalf.'

'We don't need another Keeper. Well, that's not exactly true. Another Keeper would be really helpful at the moment, but what we're really looking for is information on Bane's barrier that prevents Portals being opened in the Western Mountains.'

Ottoline sucked at her teeth. 'Then you might be in luck. Follow me.'

The three shared a look, but after a round of shrugs and nods that indicated they should keep their wits about them, they followed Ottoline as she unlatched a small gate that led from the garden. They filed down a narrow path that in turn led to the back of a building.

'What is this place?' asked Crumble, only to get a 'Shh' from Ottoline.

Pulling a key from her belt she unlocked the door and ushered them inside.

'Keep your voices down while you're in here. The walls aren't that thick and my neighbours aren't as Human friendly as I am.'

'But what is this place?' insisted Crumble.

'"The Crooked Letter Y". It's my shop and my home.'

'Really? What do you sell?'

'Knowledge.' She saw the odd look that Crumble gave her. 'Hhmpf. Here . . .' She opened another door with a flourish to reveal a shelved room heavily laden with books and scrolls. 'Knowledge from around the world.'

'You're a bookseller!' said Charlie, delighted by the sight.

'Aye, that I am, but the three of you must wait here while I close the blinds. It would do no good for hungry eyes to spy you three in my premises.'

She swiftly rolled the blinds across the large bay windows that overlooked the street, and for good measure she also unbolted the front door so she could go out and close the shutters.

Charlie, unable to restrain herself, took the opportunity to browse through the shelves. It was just like a bookshop from back home, only different in little ways. More dust for one thing, she noted, and more scrolls and unbound parchments than would be found in any shop in London, but nonetheless there was something so very similar about it that she couldn't help but feel homesick.

'All done,' said Ottoline as she relocked the door behind her. 'So long as we don't raise our voices we should be free to work without fear of detection. So you wanted to know about Bane's border, did you not? And how he prevents nosy Keepers from butting in on him unaware?'

'It would be amazing if you could help us with that,' said Charlie.

'Unfortunately I don't think I'll be able to tell you how Bane prevents the opening of Portals. That's all higher knowledge, privileged only to Keepers and not something shared with us lowly mortals,' chuckled Ottoline as she began to weave in and out of the shelves looking for a particular book. 'However, I hope that I'll be able to help you with your particular problem by . . . Aha!' Climbing on to a footstool she pulled a large book bound in wood from the topmost shelf. 'This is what we'll need: *Poodit's Atlas of the Five Empires*.'

'Five empires?' asked Crumble. 'What five empires?'

'What indeed, young man. What five empires?' said

Ottoline, adopting a teacher's tone. 'Well, Poodit was a Treman archaeologist who had a passion for ancient ruins and stories of old. His greatest fondness was for the third, fourth and fifth centuries of the second age. A time of empires – indeed a time when the Winged Ones weren't so heavily involved in governing our realm. Of course, Poodit was a scholar from the seventh century of the third age, which means this book is more than two centuries old, but that is neither here nor there. What is important is that Poodit's studies of these ancient empires are of interest to us today.'

'How?' asked Nibbler.

'Because, Hatchling, Poodit drew detailed maps of the old empires and of their old capitals. The Western Mountains – or rather the city known as the Western Mountains – is very, very old. Ancient even. In its time it has been many things. Before it became the city that we know today it used to be the basis of power for Stale the Swallower and the centre of his empire. Poodit has a map of the city and its original boundaries are in this very book. It is, I believe, along these ancient boundaries that Bane has placed his barrier to Portals.'

'Really? Will this map be accurate?' asked Nibbler.

'Well, probably not a hundred per cent accurate and I'm only basing this thesis on hearsay from other booksellers, scholars and learned philosophers, but if you're looking for a guide to base your travelling on then I would say that this is your best bet.'

Finding the page she wanted, Ottoline turned the book so Charlie could better see. It showed a gorgeously detailed map of the Western Mountains and surrounding lands that were spanned by three concentric circles. The names of places were carefully inked in an archaic language that Charlie could not decipher.

'I can't read this.'

'Of course you can't,' said Ottoline. 'It's ancient Lyllac and the names on this map are different from today's. These are the Silent Men, but we now know them as the Slumbering Hills, and this the Roof of the World, or the Western Mountains, and this, of course, was the ancient city of Ackrolisyss –'

'Which is now the city of the Western Mountains, right? See that, Crumble?' said Charlie. 'At least back in the day they were more original when it came to the naming of places. None of that New This or New That malarkey.' She turned her attention to the concentric circles on the map. 'What are these?' she asked, tracing her fingers over the lines.

'Boundaries. The largest indicates the furthest border of Stale the Swallower's Empire of Dawn, the second dictates the metropolitan border, and the smallest circle is Ackrolisyss's city border.'

'Does the city of the Western Mountains still have the same border?'

'Yes it does, which is what's so interesting about this second border.'

'The metropolitan border?'

'Yes. We believe – well, when I say "we", I mean other more educated philosophers – believe that Bane still uses the borders of old. We think that Bane has limited the opening of Portals anywhere within the metropolitan border.'

A huge grin blossomed across Charlie's face. This was just the knowledge she had been looking for! 'Thank you. Really a big thank you. You've saved us days with this.' Charlie turned to Nibbler and Crumble. 'So what do you guys think, if we Portal to just outside this border and walk from there?'

'Sounds good,' acknowledged Crumble as he looked at the atlas. 'It would only take another two days to walk from there to the city.'

'Great,' said Charlie. 'Are you familiar with this border?'

'Sure, there are still standing stones that mark the paths into the city. They've got to be markers for the old metropolitan border. I never knew what they were for, but it makes sense when you know about these old boundaries.'

'Could you describe a place near one of those stones well enough for me to be able to open a Portal there?'

Crumble paused to think about it. 'Yes. Yes I can. There's a waterfall near one of those stones, but it's not so close that we'll be right on top of the border.'

'I've got a map that you can take too,' said Ottoline. 'And if you wish you're welcome to use your Will and your Way to travel from my storeroom upstairs. It's large enough and it'll mean you'll be able to leave Shidden Vale discreetly too.'

'Please,' said Charlie. 'That would be great.'

'Follow me.' Ottoline led the way from the room, pausing once to lift a scroll from one of the shelves before herding the three upstairs into a well-lit room that held stacks of books and well-organized parchments. 'I'm sure this will be large enough for your needs and take this.' She passed the scroll to Charlie. 'This map covers the Slumbering Hills, the

Great Plains and the Western Mountains. I hope it's of some help.'

'I can't thank you enough,' said Charlie in an attempt to voice her gratitude. 'You're one of the few people who have been genuine enough to help me –'

'I appreciate what you're trying to say,' interrupted Ottoline. 'But there's no need to thank me. I owe a debt of old to the Keepers. They helped my father in his time of need so now I'm simply repaying the favour. If it means anything to you please pay it forward. Whenever you've finished whatever it is that you're attempting to do, don't forget us ordinary folk.'

'I won't,' said Charlie. She took Ottoline's strong hand in her own and shook it firmly.

'Wait a minute,' urged Nibbler. 'Er, seeing how nice Ottoline has been perhaps we shouldn't open a Portal right to the Western Mountains in case that fire and brimstone thing happens again. I don't think she'd appreciate it if we burned her shop down.'

Ottoline raised an eyebrow at that.

'Uh, good point,' acknowledged Charlie. 'Where to then?'

'Just take us back to the river near the road that leads to Shidden Vale. It seemed quiet enough and it should be easy for you to find.'

Charlie nodded. Her hands flashed gold then black and with a quick pulling motion opened a Portal. She blinked when she how dark it was by the riverside. 'Huh, it's night already.'

'Is that a problem?' asked Ottoline.

'No, I just hadn't realized how late it had grown.'

'The three of you are welcome to spend the night here. I have ample space.'

'No, we're good,' said Charlie. 'And I think that we've taken advantage of your hospitality enough as it is.' She motioned Crumble and Nibbler to go on ahead. 'Thank you for all you've done.' She gave Ottoline a final nod then jumped through, the Portal flickering shut behind her.

35

Gone Fishing

As Jensen and Sic Boy neared Little Storm's branch of the Gilded Bank, a Stoman in exquisitely tailored robes pushed the door open and, holding his robes high so that he wouldn't trip, sprinted down the main thoroughfare towards them.

'Jensen of the Willow?' he panted.

'Aye, that would be me.'

'I'm the master banker of Little Storm. Please excuse my haste, but I've just received word that Charlie Keeper was seen at Shidden Vale!'

'Me thanks,' said Jensen as he wheeled Sic Boy round. 'Me thanks ta ya and the Gilded Bank!'

Not wanting to cover the helpful Stoman in dust, Jensen waited until he was further down the street before kicking Sic Boy into a gallop.

'Why didn't you take her up on her offer?' asked Crumble. 'Don't you think it would have been wiser to spend the night under a friendly roof rather than pushing on ahead in the darkness?'

Charlie shrugged. 'We're not going to the Western Mountains. Or at least not until dawn. I don't like the idea of arriving in a dangerous land in the darkness any more than you do.'

'I don't get it. If that's the case why didn't we stay there then?'

'Because as nice as Ottoline was I don't trust her.'

'But she helped us out,' protested Crumble.

'Yes she did, and if I ever get the chance to repay her for her kindness I will. But being kind and being trustworthy are two very different things. I've been tricked into trusting deceitful people before and it's not something that I'm willing to risk again.'

'But –' began Crumble.

'Look I know what you're going to say. Just believe me when I say the stakes really are too high to take any unnecessary chances.'

'Well, do you trust me?'

'I . . . I'm not sure,' admitted Charlie. 'I think so. You've put yourself in danger for me and Nibbler so I'd really, really like to think that you're the nice guy you appear to be. But trust doesn't come easily to me any more.'

There was an uncomfortable silence broken only by the warble of the river and the occasional *twit-ta-woo* of owls.

'Soooo . . . we'll be making camp here then?' asked Nibbler, who couldn't stand the uneasy atmosphere.

'Yes,' said Charlie. 'We'll crash here and make our move first thing in the morning.'

When they were certain they were hidden from the roadside they set up camp and started a small fire, an activity

Charlie had grown used to over the past couple of days, and which reminded her of her first days in Bellania. Crumble, constructing a makeshift rod from a branch, settled down for some serious fishing.

Nibbler, led by his stomach, soon joined him on the riverbank and Charlie, not wanting to be left alone with her dark thoughts, joined them too.

'Who's Fo Fum?' asked Charlie as she replayed their earlier conversation with Ottoline in her head.

'I can't believe neither of you have heard of him,' said Crumble. 'I know you've both only been in Bellania for a short period of time, but he's one of those characters who everyone knows.' Seeing Charlie and Nibbler's blank expressions he continued. 'Parents scare their children to sleep with stories of Fo Fum. Mine always used to say: *Be good or Fo Fum will come and snatch you away. Do your chores or Fo Fum will come and break all your bones. Go to bed or Fo Fum will pluck your eyeballs from their sockets and gobble them up.* He's the most infamous mercenary in Bellania. Surely you must have heard something about him?'

Nibbler and Charlie shook their heads.

'How about the children's rhyme: "Fe-fi, Fo Fum, watch out, watch out, the bad man comes"?'

'I know that one,' said Charlie, 'but you've got it wrong. It's: "Fe-fi-fo-fum, I smell the blood of an Englishman. Be he alive or be he dead, I'll grind his bones to make my bread."'

'Where did you hear that?'

'It's part of a fairy tale that they tell kids back home.

That's the chant that the giant sings when he comes looking for the guy who stole his gold.'

'Well, be that as it may in your realm, this is no fairy tale and Fo Fum is no giant. He's a man . . . but like no other. They say he comes from the south. From far beyond the Great Deserts or the Great Veil, and that he lives in the Dark Temple of the Whispering Wind. They say that he was trained by the Blind Monks and that he's their best student: the only one to survive the Thousand Tests, the only man who can't be killed.'

'That sounds like more of a tall tale than the one we tell on Earth. Have you ever seen this Fo Fum?'

'No.'

'Do you know of anyone who has seen him?'

'No.'

'So how do you know he's real then?'

'Two hours walk from where I live lies a canyon so deep that parts of it never see the sun. My uncle took me there when I was six. Inside were these marks, craters and small pockmarks in the rock, that hadn't been made by stonesinging. My uncle said this was the site of a great battle when the Hundred Axes fought –'

'Were they any better than the Forty Swords?' asked Nibbler. 'Cos they weren't very good, were they? I mean –'

'Am I telling this story or do you want to talk about what happened in Shidden Vale?' protested Crumble.

'Uh, sorry. Carry on.'

'It was where the legendary Hundred Axes, *who were very skilled warriors* –' Crumble paused to give Nibbler a don't-you-dare-say-anything look – 'fought Fo Fum. They say the battle was so fierce that it went on for two whole days and nights and that Fo Fum was the only one to leave that place alive. They say those marks were made by his fists and his staff.'

'How do they know that?' persisted Charlie. 'Couldn't it just have been some funny marks in the rock that people made a story about?'

'Charlie, it was hand marks in the rock. You could see the fingers, the width of the palm, you could see everything. And the prints were deep in the rock. Some of them were so deep I could stick my hand in up to my forearm before I could reach the impression. I saw it. I was there and believe me when I tell you that they were real. Just think about it for a minute – Fo Fum doesn't stonesing, but he's so strong that he can punch into rock completely unaided. Now, I don't know about you, but that scares me.'

'So you think this Fo Fum was there and he really took out these Hundred Axes?' asked Nibbler.

'Someone made those marks.'

There was silence as they imagined how powerful some-one had to be to do that to rock without stonesinging or the Will and the Way. A sudden splash of water and the jerking of Crumble's fishing rod interrupted their thoughts. Grinning, Crumble hauled in his catch.

'Now that's a fish!' he said with relish. 'If we catch a couple more like that we'll have enough for a royal feast.'

Charlie's stomach rumbled at the idea. Barbequed fish also conjured up memories of her first day in Bellania: being chased by Sic Boy, falling off the waterfall, meeting all the Tremen and sharing their beautifully prepared meal beneath the trees of Deepforest. Her smile faded as she remembered how Stotch had died soon after that event. Dark thoughts so briefly pushed aside returned with a vengeance.

'Crumble, Nibbler, we'll rest tonight, but tomorrow we make our move. Things are going to have to move a lot faster from this point on.'

Nibbler looked up with a haunted expression on his face and Crumble hesitated as he lowered his fishing hook into the river.

'Crumble, will you look at the map and see if you can find –'

'Enough, Charlie, that's enough,' insisted Crumble. 'We'll both help you the best we can. I'll look at that map with you tomorrow and we'll find a safe place to open the Portal, but right here, right now, let's try to enjoy ourselves.'

Charlie frowned at him. 'Don't you get it? Don't you understand what's at risk?'

'Of course I get it, Charlie. Your parents, the return of the Winged Ones, a chance to return Bellania to a state of peace – all of that good stuff. And I'll help you get there, but not all of this has to be bad. Life's too short to dwell on sorrow. If you fill your stomach with nothing but anger, hate and regret then that's what you'll turn into: an angry, hateful, regretful person. My uncle used to say "The wound that bleeds inwardly is the most dangerous". I never knew what he meant, but having seen what you're putting yourself through I finally understand. Charlie, you're your own worst enemy.'

Charlie hesitated. She wanted to say something to defend herself, but felt that if she opened her mouth she'd only make matters worse.

'Charlie,' said Nibbler with a gentle voice, 'he's right. I can't stand to see what you're doing to yourself either and I'm afraid that I'm going to lose my best friend because of it. You've been surrounded by darkness for so long that you've taken it into yourself. You're becoming as menacing as the people we fight and that's just not who you are.'

Charlie couldn't deny that what they said had a grain of truth to it, but how could they say such a thing? Didn't she have the right to change after all that she had endured? She felt the unbearable pressure of responsibility, always bubbling in the back of her mind, build to the point where she thought her head would explode. With it came a feeling of anger and a strong need to express herself.

She opened her mouth, but before she could vent an image of her grandma's kitchen, very much unexpected, appeared in her mind's eye. It was a vivid memory of better times when her parents were still around. And although the kitchen was empty she could tell that her gran had just been in there. She could see the flour-coated kitchen top, the rolling pin so recently used. The memory was so strong that she could smell the scent of fresh baking, and lingering in the air was the aroma of her mother's perfume. With that reminder came a sudden peace that lulled her heart. Relaxing from her tense position she shut her mouth.

Then she opened it again. 'It's not easy. It's not! They've taken everything from me, even the promise of any return to normality, of ever having a regular life. All of that has been stolen from me. But you're right. You're both right, I can't go on like this.' She paused to gather her thoughts. 'I can't allow this darkness to consume me. But I can't give it up either. I need it. If I'm ever going to stand up to Bane or if I ever meet Darkmount again I'm going to need it. So help me. Help me find a balance, one where I can use this thing inside me but still be . . . me.'

'I won't leave you, Charlie,' said Nibbler. 'I'll always be here.'

'Erm . . . I can't match that.' Crumble grinned ruefully. 'I've got a family and, while I don't necessarily get on well with my father, I love my rock brothers and sisters, and there's still a lot that I can learn from my uncle. So I won't always be there for you, but I think that I'd like to be your friend, Charlie. And if I help you in the future it'll be for friendship and not out of respect for your profession.'

Crumble leaned across the campfire with an open hand. Charlie took it and gripped it and, unable and unwilling to ignore his honest smile, found herself cracking a grin too.

'So we're going to blow some steam off tonight and get back on with the game plan tomorrow?' she asked.

Crumble nodded as he added some fresh bait to his hook. 'Now that sounds like a plan. Time off every once in a while can't be a bad thing.'

'Great,' agreed Nibbler. 'I'm all about the relaxing time. So can we get on with the fishing now? I'm getting those growing pangs again.'

36

The First of War

Kelko stood uncomfortably next to the two men on either side of him. They, unlike him, seemed keen to confront Bane's army and had spent most of the last two hours boasting about how many soldiers they would vanquish and how many medals they would win.

Kelko, in contrast, felt mildly sick. He stared down at his suit of armour with twin feelings of disbelief and sadness. It was a beautiful piece of woodsmanship, crafted by the very finest Tree Singers and passed down from one of his great forebears. It bore marks and scars from famous historic battles and had been passed from generation to generation with whispered stories of what previous members of the Oak family had achieved from beneath its protective plating.

Even though Kelko had employed a Tree Singer of wondrous skill to enlarge it to fit his unique frame, he had honestly never thought the day would arise when he would have to wear it with serious intent. He didn't consider himself a soldier, nor did he believe in the merits of death and destruction

But that day had come. Now it was time for him to claim his place as a soldier of Sylvaris and defend the city of his birth and the forest he loved. That morning he had pulled the great family war axe from its mount on the wall and, slipping the heraldic shield that bore a stylized oak over his other arm, he had left his tower in Sylvaris and joined the procession of other men filing down to Deepforest.

All afternoon the Sylvarisian forces encamped on the border between Deepforest and the endless grasslands of the Great Plains had prepared for the coming of the enemy. Generals had made bold speeches; master Tree Singers had grown huge beds of strangleweed and suckerthorns to hinder the enemy's approach; sappers had dug trenches, embedded stakes in the soil and raised great ramparts; fletchers had handed out arrows; blacksmiths and woodsmiths had attended to weapons and armour; and healers had prepared medical tents.

But now everyone at the front was growing restless. Archers had checked and rechecked their flights; cavalry and canine riders had fed and watered their mounts; foot soldiers had sharpened their swords to razor edges; quartermasters had long since given out all necessary supplies; and now only potboys or juniors moved as they carried water and sweet tea to the waiting troops.

An uneasy silence settled across the Treman army as a faint vibration rocked the land. Minutes passed and the vibration didn't cease. Instead the tremor grew and with it came a faint noise reminiscent of waves crashing against distant cliffs. A smudge appeared on the horizon that slowly grew and unfolded like low hanging clouds. As this odd phenomenon grew, so too did the terrible vibration and eerie sound. Soon it was clear that the impossibly long line that spread across the horizon was none other than Bane's First Army.

To begin with the line was made up of distant specks, but as it drew closer everything eased into focus so that individuals and details could be identified. Throngs of Shades skittered and shrieked as they surged across the grass like the approaching tide of a dark sea. Stamping behind them with measured steps came proud Stoman soldiers with axes or swords clamped in their eager hands. Finally, above the rank and file, skittered the Widow Brigade. Each rider, whip and spiked pennant in hand, was carried forward by rhinospiders that, having detected the scent of Tremen in the air, clicked their mandibles together with greedy appetite.

The two men on either side of Kelko stared at each other. One took a hasty sip of water and the other chewed on his knuckles. Their earlier boasts of prowess were swiftly forgotten as they were faced with the terrible realization that the Treman army was vastly outnumbered.

With a final thump the enemy came to a standstill.

Just out of bowshot Stomen sniggered and grinned as they eyed their diminutive foes. Jeers and catcalls were hurled across the gap of no-man's-land. These were swiftly silenced as a general to the rear of the ranks snapped out a command. The Stomen raised their weapons high, then brought them crashing down against their shields.

Again and again they repeated this action and a barrage of sound cracked against the sky. Another order was screamed out and the speed with which the Stomen struck their shields changed so that it was no longer a mindless pounding but a fiery rhythm that snapped and boomed across the landscape.

Frightening. Threatening.

And then the enemy started to sing.

Rough voices joined together to weave a song of power that filled the air with a tangible potency. The ranks parted and Stonesingers swaggered forward. Gesturing with glowing hands they harnessed the song and channelled it into the ground. Creaking and moaning, the grass tore apart as gigantic fists and overly large heads squirmed free from the soil. Slowly, behemoths pulled themselves from the earth to tower over the battlefield like the stone gods of old.

The Stoman army cheered in delight as one by one the behemoths grated open their jaws and trumpeted a mindless bellow of challenge to the Treman ranks that detonated across no-man's-land.

The Tremen, not to be outdone, roused themselves and responded with a militant chant of their own that brought with it a scent of pepper, nettle and cardamom. Tree Singers, funnelling the power of their song, roused great panther-like creatures from oversized seeds that had been placed strategically upon the soil. The feline forest creatures snarled and paced back and forth aggressively. Their eyes blazed with an elemental purple light and the desire to pounce on the enemy.

But the Treman lines were thin and the pantherine creatures few and far between. Those who could count soon realized that their defences were nothing more than temporary sea walls attempting to hold back the tempest of a raging ocean.

Comprehending the futility of it all, the two soldiers took a step backwards. In contrast Kelko was shocked to realize that the shaking in his legs was not fear but adrenalin, and the tightness in his throat was caused by anger at the threat to his homeland. He was not feeling particularly courageous, but he believed that he had to do something, so perhaps with more foolishness than bravado he took a threatening step forward. The Treman soldiers up and down the line, including the two beside Kelko, mistook this as an act of bravery in the face of unbeatable odds. With a crash of arms and a shout of derision for the opposition the entire Treman army took a crunching step towards the earth ramparts and rattled their armour in a show of defiance.

The Stoman army shrieked and bellowed their reply.

Then, the ground pounding and rocking beneath their feet, Bane's First Army charged.

In response Kelko held his axe overhead and, with a roar that would have made an ice tiger proud, pushed his way forward to the front, eager to be amongst the first to exchange blows with those who threatened his beloved forest and ancestral home.

37

Fe-fi

Charlie awoke from her usual nightmares to a light morning rain. Sighing she wriggled out of her bed roll and, careful not to wake Nibbler, ducked beneath the rough canopy they had erected last night. Pushing her hair into a topknot she headed to the riverbank to watch the fast moving waters beneath the shelter of an overhanging willow, which automatically reminded her of Jensen.

'Are you always an early riser?' asked Crumble as he came to stand by her side.

'I never used to be, but since coming to Bellania sleep doesn't seem to be as easy as it was.'

Sitting down on the driest patch of ground she could find she leaned back against the willow's trunk. Crumble hunkered down beside her.

'So what are your plans?' he asked.

'Enjoy the morning quiet, practise K'Changa, eat some breakfast and then try opening that Portal.' Sitting in a comfortable silence the two enjoyed the view of the rain clouds turning a deep red as the sun tried to make an entrance. 'Crumble?'

'Yes, Charlie?'

'You've seen me fight, right?'

'Yes.'

'Do you have any advice for me? Anything that I could use or change when I face Bane or Darkmount?'

'I think you're already scary enough when you fight.'

'I'm being serious!' said Charlie and nudged him in the ribs.

'As was I.' He had to resist nudging Charlie back. 'I'm not sure what to say. Your style of fighting – the way you mix K'Changa with your Will – it's very elaborate and . . . pretty.' Seeing Charlie's look he quickly reworded. 'Look, I'm not saying it isn't effective because clearly it is. We both know that when you're charged up on your Will you could easily knock me aside. What I am trying to say is your style of fighting has a lot of embellishments and flourishes to it. The way I fight and the way that Stoman bishops fight is more . . . blunt. You flow and move like this river, but the great Stonesingers fight like they're made from rock: they're steady and direct.' He pointed to several large boulders in the middle of the river. 'That's what the bishops are like and, just like the river, you'll be able to flow round them, but I think that you'll struggle when the time comes to move them.'

'Water is supposed to be one of the most powerful natural forces,' Charlie protested, 'and if there's enough –'

'But you understand what I'm getting at, though?'

'Yes.' She sighed. 'So what would you suggest I do to stop my Will getting brushed aside next time I fight someone more powerful than me?'

'Either be more aggressive or sneakier.'

'That's it? That's your great advice?'

'Well . . . yes.'

The rising sun was obscured by more rain clouds. Feeling glum, Charlie stood and offered Crumble a hand up. Together they made their way back to the campsite. 'Did you get a chance to look at that map?' she asked.

'Yes.'

'And do you think you can . . .'

Charlie's voice petered off as she caught sight of a man staring down at them from the roadside. There was something so unusual in the way he held himself, something so silent and still that he could have passed for a statue, but the menace that he projected was palpable. Even at this distance she could sense his hostility. Charlie stumbled over her own feet and had to grab on to Crumble for support.

'Look at that man!'

Crumble followed her finger to the roadside. The man wore a wide-brimmed hat that kept his face hidden in shadow; a tattered brown cloak hung from his shoulders and he carried a long walking staff.

'What is it?' asked Charlie when she saw Crumble suddenly tense. 'What's the matter?'

'That's Fo Fum.'

'Him? But how do you know? You said you've never seen him. Wha– Slow down!'

Crumble in his haste to make it back to the camp, hauled Charlie along by the arm. 'The hat, the staff and the cloak, they all match the legends.'

'But –'

'No time for buts! We've got to get Nibbler and run!'

'Wait!'

'No, we can't –'

'Just wait! Look – he's gone!'

Crumble, hand still on Charlie's wrist, staggered to a halt. The man had disappeared.

'Oh, Fractured Diamond!' cursed Crumble. 'We've got to get out of here before he appears.'

They turned to stare at each other. 'Nibbler!' they shouted in unison.

The battle had raged for hours.

Kelko's face was covered with blood that trickled from a gash across his forehead. It wasn't life-threatening or even that serious, but because it was a head wound it bled a great deal. At times it made it hard to see, so that the chaotic world around him appeared washed with a red haze.

The tide of the battle ebbed and flowed: one minute cruel and intense, the next slow and ponderous. Taking advantage of one of the rare moments of relative peace, Kelko snatched a water flask from the corpse of Stoman warrior and upended it over his head to wash off the blood before taking a huge gulp.

'Ahh, by me beloved Oak.' Kelko gasped, enjoying the respite. 'That's gorgeous.'

Ripping a rudimentary bandage from someone's discarded cloak he wrapped it round his forehead. He was about to raise the flask for one last swig of water, but a wayward arrow punched it out of his grasp. And then, as if controlled by the flick of a switch, the battle raged once more.

Shrieking and screaming, a fresh wave of Shades darted up the earth rampart followed closely by a scampering, scuttling pack of rhinospiders. Pulling his battered shield close, Kelko raised his axe with a weary arm and prepared for yet another onslaught.

38

Fo Fum

'NIBBLER!'

'Huh, whaddya wrgg wimfa?' mumbled Nibbler as he rolled over with a sleepy swish of his tail.

'NIBBLER, GET UP!'

'I'm not leaving the ballroom until they've served dessert,' he protested. Frowning, he cracked open one eyelid, then the other. Realizing he was no longer asleep he rolled on to his back feet and yawned. 'What's all the fuss about?'

'BEHIND YOU, NIBBLER, BEHIND YOU!'

Nibbler rubbed at his eyes and blearily tried to work out why Charlie and Crumble were running hell for leather towards him. 'They'd better not be expecting me to do the dishes again,' he mumbled.

Standing, he tried to duck beneath the canopy only to trip over his discarded blanket. As he fell, he felt the wind of something whoosh past his head. He spun round, startled, to see a man with a weird circular hat, a cloak and a serious-looking pole. Nibbler had to scuttle backwards to avoid being brained as the man whipped the staff forward, its tip missing his muzzle by a hair's breadth.

'It's Fo Fum!' screamed Charlie. 'Get back, Nibbler, get back from him!'

Nibbler skittered further back, but, now feeling very awake and more confident, simply opened his mouth and let loose a jet of flame. It had almost no effect. Fo Fum's cloak didn't catch alight and the few bits of clothing that did smoulder he simply ignored. Stepping forward he again brought his staff into play and Nibbler, dazed by what he had just seen, almost didn't get out of the way in time.

'Nibbler!' screamed Charlie.

Coming to his senses Nibbler leaped away and opening his wings took to the sky. Banking sharply he turned round and, swooping low, spat out a bolt of electricity. Somehow Fo Fum managed to spin aside and in one flowing motion swept off his cloak and pulled a set of bolas from his waist – and in one, two, three rotations he released them to whirr through the air. The bolas snapped round Nibbler, the rope entangling his wings. With a cry of dismay the dragon plummeted into the river. Unable to free his limbs he struggled to stay afloat. As the current dragged him along, it dashed his body against the partially submerged rocks and repeatedly forced his head below the surface.

Charlie and Crumble sprinted for the riverside, desperate to save Nibbler before he drowned. Another set of bolas whipped round Crumble's ankles, bringing him crashing down. The Stoman boy immediately began to saw at the rope with his small knife, but the delay was costing them dearly as Nibbler was swept further and further away.

Charlie hesitated. If she chased after Nibbler it would mean leaving Crumble at the mercy of Fo Fum, but if she delayed to fight Fo Fum and release Crumble then surely Nibbler would drown.

'Can you cut yourself free?'

'Yes,' said Crumble, parting the ropes as quickly as he could. 'Just give me a second. I'm almost there.'

'Good. Get Nibbler. I'll buy you some time.'

'But –'

'Just do it!' insisted Charlie. She turned to face Fo Fum. The air of menace that had been tangible even from the roadside was much more apparent now. A cloud of hostility surrounded the man, noticeable in faint shimmers and the way it pressed the grass flat in an arc round him. Charlie had to resist the urge to take a step backwards. Gritting her teeth she forced herself to stand still.

Fo Fum slammed his staff into the ground and paused to remove his strange hat, revealing a dark green fabric that had been wound several times round his head to cover his eyes. Slowly he began to unwrap the bandage.

'Got it!' said Crumble, getting back to his feet. He hesitated briefly as he watched the strange confrontation, but then bolted after Nibbler.

Charlie watched as Fo Fum unravelled the last strip, then almost shrieked in horror at the sight of the dark, empty holes where his eyes should have been. Thick smoke began to pour out of the pits like ash wafting upward from twin volcanoes.

With a thin smile Fo Fum pulled his staff free from the ground and, falling into low stance, began to flip it from hand to hand, then back round his neck in an awe-inspiring display of martial skill. Smoke still bubbling from his empty eye sockets, Fo Fum moved towards Charlie with a smooth grace.

With no other alternative Charlie went forward to meet him.

Sic Boy had done Jensen proud. He had eaten up great distances far faster than a horse or a rhinospider would have done. But it was obvious that the fierce dog's stamina was ebbing. His large tongue lolled from his muzzle and Jensen's newly tailored three-quarter-length trousers were salt-stained with the dog's sweat. But they were close. Jensen could see their destination, Shidden Vale, in the distance.

'Keep going, Sic Boy, keep going! That's it, we're nearly there. Nearly there!'

Sensing the urgency in Jensen's voice, Sic Boy somehow managed to tap extra reserves of energy. Powerful muscles flexing, he increased his stride until Jensen's eyes watered and his topknot was pressed flat by the wind.

The road curved gently as it neared the town. On the right lay a landscape of wind-smoothed boulders and on the left a fast-paced river.

Jensen did a double take and his jaw dropped in disbelief as he saw Nibbler being dragged along by the current.

'Wot the . . .'

Snapping his head round he saw a teenage Stoman hollering as he chased the struggling Winged One along the riverbank. Looking even further upstream, Jensen caught a glimpse of movement and a flash of unruly blonde hair before the image disappeared behind the trees and foliage.

Making an abrupt decision, he pulled Sic Boy to a halt and leaped from his back.

Pointing him in the direction of the struggling Winged One he shouted his command. 'Go! Get Nibbler! Go boy!'

Sic Boy flared his nostrils, but didn't hesitate. Leaving a trail of sparks as his talons blazed across the road, he sped off in pursuit of the Hatchling.

Jensen, sword in hand and a grim look on his face, sprinted in the opposite direction.

39

Fist, Rock and Water

Crumble leaped over a fallen tree trunk, vaulted over a boulder and dodged beneath a series of branches. Sliding down the wet riverbank he landed ankle deep in water and splashed onward.

'–eeeeeeelp! Heeeelp m–' Nibbler's cries were momentarily cut off as the current slammed him against another rock then dragged his head beneath the water. 'Chaaaaaaarl–'

'I'm coming!' hollered Crumble.

Long legs kicking up a spray of water, he waded as far as he could then dived forward. With vigorous strokes he swam over to where he had last seen the dragon. Taking a series of deep breaths, he ducked down into a murky world of river weed and displaced leaves that made it hard to see. When he glimpsed a flash of scales he darted forward, but it was just a large fish startled into making a quick escape. Kicking for the surface he filled his lungs then dived back down.

This time he found a length of cord with a wooden weight tied to the end. Following it he grasped a wing and, swimming even deeper, he discovered the rest of Nibbler flailing weakly in an attempt to free himself from the bolas. Grabbing hold of a paw, Crumble kicked his way towards the surface.

Both of them drew in great lungfuls of air. With Crumble supporting Nibbler they struggled to the riverside, crawled up the bank and collapsed in a heap.

'Well, will you look at what the tide dragged in,' said a voice. 'Looks like the Band o' Thirteen might have a new clue as to the whereabouts of our bounty.'

Crumble and Nibbler twisted round to find that not only had they washed ashore next to the town of Shidden Vale, but they were encircled by a group of Humans dressed in intricate armour, all of whom had the number thirteen stamped in blood-red ink on to their breastplates.

Even partially tied-up Nibbler couldn't contain his curiosity. 'But there's only eleven of you,' he protested. 'Aren't you supposed to be a band of thirteen?'

'We're so named because if we don't get what we want, thirteen pieces is what we cut our victims into,' leered one of the men. Gold teeth twinkling through his greasy beard he loomed over the river-sodden duo. 'So what do you say, my pretties? Do you want to tell me where Charlie of the Keepers is or do me and my boys get busy with our talent for butchery?'

Fo Fum ducked away from Charlie's blow and, with the acrid smoke still jetting from his eye holes, unleashed a wave of vicious counter-attacks. Charlie blocked each with a flash from her blazing fists, but it hurt. So powerful were the mercenary's strikes that even surrounded by the shield of her Will Charlie felt like she was being struck by a sledgehammer.

Rallying, she struck back with whips of dark Will. Lashing one hand forward then another she brought great licks of flame to bear, but Fo Fum, cartwheeling backwards in a flurry of smoke, evaded her attack. Back and forth they went, each equally skilled and both equally fast, until Fo Fum's incredible strength became the deciding factor. The few blows that Charlie landed barely stunned the man, whereas each of his continued to almost knock her off her feet.

'Leave me alone!' she snapped as her sense of frustration soared.

Somersaulting sideways she tried to create some distance, but Fo Fum kept up.

'I mean it! Leave me alone! I've got enough on my plate already. ENOUGH!' Riding a wave of anger her Will exploded.

Great streams of black flames, golden light and sun-white sparks burst from her fists. Leaping forward she danced around Fo Fum battering at him with a barrage of kicks and punches.

'I'LL TEACH YOU NOT TO MESS WITH ME! I'LL TEACH YOU THE MEANING OF –'

Fo Fum suddenly screamed, 'Feeeee!' and knifed the heel of his foot sideways into Charlie's stomach.

The air was knocked from Charlie's lungs. Winded, she was forced to stagger backwards, but Fo Fum pressed forward to his advantage. With each blow that he unleashed he let loose an ear-wrenching scream.

'Fiiiiiii!'

His staff cracked against Charlie's fists in a flash of sparks.

'Fffffo!'

Smoke erupting from his nightmare face, he smashed at Charlie's defences.

'Ffffum!'

Senses reeling, Charlie barely deflected his next strike.

And then she failed altogether. Fo Fum's staff burst through her Will and landed a glancing blow across her temple. The world spun. Sky appeared where there should have been earth and trees where just before there had been rain clouds.

'Aaaaargh!' screamed Charlie as the ground came rushing up to meet her. She blacked out for a second and when she came to, Fo Fum's silhouette reared above her. He raised his staff high overhead.

'No one messes with me friends!' growled a voice.

Fo Fum twitched. His mean smile slipped as his arm fell and his staff thudded to the floor. He swayed from side to side then collapsed with all the suddenness of a puppet with its strings cut. Behind him stood Jensen, arm extended, blood-splattered Thornsword held firmly in his hand, droplets of rainwater cascading down his worried face. Confident that Fo Fum was dead, but unwilling to take any chances, he plunged his sword into the inert body and left it there.

'Hello, lass,' he said as he knelt by Charlie's side.

'J-Jensen?'

'Ya got it in one, me little Hippotomi.'

Nibbler, in his haste to lunge at the nearest Band of Thirteen, forgot about the bolas. Tripping forward into a flailing heap he struggled to stand up. Roaring with laughter at the Winged

One's misfortune, one of the Humans raised his heavy mace only to be felled in turn as Crumble tackled him round the waist. Both Human and Stoman went tumbling into the river.

The rest of the band found this uproarious, laughing and pointing at their fallen comrade. Their chuckles fell silent as Crumble, hands aglow, made short work of his foe. Knocking the man's mace from his grasp, Crumble used it against him, leaving his attacker dazed and cross-eyed from a thump to the side of his head. Wading from the water with the mace in his hand, Crumble stood protectively over Nibbler.

A hard expression crossed the remaining ten men's faces.

'Weapons out, ladies,' growled the man with the beard and golden teeth. 'Looks like we'll have to demonstrate our ability to count to thirteen.'

They stalked forward only to be met by crackles of electricity as Nibbler, still struggling to free himself, proved his worth. The men scuttled out of reach.

'Well, what are you waiting for?' bellowed Golden Teeth. 'We all know the drill. Three of you take that side, you three take the other. And don't hold back with the blades. We only need one of them able to talk!'

Split into three groups, they began to press their attack. Crumble and Nibbler, forced almost all the way back to the water's edge, did their best to fend off the Band of Thirteen. But Nibbler's lightning could only restrain one side at a time, and no matter how fast he moved the other two groups would dart forward to strike. Crumble did his best to counter their attacks with his mace and Shatterstone, but it was an impossible task.

Then the three on the left, timing their attack to perfection, reached Nibbler just as he was fending off the other seven. Crumble, desperate beyond measure, threw the mace at one of them and, shouting mindlessly, barrelled into the other two before they could raise their weapons.

But these weren't the Forty Swords; the Band of Thirteen were toughened, driven by greed and above all very experienced. Dropping their weapons so they could better grapple at close quarters, the two Humans pulled Crumble to the ground. Using their combined weight to their advantage, they forced the young Stoman's hands backwards and with a sickening pop wrenched one of his arms all the way behind him.

Crumble screamed in agony then moaned as a fist was driven under his ribs. Grinning nastily, the two men retrieved their weapons.

A distant growl gave them cause to turn their heads.

Sic Boy, kicking up a cloud of dust and pebbles, raced towards them. The deep bass of his enraged barks rumbled down the street and broke like a wave upon the Band of Thirteen.

Stunned by this sudden

appearance they tried to reorganize their ranks, but it was too late. Growling and gnashing, Sic Boy flung himself at the band. Knocking two to the ground he closed his jaws round a screaming third. The crunch of plate armour being crumpled in the huge dog's mouth was appalling for all to hear. Dashing his victim aside he fixed Golden Teeth with a glare and growled so menacingly that the leader nearly lost control of his bladder.

A fork of lightning struck one of the Humans in the back. Caught between the anvil of Nibbler's flames and the hammer of Sic Boy's untamed ferocity, the band were in a tactically disastrous position. Sic Boy encouraged their decision to flee by raking his paw across Golden Teeth's chest plate. The shriek of metal and the deep grooves left in the armour gave those still standing a chance to appreciate just how much they valued their lives.

Cursing and hollering, the Band of Thirteen made an undignified retreat.

40

Reunited

Unaware that Charlie had already been saved, Nibbler had hobbled back as fast as he could, followed by Sic Boy and finally, at a somewhat slower rate, by Crumble, who with only one active arm, had difficulty traversing the riverbank. Everyone relaxed once it became evident that neither group had suffered life-threatening injury. Jensen, an experienced hand, popped Crumble's dislocated shoulder back into place.

Once everyone had settled down, introductions were made and stories exchanged as each party did their best to bring the other up to date. Charlie was elated to hear that Kelko was OK but horrified to hear of the vast army that was now descending on Sylvaris. She couldn't bear to think of the city that she had grown to love threatened in such a way. Jensen in turn was shocked to hear of Charlie's adventures and seemed more than a little heartbroken to see her so bruised, battered and changed. He had trouble containing his excitement as he learned the pendant's secret, and shook his head in disbelief as she told him of their ordeal breaking into the Stubborn Citadel. When he heard that Darkmount had broken Charlie's leg and stolen her pendant he exploded.

'Wot? He wot? If I catch him . . .' Mid-rant he suddenly stopped.

'What is it?' asked Nibbler. 'What's the matter, Jensen?'

'I think . . . I think I know where he is.'

'Who? Darkmount?' asked Charlie, a thrill racing through her.

'I think so,' muttered Jensen, trying to piece together the image of the Stoman and his silent army and add it to the pieces of information provided by Nibbler and Charlie. 'I mean how many Stoman bishops are there any more? Bane has trampled most of his opposition under foot. It's gotta be him.'

Jensen recounted his journey across the Great Plains and the Slumbering Hills and what he had seen that strange night.

'That's got to be him, who else would be power-mad enough to attempt to build his own army?' said Charlie, balling her fingers into fists. 'Let's go and get him. Let's get my pendant back.'

'Erm . . . please tell me you don't want to go and do that right now,' said Crumble in disbelief.

'Of course right now!'

Crumble rubbed a hand over his tired eyes. 'Charlie, look at us. My arm is so stiff I can barely use it. Nibbler is so bruised that he lurches around like something dragged from a grave –'

'Braaaaaaaaaains,' groaned Nibbler, but everyone ignored him.

'And you . . .' continued Crumble, '. . . well, I don't understand how you can be moving after that beating you took.'

Charlie kept quiet. She didn't want to explain that bruising or no bruising, with the darkness pulsing inside her she felt fine. She'd been careful not to mention the change in her Will either; that was something she'd rather tell Jensen at a later date.

Jensen, however, had a calculating look in his eyes as he listened to Crumble's counsel. 'Maybe the lad's got a point. Perhaps it would be best if ya took us back ta Sylvaris. I know some amazing healers and they'd have ya right as rain in a day or two. With the Jade Circle's aid we could return with some serious reinforcements –'

'Stop that,' retorted Charlie. 'We both know that's not going to work.'

Jensen sighed. He didn't bother to push his argument any further.

'Why isn't that going to work?' demanded Crumble. He turned to Jensen. 'Please tell me you're not thinking of jumping straight in on this too? I thought you were supposed to be the wisest one here! Surely you should be counselling rest?'

'The dice have already been rolled, lad.'

'What's that supposed to mean?'

'I mean that when yer falling from a cliff there's no point in grasping at straws, yer've just gotta jump and hope the waters below are deep enough.'

Crumble narrowed his eyes to stare accusingly at Jensen. 'You've met my uncle, haven't you?'

'No, lad, but if he talks like me he's probably sound of mind.'

'Or you're just another adult who likes to quote proverbs instead of getting to the point.'

Jensen chuckled at that. 'Crumble, when an adult throws a proverb at ya that's their way of hoping yer smart enough ta understand wot they're driving at without having ta elaborate for half an hour.'

'Well, I've just had my shoulder dislocated by a crew of mercenaries who like to cut their foes into thirteen itty-bitty pieces. Surely that's excuse enough for my sudden drop in intelligence, *so would you please tell me why we shouldn't rest up until we're fully healed*?'

Jensen rolled his eyes, but took pity on the Stoman boy. 'Bellania,' he began, 'as we know it, is on the brink of collapse. Bane could quite feasibly crush it and rebuild the land in any way he sees fit. He's blocked the return of the Winged Ones, conquered Alavis and Alacorn and has sent one of the largest armies dis realm has ever seen to Sylvaris. Wot Charlie was quick ta realize is that the Jade Circle cannot help us now, nor can it afford ta divert soldiers from the defence of Deepforest. If there's any hope ta be had – any hope at all for saving Bellania – we have ta get that pendant back. If we can get it then we can free the Winged Ones, kick Bane up the backside and return Bellania ta its state of peace. And cos time is so pressing we cannot afford ta lie around. We've gotta move and we've gotta move now.' Jensen's serious expression was abruptly marred by a grin. 'Besides, from wot I hear yer not exactly the wisest of counsels either. Weren't ya about ta take Charlie and Nibbler right ta the Western Mountains? That sounds like the sort of foolhardy thing that happens in fairy tales: trying ta kill the bad guy in his own lair.'

Crumble blushed. 'That was Charlie's idea. I-I just felt honour bound to help.'

'Pfft,' snorted Jensen. 'I think we all know that Charlie is missing a few marbles in her noggin when it comes ta making sensible decisions or where her safety is concerned. Nibbler hasn't worked out what the word danger means and Sic Boy . . .' They all turned to look at the ferocious dog. 'Well, let's just say he's suitably named. I think, young Crumble Shard, that ya are deluded inta thinking yer sane, but let me tell ya dis: anyone fool enough ta hang out in dis group has ta be a few acorns short in the head too!'

The twinkle in Jensen's eyes was infectious and Crumble couldn't help but return his smile. 'OK, maybe you've got a point. And . . . to be honest, the idea of taking on Edge Darkmount and his new army sounds just as crazy as going to the Western Mountains. At least this will mean a change of scenery even if the risks are the same.'

'That's the spirit!' Jensen chuckled.

'So what's the plan then? How do you intend to reclaim the pendant?'

'I think it would be best ta ask Charlie.'

They turned to look at the bruised and battered girl.

'After all my recent fights, Crumble, I think it's fair to say that having the Will to fight is not enough,' she said with a shrewd look. 'So I've decided to take your advice: be more aggressive or be sneakier. Well, I choose being sneakier. But before we do anything I need to know a little more about these things you Bellanians call gods.'

41

From Another Realm

'The stories would have it that, throughout the ages, gods have always come and gone from Bellania. In dis case Dark-mount and Bane's gods are relatively new ta the realm,' began Jensen. 'Edge Darkmount's god appeared ninety years ago and a small but flourishing Stoman religion was built around its worship. Darkmount stems from a line of bishops who see their god and their religion as the one true faith. Indeed, rumour would have it that his father was the original founder of their religion.

'Forty years ago Bane was a merely a young bishop with dreams of power. Unable ta wrestle the existing god of the "true faith" away from Edge Darkmount and his fellow bishops, Bane went in search of something else that would grant him supremacy. Drawn towards the never-ending passages and tunnels that lie beneath the Western Mountains, he went on a three-year quest until he found his *own* god. As Tremen, we're not sure how he managed ta usurp both Darkmount's god and religion and then rise even higher until he became the Stoman leader, but succeed he did.'

'And what about the gods themselves?' asked Charlie. 'What are they? What can they do?'

'I was just coming ta that, lass. Many years ago when I was still growing my financial empire I was granted a meeting with Dridif and a Winged One and they did their best ta explain the truth of the matter ta me.'

'And that is . . .'

'They're not gods.'

'Huh?'

'Well, maybe they are, but not in the sense that ya or I would expect. The Winged Ones say that they're just creatures from another realm – and insignificant ones at that; in their own realm they're nothing more than bottom feeders.'

'Wha– You're not making any sense, Jensen.'

Well, maybe I'm not spelling dis out too clearly, although ta be honest I was never a hundred per cent clear meself when it was explained ta me. Look, from wot I can gather these "gods" ain't from Bellania or even Earth. They're supposed ta be from somewhere else altogether.'

'How can that be?'

'Uh, well the Winged Ones sometimes like ta talk about parallel realms and "united universe" theories but that's a subject for another day. Apparently, in their own realm these gods live in a world that is nothing more than a gigantic ball of gas.'

'What, like Jupiter?'

'That's that planet that can be seen from Earth, isn't it?'

'Yes.'

'Then, yes, like Jupiter. Now as I was saying, apparently, in dis realm all manner of weird and wonderful beasties exist. The Winged One said that the beasties over there treat the gas like a liquid – almost like a spherical ocean – and that these weird creatures swim, fly and float through the gassy murkiness much like our sea creatures navigate through water. Now wot's so unbelievable about all of dis is that over there the gods are at the bottom of the food chain. Literally. All the really amazing creatures swim high up where the pressure is lower, then as ya get deeper and deeper and the pressure grows, the creatures of that realm get smaller and smaller and less majestic. And there, right at the bottom, where there's no light and the gas pressure is so intense that almost nothing but the most hardy bottom feeders can live ya'll find –'

'The gods?'

'So they say.'

'B-b-but that makes no sense!'

'I know. That's wot I thought when I first heard about it.'

'But how . . .'

'How did they get here?'

'Yes.'

'Good question. The Winged Ones reckon that in their realm the gas pressure is so strong that the sheer, unrelenting, unimaginable force of it pushes them through the reality of their realm inta ours.'

'Doesn't that sound a little far-fetched?'

'Ta be honest? Yes it does and I've always had my suspicions that Dridif and that Winged One were having a laugh at my expense but oddly enough their explanation does have some logic ta it.'

'It does?'

'Well . . . yes. Just think about it, we're all familiar with the Gateways between Earth and Bellania and we know there are other realms and places that we can travel ta.'

'Like what?'

'Like the lower dominions where you retrieved Darkmount's god and then there's the Winged Dominion: the place where the Winged Ones go for their Chrysalis Period. If we know all these places are connected wot's ta say that it couldn't happen with another realm, even by accident?'

Charlie opened her mouth to laugh but paused as she considered what Jensen was suggesting. There was indeed a faint trace of logic to it. After all, wasn't Bellania a weird and wonderful place in comparison to Earth? Knowing that, who was she to say that there were or weren't other realms with inexplicable laws and physics? Then her sense of suspicion caught up with her and she looked askance at Jensen.

'Ha!' He chuckled as he saw her expression. 'I gave the Winged One and Dridif that very same look when they first told me. I wasn't sure if they were pulling my leg or not.'

'Were they?'

'They said they weren't and as odd as it sounds I do tend ta bow my head ta my more learned betters in subjects such as these. I think they were telling me the truth.'

'OK, supposing it's true, what do these gods want?'

'Well there's the rub. They want ta be worshipped. They don't care by whom or by wot, but there's something in the *stuff* of worship that they need. Something that is intangible ta ya and I, but acts like food ta them. They grant wishes and in return they get fed wot they desire most.'

Charlie scrunched her eyes shut as she tried to make sense of all the bits and pieces of information. 'So they really are bottom feeders, aren't they? I mean there's no "greater purpose" going on here is there? These things just grub around looking for sustenance and cos they're so alien they're called gods.'

'That's the crux of it.'

Charlie was caught up in her own thoughts. 'When I talked to Darkmount's god, it sounded like it was right inside my head, my nose began to bleed and I had a splitting headache . . . Do you think that maybe it feeds on thoughts or emotions?'

'I'm not sure . . . maybe. All I know is that there's supposed to be a price to be paid. They say if ya spend too long with one it changes ya.'

'Changes you how?'

'Charlie, I honestly wouldn't know. Darkmount hasn't spent too much time with his, but Bane . . . they say Bane has changed the most. The Winged Ones say that the reason why his face can never be seen and that he wraps his flesh in bandages is because all that time spent with his god has changed him irreversibly.'

'What do you think he looks like beneath that hood?'

'That's the billion shilling question, isn't it? No one knows and only Darkmount is fool enough to risk playing with a god long enough ta find out.'

Charlie shivered at the thought. The idea of allowing something so alien inside your head, to allow it to pluck and squirm through your emotions and memories for year after year seemed horrifying.

'One more question,' she said. 'What do you think these gods ultimately want?'

'We don't know. Well, I definitely don't know, and neither

Dridif nor the Winged One knew either. There's a theory that these gods are quite happy picking over the scraps and leftovers. And while they're content ta live amongst the Stomen, the Winged One and Dridif were musing that perhaps they would be just as happy amongst chicken or even shellfish. I don't think these gods care who worships them – if worship is even the right word – so long as they have the opportunity ta feed off emotion or memories or wotever it is they suck from their followers.'

'That doesn't make sense. How can something that's so powerful not care? I mean, come on, Bane's god has helped him reshape the whole of Bellania. How can something like that not care?'

'They might be powerful over here, but think about it. Where they come from they're the lowest of the low that feed on the leftovers. How boring must their lives be? How infinitely small must their minds and their imaginations be? Maybe it might help if we put it inta context: could ya imagine pulling a crab or say a squigglefish from the ocean and expecting them ta create great philosophies or paintings or scientific equations?'

'Well, if you put it like that . . . no.'

'Of course. And would ya expect a crab ta be able ta think past its next meal?'

'Um, no. But how can you compare a crab from here to something that's a god?'

Jensen shrugged. 'Different realms, but same mentality.'

'Huh . . . well, that's food for thought and that's for sure,' said Charlie. 'You've definitely given me something to consider for our next meeting with Darkmount.'

Nibbler, having finished chewing on the last of the grilled fish that Crumble had caught and cooked, shook himself and sat upright. 'So what about the rest of the beasties that live in their realm? I mean if the smallest, most insignificant creatures from their realm are seen as gods over here, what amazing things could, say, the whales and the dolphins of their world do?'

They all paused to think about that. A different realm with different laws and physics and thoughts.

'Indeed, me young Winged One.' Jensen grinned, obviously enjoying the idea. 'Wot wonders could such things accomplish? But surely thoughts and dreams like that are for another day? Right now we've got other matters that need attending ta.'

'Yes we do,' agreed Charlie as thoughts and plans started to whirr through her mind. 'I think it's time for us to get moving. It's time we paid Darkmount a visit.'

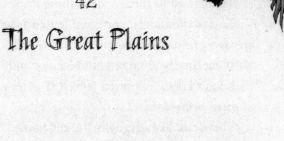

42

The Great Plains

The Portal closed, leaving them on a grassy and rain-swept ridge. Jensen indicated that they should get down on their stomachs, so one by one they wormed their way across the wet grass until they reached the hill's summit. Following Jensen's instruction they slowly stuck their heads over the top in order to see the valley.

When they saw what lay below Crumble's eyes bulged, Sic Boy growled deep in his throat and Nibbler let out a low whistle of surprise. Charlie, already expecting the worst, merely grunted.

A cavernous tent had been erected in the valley basin. Dark pennants fluttered from its supports. In precise ranks that spread from the tent like vast spokes of a wheel, was an army. An army the like of which Bellania had never seen. Row after row of brooding, bulky *things* squatted, and even though they were silent and unmoving there was something about them that screamed *violence*. Distance and rain made it hard to judge exactly what they were, but Charlie thought they looked like smaller versions of the Stoman behemoths they had encountered before, though less mannequin-like.

'Looks like our bishop has been a busy boy since I saw him last,' muttered Jensen.

'There must be thousands of those things,' said Crumble.

'Tens of thousands,' corrected Jensen as he ran a practised eye over the neat lines.

'What are they?' asked Nibbler.

'I don't know,' admitted Jensen. 'I've never seen the likes of them before.'

'They look like gargoyles,' said Charlie.

'That's funny,' said Jensen, 'I was thinking that they looked just like gorillas.'

'Gargorillas or apeogyles?' suggested Crumble, mixing the words together.

'Ape-o-gyles?' queried Charlie, unimpressed with his lack of originality.

'Gargorillas,' said Nibbler. 'Definitely gargorillas.'

'Gargorillas it is,' said Jensen, settling the debate.

A dark green pulse of light suddenly appeared beneath the canvas flaps. As it faded, four more gargorillas knuckled their way out of the tent to join the ranks.

'How many more does he need to make?' asked Charlie. 'Surely with an army that size he could defeat anyone?'

Jensen shook his head. 'No he couldn't. Bane has raised a force larger than any in history. Three armies with hundreds of thousands in each. Hundreds. Of. Thousands. And while I'm sure those big beasties down there could wreak all sorts of damage, they're still not enough ta match one of Bane's armies, let alone all three of them. Not yet anyway. Either way I think it would be wise ta get down there before Darkmount makes any more. Although with all those brutes facing outward I'm not sure how we're going ta get down there without being detected.'

'We'll just open a Portal behind the tent and slip in.'

'Wot, just like that?'

'Why not? Like you said, they're all looking away from the tent. As long as we're quiet, we can open the Portal in the gap between the gargorillas and the tent, then slip inside.'

'I like the direct approach,' mused Jensen.

'And I've got another idea,' continued Charlie.

'Which is?'

'Deception, trickery and . . .' She turned to give Crumble a wink. 'Some of that good old-fashioned sneakiness we were talking about earlier.'

There was another green pulse as four more gargorillas appeared.

'Wot d'ya have in mind, lass?'

'I'll tell you, but, first, Crumble, what's the biggest stone club you could make and wield?'

'I can make something pretty big.'

'Big enough to bring down an elephant?'

'What's that?'

'A big mammal with a trunk for a nose. Imagine something four times bigger than Sic Boy.'

'Uh . . . I'm not sure. I can make a club big enough to damage a rhinospider, but with my stiff shoulder I won't be able to wield it for long.'

'Don't worry, hopefully you'll only have to swing it the once.'

'Wot do ya have planned, me little Hippotomi?' Jensen,

although growing curious, enjoyed seeing Charlie's mind at work.

'Something big. Jensen, can you be quick and quiet?'

'Of course, lass, I'm a Treman.'

'What about me?' asked Nibbler.

Charlie looked at her friend and sighed. 'I need you and Sic Boy to stay here.'

'What? No way! You're going to need all the muscle –'

Charlie put up her hand to silence him. 'Nibbler, now isn't the time for muscle. We're going to need to be quick and silent and –'

'I'm quick!'

'You haven't recovered from your time in that river. I saw how hard it was for you to crawl up here. You're stiff and I know you're still in pain.'

'That doesn't matter. There's no way I'm letting you go down there on your own.'

'I won't be alone. Crumble and Jensen will be with me.'

'But –'

'Nibbler, please. Trust me on this. One or two more people watching my back isn't going to make a difference, not when we're facing tens of thousands of . . . whatever those things are. Smaller numbers are what's needed for this plan to work. Any more than that and we risk being detected.'

'But –'

'Please, Nibbler.'

The Hatchling didn't look happy, but finally he nodded. 'OK, but if anything does go wrong, me and Sic Boy are going to come and get you.'

Charlie rubbed the scales that ran down his neck. 'I wouldn't have it any other way,' she said with a smile.

'When were ya thinking of making a move?' asked Jensen.

'As soon as Crumble can make his club, I'll open the Portal.'

'Let's wait a bit,' suggested Jensen, his eyes tracking the distant sky.

'Why?'

'Those rain clouds are approaching; we can go under cover of the downpour.'

Charlie's wet hair was already sticking out at unusual angles. 'You wouldn't call this delightful weather "rain"?' she said, looking at Jensen as though he were mad.

'Wot, dis spring shower? Dis is just a misting! We're on the edge of the Great Plains, lass. Just ya wait until the heavens really open. Out here they know the meaning of thunderstorms.'

'OK, then. So how long do you think until it arrives?'

'Ah, that's never an easy estimate ta make. An hour and a half, maybe two?'

'All right, let's wait a bit. But if it's not here by then we need to move before Darkmount makes too many more of those things.'

Everyone nodded in agreement and they all crawled back from the ridge to wait for the right moment to ambush.

Back by the abandoned campsite the wind had changed direction, teasing the cinders of the dying fire that persisted despite the light rain. Unrelenting in its demands, the wind continued to tickle the embers with a gentle touch, fanning its ambitions until it glowed a cherry red. Unable to withstand the heated embrace any longer, a partially burnt log ignited and a lazy tendril of smoke wafted upward.

Carried along by the gentle nudge of the wind, the smoke eased over the withered and twisted corpse of Fo Fum. Bits of the smoke blew into the man's hollow eyes.

One of Fo Fum's legs began to twitch in a horrible rhythm. It kicked up and down, disturbing small pebbles and scaring nearby herons into flight. The sickening beat was joined by fingers that jolted in time as the corpse began to shudder and spasm. Abruptly, and as if with a life of its own, one of the hands scuttled up the blade of Jensen's Thornsword to grasp and paw at the hilt. Slowly it pulled the sword free. With a terrible croak Fo Fum rolled on to his stomach. Undulating forward like some misshapen worm, the corpse plunged its face into the ashes of the fire.

Long moments of stillness passed and the sickly scent of burning flesh filled the clearing. The smoke no longer spooled into the air but appeared to be sucked towards the deflated body. Fo Fum's corpse gradually started to swell, still accompanied by the awful twitching.

And then it stopped.

Fo Fum pushed himself to his knees then jerked upright. His face was a blackened mess, but the endless hollows that should have held his eyes wriggled with the spark of life.

Reaching over he pulled his staff from the floor. Snapping it across his knee he added the two parts to the rekindled fire. More smoke bubbled up and the odd aroma of burning rubber and mouldy socks filled the air. Without hesitation Fo Fum plunged his face into the smoke and slowly he inhaled the dark vapours with disturbing delight. His muscles bulged, his clothes stretched and he grew in height as the heavens opened above him and heavy rain poured down across the campsite.

Moving gracefully once more he bound his eyes with a scrap torn from his cloak. Pulling his hat on to his head he retrieved his compass from his pocket and, after checking his bearings, strode from the riverside. His purposeful stride turned into a jog, his jog into a run and then with his over-inflated muscles pumping with renewed power he broke into a sprint.

Faster and faster, his cloak flaring behind him, Fo Fum began to eat up the distance that lay between him and his prey. Using the strike of his heels as a beat he began to chant a rhyme: 'Fe-fi, Fo Fum, I come to earn my bounty sum. Fe-fi, Fo Fum, I go to kill that Keeper scum.'

With a thin smile of greedy delight the mercenary disappeared into the quickening rain.

43

Mud

The thick clouds churned overhead, dimming the landscape. The wind picked up sending formidable gusts rippling and bobbing through the tall grass like ocean waves. With a crack of thunder and a flash of lightning the deluge started. Thick blobs of rain cascaded down upon the small group.

Charlie had to shout to be heard above the tempest. 'Any last questions?' she hollered. She was answered with a grim shaking of heads. Everyone knew their role and was keen to get on with the task. 'Good! Let's go.'

She opened the Portal and with a brief but confident grin for Nibbler's sake she jumped through. Jensen and Crumble, with his almost comically large club, raced to join her.

They landed, ankle deep in mud, facing the fabric of the tent. Behind them, and behind the Portal with its view back to the ridge, were the regimented lines of Darkmount's new army. Even though they were blurred behind the curtain of rain, the gargorillas loomed brutally big. But not one of them turned to look behind. Each and every single one of them faced outward, positioned in perfect lines: Charlie could not see a single face.

She grinned.

Feeling somewhat more confident she allowed the Portal to close.

Jensen lowered himself into the mud and, careful not to make any hasty movements, slowly rolled over so that he was covered from head to toe. Charlie, then Crumble, followed his lead. With only the whites of their eyes discernible the three slunk forward. Crumble pulled out his small knife and, crouching low, they waited.

The tent glowed. Green light seeped out to briefly illuminate the gloomy downpour. They heard the thud of heavy footsteps, the scrape of a flap lifting then the tramp of feet as the army realigned itself to accommodate four new soldiers.

Crumble looked to Charlie and on her nod quickly stuck his knife into the tent and cut a large L-shape. Jensen waited for a flash of lightning to die down before crawling through the opening, Charlie and Crumble followed close behind.

It was dark inside. As their eyes grew accustomed to the low light, it became apparent that they were sandwiched between an outer and inner layer of canvas. Keeping low they shuffled forward until they were pressed against the second layer. Charlie tensed at the sound of Darkmount's familiar voice. The deluge pounding upon the roof muffled his words, but it was clear from the response that the bishop was asking for something.

'As you wish,' echoed a voice that came not from within the tent, but which was directly inside Charlie's head.

The shock of hearing Darkmount's god within their own minds caused all three to start. They turned to stare at each other, obviously wanting to say something, but too close to their enemy to dare.

The fabric that separated them from the inner confines glowed yet again. The green light cast strange shadows that danced across the canvas. Four rounded, writhing things grew from small silhouettes into large brooding shapes.

Again Darkmount's voice but not his words could be heard.

The four shapes moved, and as the thump of their foot-falls faded Charlie touched Crumble on the shoulder, giving him the go-ahead. As quietly as possible, he split the parti-tion. Charlie reached out and gave her friends a final grasping touch on their forearms before she slithered through the hole.

Her first impression of the tent now she was up close was its size; it could have passed for a circus big top. Her second was how dark it was. Only a few oil-burning lights and a paltry fire gave any illumination, all of which were on or around a small altar that lay in the tent's centre. Darkmount, hood thrown back to reveal his sharp features, stood next to the altar gazing intently at the urn, a greedy look somewhere between hunger and adoration on his face.

Charlie, glad of the poor lighting and muddy camouflage, waited for Jensen and Crumble to join her. She then watched as each sneaked off in opposite directions. Riding on a wave of growing excitement and struggling to deal with the insist-ent tick of adrenalin rushing through her veins, she stood up to make her move.

'What kind of inefficient killer forgets to check his handiwork?' she said, the abruptness of her voice making Darkmount jump.

'Charlie Keeper?'

'Got it in one,' she said, stepping into the small circle of light.

Darkmount quickly regained his composure. 'I have more pressing matters to concern myself with than one idiotic girl foolishly dreaming about the return of her pendant. I'll give you one chance to leave with your life and one only.'

'That's one more chance than I'm prepared to give you.' Charlie paused. Having narrowed the distance between them she could clearly see that the Stoman had changed since they last met. There was something wrong with his face. Little patches of darkness moved across it like windswept clouds streaming through an otherwise clear sky. Charlie blinked as she noted little lights glimmering in the dark patches; it was as if Darkmount was beginning to take on similar qualities to that of his god. He was becoming a patchwork man of flesh and starry galaxies.

'Looks like you've been spending too much time with your god, eh, Darkmount?'

The bishop reached up to touch his face. His fingers actually dipped into one of the black spots as though it was in itself a tiny window to another realm. 'I'm becoming a true holy man, Charlie Keeper. My god is bestowing upon me the holiness of his heavens.'

'Heavens, huh? I think you'd better prepare yourself to be disappointed.'

'Infantile to the last, Charlie Keeper! Are you really unable to comprehend how powerful I have become? Would it help you understand the situation if instead of burying you beneath a mountain of stone I simply ripped your spine from your body?'

'Enough with the talking, let's get on with this.'

'As you wish.' Darkmount took a step towards her.

Charlie gave him a dry laugh. 'I wasn't talking to you.'

She raised one arm high and clicked her fingers.

At her command a pair of hands snaked out of the darkness and snatched the vessel off the altar.

Darkmount, glimpsing the theft out of the corner of his eye, whipped round, but before he could cry out or summon his Stonesong Charlie clicked her fingers again.

KRUUU-KKKACK!

Taking advantage of Darkmount's distraction, Crumble cracked his oversized club against the bishop's head. Darkmount flew through the air to land in a heap. His eyes rolled up, one arm twitched spasmodically and almost immediately a rasping snore oozed from his slack mouth.

'Are we good?' asked Charlie.

'All good.' Jensen grinned, stepping forward with the urn cradled in his arms.

Crumble joined him. 'Great plan, Charlie, well done.'

'Well done indeed, lass,' said Jensen, genuine admiration shone from his eyes. 'Quick, simple and very, very effective.'

'If I'd known sneaky attacks worked so well I'd have started using them sooner,' said Charlie, her jubilation mirroring Jensen's. 'Sneakiness and good teamwork is definitely the way forward.'

While the Treman and Stoman ripped Darkmount's cloak into strips so they could bind him, Charlie went through his pockets.

'Got it!' Her grin grew wider as she held the pendant aloft. The clasp was broken, and for a moment she considered wrapping it round her wrist like a bracelet, but settled instead for stuffing it deep in her pocket until she could get it fixed or come up with a better solution.

'He's not going anywhere,' stated Crumble as he tied the last knot.

Darkmount, still snoring and twitching erratically, had been trussed into a U-shape so that his wrists were tied to his ankles.

'Gag him too,' insisted Charlie.

Jensen returned the urn to the altar then stuffed the remnants of Darkmount's cloak into his mouth.

'What are we going to do about him?' asked Crumble. 'We can't just let him go, can we?'

'After all that he's done? There's no chance I'm just going to let him go,' said Charlie, an undercurrent of anger in her voice.

'What do you have in mind?'

'Vengeance.'

Jensen, so jubilant before, examined her with worried eyes. 'Hippotomi,' he began, but Charlie put her hand up.

'I know what you're going to say, Jensen, but please, trust me. Trust my instincts this time. I won't do anything that would make you ashamed of me.'

Jensen couldn't say anything after that, but he continued to watch her. Concern for what she might do and fears about the influence of the darkness that she now carried within her was evident in his eyes.

Charlie made her way to the altar. 'Let's get reckless,' she whispered, and without allowing herself time to think, lifted the urn and stared into its star-filled depths.

44

Vengeance

'I know you're there,' she said.

The urn grew cold. One of the stars grew closer and pulsed with a sickly green light.

'Utter your request and see it done,' said the god.

'Those *things* outside. How was Darkmount going to control them?'

'They will move to his wants so long as he holds their hearts within his fist.'

'Where is this, uh, heart?'

'Here.'

Charlie, ignoring the trickle of blood that seeped from her nose, looked around, but couldn't see an object that resembled or could be called a heart.

'Where?'

'Here.'

As the star continued to grow to the point that Charlie's face was bathed in green light, it dawned on her that it meant that *it* had it. Realizing she couldn't back down, she summoned all her courage.

'Give it to me.'

'As you wish.'

The star grew and grew, the sensation of intense cold now beyond the point of bearing, and Charlie had no option but to drop the vessel. As it struck the ground, frost appeared along its length then spread along the floor in an arc. The tent grew icy, Charlie's breath misted and the starlight seeping from the urn grew to an almost unbearable glory.

Just when she thought the light couldn't get any brighter the star floated free to hang above the urn. Something stirred within the green light. A great diamond-shaped head and a pair of grasping hands appeared, but everything else, if indeed there was anything else, remained hidden inside the star.

'Come closer,' demanded the voice.

Charlie, thinking that perhaps she had finally bitten off more than she could chew, edged her unwilling feet nearer.

'Closer.'

The cold was almost unbearable, the blood dripping from her nose freezing, however a small part of Charlie's mind couldn't help but notice and be horrified that the thing, *this god,* had no mouth with which to speak.

'Give me your hand.'

Almost beyond the point of caring, Charlie thrust her arm forward. The thing reached out a thin and blackened arm and ever so lightly placed something in Charlie's palm, and then, shrinking in on itself, it returned to the urn.

Whatever it was it was repulsive. It glistened on the palm of her hand like a fat slug. Purple tendrils sprouted across its surface and it pulsed in her hand with the movement of a real heart. The little tendrils clutched weakly at her skin and Charlie almost dropped it in disgust.

'Er . . . how do I use . . . this?' she asked. The question was partly for herself, partly for Jensen and Crumble, but it was the god who answered her.

'Nurture it. Feed it. When it is satisfied it will be yours to command.'

'Uh, OK. Thank you.'

The god didn't reply.

With some trepidation Charlie placed the urn back on the altar. Gesturing for Crumble and Jensen to join her, she pulled them into a close huddle.

'I need to know two things. Where is the deepest ocean in Bellania? And where's the most desolate place?'

Jensen pondered her questions. 'I've heard it said that the Sea of Charms is supposed ta be bottomless,' he said.

'That sounds perfect. Where is it?'

Jensen told her.

'Good, and the most desolate place?'

'Um, do you want ta be a bit more specific about that?'

'I want a place that's scarcely populated and would be very, very hard to return from.'

'Fo Fum was the only person to make the journey from beyond the Great Deserts,' said Crumble, 'so I'd say that would make them a great candidate for being desolate.'

Charlie turned to stare at Darkmount's unconscious form. 'The Great Deserts sound perfect. I'll need to know where those are too.'

Hesitantly Crumble, with the aid of the better-travelled Jensen, described the geography of the place.

With a grim smile Charlie went to wake Edge Darkmount.

Tipping the liquid contents of an altar bowl across his face she waited for him to stop spluttering before addressing him.

'You used me, Darkmount,' she snapped at him. 'You broke my leg. You stole my pendant. You left me for dead.'

'Mmngg-hhnn-grrmpf!' mumbled Darkmount as he struggled against his bonds.

Charlie hunkered down so she could stare directly into his eyes. 'You almost ruined the one chance left for Bellania and –' her voice dropped to a terrible whisper – 'you almost took the one chance I have left to save my parents.' Charlie's hair began to writhe and little trickles of darkness crept from her eyes.

'Yyuuu-dnnnt-owww–'

Charlie pressed her hand over his mouth, silencing his attempts at speech. Leaning even closer she whispered into his ear: 'Have you ever heard of that old expression "an eye for an eye"?'

'Charlie –' warned Jensen, but she silenced him with a wave of her hand.

'Don't worry,' she said, addressing both Jensen and Darkmount, 'I'm not that dark. At least not yet. But Darkmount tried to take what's dearest to me so it's only fair that I return the favour.'

Fists clenched, darkness writhing round her, Charlie opened a Portal to reveal a sea of churning waves. Taking hold of the urn she held it teasingly above Darkmount, then with an almost negligent flick of her wrist she tossed it through the Portal. The urn spun head over tail to land with a soft splash. Jensen and Crumble gasped as they saw a flash of luminescence and the flicker of something tentacle-like emerge from the urn before it sank from sight.

Moans of dismay leaked from beneath Darkmount's gag as he watched his dreams literally sink away.

'I know that, given the chance, you'd probably like to curse and threaten me with promises of eternal revenge, but, Darkmount, believe you me, this is the very least that you deserve. You didn't care about the pain you brought, or the damage that you dealt, and obviously you didn't think about anyone other than yourself or that thing you called a god.'

'Grrrrtt-mnnn-nnrr!'

'What? You feel wronged? Ha! Darkmount, look what you've turned me into.' Spreading her arms wide, Charlie unleashed the full wrath of her Will. The tent billowed as she let loose the darkness held within her heart. Black waves, highlighted by a faint glimmer of gold, gushed from her hands and seeped from her eyes, sending her clothes rippling and causing her hair to stand on end. 'LOOK AT ME! Look at what you've created!' Riding on a crest of anger, she slammed shut the Portal that led to the Sea of Charms and tore open another that led to a stony desert bereft of life. Grabbing hold of Darkmount, she dragged him across the floor as though he weighed little more than a doll. She paused as she neared the Portal. 'Be glad that I still hold on to some semblance of my old self. Be pleased my friends stand strong behind me. Be thankful that they have kept some measure of light in my heart, otherwise I would be taking your life.'

With a roar Charlie flung Edge Darkmount through the

Portal. He landed in a cloud of dust and rolled several times before coming to a stop. Charlie took Crumble's small knife and a gourd of water from Jensen. She threw both through the Portal to land next to the fallen bishop.

'No matter how hard you push me, no matter how hard Bane or Bellania pushes me or how brutal the challenges that come my way, I'll never become as twisted as you and for that you should count your blessings.'

With a clap of her hands she allowed the Portal to snap shut.

45

Pigtails

The Tremen had done remarkably well. Driven by fear and anger and spurred on by the necessity of defending their home, they had thinned the Stoman ranks.

Scores of dead formed ghastly mounds that had at first slowed the approach of the enemy, tripping and entangling their legs and feet so that the endless Stoman charges had swiftly turned into blundering and poorly executed attacks. But as the numbers of enemy dead had risen this paradoxically worked in their favour. Bodies plugged the trenches and as they continued to pile higher and higher they formed ramps that were used to scale the sides of the Treman defences.

The tide began to turn. And what had at first been a simple act of turning back the enemy swiftly grew into a desperate affair. Enraged Stomen began to push past defenders and here and there small groups of the enemy managed to plunge all the way past the first line of Treman soldiers before being hurled back.

Then suddenly they were through and the Treman defence crumbled entirely.

A shocked warrior grabbed Kelko by the arm. 'Back!

We've got ta pull back!' Without waiting to see if Kelko would join him, the man sprinted off.

Others swiftly followed suit and cries of 'Back!' and 'Retreat!' filled the air.

Kelko wanted to wait for the sound of the horn that would officially signal the retreat, but it never came.

'Wot are ya waiting for, fool?' gasped an older veteran as he staggered by.

'There's been no call for retreat!' protested Kelko.

'There won't be,' shouted the veteran as he disappeared behind the trees. His voice came echoing back. 'The high command has been slaughtered! Retreat! Retreat ta Sylvaris. We'll make our stand there!'

'Blight my Leaf!' cursed Kelko.

He had to duck suddenly to avoid getting his head cut off as a rider swished his halberd through the air. Ducking and rolling, Kelko sliced off several of the rhinospider's angular legs then, bunching his feet beneath him, raced after the retreating soldiers. As his feet pounded the leaf-littered forest floor and the dappled sunlight speared through the canopy, despair slowly coiled its fingers round his heart. Deepforest had fallen.

'What?' Charlie demanded as she realized Crumble and Jensen were staring at her. 'He'll escape from those bonds. It might take him an hour or so but with the knife in easy reach it won't take him all day.'

'It's not that –' began Jensen.

'And at least he's got enough water to last him a day or two. That should be more than enough to find an oasis or something.'

'It's not –'

'Do you think I let him off too easily?'

'It's –'

Charlie sighed. 'You're right. I didn't punish him enough, did I?' Summoning her Will she reopened the Portal.

Darkmount froze as he realized people were watching his embarrassing attempts to squirm like a caterpillar towards the knife. Humiliated and infuriated he fixed Charlie with a stare that could have broken boulders.

'Darkmount?' called Charlie. 'Before we leave you for good I thought it would be best to remind you that you were beaten by me, Charlie Keeper. A fourteen-year-old girl who you liked to call "naive, innocent, stupid and immature". And just to recap that in case you didn't get it the first time: I'm a girl, I'm fourteen, I occasionally like to put my hair in pigtails and I just beat you.' Then with a final impudent wave that she knew would have him grinding his teeth for years to come she closed the Portal.

She turned to Crumble and Jensen. 'Better?'

Jensen and Crumble shared a what-happened-there look and a did-that-really-happen shrug.

'I, uh, I was going ta say that I was proud of ya for not taking it so far. I wanted ta say that if yer parents were here they would have been proud that ya haven't turned inta a bad apple.'

'So it wasn't that I didn't punish him enough?'

'Um . . . no.'

Again there was a pause as Crumble and Jensen shared yet another look.

'I did kind of like the bit about the pigtails,' said Crumble.

Jensen nodded in appreciation. 'And rubbing yer age in his face too. That was, uh . . . unusual.'

'But effective,' said Crumble.

Jensen blew air between his teeth. 'Uh . . . effective. Yes.'

Charlie decided that the less said about the matter the better. Ignoring the gestures that Jensen and Crumble were making to one another she opened her fist for a better look at the heart.

She regretted it almost immediately. The heart, on closer inspection, was even more disgusting than she had first thought. Trying to force down a sense of revulsion as it wrapped one of its tendrils round her little finger, she rummaged through her pockets. Finding nothing useful she wandered over to Crumble.

'Do you have any food on you?'

Crumble pulled a strip of dried meat from his pouch. Charlie broke off a small piece and tried to feed it to the heart, but it didn't appear interested.

'How am I supposed to do this,' muttered Charlie, 'if it doesn't even have a mouth?'

'Sweet Sap, Charlie, didn't yer parents tell ya any fairy tales when ya were younger?' protested Jensen with a woeful shake of his head. Walking to the altar he broke one of the bowls that lay on its surface. Using one of the sharper fragments to prick his finger he went to Charlie's side. 'Bit obvious when ya think about it. Hold yer hand up.'

He allowed several drops of blood to drip from his finger

on to the heart. It reacted immediately. Pulsing faster on Charlie's hand it squirmed and tried to latch several tendrils round Jensen's finger, but he was careful to keep his hand out of reach.

'Uck, it feels so gross,' grumbled Charlie. She unwrapped the tendril that had twined round her finger. 'Do you think that's it? Is that all it's going to need?'

'I don't know. Wanna try a little more?'

'Go for it.'

Jensen let drop some more blood.

Once again the heart reacted. Wriggling and writhing, it desperately tried to reach Jensen's finger.

'It wants to touch you,' observed Charlie. 'Do you think we should let it?'

'Wot? Are ya nuts? Everyone knows not ta do something like that.'

'They do?'

'Of course!'

'Why?'

'Yer joking right? Ya must have read enough myths and legends ta know better than that. Even those cheesy horror movies yer've got on Earth make it easy enough ta understand. Ya don't give monsters enough food ta grow big enough ta eat ya. Ya don't let them touch ya when yer bleeding, particularly the weird ones like this with tentacles cos they always try ta stick them right in yer veins and drink ya dry.'

'Or they control your mind,' said Crumble.

'Right,' said Jensen nodding his head in agreement. 'Or they turn ya inta a zombie.'

'Or they turn your hand against you so that you have to cut it off,' said Crumble. 'But even then it crawls around on its fingers and still tries to kill you.'

'Right!' said Jensen with another enthusiastic nod. 'Or they –'

'OK, I think I get it,' interrupted Charlie. 'So we can't give it too much of your blood. But how do we know we've got enough? Does it look satisfied to you?'

Crumble and Jensen looked warily at the heart, which continued to wriggle on Charlie's hand.

'Uh . . . no. It still looks kinda hungry ta me.'

'Me too,' admitted Crumble.

'OK, you big sissies, I've got a better idea,' said Charlie. 'Crumble do you still have all that money on you?'

'Yes.'

'Good.' Charlie opened a Portal that led to Opal Hold. 'Can you grab us a couple of steaks and another waist pouch like yours?'

'Sure.'

'Excellent. Do you think anyone will recognize you and cause trouble?'

Crumble looked down at himself. 'I think I'm a little too muddy.'

'Uh . . . good point. Hang on, will anyone serve you looking like that?'

'I've never known a merchant to turn down business as long as there's gold to be gained.' Crumble flicked a coin in the air. 'And thanks to you we've still got some money to our name.'

'Great.' Charlie frowned as she eyed the Portal. 'Don't be

long, Opal Hold is further away from here than Shidden Vale was and, uh . . . well the Portal feels a bit heavier.'

'Heavier?'

'Yeah. Harder to hold open.'

'OK, I'll be quick.' Crumble darted through.

'Think ya can hold that without having ta look at it?'

Charlie gave it some thought then nodded.

'Then follow me.'

Jensen led her to the tent opening. Together they looked out into the torrential rain and at the precise ranks of the silent army. 'Are ya thinking wot I've been thinking?'

Charlie stared at Jensen then turned to look once more at the long lines of gargorillas disappearing into the downpour.

'Sylvaris,' she said with a jubilant grin.

'Right,' said Jensen, his white teeth breaking the mask of his muddy face.

A new sense of purpose filled Charlie. Since Jensen had first broken the news of Sylvaris's imminent doom, a feeling of urgency had filled her. At first she had hoped to confront Bane in his palace, maybe stop him in his tracks. Then, learning that there was still a chance to retrieve her pendant, she had been filled with dreams of freeing the Winged Ones in time to save Sylvaris. But as the reality of the distances and time involved became apparent those hopes had slowly crumbled. All along she had assumed that she would be fighting a losing battle to save Sylvaris and Bellania from the Stoman Lord, but now in one swoop of luck she had changed everything.

Charlie's smile grew as she looked at the long line of

gargorillas. If she really could control them with that yucky heart she had a strong chance of doing some real good. 'So we get to give Bane a taste of his own medicine at last.'

'About time,' said Jensen, perhaps a little louder than he should. The idea of saving his beloved city rode high in his heart. 'Me little Hippotomi, if only Azariah could see ya now he'd be proud of ya.'

'If there's a Will there's a Way,' said Charlie as she fondly remembered Azariah's teaching.

'Yes!' said Jensen, his voice rising as he got caught in the moment. 'Yes! If there's a Will there's a Way!'

One of the stone soldiers near the tent shifted its head as the sound of Jensen's excited voice carried above the noise of the storm.

'Uh-oh,' said Jensen. He pulled Charlie back from the entrance as the thing knuckled over to investigate the disturbance. Keeping to the shadows the two held their breath as it approached.

Although the thing had definite similarities to the stone behemoth that Charlie had seen in the courtyard, it certainly had a gorilla-ness to it. Gargorilla was definitely an appropriate name. It had short, almost deformed rear legs, a narrow waist that led to a broad and powerful chest that in turn was supported by long and heavily muscled arms that thudded, fist first, into the ground with every step. Its craggy head had limited features, a crude slit for a mouth, a hint of a nose and broad eyebrows that overhung poorly defined eyes. All in all it looked like a half-baked and half-glazed pottery figure crafted by either an enthusiastic seven-year-old or a mad artist. *Or in this case*, thought Charlie, *a mad Stoman bishop*.

Brutal and at the same time eerie-looking, the gargorilla pushed its way into the tent. Charlie and Jensen, quiet as mice, tiptoed backwards.

The gargorilla saw the Portal hanging at the back of the tent. Suspecting that something was amiss it croaked out a tortured call. Two of its comrades answered and thudded their way into the tent. Making odd snuffling, sniffing noises they spread out and began to investigate.

46

The Dark Army

Jensen put his finger to his lips, indicating the need for silence. Taking Charlie by the arm he led her towards their initial entrance point. Pushing Charlie through the slit in the tent he followed after. They waited in the narrow channel that lay between the two walls.

The sniffing noises grew closer, so too the *thud-thud-thud* of heavy movement. A shadow loomed close. Charlie and Jensen pressed themselves to the floor and held their breath as it passed.

'Wot are we gonna do about the Portal?' whispered Jensen. 'And wot about Crumble? We're gonna have ta warn him somehow.'

'How about if we –'

A huge fist punched through the canvas mere inches above Charlie's face. She squawked and rolled out of the way.

'Jens–'

'Shh!' said Jensen. With agitated gestures he indicated that they should crawl further along the perimeter.

Keeping as low and as silent as possible they scurried along on their hands and knees. Charlie turned to Jensen with eyes as wide as saucers.

SSSSSCCKKRR!

A pair of stone hands pushed through the fabric and ripped away a large portion of canvas. Looming over the two with a sullen face the gargorilla growled.

'Run!' shouted Charlie.

Scuttling between the creature's legs she squeaked in surprise as she came face to face with a second.

'On yer left!' screamed Jensen.

Charlie turned left and bounced off the third's backside.

'No!' hollered Jensen, ripping at his hair in frustration. 'Don't *turn* left. There's one *on* yer left!'

Sprinting past the soldiers he grabbed Charlie by the back of her shirt and hauled her out of the way as a boulder-like fist smashed into the ground.

'Use yer Will!'

Charlie panicked when she realized she couldn't. 'I can't! I can't hold the Portal open and wield my Will!'

'Duck! Duck!' yelled Jensen, watching with horror as Charlie narrowly missed getting squished by one of the lumbering creatures. 'Well let go of the Portal then!'

Charlie, already fatigued from her fight with Fo Fum, and grown weary from holding open a Portal for so long, was in no shape for a fight. Falling back on her K'Changa skills she bobbed, weaved and sprang out of the way. She was unable to use the hand that held the pulsing heart, which severely disadvantaged her. Eluding the gargorilla's grasping paws, but becoming further exhausted by the second, she struggled to think of a solution.

'What about Crumble?'

'He's safe where he is! Let go of the Portal and we can get him later.'

Charlie, ending a series of complicated single handsprings, saw an opportunity in Jensen's argument. 'Let's forget using my Will; let's use the Portal instead! *We* can come back later.' She ducked away as a fourth gargorilla entered the tent.

Unfortunately Crumble, unaware of what was happening, chose that moment to step through the Portal with his shopping.

'Cracked Rock!' he cursed as the soldier nearest him spun round and tried to hammer him to a pulp.

'Back!' screamed Charlie. 'Go back!'

But one of the gargorillas barred his retreat. Realizing she had little choice, Charlie let go of the Portal. Calling on her Will she slammed a fist against the nearest creature. Large cracks appeared across its chest, but still it lurched on. Clenching her teeth Charlie punched it with all her might. It staggered forward for several more steps before shattering into a hundred pieces.

But Charlie's strength was fading fast.

'Crumble! Throw me your shopping!'

The young Stoman was having problems of his own. In his haste to escape the clutching hands of one gargorilla he almost backed straight into another and now found himself penned in.

'Here!'

He threw a wrapped packet at her, then, breaking into song, he dived forward to slam both glowing hands against one of the gargorilla's feet.

KRAAAACK!

The soldier's foot shattered, but Crumble's sigh of relief was short-lived as it continued to limp forward on its ruined ankle. The young Stoman was forced to scramble away.

'Charlie, if yer gonna do anything, now's the time!' shouted Jensen.

Sensing her friends' growing panic, Charlie tore open the paper, pulled out a chunk of meat and squeezed the blood over the heart. It pulsed and wriggled greedily as it feasted on the bloody offering, then reached up to snatch the flesh from her hand. The tendrils pulsed with an odd rhythm across her palm, then gripped gently at her skin. It was a disgusting sensation.

THUD!

THUD!

THUD!

The great noise was accompanied by a vibration that caused the ground to shake with each thud. Charlie, Jensen and Crumble struggled to keep their balance as the floor rocked from side to side. With shocking abruptness the tent was whipped away revealing the cloud-filled sky and torrential rain.

THUD!

THA-THUD!

Charlie felt the blood drain from her face.

The tent had been circled by a ring of gargorillas. They were pressed shoulder to shoulder, ripped remnants of the tent still gripped in some of their hands, and on their simple faces were expressions of mindless anger.

'Use it!' screamed Jensen over the roar of the downpour. 'Use the heart!'

Charlie, a horrified expression on her face, looked dumbly

down at the nasty thing that squelched in her hand. 'H-how?'

'Tell it wot to do!' shouted Jensen. 'Tell it –'

His words were cut off as one of the soldiers grabbed him round the neck. Yanking the Treman into the air it attempted to grab his writhing arms with its other hand. A second came along and grabbed Jensen's kicking legs. Pulling him so he was spread-eagled they prepared to tear him apart.

'STOOOOOOOOP!' screamed Charlie. Her voice was ragged and her chest lurched from exhaustion, but there was no mistaking the command.

THU–

All the gargorillas froze mid-step. The two who held Jensen had assumed a statue-like stillness disturbed only by the motion of the heavy rain.

'Release him!'

Jensen fell to the floor. Gasping and clutching at his throat he began to retch and dry heave.

Charlie rushed to his side. 'Jensen?'

'O-OK,' he rasped between a fit of coughing. 'I'm OK.'

'Charlie!' shouted Nibbler as he joined them in an ungainly tangle of wings. Limping forward he did his best to hurry to their side. 'Are you guys all right?'

'Safe for now, but we've all earned another set of bruises to add to our growing collection.'

'Are they going to attack again?'

'I don't think so.'

'I saw them turn round to face the tent. It was one of the scariest things I've ever seen! You should have seen them from up above; it was like clockwork in motion.'

'Where's Sic Boy?'

'There!' said Crumble. He pointed to the encircled mass of gargorillas that remained as still as statues.

Sic Boy, unable to push through their ranks, was instead nimbly climbing across the gargorillas' heads and shoulders. Leaping into the rain-drenched circle he made his way towards them. He halted by Jensen's side and, noting how pale the Treman looked, Sic Boy carefully hauled his friend off the ground and plonked him as gently as possible across his own muscular back.

'Let's see what we can do with these,' whispered Charlie.

Mouth set in a determined line, she stomped her way over to the shattered remains of the gargorilla that she had destroyed moments earlier. Clambering up the rubble she punched her hand that held the heart towards the turbulent clouds that writhed overhead.

'FORM RANKS!' she shouted.

THUUD!

THA-THUUUD!

The ground shook as the stone army reorganized itself. Crumble, Jensen and Nibbler stared first at the massed army as it stood in neat lines then to the small girl who held all that power in her fist.

'KNEEL!' bellowed Charlie.

With a rumble that was louder than the thunder the army bowed their heads in deference to their new leader.

Mr Crow, tired of haunting his cave, burst apart and flapped his way into the gloomy skies. Curiosity still unsatisfied, he flew back to the valley with an urge to revisit the Stoman bishop and the weird monsters that he'd created. Perhaps there was something he could learn from the strange god that lived in the stone urn.

Swooping over the valley ridge he paused to admire the view. Where before there had only been a few of the stone monsters, there were now thousands upon thousands. Cawing and fluttering in the strong wind, the birds swooped down for a closer look.

Crow couldn't believe his luck when he saw the new scene that awaited him. Charlie Keeper was there! Now was the time for redemption! Now was the time to take Charlie's life and reclaim his position of power next to Bane. Filled with a sense of sweet greed Mr Crow flew lower and lower.

A flash of lightning lit the night sky, then another and another, illuminating the scene below. With an abruptness the birds slowed their flight.

Charlie controlled the monsters?

Mr Crow couldn't believe it. Cowardice overcame his greed and in a flurry of inky wings he made to depart for the safety of his cave. But his old devious ways gave him cause to pause. Maybe there was some way for him to bene-fit from this odd scenario. Ignoring the wind and rain he hid himself behind the furthest row of stone monsters to wait and see what would happen.

47

Return to Sylvaris

Charlie stood with her friends by her side and the gargorilla army at her back. With a ripping motion she tore open a huge Portal, the largest that she had ever attempted. But the effort of sustaining such a giant Portal was overwhelming. Groaning, Charlie tried to hold open the Portal, but her Will failed her. Folding in on itself the Portal disappeared.

Crumble helped her to her feet.

'Lass, are ya OK?' asked Jensen, standing up beside her. It struck him just how tired his friend looked.

'I can't do it,' grumbled Charlie, angered by her own shortcomings. 'It's just too big a distance.'

'So let's think of an alternative,' said Jensen.

'Couldn't we just ride on the gargorillas' backs and pretend they're large horses or rhinospiders?' suggested Crumble.

'Now that's an idea,' said Nibbler.

'How long do you think it would take?' asked Charlie. Unravelling the map that Ottoline had given her, she examined it with interest. 'This has to be us, right? Just where the Slumbering Hills meet the Great Plains. Deepforest and Sylvaris aren't on the map, but they've got to be over there somewhere.'

'It would take a merchant wagon two weeks ta cross the distance,' said Jensen. 'That's too long.'

'Hang on, how fast can those things move?' asked Nibbler.

They turned to face the long line of stone soldiers that stood silently and expressionless.

'Good question,' muttered Charlie.

After the fracas of taking control of the army had passed, Charlie had been able to make use of Crumble's shopping expedition to Opal Hold. She had taken the waist pouch and strapped it across her shoulder so that it hung like an old-fashioned bandit's bandolier. In this she had stuffed the heart along with a portion of the remaining steaks. Disgusting as it was, it allowed her to keep the heart satisfied and her hands free.

She pointed to the nearest gargorilla. 'You. Run to that ridge and back as fast as you can!'

They watched as it charged off. Breaking into a lope it took a few seconds to reach top speed, but when it did it moved at quite a pace.

'That's almost as fast as a galloping horse,' commented Jensen, a thoughtful look on his face.

'So if we ride them as Nibbler suggests, how long would that take?'

'Five days?' suggested Jensen. 'Maybe two or three if they didn't stop at night.'

'Surely that's the beauty of using the gargorillas?' said Crumble. 'They're made of stone; they don't need rest.'

'That's true, they don't, but we do. I don't think we could go for that long without a break. Do ya think yer bruised arm would be able ta hold on non-stop for two days and two nights?'

'Even if we went all day and night,' said Charlie, 'does Sylvaris have that much time?'

Jensen paused. 'No,' he admitted.

'So we need a different solution, then.' Charlie clenched the small muscles that ran along the side of her jaw. As frustrated as she felt, she was determined not to fail the Treman city. It simply wasn't an option.

'Could ya open a smaller Portal ta Sylvaris?'

'Yes, but you saw how weak I am at the moment. I don't think I could hold it open for long.'

'It only needs ta be open long enough for the five of us ta get through.'

'What about that lot?' Charlie pointed at the army.

'I'm pretty confident that we can find more Keepers at Sylvaris. With Deepforest under such a threat some of the Keepers will have returned. They'll feel duty-bound ta defend the land. If we can get three of them together ta form a Triad they could open a Portal large enough ta bring this army ta Deepforest.'

Charlie felt a little flutter of relief. Jensen's suggestion was sound in principle and at least offered them a viable alternative.

'What about the gargorillas?' asked Nibbler. 'We can't leave them here can we?'

'Who's gonna mess with them?' said Jensen. 'They're big and scary enough not ta have ta worry about anyone. Charlie has control of that freaky heart too so they're not going ta go anywhere without her permission.'

Charlie nodded. 'They can wait here until we call for them.'

Taking a deep breath and summoning perhaps the final drop of energy in her body, she opened a smaller Portal. She quickly led her bruised and battered friends through to the relative warmth and wonderful dryness of the Keepers' Room of Travel, high up in the Jade Tower. Crumble, Nibbler and Jensen groaned as they approached the top of the great stairs.

'Stairs,' grumbled Jensen. 'If I survive this war I'm going ta give up my Willow Tower and start living in a bungalow.'

'Or you could put an elevator in your tower,' suggested Charlie. 'You're certainly rich enough to afford it.'

'That's a good point,' mused Jensen. 'They haven't been widely accepted in this realm, but now that ya mention it maybe I'm the man ta make them more fashionable.'

'Or you could just grow a set of wings,' smirked Nibbler with a flutter of his own.

'Don't push it, pickle brain,' said Jensen.

Limping and hobbling they began the descent, followed by Sic Boy who had suffered no injury on his travels, and Charlie who, although more bruised than the others, was fuelled by the darkness in her heart.

A footman followed by a maid with a mop and bucket bumped into them on the stairwell.

'Go and inform Lady Dridif that Charlie Keeper and Jensen the Willow have returned,' instructed Jensen. 'And make haste! Dis is a matter of utmost urgency. Run, man, run!'

The footman, spurred on by Jensen's stern look, scampered down the stairs as the maid continued up to the Room of Travel. It was only after she'd passed that Charlie realized that she recognized her face.

'Constantina!'

Lady Narcissa's daughter stared back down at Charlie. But it was not with the smug satisfaction that she had exhibited in their K'Changa battle. It was an odd look, one of malice mixed with resignation and a touch of humility. Looking deeper, Charlie could also detect from the set of the girl's mouth and the way she held her eyes that she harboured a sense of dread.

'They're coming for us,' said Constantina flatly. 'They say the Stoman Lord's armies are as endless as the grains of sand in a desert.' Then she thrust out her chin with a nostalgic sense of defiance. 'I-I hate you, Charlie Keeper. You killed my mother,' stammered Constantina. 'But they say you're our last hope. You're the only one who can stop us being slaughtered.'

Overcome by a variety of emotions, the girl ran up the stairs and in her haste slopped soapy water over Jensen's feet. Already soaked from his time on the Great Plains, he merely shook his head in dismay rather than causing a fuss. Charlie watched Constantina's skirt whisk round the corner.

'I think that means, me little Hippotomi, that time is running short,' Jensen advised. 'We'd best get down ta see Dridif – and fast.'

Jensen began to hobble down the stairs at a swifter pace than before.

Charlie couldn't get the image of Constantina out of her head. 'She seemed a bit . . . different.'

'Working under Dridif and the First Maid will do that ta a person. Those two won't suffer fools.'

'But it was like she was scared and humble at the same time.'

'Like I said, Dridif is a hard taskmaster. She could scrape barnacles off a ship with her tongue. Knocking an air of superiority off one spoilt brat probably didn't take too much effort on her behalf.'

'And the fear?'

Jensen paused to look at Charlie, but before he could answer the tower was fiercely rocked from side to side. Charlie staggered, lost her balance and nearly fell over the narrow railing. Crumble grabbed her wrist and pulled her back to safety.

'Wot the b-bloomin' –' stuttered Jensen.

'Lady Dridif has been told of yer arrival,' announced a pale-faced footman who raced up the stairs to greet them. 'She requests that ya meet her and the councillors with all due haste.' Tugging at his collar, the Treman appeared quite agitated. 'Please do hurry.'

The companions shared a look then bustled into motion. Moving at speed, they raced down the the stairway and passed beneath the long line of arched doors that led to the Council Chamber. Two stony-faced guards pushed open the last door and then they were there, back once more in the Jade Circle.

The room was unusually crowded. Important-looking people were pressed against the walls, scrolls and notes clutched in white-knuckled hands. The beautiful circular Jade Table was covered with maps and military markers.

Oddly enough considering the crowd, several seats were noticeably empty. Flint, Lady Narcissa's and several other seats had not been filled.

'Charlie Keeper,' said a familiar voice. 'It is good ta see yer still amongst the living. Yer a most welcome sight indeed.' Lady Dridif appeared from amongst the throng looking harassed but determined.

'Wot news do ya bring us?' asked the old lady as she moved hastily round the table. 'And have ya uncovered the pendant's secret?' Clasping Charlie's hands with her own Dridif smiled, delighted to see the young Keeper return. Her smile changed as she examined Charlie's face. 'Ya've changed since we last met. Are ya well?'

'My trip didn't go too smoothly, but we uncovered the pendant's secret. We've also –'

Charlie was interrupted as a smoke-smudged soldier burst into the Council Chamber. 'Brace yerselves!'

There was a hubbub of urgent voices and someone screamed. Before Charlie could ask what was going on the tower shook yet again. With a groan of terror everyone held on to the table and walls, desperate to keep their balance. The shaking stopped as suddenly as it had started.

'Wot's going on?' demanded Jensen.

'We're under siege,' stated Dridif.

'They're here already?' asked Jensen, mouth agape. 'I didn't think –'

Lady Dridif cut him short. 'Young lady, ya have the pendant?'

'Yes, but –'

'And ya have the secret?'

'I do, but –'

'Good. Good! Maybe we have a chance yet,' said Dridif, a wild spark of determination ignited in her eyes. 'It is a weapon is it not?'

'No, it's not a weapon.'

Dridif's jaw muscles clenched, but she kept her disappointment in check. 'Go on.'

'It's a key that we can use to release the Winged Ones.'

'I've been reliably informed that Bane has succeeded in blocking their return. Knowing dis would the pendant still be of use?'

'The Winged Ones figured that Bane would seal their Gateway so they prepared an alternative, but it needs the pendant in order to be opened.'

'How long would it take you ta get there?'

'I . . . I don't know. It's somewhere close to the Winged Mount in a place called the Serpent's Tail.'

'I've never heard of such a place. How close does it lie ta the Winged Mount?'

'I don't know. The god –'

'God?' said Dridif with a startled look.

'Long story,' said Charlie with a dismissive wave of her hand. She doubted Dridif really had time for a step-by-step account of her adventures. 'The god said it was somewhere within the Winged Mount's shadow.'

'I journeyed ta the Winged Mount once when I was young. It's a huge peak and its shadow even longer and that's not accounting for the passage of the sun nor the movement of the shadow throughout the day. That's a vast amount of ground ta cover.'

'And if Bane has blocked the Gateway,' said Jensen, adding his thoughts, 'that would mean he's garrisoned a large force there ta protect his interest.'

'Yer talking about looking fer a needle in a haystack while either running away from or fighting an armed force.' Dridif rubbed at her forehead in an agitated manner. 'No easy matter and time . . . time is most pressing.'

'Lady Dridif –'

'Ssh, child, let me think.'

'Dridif, ya need ta listen ta the lass.'

Dridif first fixed Jensen with her steely gaze then turned to Charlie with a questioning look.

'There's no time for the Winged Ones,' said Charlie.

Dridif's lips twitched with the desire to speak, but she held her tongue and merely raised an eyebrow.

'And if Sylvaris is already under attack I don't think ya can afford to lend any of yer men to confront whatever forces are waiting at the Winged Mount.'

Dridif, finally unable to maintain her equilibrium, put a hand up to stall any further words. 'Charlie, we're at a cross-roads. Sylvaris and our very way of life is under threat of extinction and we have nothing with which ta reply ta Bane's offensive other than taking a gamble. Dis is it. We have no other choice than ta send ya ta the Winged Mount –'

'Well that's the thing,' said Charlie, turning to smile at her weary friends who had risked everything to help her. 'Thanks to these guys . . . I have an army.'

48
E'Jaaz Keeper

Fo Fum paused as his compass suddenly spun to point in a new direction.

He looked east towards Sylvaris then back to his original destination.

'Fe-fi, Fo Fum, where has my fickle bounty gone?'

Not yet willing to turn from his previous path, Fo Fum jogged over the ridge so that he could see into the valley.

The slim half-smile on his lips crept slightly higher. Realizing that his target had flown the coop, but suspecting that Charlie would return at some point to revisit the silent army, the mercenary jogged down into the gorge. Sensing a flicker of movement, he fixed the pack of distant crows with his blindfolded gaze. Accepting that they were dangerous, but not necessarily a threat he dismissed them as a minor inconvenience. Padding over to the furthest line of stony soldiers he too settled down to wait.

Dridif blinked in astonishment. 'Ya wot?'

'I have an army. That's the reason we came back instead of pressing on to free the Winged Ones. I can help.'

Dridif was at a loss for words. She turned to Jensen for confirmation.

'It's big, Dridif,' said Jensen with a confirming nod. 'Maybe big enough ta give us a real chance.'

'Ya mean ta tell me that while out on yer travels ya stumbled across an army that's not only powerful enough ta put a dent inta Bane's forces but also yers ta control?'

'Yes.'

Dridif paused to search their faces. Detecting no hint of deception or tomfoolery – and not being a lady to look a gift horse in the mouth – her lips twitched into a faint smile. 'Well go get this army of yers and be quick about it.'

'We can't. It's too big and too far away for me to Portal them here. I need help. I need some other Keepers.'

'Then yer in luck. Five have returned ta defend Deepforest.'

Charlie felt a small lurch of relief. 'Where are they?' she asked.

Lady Dridif closed her eyes and when she opened them she didn't appear happy. 'Yer guess is as good as mine.' Snapping her fingers she gestured for the captain of the guard. 'Open the balcony.'

Unsure what to expect, Charlie trailed after Dridif. Sic Boy, however, detecting that he was no longer needed, ambled off to find Kelko.

Four of the guards loosened heavy brackets that were mounted on the wall and slowly, muscles tensed beneath the great weight, heaved back a sliding partition to reveal a sweeping balcony that spanned one side of the tower. Lady Dridif gestured for the companions to follow her.

'All I know is that they're somewhere down there.'

Charlie's mouth fell open, Jensen groaned in dismay, Crumble staggered and Nibbler froze as their eyes took in the sight.

Deepforest was burning.

Great behemoths lurched head and shoulders above the tall trees, tearing at towers and flailing at the once great bridges of Sylvaris. Black smoke, cries of terror and the squawk of terrified birds bubbled into the sky. Where huge swathes of Deepforest had been torn or burned to the ground battles could be seen as Bane's soldiers and desperate Tremen tore at one another. Explosions of sparks erupted amongst the treetops as treesinging collided with stonesinging. Hand-to-hand fighting swept up and down streets and boulevards as the invaders moved closer and closer to the heart of Sylvaris.

'How are we going ta find them in that?' asked Jensen. Tears of anger threatened to leak from his eyes as he watched the ruin of his beloved city.

'Captain!' snapped Dridif. 'Drop everything yer doing and have yer men scour the streets. I must have those Keepers returned here at once.'

'I'll fly down there and see what I can find,' suggested Nibbler. Bunching his muscles he prepared to leap, but Charlie stopped him by placing her hand on his shoulder.

'Wait,' she suggested. 'We're in a position of vantage. From up here we can see across most of Sylvaris. All we have to look out for is a flash of Will. A golden light is going to stand out much brighter than anything else, right?'

'Good lass,' congratulated Jensen. He pointed at the few

councillors who had followed them outside. 'Everyone, keep yer eyes open for gold. Cry out if ya see a Keeper!'

The balcony was soon fringed with bodies as those present desperately looked out.

'There!' boomed a Stoman lady, proudly wearing all her jade jewellery. 'Down there . . . no, wait.' Leaning over the balcony she pointed to a distant tower that throbbed with motion as soldiers from both sides battled across it. 'It was there I saw it . . . wait, yes! It's there again. A Keeper!'

Charlie pushed her way to the front of the balcony. Her eyes widened in triumph as she too glimpsed the faraway spark of golden Will.

'Stand back,' she commanded. Barely allowing the councillors enough time to jump aside, she opened a Portal and dived through. Jensen and Nibbler joined her. Crumble paused long enough to pinch a sword from one of the Treman guards, then he too sprang through.

They found themselves amidst a world of chaos. Screaming Humans and Tremen tore at Stomen. Rhinospiders scuttled this way and that, arrows flashed through the air, Shades snapped at swords, and axes thudded against shields.

Realizing that the bulk of the defenders were pressed back against the tower and that the majority of the invaders had pushed their way along a narrow bridge, Charlie let loose a torrent of blackened Will that shot across the end of the overpass. Nibbler joined her efforts with a blistering wave of flame. The enemy fell back, cursing and shrieking.

'Here!' hollered Crumble, pointing at the tower.

Surrounded by a cadre of Human and Treman soldiers

in torn and bloodied armour was a Keeper. A halo of gold fizzed and flitted above his fists, both of which clutched an arrow that had pierced his thigh, pinning him to the building's stonework.

As Charlie and Nibbler struggled to keep Bane's forces at bay, Jensen rushed to the Keeper's side.

'How bad is it?' he asked.

The man, teeth clenched against the pain, somehow managed to force a grin. 'I think it might put a crimp in my dancing style.'

Jensen, always one to appreciate a foolhardy spirit, grinned in response. 'Any reason why yer haven't pulled yerself free or were yer simply enjoying the opportunity ta rest against the wall?'

'I don't think it's near the artery, but I've been too busy trying to keep those Shades away from my boys to take a look.'

'Let's take a peek.' Jensen hunkered down to peer behind the man's trapped leg.

'Whatever you're doing,' screamed Charlie, tendons sticking up on her neck as she struggled to hold back the tide, 'you'd better hurry it up!'

Jensen paused in his deliberations to look over his shoulder. 'Whoops,' he said as he caught sight of a behemoth wading along the bridge towards them. 'Better make dis quick!' Helping himself to a knife that hung from the Keeper's belt, he reached around to feel for the arrow head embedded into the tower wall. 'Sorry, friend, no time for niceties.' With quick strokes he sawed through the shaft. Once he had parted the arrow from its head he gripped the man by the thigh and with another 'sorry!' yanked the arrow free of his leg.

The man groaned and only by holding on to Jensen's shoulder prevented himself from keeling over. 'That wasn't the lightest of touches,' he protested.

Jensen grinned as he put a supporting arm round the man's waist. 'We could always wait for ya ta get shot in the other leg. Who knows I might get better with practice.'

'No, no, you're good. Thanks.'

'Jensen!' screamed Charlie as, with arms spread wide, she tried to slow the approach of the behemoth.

'OK! We're done here!' he replied.

'All right, boys!' hollered the Keeper. 'We're not winning any ground here, let's regroup and try hitting them from somewhere else.'

At his command those of his men still capable of standing dragged those who couldn't through Charlie's Portal.

'Clear!' hollered the last of the Treman soldiers as they disappeared through to the Jade Tower.

Charlie commenced her retreat. Step by step she did her best to keep both the Stomen and lumbering behemoth at bay, all the while slowly inching back.

'The bridge!' shouted Nibbler. 'The bridge!'

With both her hands full and her mind focused on fighting the behemoth Charlie didn't grasp what Nibbler was driving at. It was only when he sent bolt after bolt of lightning into the arch of the bridge that Charlie finally understood what he was suggesting.

And she wasn't happy with the notion.

She saw Bane's forces rioting across the city, she saw the

smoke, the fire and the Stonesingers rampaging through Deepforest, but until now it simply hadn't dawned upon her that they were fighting a losing battle. She couldn't bring herself to strike against the city that she saw as a second home, she simply couldn't raise her hand to damage something that had bewitched her with its sheer beauty.

It was the Keeper they had rescued who made the decision for her. Sending a sheet of golden Will to strike in tandem with Nibbler's lightning, he brought the graceful bridge, the behemoth and all the Stoman forces upon it tumbling down. With barely a pause Jensen dragged him through the Portal, grabbing Crumble as he went. Nibbler flapped in behind them.

'Charlie!' he shouted. 'Come on!'

Charlie took one last look at the scene before her. With her heart heavy in her chest and the taste of ashes upon her tongue, she leaped after the others.

49

Marsila the Fierce

With one hand pressed on his wound the Keeper extended his other towards Charlie.

'My name is E'Jaaz. I believe I owe you a debt of gratitude.'

Charlie took his calloused hand in her own and they shook hands. She was fascinated to note that this Keeper was dressed very differently from Azariah; indeed there was something about him that made her think of a Persian knight. He had brown eyes and long dark hair that was held in check with a braided cord. Strange tattoos were inscribed across his bronzed cheeks. His billowing black trousers were tucked into shin-high boots and his loose open shirt was tied with an embroidered sash.

'That's a debt that I might want repaid sooner than you think.'

'Ha!' chuckled E'Jaaz. 'So you've noticed it's the end of the world and you want to collect what's owed to you while you can? I like your style!'

Charlie eyed the man. His leg was bleeding, the city was burning around him and he had the courage or the madness to grin. What kind of man was this Keeper?

'E'Jaaz,' said Dridif, interrupting the conversation with a commanding tone. 'Charlie brings Sylvaris hope, but we need one more Keeper. Where can the other four be found?'

'Hope?' said E'Jaaz, shocked to realize that this might not be the end. ''Tis a fine thing. A fine thing indeed.' He turned to Dridif. 'I'm not certain regarding the whereabouts of Hikmat, Jericha and Roxana, but Marsila I know has chosen to hold back the tide at the Whispering Heights. I can get us –'

'I'll do it,' insisted Charlie. 'Get that leg looked at. You'll need it where we're going.'

E'Jaaz chuckled as he watched Charlie sweep open a Portal. 'Charlie, you're something new, you know that?'

'Fetch a healer!' snapped Dridif.

E'Jaaz shrugged and allowed himself to be pulled into a chair. 'Keep your Will bright!' he called out as Charlie, Jensen, Crumble and Nibbler disappeared through the Portal.

Mr Crow was growing nervous. He didn't like the look of the stranger with the wide oriental-looking hat. The man had a definite air of danger to him. That, combined with the multitude of looming stone monsters – which Mr Crow knew were just waiting to lumber into motion – were almost too much to bear. His natural instinct for survival and his constant cowardice were screaming at him to depart the scene. To leave while he still could.

But the lawyer knew that he couldn't return to Bane

empty-handed if he wanted to live. The Stoman Lord would rip him into a thousand pieces for his failures. Better to return late and triumphant or not at all.

Becoming increasingly fraught, Mr Crow strode up and down, racking his brains in an attempt to come up with a plan. What could he offer Bane? What could he give the Stoman Lord that he didn't already have?

A nasty grin crept across the lawyer's face. Breaking into a trot, then a sprint, he leaped into the air and dissolved into a flock of shrieking black birds. Whipping into a frenzy, they settled round one of the statuesque soldiers. Grasping its rocky skin, they tried to lift it into the air, but it was simply too heavy a weight.

Darting upwards to a higher altitude they hesitated for a moment then descended with the power of a sledgehammer. Slamming repeatedly against the gargorilla's waist they broke it into two. Grabbing the topmost piece they again attempted to take to the skies.

This time it worked. Flapping and cawing, they headed westward with their prize clutched in their talons.

Charlie and her friends pushed against the flow of terrified people. There were Tremen with bags upon their backs, Humans with children upon their shoulders and Stomen heaving over-laden carts full of belongings, food and hastily gathered medical supplies.

It was by no means easy pushing through the refugees, but Charlie had miscast her Portal so that it fell a bridge away from the three towers that comprised the Whispering Heights. Gritting their teeth the three friends plunged ahead while Nibbler flew above them.

There were sudden screams and a slackening of pressure. The crowd parted as a carpet of Shades, screeching and hooting, forced their way past the defensive line of Treman soldiers. Young children shrieked in terror, old folks tottered desperately forward and terrified parents dropped their belongings in a bid to escape.

'NO MORE!' howled a voice. 'NO MORE I SAID!'

A sheet of gold light sheared into one of the three towers, ripping free several flights of stairs, a couple of balconies and two of the celebrated gardens of Sylvaris. Cracking and groaning the great mass cascaded free to slam into the writhing pile of Shades.

A woman in tight-fitting clothes and black lacquered armour clambered up the rubble to strike and claw at the few surviving Shades with golden hands.

'Marsila?' hollered Charlie.

The Keeper, a Shade dangling lifelessly in one hand, her other arm poised to strike, paused in her efforts.

'Who are you?' she shouted.

'Charlie. Charlie Keeper.'

'Elias and Mya's girl?'

Charlie started at the sound of her parents' names. 'How do you know my parents?'

Marsila nodded in appreciation as Nibbler swept low to finish her job with a wave of flame that sent the last of the Shades writhing and clawing to plummet from the bridge to the chaos that lay below. 'We Keepers are a small community.' She watched with a bleak expression as a distant behemoth tore down a once graceful tower. 'Much smaller now that Bane has had his way.'

'Marsila?' said Charlie, noting that the lady in black appeared distracted.

The lady blinked. A ribbon of red warpaint covered her eyes and the bridge of her nose. This, the dead Shade in one hand and the stink of war upon her clothes made her appear fearsome indeed. 'Apologies. It has been days since I slept and my mind has started to wander. What can I do for you Charlie?'

'I need help. I need a Triad of Keepers.'

Marsila allowed a sad smile to reach her lips. 'That has been tried already, but Hikmat, Jericha and Roxana fell within the first two hours. A Triad will not save the day. This is the end.' She cast the Shade over the side of the bridge. 'Make your last stand how you will.' Marsila began to walk away.

'Wait!' shouted Charlie, chasing after her. 'Wait. There is a chance. There is. I have an army waiting out of reach. I just need your help to get it here.'

Marsila fixed Charlie with a questioning gaze. Having had a bellyful of death and destruction, she was uncertain as to whether the young Keeper was telling the truth or merely waving a vague promise of hope as a final banner to rally around. She turned to Jensen. 'Is this true?'

'Sweet Sap, yes it is, but we need ta make a move on dis while there's still some city ta be saved.'

'Then let's get to it.'

'Before ya go,' urged Jensen, 'cut the bridges. It'll slow the tide and buy those folks some time. If we can . . .' Jensen's voice faded as he stared into the distance. He staggered to the side of the bridge to grab the railing with white-knuckled hands.

'What is it, Jensen?'

'Me, me tower . . .' He pointed towards a clutch of buildings on the other side of the city. Jensen's beautiful tower, taller than the others, was easy to spot.

A behemoth pulled itself above the forest canopy. Using Jensen's tower as an improvised ladder it clambered upward until it was high enough to swing both feet on to one of the broad bridges. Pushing itself upright with mechanical motions it started to lurch towards the city centre, only to pause mid-stride. Slowly it lowered its foot then twisted round one hundred and eighty degrees until it faced back the way it had come.

'No,' whispered Jensen.

The behemoth lumbered back to the Willow Tower.

'No, no, no . . .'

Slamming its fists like a wrecking ball, it tore free great chunks of debris from Jensen's beloved home. Furniture, rare books, prized possessions and family heirlooms cascaded free to fall like an obscene waterfall into the forest fires far below. And still the behemoth didn't stop. Battering away it shovelled its palms ever deeper until, with a great crack, the Willow Tower leaned drunkenly to one side. The behemoth paused. There was a glimmer of faint but excited motion as nearby Stonesingers spurred the giant into motion.

It raised one hand high and brought it chopping down. The few remaining supports snapped and Jensen's tower came plummeting down.

Wide-eyed and heartbroken, the Treman stared at the broken stub of his once great tower. 'Salixia?' he gasped. 'SALIXIA!'

50

Harsh Realities

'She wouldn't have been in there,' insisted Charlie as she stared at the broken remnants of the Willow Tower. A pang of loss filled her as she realized she'd never again share breakfast with Jensen in his home or watch another sunrise from what she thought of as her bedroom balcony. 'There's no way the sister of Jensen the Willow would have remained at home in a battle like this. No way.'

Stuck in a stare, Jensen reached out to grab Charlie's shoulder with a shaking hand.

'Did you hear me, Jensen? I said there was no way Salixia would have been in your tower. Not at a time like this.'

With a great start Jensen shook himself free of the moment. 'Yeah . . . yer right. She was always one ta think more about others than herself. She'll be off with the healers or somewhere.'

Just how far had the bedlam and chaos reached? Even if Salixia hadn't been in the tower would she still be safe? Was there anywhere in Sylvaris that was beyond Bane's reach?

'Bless me Leaf,' muttered Jensen. Finding some strength in the words he said it again, 'Bless me Leaf, Charlie, let's get dis done! Let's get that army of yers while there's some towers still standing!' Grabbing her hand he dragged her over to Marsila. 'No more waiting around. We've gotta go and we've gotta go now.'

Marsila, rocked from her lethargy by Jensen's fierce expression, and armed with the hope that Charlie's news brought, she gestured for Charlie to go ahead and open her Portal. As Charlie set her sights on the Jade Tower, Marsila sheared free the remaining bridges, slowing the approach of the Stoman army and buying the fleeing civilians some extra time.

'Let's go!' called Charlie.

Together they leaped back to the relative safety of the Council Chamber.

There they found E'Jaaz gingerly testing his weight upon his wounded leg. By his side a Treman healer looked on thoughtfully, ready to offer his professional opinion, but it seemed that none was needed. E'Jaaz's smile grew as he caught sight of Marsila.

'Although I still think it a shame to hide such pretty eyes behind warpaint I'm glad it succeeded in scaring off the opposition and kept you alive for another day,' he said with a roguish grin.

Marsila rolled her eyes. 'What was that?' she asked with a nod to his bandaged leg.

'Arrow.'

'Shame they missed your big mouth and stuck you in your scrawny leg,' retorted Marsila. 'How anyone could miss such a big flapping target is beyond me.'

'Be glad our enemy's aim is so poor, otherwise I'd never have the opportunity to claim that dinner date you owe me.'

'Keep dreaming, wool-for-brains.'

'Dis is no time for idle flirting,' snorted Lady Dridif. She stared sternly at the two Keepers. 'Now, time is ticking. Are ya all aware of wot is required from ya?'

'I think you've all been a little light on the detail, but I think I grasp the gist of what's needed.' E'Jaaz held up a hand to count off points. 'One, dispense with years of training and teach Charlie how to initiate a Triad of Keepers. Two, cut a giant Portal to the far side of the Great Plains. Three, take control of some monster army, and four, transport them back to Sylvaris and save the day.'

The councillors, Lady Dridif, Marsila and even Jensen gave the man a dark stare for his disrespectful attitude.

'What? Did I forget something?' E'Jaaz made a pantomime of putting his hand over his mouth. 'Oh yes: five, whisk Marsila off her feet and claim that kiss I've always been waiting for. What?' he protested. 'What better time for a kiss than the end of the world?'

The tower shook and in the distance someone screamed.

'Enough tomfoolery,' demanded Dridif. 'Get ta it.'

'Wait,' urged Jensen. 'The Winged Saddles. Get them out of storage; we'll need them.'

Lady Dridif turned to the nearest footman. 'Get them,' she instructed. As the man scampered off with several soldiers and footmen in tow, the First Speaker gave the group a contemplative stare before her gaze rested upon Nibbler. 'I won't put all ma eggs in one basket,' she muttered to herself.

'What was that?' asked Nibbler, who felt uncomfortable beneath the weight of her attention.

'Charlie?'

'Yes, Dridif?'

'Give Nibbler the pendant.'

Charlie hesitated. 'I don't have a problem giving it to Nibbler, but are you going to tell me why?'

'Should ya die today we need a second chance. A hope, no matter how faint, that Bellania will still recover from Bane's shadow.'

'You, ah . . . you lost me there.'

'We don't know if the pendant was intended for yer sole use or not. If ya perish then Nibbler is our one other hope of using that pendant and returning the Winged Ones ta our realm. If there are no other Keepers left then a Winged One would surely be the next logical choice.'

Charlie tentatively pulled the pendant from her pocket. 'I'm, er, still not up to speed with what you're trying to suggest.'

Dridif, her hard face a direct contrast to many of the other terrified people in the room, straightened. 'I mean for yer companions ta split. Ya must send Nibbler and Jensen ta the Winged Mount with yer pendant. There they can pursue our hopes of reuniting the Winged Ones.'

'Wot about Charlie?' demanded Jensen.

'Her chances are more than fair. She is a Keeper, joined by Keepers and she will have an army at her back.'

'An army that might not be able ta match the might of the Stoman army!'

'Precisely,' said Dridif.

'Huh?' Jensen twitched his head to one side so he could better hear the First Speaker. He was certain that he had misheard.

'Do not be naive, Jensen! Ya are the first Merchant Prince of Sylvaris. Yer wealth and business acumen is renowned across Bellania. Ya juggle figures and manipulate markets ta better reap profit. I know yer brain is not slow so open yer eyes and acknowledge the truth! We are more than dying! We, our people, our way of life, our hopes, dreams and fondest wishes are close ta extinction! We must prepare for every opportunity. We must allow every seed of our culture a chance ta take root. Charlie is but one seed. Nibbler, ya and the pendant are another. Two chances, two hopes, two dreams for our future are far better than a solitary gamble.'

'Hang on –'

'No!' snapped Dridif, preventing any further protests. 'I am the First Speaker and I have spoken!'

At that moment the footmen and soldiers returned dragging six ornate but overly large leather saddles.

'We will only be needing three of those,' commanded Dridif.

The exhausted footmen gratefully dropped three.

'Where do you want these two sent?' Marsila gestured at Jensen and Nibbler.

'These *three*,' corrected Crumble in an unexpected display of loyalty. 'I'll watch out for them, Charlie.'

Charlie, still perplexed by Dridif's abrupt decision, nodded her thanks to Crumble Shard.

'A day's walk from the Winged Mount,' said Dridif after a moment's contemplation.

'Wait!' protested Jensen, a tortured look on his face. 'Just wait a Blighted minute.' He moved to Charlie's side and with a frustrated expression on his face pulled her into a tight embrace.

'Once yer've finished off Bane's army – *which I know ya'll do* – I want ya ta keep an eye out for me sister and that fat oaf of an Oak, Kelko.'

The clash of arms sounded closer.

'I promise,' whispered Charlie, clasping her friend as tightly as she could.

'I love ya, me little Hippotomi.'

'Charlie –' began Nibbler. Behind him stood Crumble, eager to get one last word in too.

'There's no time for dis!' said Dridif, brusque and formal. 'Every second is someone's life! Marsila, get ta it!'

As much as Marsila sympathized with Charlie's tangled emotions, she couldn't help but agree with the First Speaker's prognosis. She opened a Portal. Fresh air, cool mountain scents and the call of birdsong flooded into the chamber.

'Go!' commanded Dridif.

'Charlie come for us as soon as –'

'Go!' insisted Dridif, cutting Nibbler's words short.

Nibbler, Crumble and Jensen forlornly made an exit.

'If there be any man or woman here that cannot wield a sword I command that ya leave too.'

There was a rumble of vague protest.

'This is no time for empty words. Survival is at stake! Hericho, Jaylance, Treddit. I know yer minds are sharp, but it has been years since ya took part in any sport. Go! Pheranice, Lago and Stupper – yer services over the years have been great, but it is time for ya ta take yer leave.' One by one she singled out councillor and servant alike until there was a steady stream of old faces retreating from the room. 'Captain.'

'Ma'am?'

'Send a third of yer men and the wounded who can walk with them. I would see that our young Hatchling has some protection on his quest.'

'Ma'am.' The captain barked some orders and soon armed figures joined the others on the far side of the Portal.

'Charlie!' cried Nibbler. 'I –'

Marsila let the Portal go, cutting short any further good-byes. Charlie scowled, but Marsila ignored the look.

'Where's this army of yours?'

Charlie stood tall, realizing that she had duties to attend to rather than bemoaning absent friends. 'Let me show you.'

She opened a Portal then staggered beneath the sudden weight.

'Be careful,' muttered Marsila. 'Open too many Portals too quickly and your energy will swiftly deteriorate.'

'Uh,' grimaced Charlie. 'Yeah, I'm kinda familiar with that.'

'Captain, take those saddles through,' said Dridif.

Once the guards had deposited the saddles they tried to return, but Dridif held up her hand. 'Stay with the Keepers, assist them with the saddles then aid them as best ya can.'

'Is this it?' enquired Marsila. 'Are we good to go?'

Dridif nodded. 'Ya are.'

'Any last words of wisdom?'

'Grind the enemy ta dust.'

Marsila gave the First Speaker a grim smile. 'You've got it.'

51

Triad

It was still raining on the Great Plains.

The stone soldiers, standing in the long ranks where Charlie had left them, disappeared into the gloom.

'Seven Heavens,' muttered E'Jaaz, 'those are big.'

Marsila spun around in a slow, disbelieving circle as she tried to count the gargorillas in their entirety. 'It's like one of those fairy armies the Winged Ones used to tell me about when I was a child.'

A roll of thunder boomed overhead.

'Let's get to it,' said Charlie, a determined expression on her face. She could feel the seconds ticking by and with it came a helpless sense that Sylvaris, beyond the horizon and beyond her reach, was being crushed into oblivion.

The Treman captain instructed his men to fasten the saddles round three of the silent gargorillas. Once their task was complete he hesitantly approached Marsila.

'Wot of us, my lady?'

'Wait until we've gone through, then you and your men can take care of any stragglers that this lot leave behind.'

The captain nodded gratefully then went to attend to his men, leaving Charlie alone with the two Keepers.

'All right, Charlie,' began Marsila. 'I don't know what training you've had, if any, but working with two other Keepers to form a Triad is not something that is easily learned. And today of all days, time is the one thing that we don't have . . .'

'Just tell me what needs to be done.'

'We need to share our Wills: one common goal, one shared ambition.'

Charlie, growing more and more impatient as each minute passed, had to subdue the urge to scream with frustration. She had to stay calm. She had to stay focused. If she lost her cool now people would pay for her mistakes. But knowing that didn't help; if anything it only added to her overwhelming sense of burden. Biting her lip and digging her nails into her palms, she did her best to control her breathing. 'OK: one goal, one ambition. I've got that.'

'Are you sure?' asked Marsila.

'No, of course I'm not sure!' retorted Charlie. 'But we've got no choice. Look, if you and E'Jaaz just start doing whatever needs to be done I'll watch and see if I can learn.'

E'Jaaz shrugged. 'That's worth a try.'

The gargorillas on either side of the small party glowed with a warm reflected light as both adults summoned their Wills. Golden fists raised, they turned to face the east.

Charlie blinked. She could feel it. Something that tugged at her. A sense of wanting filled her and, not knowing quite what was happening, but realizing that she had to go with the flow she stepped forward and added her dark light to the Keeper's warm glow.

'Feel it?' asked E'Jaaz, a smile of delight wrapped across his face as he revelled in the shared power.

'Yes!' said Charlie. The fine hairs along her arms and the back of her neck stood up as arcs of Will crackled round her. 'Yes!'

'Sylvaris! We have to open a Portal to Sylvaris!' shouted Marsila as she struggled to be heard above the growing hum of energy.

The three were encompassed by a halo of light, predominantly yellow and gold, but in places dark and almost black as Charlie's Will interlaced with the others'. The rain evaporated as it came into contact with the sphere of power. The gargorillas on either side of the three Keepers cast odd shadows and the Treman guards had to stagger back with hands held high to shield their eyes.

'Got it!' acknowledged Charlie as she felt a shared consciousness.

With a great crack a Portal shimmered open. It was far larger than Charlie had expected and stretched for metres in each direction. Bright daylight sheared into the gloomy rain and with it came the sounds and terrible sights of a rampaging battle.

'Mount up!' snapped Marsila.

Charlie, copying the other Keeper's movements, scaled the back of one of the gargorillas and wriggled her way into the saddle.

'Now what?' asked Charlie.

'You're the one in control!' snorted E'Jaaz.

'I know that!' said Charlie, 'but what are we going to do? I've never been in a battle before.'

E'Jaaz cleared his throat. 'I believe the traditional word is "charge".'

Charlie gave him a dirty look. Standing in her stirrups so she could be seen she shouted, 'LISTEN TO ME!'

The gargorilla army lurched upright and even though they had no ears they gave the impression that they were paying attention.

Charlie opened her mouth to issue her final commands, but as she looked through the Portal at the massed ranks of Stoman soldiers intent on tearing Sylvaris to the ground, she paused. The darkness in her chest pulsed. Anger, now a constant in her life, began to surge, filling her veins with tempestuous warmth.

'Charlie,' began E'Jaaz with a concerned look. 'Don't let that darkness consume you. You musn't –'

'This is a war, is it not?' said Charlie, riding roughshod over his worries. 'What better place for anger? Look at that – look!'

She pointed through the Portal to the backs of the armoured Stomen. Shades snaked through their feet in their eagerness to be the first to kill Treman children. Rhinospiders danced across spears and shoulders in their haste to carry their riders forward. Arrogant Stonesingers strutted about, urging behemoths to inflict more and more damage on the once beautiful city.

'I can think of no better place for my anger. I will wipe Bane's army from the face of this realm!'

'Charlie –'

'No!' Once again Charlie cut E'Jaaz short.

The Keeper was shocked by the commanding tone in Charlie's voice. He was twice as shocked to realize that he was obeying her.

'E'Jaaz, you will take a third of our forces and push back all that you find in Deepforest. Marsila?'

'Yes, Charlie?'

'You're with me. We're taking the other two thirds up into Sylvaris.'

Marsila tried to say something, but Charlie turned to the Treman captain. 'What's the quickest route up to the streets?'

'There's a ramp about half a mile from here. It's in that direction.' He pointed past the Stomen still wriggling and churning like a mass of maggots fighting to be the first to chew on decomposing flesh. 'Just stick ta the road when ya find it and it'll lead ya there. It's a main thoroughfare inta the city. It should take six of these big beasties marching abreast.'

Charlie leaned down to shake the man's hand. 'Thank you. Stay safe and survive today.'

'Ya too, dangerous lady.'

'Charlie –' began Marsila, trying one last time to be heard.

Charlie, fuelled by the rising rush of bleak anger, ignored her elder. She fixed her army with an intent gaze. The long lines of stone soldiers, realizing that the time had come, stood even straighter.

'Go to Sylvaris and drive out Bane's soldiers!' shouted Charlie. 'Crush them and send them reeling back to the Western Mountains! Do not stop until Sylvaris is free. Go! Go! GO!'

She was almost jolted out of her seat as her gargorilla lurched into motion. Heaving forward on all fours, it was the first to leap through the Portal. A thunderous rumble accompanied Charlie as the rest of her army followed.

Accelerating to a gallop, the gargorillas erupted from the rift and exploded into Deepforest. Kicking up a flurry of leaves they charged towards the Stoman ranks. Several Shades turned to shriek in horror, but most never got a chance. With an almighty crash Charlie's army struck and didn't slow at all. Shades were flung through the air, armoured Stomen trampled underfoot, behemoths crushed to dust and the swollen abdomens of rhinospiders squashed with a squelchy 'pop'.

'Left! To the left!' screamed Charlie as she saw the road. The raging torrent of stone soldiers swerved round tree trunks and pounded their slab-like feet along the road. Seeing the ramp approach Charlie waved at E'Jaaz. 'Good luck!'

E'Jaaz, powered with Will to the point where even his mount glowed, waved back. 'Luck be with you!' he hollered.

As Charlie and her troops clattered up the ramp, the tattooed Keeper angled off with his third of the army. The last Charlie saw of E'Jaaz before the trees hid him from sight was him and his gargorillas spreading out in search of further combat.

Charlie turned to Marsila and nodded. Not certain that she could be heard above the din, the fierce lady returned the gesture. As they crested the top of the ramp, Sylvaris swept into view. Shattered towers, flames and smoke filled the skyscape.

'On!' screamed Charlie, determined to save what she could of the city. 'Onward!'

Fo Fum remained hidden on the rain-swept plains. Ducking behind the last line of gargorillas he patiently waited as the Keepers charged through the Portal. He hesistated for several additional minutes to ensure that there was no chance of being spotted. During that time many thousands of the stone soldiers thundered through the Portal, the combined weight of their footfall causing the ground to shimmer and shake.

Fo Fum, holding the brim of his hat low over his face, rode the tempest calmly. Then, judging the moment to be right, he grabbed the shoulder of a passing gargorilla and leaped on to its back. Cloak streaming behind him, mercenary and gargorilla punched through the Portal into a chaotic world of war.

Stomen and Shades shrieked as they were pummelled into the ground, soldiers panicked and Stonesingers tried futilely to battle Charlie's dark army.

Fo Fum ignored it all. Using his mount's head to haul himself upright he bunched his legs beneath him and . . . jumped. Landing lightly on the shoulders of another gargorilla he repeated the motion again and again until he had built enough momentum to *run* across the backs of the stone soldiers. Gathering speed, he began to move in front of the army. Focusing on what lay ahead, he was finally rewarded with a glimpse of Charlie's messy hair as she rode the lead gargorilla.

His empty grin growing wider and meaner, Fo Fum continued to push his way ahead. He was determined to grasp his elusive prey while she was unaware that she was being stalked and the advantage was his.

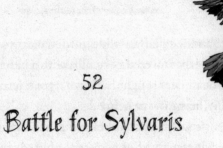

52

Battle for Sylvaris

At each junction a steady stream of gargorillas split from the main force to engage the enemy. Street by street and bridge by bridge Charlie's army swept clear the Stoman army, leaving a carpet of armoured corpses, broken behemoths and writhing scraps of Shades.

But not everything went their way.

Gargantuan behemoths stamped, gnashed and thumped their way through great swathes of Charlie's soldiers before they in turn could be brought to their knees. Shades working in wriggling, writhing packs pulled gargorillas beneath their shadowy embrace, never to rise again. Stomen fighting for their lives smashed clubs into stony heads, axes into barrel chests and maces into rocky backs.

Bit by bit the enemy was forced back, but in return Charlie's army was diminished, leaving nothing more than a pile of shattered rock or a trail of fractured limbs to mark their passing.

'The Jade Tower!' called Marsila.

Charlie, sheathed in a dark cloud of tempestuous Will, turned in the direction of Marsila's outstretched finger. The tower was a hive of activity. Rhinospiders clambered up the walls, Shades tried to slide into windows and Stomen pounded at the lowered portcullis with a battering ram. The tower's defenders fought back with great ferocity, but were gradually being overwhelmed.

'Go!' shouted Charlie. Heeling her mount round she urged what remained of her army towards the tower.

Something suddenly yanked her from her mount. Cartwheeling through the air Charlie landed in a heap. Scrambling to her feet, she went white in shock as Fo Fum appeared, bigger and larger than ever, dancing towards her across the backs of her stone soldiers.

Marsila dragged her gargorilla to a halt.

'No!' said Charlie. 'I've got this. Clear the Jade Tower.'

The older Keeper paused. The screams coming from the Jade Tower spurred her decision. Tight-lipped and with a scowl marring her beautiful face, Marsila made for the tower.

Fo Fum raced across the gargorillas then leaped lightly to the ground as the last few ranks converged round the Jade Tower. Still wearing his hideous little half-smile on his burnt and blistered face, he turned to Charlie.

'Fe-fi –'

'Fo Fum, better watch out,' said Charlie, finishing the mercenary's chanted ditty, 'cos the bad girl comes.' In a gesture of defiance she raised her shadow-wreathed hands.

Though Marsila had concerns about leaving Charlie to fight the blindfolded stranger alone, she had no choice in the matter. The Jade Circle had to be saved.

She leaped clear as her mount and the others slammed into the pushing, swearing, bloodthirsty mass of Stomen that until now had been preoccupied with forcing their way into the Jade Tower.

Squealing in pain and rage they turned to face their new attackers.

Stonesingers commanded behemoths to punch and pummel at the gargorillas. Shades twined their way past rocky feet, tripping and trapping the stone soldiers then tearing them to shreds when they tried to struggle upright. Stoman soldiers cracked warhammers against arms, chests and legs and, bit by bit, tore gargorilla after gargorilla into piles of shattered stone.

But this was not a one-sided battle. The last of the behemoths was heaved off the walkway and disappeared beneath the smoking canopy of Deepforest. The battering ram was dropped as the Stoman soldiers were forced to aid their brothers-in-arms in defeating the gargorillas. Rhinospiders that had been scaling the sides of the Jade Tower were forced to abandon their siege in order to drop down and attack their foe.

And then the gargorillas were gone, with nothing to show for their passing other than trails of stone and mounds of shattered limbs and cracked heads.

Marsila was left to stand alone. Behind her red warpaint her eyes widened then calmed. A smile even teased across her lips.

'So it's like that then?' she snorted. 'Well, if you've got to go, you've got to go . . .' Raising her blazing fists she started to stride forward, keen to close the gap between her and the enraged Stomen who had ringed her in.

Screams of shock arose from the back of the crowd. Several of the more experienced Stomen turned to see what the confusion was. When they saw the cause of the unrest they cursed and hastily turned to meet the new threat.

It was the Jade Councillors, servants and guards. Having broken out of the besieged tower, they were hurling themselves against the Stomen and Shades in a desperate bid to turn the tide.

'Cut them down!' roared Dridif's familiar voice. 'Fling them from the bridges and pound them inta the ground! Sylvaris! Sylvaris!'

Marsila, hands bright with the flame of her Will, decided that if Dridif and the Jade Circle were going to be the anvil then she was definitely going to be the hammer.

'Sylvaris!' she bellowed. 'For Sylvaris!' Leaping forward she joined the fray.

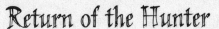

53

Return of the Hunter

Fo Fum's fist smashed one of the large ornamental vases that lined the bridge, sending showers of soil, pottery and orchid petals through the air.

Charlie, fuelled by her anger, danced out of range. 'Is that the best you've got?' she taunted.

The mercenary didn't reply. Sliding forward he whipped his heel towards Charlie's face. Once again she ducked and somersaulted out of the way. Fo Fum matched her move for move, chasing her across the bridge. Dancing over fallen behemoths and springing off the broken remnants of once-mighty gargorillas, he pursued the small girl back and forth. But not once did he manage to connect or land a solid blow. Undeterred, he continued to wreak a trail of havoc.

'You're as bad as Mr Crow!' snapped Charlie. Suddenly moving into the mercenary's range rather than away, she ducked beneath a punch and drove the ball of her foot deep into Fo Fum's gut. She followed this with a flurry of upper-cuts. Confident that she could win this fight she stalked forward, trailing little puddles of darkness behind her with each step.

'Money. Power. Titles. There's always something, isn't

there? And it always has to come at the cost of someone else's pain.'

Growling, Fo Fum lunged out, but Charlie grabbed his fist.

'Everything changes when you meet someone stronger than you, doesn't it?' Trickles of inky light oozed from Charlie's eyes and her hair writhed like an angered goddess's. 'And I bet that just like Mr Crow you'll try to run when you realize that you've finally met your match. So what are you going to do, Fo Fum? Want to come quietly?'

On his knees and wheezing, Fo Fum raised his ruined face. 'Fo Fum will show you what he will do!' Ripping the bandage from across his eyes he pushed Charlie aside and with the last of his strength threw himself into a burning tower.

'Huh?' Charlie stared with confusion at what she assumed was the man's funeral pyre. 'That was . . . easy?'

Uncertain what had just happened but glad of an anticlimax rather than a brutal fight she wearily trudged towards the Jade Tower. Apparently, the battle was over and they had won! She could see Jade Councillors armed with whatever had been close at hand emerge from the damaged but still-standing tower. Slowly she began to unwind. The anger that had fuelled her for so many days no longer seemed necessary. In fact, when she thought about it, the anger seemed more of a hindrance than a boon.

As Charlie stared at the place that she had once considered to be a fairy-tale city, her mind started to turn over and over. Little cogs of emotion and small wheels of logic that hadn't been used in a while began to spin.

What had all of her rage achieved?

She hadn't stopped the city from burning. She hadn't preserved the wondrous architecture of Sylvaris. She hadn't prevented the unimaginable and uncountable deaths of thousands of people, regardless of whether they were invaders or invaded. She hadn't helped the refugees flee to safer locations and she had done little to stem the misery.

'And I haven't stopped Bane and I haven't freed my parents,' said Charlie, adding to her list of failures in an emotionless voice.

She looked down at her hands and examined the black Will that flickered from fingertip to fingertip. There were very few golden sparks left. Lifting her hands against the backdrop of fire, she realized that there was very little difference between the black smoke that filled the sky and the darkness that she now wielded.

Charlie suddenly felt very sick.

Lurching over she grabbed her knees as a wave of cramp clenched at her gut. Staggering over to grasp a railing for support she began to heave. Something clutched at her heart, then clawed at her stomach. The sensation tore at her throat and, still heaving as cramps gripped her body, she felt something fill her mouth.

'Cluuuuurgh!'

Charlie vomited a thick oily substance on to the ground. Bent over and still struggling from the effects of the nausea she stared in horror and fascination at the puddle of black goo. It moved sluggishly like a sea anemone stretching its tendrils in search of food.

Disgusted, Charlie lurched back. As she moved, the puddle, no longer in her shadow, writhed and hissed as sunlight struck it. Wriggling and twitching, it crinkled up on itself, finally fading away to nothing more than a faint stain.

'Eeeurgh.' Charlie wiped her mouth clean and slowly straightened. 'What was that?' She stopped, suddenly aware that something felt different. Hesitantly she put her hand to her chest. Feeling nothing there and uncertain what to expect, she summoned her Will. Raising both her hands, she stared in wonder and more than a little delight at the yellow flames that danced merrily across her wrists, fingers and knuckles. Once more her Will was golden.

'Charlie!' called Marsila from the far side of the bridge. Shattered armour, fallen foes and discarded weaponry lay scattered by her feet. Behind her milled the survivors from the Jade Tower, all of whom appeared slightly shellshocked but nonetheless ecstatic to find themselves still alive. Marsila, overjoyed in victory and thrilled to see that the young Keeper had shed her darkness, waved, genuine happiness etched on her face.

Charlie smiled and waved back. Eager to speak to both Lady Dridif and Marsila, Charlie began to walk towards the Jade Tower. As she did so, the aches and pains, bruises and sprains that she had suffered over the past week, no longer held in check by the force of her anger, returned with a vengeance.

But Charlie didn't care. Limping slightly and gritting her teeth until she grew accustomed to the pain, she continued on, surprised at how content she felt. She began to think of all the things that needed doing, the preparations that she would have to make in order to find this mysterious Serpent's Tail and what she would say when she finally met up with her friends. As her brain continued to pick over ideas and plans, a terrible thought came to her.

'Wasn't Fo Fum already dead?'

In the excitement of battle she had completely overlooked this obvious truth.

'How did he . . .'

As she turned to look at the wrecked tower, it exploded. Fo Fum, far, far bigger than ever before, stepped on to the bridge. Clutched in his hand was one of the wickedly sharp spears that the behemoths had been using. And erupting from his disfigured face, with all the speed and power of an industrial chimney stack, was a jet of smoke that boiled and bubbled upward to poison the sky.

E'Jaaz laughed aloud as the thrill of the fight filled him with an unquenchable thirst for life.

His third of the gargorillas had diminished as they had swept through the burning foliage of Deepforest, punishing and pushing aside what was left of the Stoman army. One by one his army had dwindled as they succumbed to the ferocity of behemoths and Stonesingers. But he cared not. For each of his losses Bane's First Army had lost many, many more. Surrounded by a nimbus of golden Will, he watched with shining eyes as Shade, Stoman and rhinospider scrambled from his path, desperate to flee the crunching fists and thumping teeth of the gargorillas.

E'Jaaz's white teeth sparkled as he grinned. Victory down on the Deepforest floor, he was certain, was his.

54

Panic

Charlie's legs shook. She stared at them in disgust, unable to believe that they were betraying her. But as she looked back at Fo Fum she couldn't fault her body's reaction. He was a fearsome sight.

Standing with feet planted on either side of the bridge he stood nearly as tall as a behemoth. Ash and cinder from the still-burning towers billowed towards him like iron particles attracted to a magnet. Smoke too rolled round him like a dark whirlpool and with each and every breath he seemed to suck a little bit more into his lungs, only for it to seep out of his eyes in a paradoxical circle of power. Swinging his stolen spear in great arcs that made the blade thrum as it cut the air, he slowly turned his head from side to side.

Searching for his foe.

Searching for Charlie Keeper.

There was a hushed moment of disbelief as those who had survived the battle for the Jade Tower eyed this prodigious new foe that stood above their city like a demonic thunder god.

'Feeeee-fiiiiiii FO FUM!' he bellowed, his voice booming across the city like an avalanche. 'I will not rest until Charlie Keeper's life has flown!'

Charlie stumbled back, tripped over the shattered remnant of a gargorilla's foot and landed on her bum.

'By the Seven Hells,' swore Marsila as she helped Charlie stand. 'What the . . . what is . . . is that thing really Fo Fum?'

'Y-yes,' stammered Charlie, unable to stop staring at the looming ruin of a thing that used to be a man.

As it craned its muscled neck from side to side in its attempts to locate its prey, the two Keepers got a proper look at its face. Or what should have been a face. It had been so badly burned that now it was just one big mess of red blistered flesh.

'Ugh,' said Marsila, recoiling from the sight.

Charlie wanted to say something too, but she felt like she was close to panic. She reached deep, trying to find the anger that had fuelled her for so long, but it was gone. She had let it go and now she felt as though she was running on empty. Summoning her Will she stared at her golden hands. She had been overjoyed to see it mere minutes ago, but now she eyed it uncertainly. If she hadn't been able to beat the regular Fo Fum with her dark Will what chance did she have of defeating this upgraded version?

'Ha!' roared Fo Fum as he caught sight of Charlie. Whipping the spear overhead he lumbered forward, his ruined lips splitting into an ugly approximation of a smile.

Both Keepers, reaching the same conclusion, turned and ran. Leaping from bridge to bridge and vaulting from roof to balcony to boulevard they tried to outdistance their enemy.

'Any plans?' gasped Marsila.

'Me?'

'Well you're the one "in charge", aren't you?'

Charlie opened her mouth to reply, but decided it was best to keep running and try to come up with some sort of a strategy while she still could.

A behemoth's arm whisked past her head to shatter against a tower. Charlie spun round. Fo Fum, still lurching towards them, picked up another remnant of the earlier battle, a gargorilla head. He flung it with all the speed and power of a cannonball. The Keepers were forced to dive out of the way.

'Keepers!' roared E'Jaaz. 'This way!'

He still rode his original gargorilla, which was badly dented and chipped. About thirty more ran, lumbered and limped by its side. Some were missing limbs, others had large cracks across their torsos, all proof of the viciousness of the battle for Sylvaris.

'Yaaa!' shouted E'Jaaz, slipping from his mount. He slapped it on the back, urging it and its brethren on. Running to Charlie and Marsila's side he watched as the gargorillas converged on Fo Fum.

'Do you think that will work?' asked Marsila.

E'Jaaz watched as Fo Fum sliced one in half and smashed another two into rubble with a stamp of his huge foot. 'Er . . . I think the answer is going to be no. What's next?'

Marsila and E'Jaaz shared a look, then both turned to Charlie. She stared back at the adults with an open mouth.

E'Jaaz frowned. 'Really? No ideas?'

'We could always go out in style?' suggested Marsila, her old scowl returning.

'What?' scoffed E'Jaaz. 'After all we've gone through? Not a chance. Besides you still owe me a kiss.'

'Brain-rattled fool, you were asking for a dinner date in the Jade Tower and now you want to up the stakes to a kiss?'

Charlie wanted to sit down and rest for a minute. She needed the chance to recuperate, to think and to plan. The cost of sustained action over the last few days was taking its toll, but she suspected that if she lay down she might not be able to stand again. She didn't think that would be a dignified way to go; being beheaded by a raging smoke-filled giant while she sat on her backside.

Rubbing thoughtfully at her head she did her best to block out the clumsy attempts at witty interaction between Marsila and E'Jaaz and tried to think.

'Got to have a plan. Got to have a plan,' she whispered.

An image bubbled up from the deep recesses of her tired brain. Slowly it swirled into focus. She and Crumble by the riverside, discussing her fighting style. Charlie rubbed harder at her head in an attempt to hasten the process.

Slowly, like a musical chord echoing over the distance, Crumble Shard's words came to her.

'Be sneaky or more aggressive!' she cried.

E'Jaaz and Marsila gave a start.

'Oh my gosh! OK, OK,' gushed Charlie, her tongue suddenly unable to keep up with brain. 'We've got to . . .' She paused to look around. 'We've got to get out of the city. We need more room and less people.'

The last of the gargorillas flew through the air, knocking E'Jaaz off his feet. Rolling over and over in a cloud of dust and a nimbus of Will, the Keeper eventually staggered to his feet. They all turned to watch Fo Fum. Smoke still haloing round his head, he dipped his hand into the pile of gargorillas that lay broken at his feet. Grabbing an assorted handful of bits and pieces he flung them at the Keepers. Hands up, Will blazing, they were forced to retreat from the onslaught.

'We've got to –' Another deluge of missiles punched Charlie further back. Her shield of gold flashed and sparked as it was struck. 'Ah forget it! Just follow me!'

Pushing her tired limbs into motion and using her Will to the very best of her ability, Charlie led the two Keepers through Sylvaris. Tumbling and spinning, jumping and somersaulting they pushed their way across the city, leaping over broken bridges and ducking through towers with gaping excavations. The *crunch, crunch* of Fo Fum's measured step pursued them as did the occasional projectile of a flung wall, behemoth limb or Stoman corpse.

'What are we doing?' panted E'Jaaz.

'Getting rid of –' Once again another thrown missile cut her short. Charlie smashed the next aside with a flurry of Will.

'Getting that –' The bridge they were running on crumpled and partially collapsed as Fo Fum put his weight on it. Helping each other they clambered on to another.

'Just run!'

Onward and onward they went until they reached the city limits and the towers grew further and further apart. Sliding down the outside of a severely damaged building that leaned at an extreme angle, they tumbled into Deepforest. Checking that Fo Fum was still chasing them they raced across battlefield debris, past groups of Treman soldiers who were being assisted by healers, skipped past still-burning fires and out on to the grasslands of the Great Plains.

'How-much-longer,' gasped Marsila, holding her hand to her side in an attempt to calm a stitch, 'do-we-have-to-run?'

Charlie, realizing that they were now free of the city and the possibility of harming any innocent civilians, skidded to a stop. 'This is far enough.'

Panting, they looked back to Deepforest.

Fo Fum's spear spat through the trees and buried itself right between the three Keepers. Clods of dirt and clumps of grass rained down on them from the near miss. Fo Fum came next. Having feasted on the smoke of Sylvaris he was now large enough to push the trees of Deepforest aside like a farmer stepping through a field of corn.

The Keepers were forced to crane their heads right back in order to see the giant's tortured face. His clothes had fallen from him long ago, leaving him coated in blood and ashes.

'Feeeeeeeeeeeeee!' he screamed in delight as he saw his prey.

Charlie was so shocked by the change in his appearance that she nearly lost sight of her plans.

'Charlie?' E'Jaaz nudged her in the ribs. 'If you're going to do anything, now's the time.'

'A T-T-Triad,' stuttered Charlie as the fear threatened to get the better of her. 'Form a Triad.'

The two Keepers nodded. Wills shimmering, the three merged their strengths.

'Where do you want us to open the Portal?' shouted Marsila over the footfall of the approaching giant. 'Beneath his feet?'

'No, I want you to open it –' Charlie was cut short as Fo

Fum's gigantic hand lashed down, knocking her off her feet. It smashed a cratered imprint in the soft earth. Charlie pulled herself upright, doing her best to maintain the Triad. 'I want you to open it above his head!'

E'Jaaz and Marsila stared at one another, sharing a look of confusion.

'*Where* do you want us to open it?'

But before Charlie could reply Fo Fum plucked her off the grass as easily as one might bend down to pick up a fallen grape. His dark chuckle filled the sky. 'I've got you now, my scuttling fugitive! Fiiiiii!'

Delighted with his catch, he tossed Charlie from hand to hand. Charlie had to fight vertigo as she was jolted through the air. Gritting her teeth she fought to hold the Triad of Wills together. She couldn't afford to let it go.

'Open the Portal!' she screamed.

'Where?' bellowed E'Jaaz, his voice cracked with frustration. 'To *where*?'

'To the Western Mountains!' screamed Charlie.

Fo Fum paused. Snatching Charlie out of the air he lifted her to head height so he could better examine her. Charlie almost gagged at the close proximity of the giant's ruined face. The thick smoke bubbling endlessly from his eyes and the rotten stink of his wounds were almost more than she could bear.

'Fe-fi, Fo Fum –' began the mercenary.

Charlie was unable to stand it any more. 'Enough with the Fe-fi, Fo Fum chant!' She wriggled round so she could shout to the Keepers below. 'Just open the Portal to the Western Mountains!'

Still screaming, she struggled to tear open her own Portal. At first it felt as though Marsila and E'Jaaz, confused by her request, were fighting her. Gritting her teeth she Willed them into motion.

A line of gold slashed above Fo Fum's head. Rotating, it sheared through a different axis then spread open into a wide rectangle.

'Ffffo?' The giant gazed at the golden light in confusion.

The Portal began to shake. Vibrating and groaning it roared and reverberated as it fought the Keepers. Jerking faster and faster it began to oscillate.

WHHHHUUUUUUSH!

Fo Fum had only a second to react before the magma erupted from the Portal. Gushing and slurping, rushing and splattering, the lava swept across Fo Fum's head. It streamed down his shoulders and over his chest. The terrible scent of burning flesh filled the air and the mercenary's gurgling scream cracked across the Great Plains, echoed over Deep-forest and pounded against the towers of Sylvaris so that those brave enough to stick their heads from ruined towers swiftly ducked back inside.

Charlie, desperate to free herself from the giant's hands before he clenched them in agony, kicked herself free. Tumbling through the air she braced herself with Will in the hope of minimizing her impact, only to be pleasantly surprised when Marsila cushioned her fall with a trampoline of thick golden light.

Grabbing the younger Keeper by the arms, the two adults scampered to a safe distance with Charlie held between them. There, with their hands pressed to their ears, they turned to watch Fo Fum's demise with a mixture of awe and disgust.

Screaming, bellowing and writhing, the giant folded himself into a ball in an attempt to protect himself from the terrible heat. But it did little good. The lava continued to spew from the Portal like a vengeful red rain. With no smoke from which to draw added energy, the giant's body succumbed and broke down in the volcanic stream. As Fo Fum stopped moving, the Portal finally shuddered one last time then collapsed in a flash of sparks.

55

Burial at Sea

Thinking that it was over, Marsila and E'Jaaz edged closer to Fo Fum's body.

'No,' said Charlie. She had to repeat herself when the two adults, slightly deafened by the cataclysmic event, failed to hear her the first time. 'No! Don't go near him. I thought we'd killed him once before and that didn't work. Let's not take any risks.'

'What?'

Charlie sighed. Doing her best with a mix of poor panto-mime and hand gestures she indicated the risk to the dazed Keepers.

'SO WHAT DO YOU WANT TO DO?' bellowed E'Jaaz.

'I'm not deaf!' protested Charlie.

'WHAT?'

'You don't have to shout!'

'WHAT?'

'Oh for crying out loud,' muttered Charlie. Using the last scraps of her strength she opened a Portal back to the Jade Tower.

'Charlie?' said Lady Dridif. She paused so that one of the

guards could take the arm of the wounded councillor who she had been helping. 'Is it over?'

'Yes. Well . . . almost.'

'Thank ya, Charlie. For all that yer've done. We owe ya a debt of gratitude that –'

'Uh, Dridif?' groaned Charlie as she struggled beneath the weight of the Portal.

'Wot is it?'

'Portal. Kinda heavy.'

'Sorry. Wot do ya need?'

'Can you come through? Bring ink, paper, as many guards as you can spare and all the fans that you can find.'

'Fans, ya mean the ones on our ceilings?'

'Noooo,' grumbled Charlie, really struggling beneath the pressure. 'The ones that you flap with your hands. Please hurry, I can't keep this open all day.'

Seeing the sweat on the girl's brow Dridif bustled into motion. With several swift commands, a few raised eyebrows and the occasional acidic remark she spurred a mixed crowd of Tremen, councillors and servants into motion.

'Quick! Quick! Ya there, run!' urged Dridif, berating the last of the guards through the Portal. 'And ya, stop pretending yer foot's twisted. I saw yer run fast enough when the Shades came for ya. Jump, all of ya!'

Dridif was the last to step through the Portal. Charlie, drenched in sweat, sighed with relief as she could finally allow it to close.

'Ya got him,' said Dridif with an appreciative smile as she stared at the lumpy remains of Fo Fum.

'Maybe, maybe not.'

'Charlie, that's just a big lump of charcoal. How can ya be worried about that?'

'Jensen finished him off once before, but he came back from that. And you saw what happened earlier. I just don't think it would be wise to take any chances.'

Dridif gave the cremated remains of Fo Fum a measured look. She was certain that the giant posed no threat, but she hadn't reached her position of power by taking thoughtless risks. 'So wot do ya have planned?'

Charlie told her. Dridif nodded in agreement and ordered those who had brought fans into motion. They formed an arc round the gigantic corpse and, waving the fans up and down, kept the smokes of Deepforest and Sylvaris at bay. Each councillor, guard or servant was careful in their duties. Indeed they might not have been a hundred per cent sure why they were doing what they did, but Dridif with her iron words and scathing look had ensured that each carried out his or her task to the best of their ability.

Charlie used the pen and paper to write down instructions for E'Jaaz and Marsila.

'WHY DO YOU WANT TO OPEN A PORTAL TO THE SEA OF CHARMS?'

'Oh, my days, would you two please stop shouting!'

'WHAT?'

'Stop shouting! Ooh hang on . . .' Charlie scrawled Stop shouting! in capitals on a piece of parchment and underlined it three times. Grabbing both Keepers she held the paper under their noses.

'Oh, sorry,' said Marsila, shrugging. She stuck a finger in her ear in an attempt to clear her hearing. 'We didn't know.'

'So why do you want to open a Portal to the Sea of Charms?' asked E'Jaaz.

No smoke underwater, wrote Charlie and held the paper up so they could see.

'Ah, good idea,' said E'Jaaz, finally understanding what Charlie had been driving at.

Charlie gestured at the food and drink that Lady Dridif had thoughtfully brought with her. She thought it would be a good idea to boost their lagging energy before attempting to undertake the Portal opening.

While she ate, a terrible, if improbable, image of Fo Fum meeting Darkmount's god miles beneath the waves of the Sea of Charms sprang to mind.

'Dridif?'

'Yes, Charlie.'

'What's the second deepest ocean in Bellania?'

When the Keepers had eaten their fill and recovered somewhat from their labours – and, more importantly in Charlie's opinion, also recovered their hearing – they set to work.

The three Keepers formed an informal triangle with Charlie at the front. Shutting their eyes they summoned their Will and formed a Triad. Gesturing in unison they opened a Portal that led to a calm ocean. The waters were dark blue and although it was of course impossible to tell how deep they were, they nonetheless gave the suggestion that beneath the surface there lay a great depth.

'OK, are we ready?' asked Charlie.

'All right, ladies, gentlemen,' instructed Lady Dridif in an iron voice. 'Roll up those sleeves and let's get ta it. Push! PUSH!'

The faces of the guards, councillors and servants wrinkled in disgust as they began their unpleasant task of manhandling the crispy remains of the burnt giant. Charlie, taking control of the Portal, indicated that E'Jaaz and Marsila should apply their Will to aid the effort.

Struggling and grimacing, pushing and straining, everyone slowly pushed Fo Fum's remains forward. Groaning with difficulty, they finally succeeded in pushing it up to one edge, then with a final shout of 'Heave!' they shoved it so that it teetered for a second before gravity pulled it into the ocean with a great splash.

Everyone turned to watch as several fins broke the water's surface. Wriggling through the waves, great sharks with razor-sharp teeth began to attack the corpse. Slowly the great lump began to sink with the sharks following it into the depths.

Charlie watched until the ocean waves grew calm once more. Almost as an afterthought she unfastened the belt that held the gargorillas' controlling heart. Realizing that without an army to control it was useless, she cast it into the waves too. Satisfied, she closed the Portal.

'I wonder if he ever thought he'd end up like that?' said E'Jaaz.

'Like what?' asked Marsila.

'As barbecued Fo Fum.' E'Jaaz chuckled. 'It almost sounds like the name of a real snack.'

Lady Dridif put her finger to her lip and nodded appreciatively. 'I think that would be a suitable revenge,' she mused. 'I'll have all the street food vendors in Sylvaris rename their barbequed Hoodwinks Barbequed Fo Fum.'

'What's a Hoodwink?' asked Charlie.

'A type of tree rat,' said Dridif. Seeing the look on Charlie's face she added, 'They taste nicer than ya think.'

'You want to name a street food after Fo Fum?'

'Why not? Fo Fum added to the destruction of our city so dis way our citizens always get the chance ta bite back. With the addition of Barbequed Fo Fum ta our diet Sylvaris will always have the last laugh.'

Charlie stared at Lady Dridif, uncertain whether she should be horrified or amused. Seeing the twitch of a victorious smile on the old lady's face, Charlie realized that she liked the idea. She chuckled in delight, enjoying the idea that the joke would become part of Sylvarian folklore.

'So, young Keeper,' said Dridif, interrupting Charlie's thoughts, 'how do ya and yer colleagues feel about cutting us a Portal back ta the Jade Tower?'

Charlie stared at the two adult Keepers, who were once again arguing as to whether or not E'Jaaz was to get a dinner date, a kiss or a fat lip from Marsila. Shrugging, she turned back to Dridif.

'If it's all the same with you I'm knackered. I'd rather save my Will and Portals and fighting for another day. What do you say to joining me in a *walk* back to Sylvaris?'

'Wot do I say? Young Keeper . . . that sounds like a plan.'

Shoulder to shoulder, Charlie Keeper and the First Speaker of Sylvaris walked, or in Charlie's case limped, towards the trees of Deepforest.

56

A Fallen General

The Shades had already informed Bane of all that had occurred at the battle of Deepforest. His fury had been significant upon hearing the news. The Throne Room bore the marks of his temper: statues lay strewn and broken across the floor and several of the great columns displayed fist-shaped cracks.

Yet, as elemental as Bane was, a strategist's mind lurked beneath his shadowy cowl. He had already taken steps to prevent his barrier against travel being used as a weapon. Charlie Keeper might have made use of it once, but after conferring with his god, the barrier's properties had been lifted. Any Keeper thinking of repeating the actions that had resulted in Fo Fum's demise would surely be disappointed. He had also taken steps to prevent the news of his defeat from causing any damage to his growing empire. In a show of strength he had doubled garrisons throughout his territory and increased executions as a deterrent to any who thought they could take advantage of his loss.

There was one other vital piece of information that he intended to take advantage of: Sylvaris and Deepforest were now without defences. It was true that he had lost his prime fighting force, the First Army, but Deepforest had lost two. His Shades had reported that not only had the Treman army been decimated but that the strange dark army led by the Keepers had also been destroyed.

Sylvaris was now ripe for the plucking.

'Bring in my generals.'

Men-at-arms pulled open the heavy doors and footmen ushered in the generals. There were noticeably only two. The largest of the three – the leader of the First – was absent. The two generals clicked their heels together and saluted with a chorus of 'My lord'.

'The Jade Circle has expended all their forces and now lies defenceless. You will take both my Second and my Third Armies and you will crush Sylvaris. Crush it! I want that Treman city gone. Splinter its towers, harvest its citizens, burn the trees and salt the earth! I will have all traces of that city swept from my empire. See it done.'

'Aye, lord,' said the general with the milky eye.

'Your will, my lord,' said the one with the cleft in his jaw. They both turned to go.

'Wait,' commanded Bane. 'I think it only fair that you taste how I reward those who please me.' The Stoman Lord snapped his fingers. At his bidding, twelve servants struggled forward, pushing four barrels that twinkled and sparkled with diamonds, sapphires, rubies and emeralds. 'Your baths will be filled with these and tonight you will wash in wealth.' Bane snapped his fingers a second time. A long line of slaves from all three races were led forward. 'These will attend your every wish.'

The generals' eyes glittered with greed.

'My lord.'

'My thanks, my lord.'

'Enjoy tonight, let my generosity spur your ambitions, and when you return after crushing Sylvaris I will gift you more jewels than you can imagine. Return to me as victorious generals and I will let you *swim* in your reward. Now go.'

The two generals swaggered out of sight.

Bane waited for their footfalls to diminish before gesturing a footman forward. 'Bring him in.'

There was a clink and rattle of chains as a large Stoman pressed beneath a great weight of shackles lurched his way into the Throne Room. The strain of the action was evident in the tensing of the tendons in his neck and the play of muscles round his clenched fists. Even though his head was held high, the man's eyes betrayed his fear. He was none other than the disgraced general of the First Army.

Slowly and ponderously the man made his way to the foot of the raised dais where he knelt before the Devouring Throne. Pressing his forehead to the floor he failed to notice Bane's fury rekindle itself as a dark halo that spat and boiled.

'My lord, I did everything in my power to achieve your desire, but I simply could not –'

His words were cut off in a squawk as Bane leaned down and grabbed him by the throat. Holding him up so that his feet dangled above the floor, Bane growled, 'You think that I will let such an error go unpunished?'

'I-I face my death with honour intact, my lord,' gurgled the general as best he could with Bane's gigantic fingers pressed round his neck.

'Honour?' hissed Bane. Grabbing the chains he snapped them one by one. The links clanked as they struck the floor. 'You think I will allow you to die with honour after losing my prime army? Gah!' He flung the general across the room as though he was nothing more than a rag doll.

The disgraced Stoman rolled several times before coming to a stop in a darkened corner. There was a sibilant hissing and slowly the shadows unfolded. Shades reached out and entwined their dark tendrils round the general's wrists.

'For such a failure you will die a lacklustre and honour-less death! You lost my First Army and for that you will be the first adult that I will devour. Shades, take him to my kitchens. I will eat him tonight!'

The general's eyes widened, but before he could cry for mercy his mouth was stuffed with shadowy limbs. Legs kick-ing and drumming, he was hauled into the darkness.

'Ya be the best Tree Singers. The best of all Sylvaris, of all Deepforest and of all Bellania, and it is for yer skills that I have had ya gathered here today,' said Lady Dridif in solemn tones.

The men and women in front of her had all been deeply affected by the battle. Some had had their homes torched, others had lost family members, but each had in their own way made an effort to look as presentable as possible. Hair had been tied into the neatest of topknots, clean clothes had been borrowed and jade jewellery was worn with obvious pride. Now they stood on the sweeping balcony that allowed the Jade Circle to look out across the ruins of Sylvaris.

The fires had been put out and the rubble had been cleared from the streets in a remarkably short time, but it was evident that Sylvaris was a broken city. Towers leaned at drunken angles, some had had floors and balconies ripped clean off, and others were little more than ruined stumps. In Deepforest great swathes of land had been burned to the ground and many of the beautiful and almost impossibly grand trees had been turned into piles of ash.

But there was hope. Many of the forest beasts and wild creatures that had fled during the chaos had started to return. Monkeys scampered through the remaining branches, the great flamingo-like birds that had always graced the Treman capital flew through the air in flocks, and other strange and magnificent creatures made a timid reappearance in the land.

Lady Dridif, caught in a stare as she examined her city, cleared her throat. 'As I was about ta say, ya Tree Singers are gifted with wondrous skill and it is for dis reason that our once fair city of Sylvaris needs ya now. I charge ya with the rebuilding and regeneration of our way of life. It is in yer hands that Sylvaris shall be reborn. I would see our great towers arise from the ashes, our sweeping bridges rebuilt and the highways and boulevards that are the arteries and veins of this city reshaped. Tree Singers, I humbly bid ya, please repay our city for the shelter and happiness that it has provided us over the millennia. Please go forth and breathe new life inta our slumbering city. Go forth and make Sylvaris great.'

There was no applause or cheers from the throng for Dridif's words, but there was an unspoken yet strongly felt sense of purpose. Bowing low, the men and women silently filed from the room. As they left, some of those who had been hardest hit by loss even managed to gently smile. Sylvaris would rise.

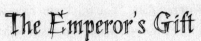

57

The Emperor's Gift

The silence of Bane's Throne Room was broken by the faint flutter of wings.

The sound was not loud or persistent enough to alarm the men-at-arms, but Bane was a different breed. Clenching his hand into a fist he banged it against his throne.

'Crowman!' he snarled. The fury of his voice spat around the room and caused the knees of footmen and servants to buckle. 'Get down here!'

The flutter of wings grew louder. Swooping out of the darkness in a trail of feathers came Mr Crow. As he landed lightly, the broken remains of the gargorilla thudded next to his feet.

'You dare,' hissed Bane, 'you DARE show your face back here after failing so spectacularly? I should rip your soul from your flesh and leave it dancing and flapping by your feet.'

'Lord –' began Mr Crow, but was cut short by Bane's thundering voice.

'You would *beg*?' Looking for something to crush, but finding nothing within arm's reach, the Stoman Lord settled for pounding both fists against the Devouring Throne. 'You snivelling, squishy little Human.'

'M-m-my lord,' stuttered the terrified lawyer, desperate to get a word in before it was too late. 'I might have missed the chance to kill Charlie, but I can still prove useful.'

'Worth?' sneered Bane. 'You think you have worth? What use is a tool if it cannot complete a task? What need do I have for a dog that cannot sink its teeth into meat? Bah! Even with your new powers you are as weak and as blubbering as the rest of your soft and fleshy race.'

'Maybe that's true, my lord, but if I failed in one way perhaps I can make you stronger in another.'

Mr Crow placed his foot on the gargorilla and, with a heave, kicked it across the floor. It spun several times before coming to a standstill at the foot of Bane's raised dais. The one remaining arm of the gagorilla spasmed slightly so its fingers curled, then it stilled and moved no more.

'What is this broken thing? Is this your idea of a gift?'

Mr Crow's eyes sparkled with the glint of nasty intelligence. 'It is, my lord. But before you pass judgement on the matter you should know that it was an army of these that overcame your First.'

There was an intake of breath as the footmen feared that the weird lawyer was in some foolish way trying to bait the wrath of their lord. But surprisingly Bane kept his composure.

'Go on,' he growled.

'Charlie Keeper led this army, but it wasn't she who created them. That was done by a Stoman and a god. A god similar to the one that dwells beneath this Throne Room.'

Bane remained silent and Mr Crow, sensing that he only had moments left in which to make his point, hastened on.

'Charlie Keeper still has the pendant and with it a chance –'

Bane rumbled, deep and low in the back of his throat.

'A faint chance!' squealed Crow. 'Only a faint chance of returning the Winged Ones to Bellania. But that matters not!'

Bane, having grown tired of this tirade, stood and slowly marched down the steps from his throne.

Gabbling his words Mr Crow spat out his last message. 'If you were to create your own stone army with your god you could match their might and never have to worry about losing your throne!'

'Stupid. Ignorant. Weak.' Bane punctuated each of his steps with a word. 'Is that the best you can offer? My Shades have reported the value of Charlie Keeper's dark army. They might have won the battle of Sylvaris but in doing so they were extinguished. Not one of these things –' Bane stamped what remained of the gargorilla into shards with one blow of his foot – 'remains. If they couldn't stand against the might of one of my armies what hope would they have in facing the power of the Winged Ones?'

Bending down, he pushed his shadowy cowl close to Mr Crow's face. The lawyer, even though he was more powerful than he had ever been back on Earth, quaked in terror. Summoning what remained of his rapidly departing courage he blurted out his last gambit. 'The Stoman who created those stone soldiers had one major flaw: he had no imagination! All he could come up with was the idea of crossing behemoths with gorillas.' Crow squeaked as Bane's fingers wrapped round one of his arms. 'We – uh, I mean you – could do so much better. Just think what would happen if you were to merge the power of a behemoth with the viciousness of a Wyrm! You would have an army that could govern the skies and match the Winged Ones power for power. You'd be unstoppable.'

Bane slowly released his fingers from round the lawyer's skinny arms. His silence was deafening as he pondered the logic. Finally the Stoman Lord spoke. 'Your idea . . . has merit.'

And even though it was impossible to tell beneath the eternal shadows that covered Bane's face, Mr Crow got the impression that his master was smiling.

58

Friends

'Charlie? Charlie! Oh, thank my beloved Oak yer all right!'

Charlie didn't get a chance to turn round before she was pulled into a bear hug. She did, however, instantly recognize her old friend by the weight of his stomach and familiar scent of vanilla and forest berries.

'Kelko, you big lummox, put me down!'

'Wot?' protested the chubby Treman. 'Wot's the matter?'

'Nothing, but I can't return the hug if you've got me hanging half upside down, can I?'

Feet returned to floor, Charlie grinned and hugged Kelko properly. After all the turmoil of the past week his soft face was a welcome sight.

'I missed ya, Blossom,' he whispered. 'And I'm glad yer safe. Yer like a little light in this time of darkness.'

'Er . . . are you sure about that?' asked Charlie as she remembered how dark she had turned and how black her Will had become.

'Wot?' protested Kelko. Pushing Charlie to arm's length so he could better stare her in the eyes, he shook his head in disbelief. 'Charlie, yer one of the best things that has happened ta me, or for that matter Jensen or Sic Boy.'

A growl came from behind his back. Leaning to one side Charlie was happy to see Sic Boy, hidden by Kelko's girth, calmly sitting on his haunches and scratching the spot behind his ear with one paw. The dog paused in his action to 'groof' at Charlie. She grinned back.

'So you, er, haven't heard anything bad about me?'

'Other than yer sad inability ta comb yer hair, everything else sounds peachy.' Kelko paused to consider the young Keeper. 'Wait a minute. Yer talking about yer Will, aren't ya?'

Charlie mumbled something under her breath.

'Yeah, well we did hear about a Keeper whose Will had turned as black as night and who rode inta town on the back of a dark army . . .'

Charlie's face blanched.

'And we also heard that this mysterious Keeper snuck inta an impenetrable fortress of the Stubborn Citadel, retrieved a god from hell, bested Lallinda the daemon queen, kicked the Forty Swords up and down a street, defeated Fo Fum the undefeatable bounty hunter, saved Sylvaris from Bane's First Army, beat a backstabbing Stoman bishop at his own game and helped her friends in their time of need . . . and all of that before dinner. Charlie, ya ROCK!'

'So you're not worried about me turning all dark and dangerous?'

'Dark? Ha! Sweet Sap, after everything that ya went through I'd have thought that ya were more than entitled ta a little grumpiness. Besides ya used yer anger ta yer advantage, and when it threatened ta become too strong ya overcame it. Charlie, I know many, many adults who have trouble letting go of their hatred and anger. Yer've succeeded where many have failed. Seriously, sweetheart, I can't say dis often enough or heartily enough: ya do me proud and if I didn't know that one day soon we're going ta reunite ya with yer parents I'd want ta adopt yer myself. Yer a daughter who would make any father happy.'

Something welled up in Charlie. Rather than waiting for tears to spill across her cheeks she grabbed Kelko and allowed herself be pulled in for another hug. Sic Boy padded over to nuzzle her shoulder.

They stayed like that for a long minute.

The moment was finally broken when Kelko's stomach gave a cheery grumble.

'Right!' said the Treman, smacking his lips together with relish. 'Yer've saved Sylvaris, right?'

'Check,' said Charlie, following his lead.

'Yer've beaten Darkmount and freed Bellania from a dark god?'

'Check.'

'Yer've left Bane spitting and cursing after destroying his prized army?'

'Check.'

'Yer've retrieved yer pendant and have firm plans for joining Jensen and Nibbler in the morning?'

'Check.'

'Yer've been ta the celebration feast and taken pride of place at the head of the victory parade?'

'Che–' Charlie paused to stare at Kelko with a look of suspicion. 'What feast? And what parade?'

'So ya haven't been ta the celebration, yammed on lots of yummy food or walked in front of adoring crowds?'

'Stop playing, Kelko.'

'Can ya hear the rumble of my stomach? Does that sound like the gurgle of a man that's willing ta joke about food?'

'I-I . . . look, I don't have time to stand in a parade.'

'It's not *stand* in a parade, it's lead a parade from the front. Place of pride, remember?'

Charlie squirmed. 'Look, we've got more important things to do. I'm supposed to find Salixia and after that I've got to prepare for tomorrow's Portal to meet up with Jensen –'

'Salixia? Who do ya think helped arrange dis celebration?'

'What, you've found Salixia?'

'Of course,' snorted Kelko. 'Do ya think I'd forget the sister of my best friend?'

'She's safe?'

'Of course she is, although ya won't be if ya turn down all the hard work she put inta dis.'

Tucking one hand behind Charlie's back Kelko began to push her down the street. Sic Boy, yawning contentedly, followed after.

'But –' began Charlie, only to be cut off by Kelko.

'Charlie, yer doing dis. If not for yerself then yer doing it fer the city. The people of Sylvaris need a chance ta smile.' A loud rumble came from Kelko's midriff. 'And if ya won't do it fer the city ya better well do it for my stomach!'

Charlie vaguely tried to protest. The idea of leading a parade went against her perception of good taste. Her concerns were silenced by a long drawn-out word that was uttered with complete warmth and total compassion by Kelko.

'Foooooooooooood!'

Sic Boy, finally having had enough of all the tomfoolery, bounded up to help Kelko haul Charlie down the street. They had a celebration to attend.

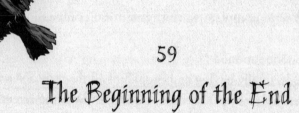

59

The Beginning of the End

'Lord,' said a footman, bowing low. 'There are two . . . men who would beg an audience with you. They appear to be skilled and more than a little dangerous. They wish to offer their services to you, O Lord.'

Bane stirred from his thoughts. 'Send them in,' he said with a negligent wave of his hand.

The great doors to the Throne Room were pulled open and two figures – one little, one large – entered. They moved with the grace of predators. Self-assured and dangerous, they ignored the men-at-arms who guarded the room. Their gaze was reserved solely for the Stoman Lord.

Bane stared them up and down, their appearance stirring a memory. 'I have heard of you two, have I not?' he said.

'I would hope so,' said the shorter one. 'My name is Stix and this is my brother, Stones.'

'Ahh, the Delightful Brothers,' said Bane in his rumbling voice.

'The Delightful Brothers indeed,' stated Stones as he stared at the menacing figure who nearly dwarfed the huge Throne Room with the weight of his presence.

'For what reason would you two dare to enter my

domain? I believe your mother failed in her task to serve me.'

'And for that incompetence she duly paid with her life,' said Stix, the harsh scar standing out on his emotionless face. 'We come to offer our services to the Stoman Lord,' he rasped.

'Yes, to offer our services,' agreed Stones, clenching and unclenching his fists, 'in the hope that we may yet tear the teeth and skin from that little pest Charlie Keeper.'

The dovecote was one of the few parts of the Jade Tower that had not suffered any damage. Its white-washed walls were still intact, as too were the many pigeonholes where birds now resumed their soft cooing. The aviarist was more than a little tipsy, having already enjoyed his fill at the street celebration and victory parade. If he was quiet he could still hear the cries and cheers of partygoers living it up on the boulevards and floors below.

Hiccupping, the bird-keeper blinked in mild surprise as an unfamiliar messenger pigeon fluttered its way towards the roosts. Swaying over to the bird he unravelled the scroll from round its foot.

'Oh, by Sweet Sap and New Leaf,' he whispered in disbelief.

Shock driving the celebratory fuzz from his brain, he hastened towards the door, determined to alert the First Speaker to this new calamity. The sound of another bird arriving halted him in his tracks. Hurrying over he removed the message from his second visitor. With shaking fingers he unrolled the scrap of parchment.

'No. No, no, nooooo,' he moaned. Collapsing back against the wall he sank down until he was crouched in ball. Stifling a sob he pushed himself to his feet and ran from the dovecote.

He had to warn the First Speaker and the Jade Circle. Sylvaris was under threat from not one but two new armies, and they were coming . . . and coming soon.

Bright and shiny and sizzling with fun stuff ...

puffin.co.uk

WEB CHAT

Discover something new
EVERY month – books, competitions
and treats galore

WEB NEWS

The **Puffin Blog** is packed with posts and photos from
Puffin HQ and special guest bloggers. You can also sign up
to our monthly newsletter **Puffin Beak Speak**

WEB FUN

Take a sneaky peek around your favourite **author's studio**,
tune in to the **podcast**, **download activities** and much more

WEBBED FEET

(Puffins have funny little feet and
brightly coloured beaks)

 Point your mouse our way today!

WANT MORE ACTION? MORE ADVENTURE? MORE ADRENALIN?

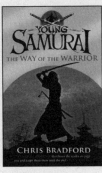

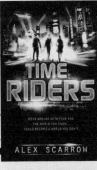

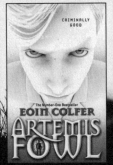

GET INTO PUFFIN'S ADVENTURE BOOKS FOR BOYS

It all started with a Scarecrow.

Puffin is seventy years old.
Sounds ancient, doesn't it? But Puffin has never been
so lively. We're always on the lookout for the next big
idea, which is how it began all those years ago.

Penguin Books was a big idea from the mind of
a man called Allen Lane, who in 1935 invented
the quality paperback and changed the world.
**And from great Penguins, great Puffins grew,
changing the face of children's books forever.**

The first four Puffin Picture Books were hatched in 1940 and the
first Puffin story book featured a man with broomstick arms called
Worzel Gummidge. In 1967 Kaye Webb, Puffin Editor, started the
Puffin Club, promising to **'make children into readers'**.
She kept that promise and over 200,000 children became
devoted Puffineers through their quarterly instalments of
Puffin Post, which is now back for a new generation.

Many years from now, we hope you'll look back and
remember Puffin with a smile. **No matter what your age
or what you're into, there's a Puffin for everyone.**
The possibilities are endless, but one thing is for sure:
whether it's a picture book or a paperback, a sticker book
or a hardback, **if it's got that little Puffin
on it – it's bound to be good.**